Praise for

WHE
WE
WERE
KILLERS

'*Saltburn* meets *The Secret History* in this
gripping tale of alchemy and academia.'
IAN RANKIN

'I was blown away by this visceral roar of a novel: erudite,
pacy and deeply moving. Think *The Secret History* on acid.
Beautifully written and impossible to put down.'
J.S. MONROE

'C.F. Barrington's tale of obsession, grief, toxic friendships and
drug-fuelled violence gripped me in its berserker paranoia,
dragging me inexorably towards its heart-achingly poignant
conclusion. *When We Were Killers* is a splintered gem of a
book. Dark Academia at its seductive, shadowy best.'
MATTHEW HARFFY

'A stylish and darkly evocative thriller that had me racing
through the pages to reach the brilliant and unsettling
conclusion. Chris is such a natural storyteller and his
characters are relatable, yet complex and fascinating.
Another absolute corker!'
RUTH HOGAN

WHEN WE WERE KILLERS

The Pantheon series
The Wolf Mile
The Blood Isles
The Hastening Storm
The Bone Fields

WHEN WE WERE WERE KILLERS

C.F. BARRINGTON

HEAD
ZEUS

An Aries Book

First published in the UK in 2025 by Head of Zeus,
part of Bloomsbury Publishing Plc

9 7 5 3 2 4 6 8

A catalogue record for this book is available from the British Library.

ISBN (PB): 9781804545751
ISBN (E): 9781804545737

Cover design: Matt Bray | Head of Zeus
Typeset by Siliconchips Services Ltd UK

Printed and bound in Great Britain by
CPI Group (UK) Ltd, Croydon CR0 4YY

Bloomsbury Publishing Plc
50 Bedford Square, London, WC1B 3DP, UK
Bloomsbury Publishing Ireland Limited,
29 Earlsfort Terrace, Dublin 2, D02 AY28, Ireland

HEAD OF ZEUS LTD
5–8 Hardwick Street
London EC1R 4RG

To find out more about our authors and books
visit www.headofzeus.com
For product safety related questions contact productsafety@bloomsbury.com

To Dave F – friend and 'first reader'.
Your insight and enthusiasm lift my stories.

"Are you sure that we are awake?
It seems to me that yet we sleep, we dream."

William Shakespeare
A Midsummer Night's Dream

Prologue

L *ife lingered in her.*
 For thirty years those words have tortured me. They've burned holes in me and gnawed at my soul. Even now, I still wake in the small hours to find them circling my head, like vultures waiting for something to die.

Life lingered in her.

What the hell was a remark like that even doing amongst the spartan narrative of an incident report in the *Edinburgh Evening News*? A phrase so prosaic, so colourful, so damn subjective. Perhaps, if the copy editor had been doing their job properly, they might have saved me half a lifetime of pain.

Life... lingered in her.

So many questions.

How long did it linger? Time enough for the five of us to reconsider and scramble down the rocks to save her? Was she conscious? Could she see us far above, silhouetted against the first smudge of dawn?

Since that night, I've lain beside her a thousand times. I've felt the implacable cold of the stone beneath our spines and tasted the iron tang of blood in her throat. Together we've stared up at the Pole Star and Ursa Major, then watched the weather change. A frontier of cloud creeping from the west like a surreptitious army, extinguishing the stars one by one. Then the arrival of a squall. Raindrops pummelling the rocks and punching our upturned faces, telling us this is a bloody stupid place to die.

The rain really did hit hard that night and only receded in the first pale inkling of morning, as we peered one final time over the edge, then fled for the car. She *looked* dead. That's what we convinced ourselves as we cursed each other beside the lay-by and clambered into the vehicle. So that was all that mattered.

In the decades since, I've wondered time and again if the others are still haunted by their actions in those pivotal moments or whether, long ago, they shifted seamlessly into the privileged lives they were always supposed to lead, forging enviable careers and raising beautiful families?

Maybe it's just me who lies beside her each night, broken, depleted, waiting for life to linger no more.

PART ONE

MARTINMAS

I

My life has been defined by tragedy and yet I begin with hope.

Hope Finola D'Angelo.

An odd name for a soul so grave, so lost in her own memories.

I think of her around our fires, flames dancing in her titian eyes and making them sparkle copper. Long legs pulled up in a protective hug. Raven hair cascading onto her shoulders. Her delicate nose scrunched and her brow furrowed.

A woman who captivated me from the moment we met.

'Humans have forgotten how to be nocturnal,' she said once, her breath spiced with wine and warm against my cheek. 'Everything thrilling happens under night skies.'

It was a typical Hope declaration. Earnest, carefully deliberated and strangely indisputable. Those words have stayed with me because they summed up everything we shared during that crazy period. The thrills, the tragedies and the endless crepuscular heavens.

Hope would speak to us of equinoxes and solstices, of Imbolc and Beltane, Lughnasadh and Samhain, of spring growth, summer fertility, autumn harvest and winter death. If she were here now, she would examine me with her nose upturned and that little frown between her eyes, and then declare that my story has no beginning because we are all part of an endless wheel of life. Perhaps she's right, but I must start somewhere.

I've wondered about beginning in the ice-cold grasp of Solway surf, the sand sucking ravenously at my boots, my jeans heavy as lead, and the diabolical sting as the salt water finds my bleeding wrists.

But I'm not ready to tell you about that yet.

So instead, I'll begin on Monday 5 September 1992, on the first afternoon of the Martinmas Semester at the University of St Andrews, on the north-eastern coastline of the Kingdom of Fife.

II

I never want to lay eyes on St Andrews again.

For a brief snippet of time when I was nineteen, it was my whole world. It gave me the greatest highs I've ever known. It opened my eyes to the wonder of friendships and to the possibilities of a new life.

And then it tore them all away.

'Am I in the right building? St Salvator's Hall?'

It was the early Nineties. No one had Google Maps or even a mobile phone. Instead, I clasped a sheet of paper which comprised my arrival instructions. I had stopped for coffee on North Street and managed to spill most of the beverage over it. Then the sea breeze had whipped the instructions back and forth as I loitered on corners to get my bearings. So now I stepped – wind-blown and tired, holding a wilting, turd-coloured scrap of paper – into the most beautiful marble-floored entrance vestibule I could ever imagine. Sandstone arches stretched above me and where they embraced, chandeliers sprouted. Beyond, were regimental lines of pigeonholes and a grand staircase rising to higher floors.

It had taken me seven hours of complicated rail connections to get from rural Dumfries. The final leg had been on a bus surrounded by fellow new students. As they had sprinkled themselves in the seats and begun to chat and ask questions and bond, I had sat rigidly silent. You see, I was what the University of St Andrews called a 'care-experienced applicant'. What this really meant was that I was a fucked-up orphan who lived with my nan and had somehow survived the trauma of my early teens, and on that bus I had been convinced that my fellow passengers – with their soft upbringings and fine-honed social skills, expensive schooling and easy A grades – could tell. Perhaps they could read it in my clothes or sense it in my posture, or even damn well smell it on me.

'You are indeed,' said a man with floppy hair and small round spectacles. He was wearing a scratchy tweed jacket, corduroy tie and bright red academic gown. 'Welcome to St Salvator's – or Sallies, as we call it. You're one of the first to arrive. Have you come far?'

'Newton Stewart in Dumfries.'

'A fellow Scot. We're becoming a rarer breed in this place.' The man laughed and extended his hand. 'I'm Roy.'

I took his hand, conscious of the delicate ridges tracing across the veins of my inner wrist, which encapsulated the end of one part of my life and the beginning of something new. 'Finn.'

'Hello Finn. I'm a post doc in Earth Sciences and I'm one of the assistant wardens at Sallies. It's my turn to do the meet-and-greet this afternoon.' He ushered me to a side table, where he leaned over a clipboard. 'Now, let's check we have you down. What's your second name?'

'Nethercott.'

'That's not so Scottish.'

'I'm from Sussex originally.'

'Let me see… Nethercott, Nethercott.' His finger went down the list, then up, then down again. 'Ah, yes, there you are.' He sounded surprised, as though he had already decided I was not the right fit for St Salvator's. 'Finn Nethercott, Room 138. That's the top floor and – oh, you are the lucky one, it's a single. Most undergrads have to share, at least for their first year.' He swivelled and ran his finger along several rows of keys hanging from the wall, found 138 and turned back. 'Rather *bijou*, I'm afraid, but what can you expect for a single room? Up the stairs for as far as you can go and then left along the corridor to the end.'

He handed me the key and I nodded thanks.

'Oh,' he added, as if suddenly remembering a vital question. 'What are you reading?'

'Divinity,' I said quietly and he raised his eyebrows.

'Oh.'

'MA in Bible Studies and Early Christian Culture.'

'Well… How interesting. I wouldn't have had you down for…'

He saw my scowl and faltered into silence.

No, I'm sure you wouldn't. People like me don't read Divinity and we don't come to places like St Bloody Sallies.

I waved the key at him. 'Thanks anyway. I'll see you later.'

'Yes, yes,' he called after me. 'Get yourself settled in.

Tomorrow there are drinks in the Common Room at six and then formal dinner in Hall when you can meet your fellow Freshers. Welcome aboard, Finn. Sallies 'til we die.'

Yeah, right.

III

Roy was correct about my accommodation. *Bijou* was too generous.

Room 138 was about as high into the eaves of St Salvator's Hall as it was possible to get and its corner plot meant that the walls sloped down on two sides. A pine chest of drawers crouched behind the door and a series of empty bookshelves ran along one wall above an ink-stained desk. In the corner was a sink, illuminated by September light filtering from a tiny window.

I heaved my bag onto the bed and listened to the springs groan, then climbed onto the mattress and peered through the window. If I craned my neck I could just make out the Sallies front lawns. The panes themselves were grimy and full of webs, and a fat pigeon was squatting in the gutter, blocking half the view. I tried to open the catch, but it was unyielding, so I tapped on the glass to shoo the bird, but it didn't even glance my way.

So this was to be my home for the next two semesters.

Somehow I'd expected more. But at least I wasn't sharing. Thank God I wasn't sharing.

Voices echoed down the corridor as new students arrived. A door slammed and someone laughed. I stepped over to the sink and checked myself in the mirror. Boy, I looked shit. Stubble darkened my chin where I'd not bothered to shave that morning before the early start. My eyes were bloodshot, my cheeks pale and my hair hung lank to my shoulders. I rummaged in my bag for a towel, then stripped to the waist and rinsed my face, hair and armpits.

By the time I was done, my stomach was rumbling. Roy had said about the Freshers Dinner tomorrow, but nothing about meals in Hall tonight, so I grabbed my wallet, pulled a coat from my bag and shoved a pack of cigarettes and lighter into my jeans, then exited and strode back along the corridor. Another new arrival was just wrestling his suitcase through a door.

'Hi,' he said hopefully, but I just shot him a terse smile and passed in silence.

I trotted down the stairs to the marble entrance, where a queue of students now waited with their luggage for Roy's attentions. He gave me a quick wave.

'Enjoy your evening.'

Outside, the front lawns of the Hall were already gloomy. In summer the borders would be resplendent with colour, but now they were a mess of browning stems. There was a smidgen of rain in the air and I turned up the collar of my coat and thrust my hands into my pockets, then rounded the back of a university building and came out upon a spacious quadrangle. This was the heart of academic St Andrews. A rectangle of perfectly manicured grass cosseted on two sides by Renaissance architecture and, on my left, by the Gothic buttresses of St Salvator's Chapel.

I swung under an arch and came out on North Street, where I stopped and looked up and down, wondering which direction to take.

'You can't stand there,' came a tart American voice over my shoulder. 'You need to get off right now.'

I turned to find a girl a few yards behind me, clutching a handful of books to her chest and glaring at me. She was tall, almost my height, with long obsidian hair parted in the centre. A vast university scarf was wrapped around her throat and her sturdy Doc Marten boots only served to emphasise the stick-thin contours of her legs. Her brows were drawn together in opprobrium and her eyes... oh, her eyes. I swam in their anger.

For a moment my mind was blank. Not a single neuron stirred.

'I said you need to get off.'

'What?'

She balanced her books with one hand and pointed at my feet. 'That! The PH, you mustn't stand on it. It brings bad luck. Lots of bad luck. Every student knows that.'

These last words were expressed with such withering contempt that I stepped back automatically and peered at the pavement. Sure enough, between the cobbles was some kind of design. The letters P and H, but woven together to make them appear one.

'I didn't know.'

'Patrick Hamilton,' she informed me brusquely. 'He was an abbot who carried the teachings of Martin Luther to Scotland. But the archbishop, James Beaton, considered them heresy and sentenced Hamilton to death in 1528.'

I adjusted my gaze back to her. She was looking at the initials. One finger of hair hung forward over her left eye, but the frown had eased and her tone softened as she got into her story.

'They burnt him at the stake on this very spot and the fire consumed him for six hours.'

Her eyes came up to meet mine and from their depths smouldered a fire of their own. 'Can you imagine taking six hours to die?'

I shook my head, but speech would not come.

'At some point through his agony, Patrick Hamilton unleashed a curse on all future students. If any should set foot on this place of his death, they would bring upon themselves a lifetime of bad luck.'

She studied me for a long, silent moment, then repeated with the utmost gravity, 'Everyone knows that.'

These final words threw me from my stupor and resentment swelled in my veins. 'Well, not me.' I swung away. 'Thanks for the history lesson.'

Thrusting my hands back into my pockets, I hunched my shoulders against the thickening rain and stalked west along the pavement. Eventually, my nose drew me to a takeaway nestled in a backstreet and I found a bench where I tucked moodily into battered sausage and chips.

Dusk settled outside, but my mind was still filled with her. Her frown, her deprecation, her bloody imperious judgement. I didn't give a toss about her story. I'd already had more than a lifetime of bad luck without old Patrick Hamilton thinking he could make it worse. But if there was anything that could alienate me more on my first day, it was the wither of her gaze and the tone of her words.

IV

On the second evening in my cubbyhole in the roof of Sallies, I was checking my reflection in the mirror before the Freshers Drinks and Dinner. I hated the heavy constriction of my suit and the way it made me feel like an undertaker. My shirt collar curled at the corners, my red tie throttled me and my shoes felt like they had been forged in iron. But my tie went well with the gown over my shoulders and I'd shaved and washed my hair in the bathroom down the corridor and I thought, *maybe you'll do*.

Holding on to this seam of self-belief, I paced along the hall and made the long descent to the ground floor. As I approached the Common Room, a wave of voices rolled out and every pore in my body began to sweat. If the noise had been a hedonistic mix of laughter and shouting, I might have been able to deal with it. I could have slipped in and released myself amongst the anonymous chaos. But these voices were genteel. A heavy hum of strangers forced to make small talk in a confined space until someone said they could stop.

A trickle ran down my back and suddenly my suit was the worst attire in the world. Heels echoed behind and a couple of girls in beautiful dresses passed me and entered the fray. Then another guy drew next to me and I snatched a glance. He looked as terrified as I did and seemed on the point of saying something – some kind of male bonding – but there was no way I needed that, so I forced myself into the room.

The noise engulfed me. People stood in little groups, sipping wine and nibbling *hors d'oeuvres*. Chairs lined the perimeter. Bay windows looked out onto the lawns. A grand piano sat solidly in the centre and some wag was tinkling the keys. Everyone else was deep in small talk. A few glanced my way, but no one smiled or offered a welcome.

Finally something clicked in my brain. I spotted a chart on a stand and stalked over to find a diagram of the Common Room showing the windows and doors and the central piano. Onto this, someone had plotted the precise locations of each degree subject in thick felt pen, like a strategic map of battle lines.

'You look lost.'

The voice was cut-glass and disarmingly close. I turned to find another student behind me, her brunette hair streaked with premature silver and a teasing glint in her eyes.

'Sorry,' I blurted.

A smile flickered across her lips. 'Don't be. This place can be pretty alien at first.' It was not a warm smile, nor one of welcome, but she came next to me and peered at the chart. 'So, what are you reading, Fresherboy?'

'Divinity. Early Christian Culture.'

She had been preparing to help me decipher the chart,

but now her brows raised and her eyes ran slowly down and then back up me. 'Whoa. Are you going to be a preacher?'

'Hell, no.'

'So it's the history that draws you?'

I considered my reply. 'I like things from the past. They give us perspective. They ground us.'

She seemed to appreciate this response and graced me with a more genuine smile. I noticed she was wearing a black T-shirt with a flowing, interlinking design on the front like something on ancient Celtic crosses.

'What about you?' I asked. 'Are you a Fresher too?'

She shook her head. 'Third year. Come to see what the pickings are like.'

'And what do you think?'

She shrugged. 'The usual.'

I thought she would elaborate, but she left the description hanging and studied me with that teasing glint again. 'I'm just playing with you. I volunteered tonight to help confused Freshers find their bearings. There's a few of us floating around.' She turned her attentions to the chart and tapped on it with one black-painted nail. 'Here you are. Divinity is in the far corner beside the second bay window.'

I peered that way and could see two of them, hovering shoulder to shoulder, casting imploring looks for someone to come and rescue them.

'Thanks,' I said and began to move.

'Anytime, Preacher.'

When the pair saw me advancing, they broke into nervous grins and opened their bodies in greeting.

'Hi,' exclaimed a girl with scarlet cheeks and a glistening forehead. Her ginger hair was combed into waves and cut in a severe line from her lobes to the back of her neck. She was squeezed into a flowery dress with a high neckline and long sleeves, and her hand was damp when she grabbed mine. 'I'm Anna.'

'I'm Finn,' I mumbled. 'Is this… is this Divinity?'

Please say no.

'Absolutely.' She laughed slightly hysterically. 'The holy corner.'

I hoped she was being ironic. Her accent was North American and I had a horrible suspicion that she hailed from one of those happy-clappy ultra-religious communities in Nashville or Utah or wherever the hell those types hang out.

'And I'm Charles,' said the man next to her, also offering his hand.

Where Anna was large in frame and personality, he was angular, bony and reserved. He wore a suit that swamped him and his eyes were set too closely on either side of a beaked nose. His chestnut hair was flattened across his scalp like a 1940s schoolboy and his tie was dotted with tiny shields emblazoned with crosses. A monk-in-waiting.

'Finn,' I repeated.

'Is that with two n's?' he asked.

Yes, it was.

'Not like a fish,' Anna hooted.

A member of the waiting staff appeared in my periphery. 'Would you like a drink, sir?'

Damn right, I would.

I accepted a glass of red wine and took a giant gulp, then realised the other two were cradling orange juices.

'You not partaking?'

Anna looked disappointed in me. 'No, I don't like the taste.'

I glanced behind and hoped to catch the eye of the third-year student again, but she had disappeared. The rest of the room seemed to be getting on swimmingly. There were people out there who looked cool, who were laughing with each other and having a good time, and sparkling wonderfully in their smart attire.

And here I was, chained in Holy Corner.

'Are you reading straight Divinity?' enquired Charles.

'No, Biblical Studies and Early Christian Culture. But I'm mostly doing the former during this first semester. What about you?'

'Single honours.'

'Joint for me,' piped Anna. 'Biblical Studies and Ancient Philosophy. It's the history that fascinates me.'

Perhaps I had been too quick to judge Anna. I toyed with saying more about my own complex love affair with history, but the words would not come. For a terrible few moments, none of us could think of anything further to say and the exuberance of the rest of the room only made it worse.

We were saved by the approach of a stooped, elderly man swathed in the sort of black robes that would have been high ecclesiastical fashion in the fourteenth century.

'So this is my new Divinity team,' he observed in a voice so scratchy that they sounded like the first words he had uttered since a vow of silence. 'Welcome to Sallies. I'm Father Haughton, your tutor for this semester.'

Oh, heaven forbid.

He held out a bony hand and I was half expecting his touch to bear the cold of the risen dead. I realised, disconcertingly, that his pupils did not align. He released my hand and exchanged introductions with the other two, then asked each of us where we were from.

'Near Kirkcudbright,' I replied.

'You don't sound Scottish,' remarked Charles.

'My dad was from Sussex and I was raised there.'

'What brought you north?'

'My mum was from Dumfries.'

Was. I had referred to both my parents in the past tense, but Charles did not seem to notice. I realised, however, that Father Haughton was regarding me shrewdly and it struck me that he might well be aware of my 'care-experienced' application channel, perhaps even knew the details of my heartbreak.

I subsided into silence and let the others talk. Anna seemed happy to voice plenty. I nodded and smiled occasionally, but I could feel my heart curling in on itself. I resented being made to mention my parents. I should not have to refer to them in the company of strangers. Not here, not this night.

I drank my wine at an unholy rate. The others were talking theology and I assumed they did not require my input, but I noticed that Father Haughton did not angle his body away from me and he kept checking on me with his lopsided stare, seeing if he could draw me into the exchanges.

There and then, I decided I did not dislike Father Haughton.

V

A bell cut through the chatter. Not like a fire alarm, but the tinkle of a genuine handheld bell.

'Ah,' observed Father Haughton. 'Supper calls.'

The crowd began to syphon from the room and I traipsed behind Anna back past the marble entrance vestibule and into the Grand Hall.

For the second time that evening, I came to an abrupt halt in a doorway. Before me was a substantial oak-panelled room, with stained-glass windows along two sides and a high table at the far end. Between the windows were gold-framed portraits of pompous men, gowned and primped, their expressions pinched sternly as though sick of listening to student conversations for the past three centuries. Oak tables and benches extended along the length of the hall and flames flickered in lamps down the centre of each.

The effect was magical. The entire hall was bathed in a soft glow. Silver cutlery twinkled. The colours of the stained-glass windows glistened. Shadows fluttered like bats between the beams. I might have described it as Hogwarts-esque, if Hogwarts had been a thing back in 1992.

With a flush of exhilaration, I followed the robed figure of Father Haughton to our places at the end of one table. Freshers studying other subjects joined us, but they left our little group alone. Father Haughton lowered his bony frame into the end seat and listened to Anna, who was still in full voice. Charles perched opposite me, upright and gathered, as if waiting to pray before we ate.

A hand materialised over my shoulder and filled my glass with wine. The other two were still on the orange, but I was pleased to see Father Haughton accept a glass of the good stuff. I let my mind wander and my eyes rove. I contemplated the oil paintings flickering in and out of the lamplight and I thought to myself that maybe this was special. Maybe this was extraordinary. Look at me. Finn Nethercott. Suited and booted, sipping vintage in the Grand Hall of St Salvator's Hall.

At that moment someone eased themselves over the bench and sat down beside me. I broke my thoughts and turned to look into the eyes of the third-year student again.

'Thought I'd join you,' she announced conspiratorially. 'Do you mind?'

'Be my guest.'

One of the serving staff proffered red wine and she took a moment tasting it, then pulled a face. 'I've had better.'

'So your remit tonight includes wining and dining?'

'We're told to scatter ourselves amongst the throng and I saw this space beside you and decided that so far you've been the most interesting person I've met.'

'That doesn't say much for the competition.'

She cast her eyes around the other diners to check that no one was paying us any attention, then leaned into me. 'You fancy making this even more interesting?'

I felt her fingers on my thigh and a flush of timidity blossomed through my veins. Then I looked down and saw she was holding a small pill. 'What's that?'

'Just something to oil the cogs. They told me my job tonight is to make things go smoothly.'

She fixed me with her blue eyes and I took the pill from her, then watched as she produced a second and swallowed it with a sip of wine.

'What are you waiting for? You're in the big world now, Preacher. All grown up and left home. So you've got to live a little dangerously.'

I could have told her that I'd had my share of pills back in Dumfries; that I'd spent too much of Nan's money on them because they liberated me from the seam of grief that always lay in the pit of my stomach. But there was something in the challenge of her expression that stopped me. I checked that Anna and Charles were absorbed in their theological discussions, then slipped the pill onto my tongue and drank. The third-year student watched intently and bestowed a wide grin on me.

Prawn cocktail starters arrived, delicately placed in front of each diner. This was a professional operation. In the shadows beyond the lamplit guests, I sensed an army of waiting staff slip smoothly into gear.

'So, what's your name?' she asked as she dipped a fork into her prawns.

I told her and she placed her fork aside and offered a hand for me to shake.

'Well Finn, I'm Madri.'

'Madri?'

'Short for Madrigal.' Stated with throwaway contempt.

'Oh, wow. That's like a song, isn't it?'

'Something else to thank my parents for.'

Her voice and diction were perfect, like royalty. They daunted me.

'Are you English?' I asked and she scoffed.

'Posh Edinburgh, pal. Don't you know a New Town accent when you hear it? My family has a rather extravagant pad on King's Street and a rather pokey estate in Perthshire.'

Roast beef and all the trimmings arrived, although Anna opted for an anaemic quiche. While she examined it, Father Haughton took the opportunity to fork a smidgen of flesh shakily into his mouth and turn his disconcerting gaze on me.

'What about you, Finn?'

I shifted away from Madri and gave him my attention. 'What about me?'

'Are you – like Anna – planning to go into the ministry one day?'

'Bloody hell, no.'

I was pretty well oiled up by then and the words blurted out without thought, but Father Haughton simply chewed on the beef, a globule of gravy on his chin.

'Then why Divinity?'

Beneath the alcohol, I could sense the pill beginning to work. I didn't know what Madri had given me, but its effects were subtle and uplifting. I felt less tongue-tied, less weighed down by reservations.

'Because my dad was a reverend in Sussex. He had a parish outside Chichester.'

Father Haughton placed his fork down, picked up his glass and took a long sip, then angled his bony frame towards me. The other two got the hint and began to talk amongst themselves, but I sensed Madri listening intently.

'So you do have faith?'

I thought about this for a long time, uncertain how much I wanted to divulge to him – and to her. 'Not the Christian type. Not what the Church preaches Sunday after Sunday to bored congregations who only want to get their blessing and then disappear. My dad was different. He tried to take his congregation out of their comfort zone. He composed sermons that tested them – made them actually think a bit. But they didn't like it and some of them complained to his boss – the bishop or whoever he was – because they didn't go to church to have their religion tested.'

When Father Haughton replied, he mirrored my cautious tone. 'Testing our faith is vital. It's exactly why we study Divinity at St Andrews. And if the answers to your questions leave you with no faith, then so be it. Divinity is a practical academic discipline.'

'But if it's a practical academic discipline, why do we come out of it with different answers?'

'That's the nature of studying faith.'

I wrinkled my nose, unconvinced. 'They say there are only three things about Jesus that can be historically verified. He lived – there are censuses that show that. He must have been a great speaker because he certainly became famed around the lands of Judea. And he was crucified. Roman records confirm that. So what about everything else?'

'Everything else is a matter of faith.'

I stoppered a cynical reply with a gulp of wine.

He waited until I had settled, then leaned even closer and asked softly, 'So if your faith is not a Christian one, where does it lie?'

It was the perfect, incisive question and I knew I must answer it well. I let my mind fill with memories of the last few years in Dumfries, the rollercoaster of emotions and the beauty I discovered that redeemed me.

'In the natural world and in history.'

I thought I heard a soft intake of breath from Madri.

Father Haughton's rheumy eyes explored me, then he prodded. 'Go on.'

Whatever chemicals were in that pill, they were running through my veins now, invigorating me, emboldening my words. *Okay, here it comes.*

'I feel happiest when I'm in places that are really old, those that have spent centuries watching each generation go by – ageless stone circles, forgotten hillforts, shifting rivers, crumbling chapels. I get inspired when I see ancient trees and I think about their long lives. I listen to the rhythm of the sea and it makes me sure there must be some kind of god. It's when I'm alone with nature, and when there are wide open spaces around me, that I feel most religious.'

Father Haughton was silent for an interminable time and I could smell the wine on his breath. 'In other words,' he said at last, 'your faith lies in a world that has been structured by a higher power.'

I thought about the utter chaotic mess of my life and shook my head.

'No. Not structured. There's no structure in this life. But I believe in a power that created the most incredible design for the world, gave it vitality and beauty and complexity – and then abandoned it.'

VI

The Freshers Dinner was over and the Grand Hall emptying.

Father Haughton bid us goodnight, which disappointed me more than I expected, and Anna and Charles also made their excuses. Maybe it was vespers or something.

But Madri did not budge. Her shoulder was pressed against mine and I knew her eyes roved over me, though I could not bring myself to look back at her.

'That was pretty intense, Preach,' she said in a husky, wine-slick voice.

'I think I sounded like a precocious prick.'

'Nothing of the sort. When I guessed you might be the most interesting person to sit next to tonight, I sure made the right decision.'

'It was your pill making me talk like that.'

'That particular pill simply releases the real person. It lowers inhibitions and gives you the confidence to be yourself.'

'I hope my tutor saw it that way.'

'Don't you worry about that. You've made two fans tonight.'

Now that the meal was finished and the hall was emptying, some of the remaining occupants were lighting up cigarettes and cigars and a smoky fug burgeoned above the tables. I pulled out my own pack and offered her one. She nodded and when I flicked the lighter, she leaned forward and held my wrist with her free hand. She took her time and I was struck by the contrast in her features. Her hair was luxuriant, yet prematurely silver; the impish curve of her mouth sat incongruously beneath a patrician nose; her eyebrows and lashes were black against skin so pale it was almost translucent, matched by the black-painted nails around my wrist. Her cigarette alight, she eased back and let her fingers trail over my skin. With a sudden convulsion, I realised she had felt my scars. Not only had she felt them, she understood what they were.

Her eyes fell on mine for interminable seconds as she drew my secrets from me.

'You have stories to tell,' she murmured.

I had no response to that, so I lit my own cigarette and tried to break the moment. 'What about you? What are you reading?'

She released me from her stare. 'What do you think?'

I took in her striking hair and arch expression and decided she was no scientist. 'Something to do with the mind? Psychology, maybe. Or Philosophy.' Then my eyes drifted down to the Celtic design on her T-shirt. 'Or perhaps you're a historian?'

She raised an eyebrow, but then changed the subject. 'Do you have an academic mum?'

WHEN WE WERE KILLERS

'If that's some kind of chat-up line, it's weird.'

'St Andrews encourages second- and third-year students to act as academic "parents" for new undergrads. Show them around, answer any queries they have.'

'And you can just select someone over dinner and offer these services? That seems like a system that's open to abuse.'

'I didn't offer, I just asked if you had one.'

I gazed at her and tried to decipher her motives. 'No, I don't. I think I'm fine without.'

She smiled. 'Perhaps you're right. I'm not sure you're the type who wants to be parented.' She dragged on her cigarette, then dropped it into her wine. 'Well thank you for the company, Finn. You made a mundane duty considerably more compelling.'

'You're going?'

'It's always more fun to leave when we're wanting more, don't you think?' She gave me a wink and swung her legs over the bench. 'But don't worry, I'll see you around, Preacher.'

With that, she weaved around the tables and left the Hall.

VII

It was three days before I encountered Madrigal again.

Three days in which I took my first faltering steps into my new university life. On the Wednesday, I spent the afternoon at a 'Freshers Fayre' in the University Sports Centre, where a rich assortment of student societies had set up stalls and were attempting to seduce first-year students into joining. I wandered around in silence and decided none of them offered what I was seeking.

On Thursday night there was a rave in a nightclub called The Bop beneath the Student Union on North Street. It was like a huge gym hall painted entirely black and heaving with sweating bodies. I had hoped Madri might be there, but it was impossible to see or hear anything other than the music and the strobes. I smoked and drank and loitered at the edges, watching the gyrations of the dancers.

On Friday, I discovered the university's main library with Anna and we went through the complicated registration process to gain access, including some ancient pledge not to burn the place down. I had hoped it would be a centuries-old citadel filled with leather tomes and lit by candles, but disappointingly it was a 1970s concrete oblong arranged over four floors, with fluorescent lighting and endless metallic shelving. It did, however, have awesome views of the North Sea, and I decided a seat at one of the desks beside these windows would not be a bad place to study.

I wandered around the Divinity stacks with Anna and she showed me books she had already read back in Knoxville, Tennessee, and pulled out others with an enthusiasm that was contagious. I bought her a coffee in a little café off Union Street and I realised that when she could overcome her natural social nerves, she was a generous and incisive companion.

That evening, I sat with Charles at one of the benches in Hall, tucking into a dinner of sausages and mash. He was telling me something or other about the Gospel of Luke, but I'd sure had enough divinity for one week. So I was toying with him about whether he believed in sex after ordination, but he wasn't amused.

A loud hail broke me from my meal. 'Hey, Preacher.'

She was standing across the Hall, looking just as striking as before, even though the effect was slightly tarnished by a plate of mash in her hands.

I rose and went to her, and she threw a dazzling grin at me. 'How's the world of the virtuous?'

'You're asking the wrong man.'

'Yes, I probably am. It's not exactly virtuous to accept a pill off an unknown woman just before a first discussion with your new tutor. Do you regret it?'

I shook my head. 'Whatever was in that thing helped me grasp feelings I can't usually put into words. For a few precious moments, I thought I could decipher the sacred.'

To this day I've no idea where that phrase came from. It just sort of popped out.

Her eyes bulged and she drew a breath. 'Whoa. You see, that's what I like about you. You walk over here and then you come out with something like that.' She leaned in and tapped my chest with a fingernail. 'You got me thinking about you, Preacher.'

I reddened and shifted my feet. 'Er, well, would you like to join us?' I waved over to our places.

'Who's your friend?'

Charles was gaping at her.

'He's a Divinity colleague.'

She smiled and returned her gaze to me. 'No, you're okay. You keep reciting your psalms.'

'Seriously, it would be no bother.'

She stepped away and winked. 'Another time, Preacher.'

I watched her slip down the Hall, then traipsed disappointed back to Charles, who seemed so bewildered by the whole episode that he could hardly speak. We ate in silence and, when I eventually regained my composure, I glanced over the rows of heads.

Madri was sitting amongst a group on the furthest table. There were four of them, huddled together, impervious to the rest of the room. One man had his back to me and I could make out nothing of him, but when some of the nearer heads moved, I saw the other one facing me, the one Madri sat beside.

He was one of the most striking men I had ever laid eyes

on. Even sitting, I guessed he was a head taller than me. His hair was pure ebony, cut short at the sides, but piled on the top into a mass of voluptuous waves, exaggerating his height. His skin was sun-kissed despite the season and his cheekbones and jawline as delicate as a woman's. He had poured himself into an immaculate black shirt and charcoal jacket, and he sat straight-backed with one hand on a glass of wine, listening to his companions and yet somehow removed from their conversation.

Some part of me was wondering where he had got the wine from. The other part was noticing how Madri had her hand on his arm and was leaning towards him, needing an attention that he was not providing. I wanted to dislike him, but I found I could not. He was irresistible, and I really did not know how I was supposed to feel about that.

Madri gave up her pawing and turned to the person on her other side, the fourth member of the group. My heart spiked. It was the American girl, the one with the exquisite frown. The one who was so certain I had brought upon myself a lifetime of bad luck.

Madri was saying something and suddenly they both looked up and stared across the Hall at me. I gasped so loudly that Charles stopped dissecting his sausage. Madri was laughing and the other girl's brows were rising up her forehead.

I could not maintain their gaze and dropped my head back to my plate. My pulse was pounding and my breathing ragged.

'You okay?' asked Charles.

'Yeah, yeah. Fine.'

I steadied myself and summed up the courage to look

back once more, but they had turned away and moved on to something more interesting.

I clattered my cutlery onto my plate and eased a leg over the bench. 'I'm done. See you later.'

I stalked from the Hall and went outside in search of some cleaner air. I found a dark corner of the main quadrangle and lit a cigarette. The smoke smoothed my irascibility and I peered up at the stars and scolded myself for acting with such petulance. I had just stubbed the butt out, when I recognised the tinkle of Madri's laugh and saw the four of them pacing along the opposite side of the quad. They disappeared through an arch onto the pedestrian walkway of Butts Wynd.

Forcing myself to forget them, I lit another smoke and stood for several minutes trying to convince myself that I was fascinated by Renaissance architecture. But who was I kidding? With a low curse at my own frailty, I stamped out the ciggy and marched onto the Wynd and then north to a road called The Scores. By the time I reached it, I had lost them. I kicked tetchily against a paving stone, shoved my hands into my pockets and wandered eastwards for want of anything better to do. I passed Edwardian faculty buildings and reached the hulking ruins of a castle on a promontory.

A large *No Admittance* sign hung on the railings and for some reason this stoked my irritability. Purely because I shouldn't, I hoisted myself up, got a boot between the spikes and leapt onto the grass. The fall was harder than I expected and my knees jolted, but I shook them out and wandered towards the first battlements.

I touched the stones. They were cold and moist, rinsed

by maritime air. I let my senses adjust to the texture against my palms and wondered who else had touched these very same walls over the years. Townsfolk perhaps. Sentries on duty. Kids playing hide-and-seek. Dogs urinating. Farriers. Leatherworkers. Fishmongers. Churchmen. Perhaps even attackers. Soldiers besieging these very battlements, probing at their strength, slamming ladders against them and urging their comrades upwards while the sky rained arrows.

I strolled deeper into the ruins and caught sight of the sea lurking beneath pale moonlight. Perhaps the attackers came from that direction. Sails on the horizon sending panic amongst the community. A rush to get inside the protection of the walls. Longships coming, silent and implacable. There would be terror coursing through the populace. Screaming and arguing. Sergeants spitting orders. Horses whinnying. The great doors wrenched closed.

I meandered through the remains and set a course towards the ocean.

And then I noticed a glow on a far wall. A flicker of flame. It was coming from a dip in the land and I caught the murmur of voices. I slipped onto a nearby stone to get a better view and my breath snagged in my throat.

It was the group from Sallies.

They were scattered on the grass around a fire in an iron brazier. I could see Madri's face clearly. She was sitting with her legs stretched languidly towards the fire. The silver in her hair sparkled almost as much as her pendant and earrings. She was contemplating the flames but listening to the soft tones of one of the men who sat on an outcrop with a cigarette burning in his fingers.

The other girl perched furthest from the fire, her thin

legs pulled up so that her chin rested on her knees, her hair darker than all the night's shadows, framing her delicate features and the serious line of her lips.

The tall man was between them. He was stretched out listening to the voice of the second man. I thought he might have his eyes closed because I could see no glint of them.

I was wrong.

'Who's there?' he demanded and, in a blur of movement, all of them sprung to their feet.

I realised I must be silhouetted against the lights of the town and I held up a placatory hand. 'I didn't mean to disturb you.'

'Get down here into the light,' the man ordered, although behind his bombast he sounded rattled.

I dropped from my perch and approached their hostile stares.

Then Madri's lips split into a grin. 'Why, it's Preacher.'

'Yes, it's me again. Hi, Madri.'

'You know this fellow?'

'He's the one I pointed out in Hall.'

'*He's* the Preacher?' The man's eyes had not left me and there was a long silence as he examined me. Evidently, it was his judgement – and his alone – that would determine how the next few moments unfolded. 'Did you follow us?'

'I fancied a walk.'

'And you just happened to end up right here.'

'It's a free country.'

'On the contrary, this specific piece of the nation is out of bounds after dusk. Can't you read?'

'I saw the sign, but to be honest I don't care to be told

where I can and can't go. Seems you feel the same way or do you have some special dispensation to be here?'

He greeted my question with another silence. Then, finally, he relaxed his posture and sank back onto the grass and the others did likewise.

'If you weren't following us and you weren't eavesdropping, how did your walk bring you here?'

I sensed that it was best to stop being evasive and indulge them in some truth. 'I like this place. Something about old buildings always puts me in a good mood. If you get what I mean.'

I glanced at the man with the cigarette, but he immediately flicked his eyes away, as though nervous of my attention. He raised his chin, puffed out smoke and stared towards the sea. Though he had been holding their rapt attention before, it would appear he had nothing to add to this conversation.

'Yes, I do get what you mean.' The tall man's focus was unwaveringly on me, but his tone was gentler.

The thin girl had curled herself up tight again. Her chin was balanced on her knees, but her eyes stared at me unblinking, like twin moons.

Eventually the pressure of their examination got the better of me. I found my own tongue moving and the first stupid thing I could think of spurted out.

'So do you do this sort of thing often?'

I was not prepared for the mirth that greeted this question. Madri put back her head and laughed and even the tall man smiled.

'Yes Preacher,' said Madri. 'We like to mark special occasions.'

'Skammdegi,' said the tall man slowly, letting the syllables extend. 'And the beginning of Gormánuður.'

I knew that first word. *Skammdegi*. I had come across it while I pored over my history books. I tried to fire up my brain. *Skammdegi*. It came to me.

'The dark months of winter in the Viking calendar.'

'And the first days of Gormánuður, the Slaughter Month. You know your Norse history.'

'Some of it.'

He kept his eyes on me, but addressed Madri. 'I thought you told me he was Divinity.'

'He is, but with a healthy fascination in the history of the times.'

Now that he had relaxed again, there was an authority coming from the man. The natural confidence of wealth, of prestige, of power.

'What's your name?'

'Finn Nethercott.'

'So it seems, Finn Nethercott, you're a rule-breaking, gate-climbing preacher, who knows his heathen Norse calendar. An interesting mix.'

'See, I told you,' said Madri. 'He's interesting. Even more so when he's got some stimulants into his bloodstream. Could be just what we're looking for.'

The man made an irritated noise in the back of his throat to hush her, then released me from his gaze and focused back on the fire. 'Well, Preacher, we cherish our privacy and we loathe eavesdroppers, so I suggest you stop creeping around in the shadows and run along back to Hall. We do not wish to be disturbed again.'

And that was it. With one simple pronunciation, I had

been dismissed. Their eyes dropped from me, their postures shifted away and they expected me to comply.

I hovered for a few seconds, then offered a final salutation. 'Happy hunting.'

As I strode away my pulse thumped with indignation. How dare they dismiss me like a schoolboy?

I marched through the ruins to a spot further along the coast and far enough away to lose sight of them. There, on the edge of the drop to the beach, I hunkered down with my back against a segment of battlement and stared at the undulating water.

I lurked there for an age, adamant that I would not cross the ruins again until I was certain I would not bump into them. But I was wearing only a shirt and eventually I began to shiver uncontrollably. So I picked my way through the castle on a route that circled far from them. I had made it to the railings when I heard a strangled moan. I stopped dead and listened. It came again. A keening and then a soft sob. I stared back into the dark and strained to listen. But now there was only silence.

It had been a female voice and my mind was filled with the face of the thin girl. Despite my better judgement, I retraced my steps. This time I made certain my approach was not silhouetted by the town's lights. I advanced on my knees until I could peer over a low wall and down into the dip.

They were still there. The fire was little more than a smouldering glow that cast only the weakest light, but it was enough to make out their figures.

The thin girl was lying stretched on the grass next to the embers, her back arched up from the ground. She moaned again, wailing softly towards the sky. The others were on their feet and they seemed to be arguing. Madri was gesticulating and the tall man was pointing an accusatory finger back at her. The other man had his arms wide and was attempting to placate them, but real anger had ignited. Madri knelt beside the prostrate girl and shook her gently. The light was poor, but I saw enough to recognise the fear scrawled across Madri's face.

Then the girl jolted awake. She sat up, ran hands over her face and waved that she was okay. Madri spat some words at the tall man and he rumbled something darkly back. The other man stalked away to light another cigarette.

I did not know what I had witnessed, but I had seen enough. Whatever they had been doing to mark the start of the Slaughter Month, it had gone awry. Heart banging, forcing my breathing to steady, I retreated quietly and slipped back into the embrace of the town.

VIII

The next morning, I joined Anna and Charles for our first visit to the School of Divinity. We gathered in the sunshine outside Sallies to study Anna's map. She was wearing baggy jeans and a lemon jumper, which clashed with her red hair. Charles had daringly removed his tie, but otherwise still wore the suit that had swamped his frame at the formal dinner.

We crossed North Street and walked down Union Street, then discovered a pleasant pedestrian cut-through called Baker Lane, which spilled us out on South Street. It was just before ten in the morning and the pavements were filled with students heading to lectures. Anna consulted her map and led us across the road to a pedestrian passage called The Long Walk. We passed under an arch and broke out onto a beautiful green space.

The Long Walk continued winding its way between lawns towards the university's Zoology museum, but where we stood the space was bounded by more intimate buildings. Sandstone walls shone warm in the sun. Leaded and colonnaded windows reflected the greenery. Wisteria fingered its way towards slate rooflines. A vast oak tree, as old as history, stood proudly at the heart of the quadrangle. It was all I could do to stop myself stepping over the encircling boundary to place my hand on its bark.

'Well, we're here,' announced Anna as she consulted her booklet.

'*This* is Divinity?' I challenged.

'St Mary's College. Says here, it houses the School of Divinity's offices, seminar rooms and library.'

'*Principio Erat Verbum*,' intoned Charles.

'What are you spouting?'

He turned and pointed back to the arch. 'It's inscribed on that. *In the Beginning was the Word*.'

'You read Latin?'

He grinned. 'Not much, but I know the School's motto. We're in the right place.'

A thin voice hailed us from a doorway and there was Father Haughton. He herded us into his office and waved us into armchairs. The place smelt of age and decay. A grandfather clock ticked in one corner and an antique desk was piled high with student essays. Books lined the walls. Outside, the boughs of the oak stretched towards the windowpanes and I noticed the leaves were dark and waxy.

'It's a holm oak,' said Father Haughton. 'It's leaves are evergreen and do not drop. This one was planted around 1650, when I think Charles the First reigned.'

'Not unless he reigned without a head,' I corrected. 'He was executed in 1649.'

He threw me a fleeting smile, then waved a gnarly finger at a pot of tea and we helped ourselves. He took us through a lengthy introduction to the School of Divinity, then steepled his fingers and asked us the value of theology. Charles gave a guarded reply and Father Haughton nodded encouragement and gradually the discussion evolved over the next hour. At the end he presented us with a reading list and an essay title – *How is Theology Related to Religion?* – and asked us to submit two thousand words on the subject by the following Monday.

Tutorial over, he levered himself out of his chair and led us along the landing to an oak door.

'The King James Library,' he said and led us in.

Arched windows looked out over South Street. Between them, imposing bookcases, painted white and gold, stood proudly. Desks were positioned for the best views. A gallery ran around three walls, with more bookcases and ladders to reach the upper shelves.

'Commissioned by King James VI and completed in 1643, this is one of the oldest libraries in the town.' Father Haughton's voice was hushed, although no one seemed to be studying at that early hour. 'It was the primary library for the whole university, but it is now a dedicated Divinity resource and you may use it as your reading room at any hour, day or night.'

He let us explore and then finally dismissed us back to Sallies.

IX

Over the next few weeks I traipsed to my lectures behind Anna and Charles. I mastered the filing systems of both libraries and found the reading-list books. I pulled caffeine-fuelled all-nighters and wrote the essays I was set by Father Haughton. I sat with Charles for meals in Sallies, and I shared coffees and reading sessions with Anna.

Though I could barely conceive of two people more different from me, I liked them. Charles was a tightly stitched prude who seemed genuinely taken aback by most of the things I said, even when I wasn't trying to shock him. But he had a brilliant academic mind and a dry wit that just occasionally broke its bonds and floored me. He would, I decided, make a good minister for his future Christian flock.

Anna's whole world revolved around her faith. She believed fervently in the scriptures and lived life accordingly. I doubted she had entertained a sacrilegious thought in her life, but kindness ran in her bones. She would bring me cookies in the library and help me structure my essays and readily discuss the underlying concepts. I gravitated towards her.

'Here we are,' said Anna one day, running her finger along a row of books and pulling out a slim volume. 'Kierkegaard, *Fear and Trembling*.'

We were on the third floor of the main library and had been wandering the stacks in search of the last titles on our reading list. The place was crowded and yet hushed, like a church. Heads sprouted from every desk as they leaned over paperwork, scribbled notes and forced their brains to absorb information. We exited the stacks and I read the essay title that Father Haughton had set us. 'I don't really get this one. *Is faith a gift or a conclusion?*'

'In the ancient world, there were two main forms of theological thought – Jewish and Greek. The Jews believed in a revelation theology. Every time they learned something it was because God had decided this should be, and anything that was beyond their understanding was because God did not wish them to know.'

'So their knowledge and their faith were *gifts* from God?'

'Precisely. Whereas the Greek idea was that everything known about God came through man's own advances in understanding. So their faith was a *conclusion* of these efforts.'

I nodded slowly as I tried to grasp these concepts.

She pushed one of the books at me. 'Read the Kierkegaard. Chapter four. Then we can meet tomorrow and discuss. I'm going to head back to Hall and make a start on Paley. You coming?'

'No, I'll stay here. Fewer distractions.'

I pondered her retreating figure, then tucked

Mr Kierkegaard under my arm and wandered to a free chair at one of the communal tables.

Ten minutes later, I was still stuck on the second paragraph, and I sighed and dragged my eyes away from the page. Low sun was slicing through the windows, bouncing off the white walls and the metallic stacks. The girl opposite was drowning in scribbled algebra notelets. The man one along had a face full of acne and jotted notes using a gold-nib fountain pen. His eyes caught mine, then fluttered away to stare sheepishly at the ceiling.

Something about the action tugged at my memory. Where had I seen that before? Of course, the castle. The man with the cigarette who had been holding the attention of Madri's group. It had been too dark to make out his features, but he had averted his eyes in same awkward manner.

He was a strange fellow. Nothing about him seemed to fit properly. His eyes were strong blue, but they were set too close together and never stopped flitting and twitching. His nose was straight, but it flared at the nostrils. His teeth were good, but his chin weak and his lower jaw too far back. His rampant spots made him look young, but his floppy hair had the wispiness of an older man. He wore an expensive tweed jacket, but it was too big in the shoulders and hung slack on him.

He was conscious of my examination, so I returned my attention to my reading. When I looked up again, he was gone.

Goddamn. I grabbed my belongings and propelled myself around the table. The algebra girl glared at me, and I mouthed an apology, then strode for the stairs. I dropped three flights and checked each floor, but there was no sign of him, so I exited and watched students filing back into town.

I was about to join them when some instinct made me turn along the far side of the building and follow a path to reach the rear of the library where smokers often congregated. Sure enough, there he was, seated on a bench, cigarette hanging from his mouth, contemplating the sweep of the grass. His eyes flitted up at my approach and he tensed, but he was cornered now and he knew it.

'I think we've met,' I said.

'Aye, I think we have.' He spoke with the cigarette still dangling from his lips. 'You're the Preacher.'

His voice was the most melodious Scots I had ever heard. Deep and lyrical. Gentle and resonant. The *r* in Preacher rolling softly.

'That's not a name I go by. I don't have a religious bone in my body.'

For a moment his awkwardness vanished and his face creased into a smile. 'A heathen in the Divinity department,' he purred. 'How delightful.'

'My name's Finn.'

'Aye, I remember. And I'm Laurie.' The smile had gone and he didn't offer his hand. 'Now perhaps you can tell me why you've followed me out here?'

'I stayed in the ruins that night and heard things that worried me. One of the girls seemed to be in pain. Is she okay?'

'You should mind your own business.'

'I'll mind my business when I'm not witnessing someone in distress. I don't know what you were doing, but it looked pretty heavy to me.'

'The person in question is fine. We were merely indulging in some fun.'

49

I bit off a sharp response, and I think he expected me to leave, but I stepped past and sat on the other end of the bench.

'Can I cadge a ciggie off you?'

Reluctantly, he pulled a pack from his jacket and I lowered my head as he flicked his lighter. Then he crossed his legs away from me and stared at the distant sea.

'So, Laurie, what are you studying?'

'I'm a postgrad. Five years in this town now. Early Medieval Scotland, specialising in the Gaelic, Celtic and Viking kingdoms of the north and west coasts.'

'Oh wow!' I was impressed and I couldn't help showing it.

'You know about ancient Scotland?'

'I'm fascinated by the ancient world in general. It's sort of what got me into the Bible and early Christian cultures.'

Laurie took a thoughtful pull on his cigarette, then said through the smoke, 'Magnus was impressed that you knew about *Skammdegi*.'

'Was he the tall man?'

'Aye, I think he liked you.'

'I get the impression his opinions are pretty important. Is he your leader?'

'He thinks he is. He suggested once that we call him Jarl.'

'A Viking chieftain. And do you?'

Laurie chuckled. 'He's obsessed with Viking culture, but we told him what he could do with that particular proposal.'

I grinned. 'So what does this group of yours do?'

'We talk, we share stories, we eat special foods and drink fine wines.'

'From what I witnessed, you also indulge in chemical taking.'

'Perhaps, sometimes. They add an edge to our storytelling.'

'And that's it?'

'Isn't it enough?'

I mulled over his words, frowning across the lawn. 'Do you usually hang out in places like the castle?'

'If memory serves me correctly, you said yourself that *old buildings always put you in a good mood*. Seems we feel the same. But what did you mean by it, Finn?'

I shrugged. 'I was feeling crap about university that night and I found myself drawn into the castle ruins because they seemed like somewhere removed from it all. Does that make sense?'

'Perhaps.'

'My dad used to take me on trips to little rural churches and sit in the pews while I wandered around checking out the statues and the crosses and the paintings. Those shared times shaped my beliefs about the power of historic locations. And I think my dad visited the little churches to find his own reassurance. I think, as he sat in those pews, he was an unhappy man trying to ask his own God for the right direction forward.'

I glanced self-consciously at Laurie. 'Anyway, something rubbed off, because here I am reading Divinity. And I like that it's the study of ancient documents, ancient customs, ancient languages and ancient places, searching for perhaps the most important truth of all. It feels pretty relevant to me.'

'It certainly does. And you tell a good tale.'

'A bit over the top.'

'Oh, I think over-the-top is an underrated attribute.'

I felt stupid. I'd followed him from the library full of questions, yet had mostly answered his. I rose and stamped out my butt. 'Anyway, I should probably be going. I'm glad we cleared a few things up. Maybe I'll see you around.'

'Aye, Finn. Maybe you will.'

X

I was deeply unconscious when there was a rat-a-tat on the door.

Befuddled, I peered groggily at my watch. It was 5.31pm on the fourth Wednesday of term and bang in the middle of my post-tutorial kip. Goddamn it, I should have put a note on the door saying, '*disturb at your peril*', but I never expected visitors.

In the tutorial, Father Haughton had returned our latest essay efforts. Anna beamed as she waved a red-inked A– grade and Charles had a B+. I was pleasantly surprised to see a B– scrawled on mine, but the comments hit me hard.

Clear and well argued, but a little lightweight. Try to write more like a theologian and less like someone making a speech at a Church Youth Group.

I would have liked to ask him just what the hell he meant by that, but instead I sulked through most of the rest of the group discussion.

I suspected my visitor was Anna, come to see if my mood had lifted.

'Hold on.' I straightened my shirt, ran a hand through my hair, opened the door and stopped.

It was not Anna.

'Hello, Finn.'

For a long moment I could think of nothing to say. Not a damn thing.

Finally, two words. 'It's you.'

She frowned, then made a play of looking down at herself. 'Last time I looked, it was. And what about you? Not been standing on any unlucky initials lately?'

'Er, no. Thanks for warning me about those.'

She shrugged and unknitted her brows. 'I'm Hope.'

'*Hope,*' I breathed.

'Hope D'Angelo.'

Coming to my senses, I extended a hand. 'Hello, Hope.'

Her clasp was light, her fingers warm and delicate.

'You're American,' I observed banally.

Her frown returned.

'You might have noticed that's not a rarity in St Andrews.'

Her tone contained the same hint of disdain that I had detected when she first accosted me on the Patrick Hamilton initials and I felt my defence barriers rearing, but then she retreated. 'Anyway, it's just my obstreperous half.'

Ideally, I could have done with a twenty-minute pause to shoot to the library and look up what the hell *obstreperous* meant, but she didn't seem in the mood for waiting.

'And you,' she added coolly, 'sound as Anglo-Saxon as they come.'

She made it seem like a character flaw, but I forced a thin smile and replied, 'Just my intransigent half.'

A twinkle behind her pupils acknowledged the parry, and

I used the truce to move back from the doorway. 'Would you like to come in?'

She took in the scene with one sweeping gaze, her nose testing the air and her eyes gliding over the rumpled bedding. 'Did I disturb you?'

'Just having a bit of down time.'

'You're lucky to bag a single in your first year. I had to share during mine.'

'To be honest, I sometimes wonder if I'd prefer to share. It's pretty cramped in this little place and hardly any visitors make it up here.'

'Well, I did.'

I tested a smile on her. 'And I'm glad. Would you like a cuppa?'

'Maybe another time.'

She was dressed much the same as when she had stopped me on that first morning. An oversize sports hoodie over leggings encasing her long, thin legs, and Doc Marten boots. Wrapped around her throat was a big university scarf and on her shoulder a canvas bag. Her hair was tied in a thick ponytail that dropped down her spine to her waist.

She finished her examination of the room and refocused on me. 'So, do you have plans tonight?'

'Plans? Not really, no.'

'Would you like to come with me?'

I swallowed and found myself nodding dumbly.

'Good. Well, grab what you need.'

'Right now?'

'Yes, right now.'

There were probably reams of ramifications, but now that I had her company, I didn't want to lose it, so I flustered around the room, banging my pockets, grabbing my wallet and the keys to access the Hall, not giving my brain a chance to consider. 'Okay, I think that's all.'

'Bring a coat. It's going to get cold where we're heading.'

I unhooked my long wool overcoat from the back of the door and then she placed a hand on my arm and indicated towards the bed. 'Maybe that blanket too. It might be a late one.'

Hardly daring to imagine what she might mean, I bundled the blanket into a roll and followed as she strode down the corridor.

She led me out of Sallies and through the gardens, around the main quadrangle and then north along Butts Wynd to The Scores. I thought we must be heading to the castle again, but she turned in the opposite direction and marched west until we could see the clubhouse of the illustrious Royal and Ancient Golf Club of St Andrews. Perhaps we were going to skirt the manicured fairways and drop into the dunes beside West Sands beach, but as we made our way through a public parking area, she skewed right and unlocked an old Volvo estate.

'Throw your things in the back.'

The rear seat was folded down and I noticed she had a sleeping bag rolled out, as well as a crate of wine bottles and a basket with foil-wrapped contents. I thrust my belongings in and then the old diesel engine grumbled into life, and she took us through the backroads to join the A91 out of town.

'Am I allowed to know where we're going?'

'Somewhere quiet.'

She seemed too slight for the big car. She perched

forward, her hands gripping the wheel and her chin thrust out towards the dashboard as she concentrated on the road. We headed into a landscape of hedgerows and livestock, followed signs for Cupar, then turned onto smaller lanes and set a course towards low hills on the horizon. She kept her eyes fixed ahead and the silence extended. I could not decide if she was a timorous driver or simply ill-disposed to making conversation with me.

'You don't seem very happy to be my escort,' I ventured.

'Magnus asked me.'

'Oh, *Magnus*. I get the impression the opinions of Magnus are held in the utmost regard by everyone.'

'Actually, it was Laurie you made an impression on. He's the reason you're coming tonight.'

'Are the others going to be there?'

'They are.'

'But... *you're* not so sure I should be joining.'

'I don't know you well enough to have an opinion.'

'Are you worried that I carry bad luck after my misadventure on the PH initials?'

'Don't be flippant. I'm just not sure a Divinity undergrad is the best fit for our little outing.'

This took me by surprise and I snorted. 'Why? Are you Satanists? Are you going to sacrifice a goat and drink its blood?'

'No,' she answered grimly, staring ahead at the winding lane. 'Not that.'

Eventually she turned off and we rumbled along a stone track for a mile until it petered into nothing, where a VW Camper and an older Fiat Ducato van were parked. A footpath wound down the sloping land, through a stand of conifers and onwards to a small loch nestled between the hills.

We alighted and she thrust open the boot so I could get my things. Then she handed me the crate of bottles, shouldered her canvas bag and turned to stare back along the lane with her head cocked for any sound.

'Are we waiting for someone?'

'Be quiet.'

For long moments, she did not move and a seam of unease blossomed up my spine as I watched her. At last she shifted.

'What were you doing?'

'Checking we weren't followed.'

'Out here, in the middle of nowhere?'

'I've learned it pays to be cautious. But just forget about it. Come on, this way.'

We picked our way down the path, the bottles chinking softly. The evening was cooling, but the air was breathless against a soft pastel sky and shadows stretched to breaking as the sun took a final peek over the western slopes. We progressed through the stand of conifers and came out above a stony shoreline. There were figures further along and a female laugh broke the silence. A pile of timber and branches had been hauled into a pile ready for torching. Then, oozing across the glen, came the scintillating scents of barbecuing meat.

'Is that the goat?' I asked facetiously.

She dropped her bag near the pile of wood and yanked off her boots.

'Preacher!' Madri waltzed towards me, a glass of wine in her hand and her lips parted in a blazing smile. 'You came.'

'Yeah, though I'm not sure my driver's too happy about it.' I plonked the crate of bottles down.

'Better to be invited this time than to be spying on us.'

I harrumphed, but stoppered a reply.

'All clear?' Madri asked Hope, suddenly serious, and the other girl nodded, then marched off towards the other figures, her basket in the crook of her arm.

Madri's grin returned and she slipped a hand through my arm. 'Don't worry about her. She's always the last to lend her trust to someone new, but once she does, you have it forever.'

Madri had removed her footwear too and I wondered how they managed to walk on the stony ground. Her toenails were painted the same black as her fingernails and she had extended her eyeliner in horizontal bars towards her hairline, like a modern Cleopatra, Queen of Kings, last ruler of the Ptolemaic Kingdom beyond the Nile. Despite the autumnal sting to the air, she wore a thin white dress that revealed her pale throat and shoulders, and she had plaited grasses into bracelets on both wrists.

'Are you celebrating Gormánuður again?' I wondered aloud.

'Not this time, Preach. Tonight we're just having a bit of fun.' She bent and extricated one of the wine bottles from the crate. 'Come on, let's get some spirit in your veins.'

For some reason, I had expected to find more people, but as we crossed the shoreline and climbed onto a bank of cropped grass, it was just Laurie and Magnus perched on stones, conversing softly. Laurie raised a whisky glass to salute my appearance and Magnus pulled himself up to his full height. He was wearing a close-fitting wool polo neck, well-cut chinos and boots and, as always, every item was as black as the hair that curled abundantly over his scalp.

'Welcome, Preacher,' he said and took my hand in a grip.

'My name's Finn.'

'Indeed, it is.'

'And you, of course, are Magnus.' I leaned close so that only he could hear. 'Or should I call you Jarl?'

For a moment his face tightened, then he blinked his dark eyes once and released my hand. 'No formalities tonight. Come and sit.'

He led me to the others and I lowered myself onto the grass. Madri skipped over and handed me a giant glass of wine. I murmured my thanks and took a gulp. It was deep and succulent, heavy as blood and, quite probably, the most exquisite I had ever tasted.

'Wow,' I croaked and Magnus smiled.

'From my own cellars.'

'He means his family's cellars,' Madri teased. 'Magnus' father owns most of Argyll.'

'Wow,' I repeated and Magnus dipped his head in acknowledgement. Then his gaze took in the glen and the darkening waters of the loch. 'It's beautiful, don't you think, Finn?'

'It is indeed, though I liked the castle too. Much more history there.'

'The castle has its purposes, but we wanted to bring you somewhere more quiet, where there's less chance of unwanted eyes. Besides, there's plenty of history here too if you look for it.'

'We await the lunatics,' murmured Laurie inexplicably, a

lopsided grin breaking through the acne, but his eyes flitting away as soon as they made contact with mine.

'Our resident expert on ancient lore,' said Magnus. 'But he'll need a few more drams before he gets into his stride.'

I glanced across the grass to where Hope was tending three disposable barbecues balanced precariously on a boulder. Madri joined her and then declared, 'We're ready.'

Magnus looked at me. 'Time to feast.'

And so we did.

In truth, there was nothing special about the food. Distinctly average burgers were served into white baps and blasted with various sauces, then thrust onto paper plates with a heap of coleslaw, but I ate readily enough and the group sat in a companionable circle and munched and wiped their glistening lips and nattered about irrelevant things. Magnus filled my glass with more wine, and I drank appreciatively, and evening crept around us.

And I couldn't help feeling that this was all just a prelude to something more. Something deeper.

XI

When my stomach was full, I rose and took my wine down to the shoreline. A jetty inched out into the water and two old canoes were secured to it. I walked to the end and sat down with my legs over the edge. I could hear the water lapping beneath me and the cry of gulls from somewhere further out. The sun had long gone, but a few ripples still glinted and shreds of cloud were blossoming pink.

The jetty creaked and Magnus eased his long frame down beside me. For several moments, we enjoyed the peace.

'You know how to pick great locations,' I murmured eventually.

'We pride ourselves on finding them. If you get the right place and the right stories at the right moment in time, then you can go deeper inside yourself and discover new emotions. Do you understand?'

'Perhaps.' I looked at him. 'I haven't asked you what you're studying.'

'I'm working on a doctorate about Scottish governance

in the eighteenth century. To be precise, I'm examining the hypothesis that Britain's "long" eighteenth century, which began with one aristocratic revolution in 1688 and ended with another in 1832, was a pageant of success.'

He lapsed into silence, but I could tell he wanted to say more. At last, he spoke again.

'The thing is, Finn, I've also become interested in another *informal* hypothesis. One that sits at the heart of some of the things we enjoy together as a group. It's a discovery that would make waves amongst the wider historical community and one that keeps me awake at night because the answer is so maddeningly close.'

He clammed up and deliberated for long seconds. 'Can I trust you?'

'You've trusted me enough to bring me here.'

He accepted this and thought about his next words. 'Have you heard of berserkers?'

'Of course. Viking shock troops with a talent for working themselves into frenzies.'

'If you were a Pict on the northern shores of Shetland or Orkney in the year 850, imagine your terror when the first Viking longships broke the horizon. Sleek, dragon-headed vessels of war, filled with warrior hordes from the wastelands of Scandinavia. They came to plunder, to take what they wanted and kill anyone who stood in their way.

'As these new invaders increased their range and raided further west along the coastline of Alba and the Hebrides, the only thing that perhaps moved faster than their ships was their reputation. No doubt fearful tongues painted the invaders as demons. Today, we know that these early impressions were one-dimensional and simplistic, but some descriptions have stood the test of time.

'When terrified villagers spoke of wild and crazed men, howling for blood and baying like wolves, it is now widely thought to be true. Contemporary written accounts, including the Hrafnsmál and the writings of Snorri Sturluson describe specific groups of troops who acted as if they were possessed, who led the attacks, who fought like beasts, and seemed immune to pain. The sources tell of men – and perhaps even women – "strong as bears and wild oxen" and "mad as wolves". Accounts claim that these warriors could work themselves into trance-like furies that lent them superhuman strength, so they could kill with a single blow and were unaffected by edged weapons. Before conflict, they might strip or prance and gesticulate, spitting and moaning and goading their victims.'

'And they wore bearskins,' I interrupted, 'to mark them out as elite troops.'

'Exactly, hence berserkers from the Old Norse *beserkr*, meaning bearskin.'

'So, you're informally researching these troops?'

'More specific than that. I'm trying to determine *what* turned them into moaning, shrieking beasts. *How* they switched these fits on and off. *Why* they seemed to be in a trance and immune to pain.' He fixed me with an intense gaze. 'Tell me, Finn, when you hear the description of these berserkers, what does it make you think?'

'Sounds like they were on something.'

'Exactly. Historians have proposed various hypotheses for this behaviour – mental illness, self-induced hysteria, even epilepsy. But it's blindingly obvious. The berserkers were *on something*, and I intend to find out what.'

I remembered Madri slipping a pill to me. 'And you think you'll find it with this group?'

'Maybe, but this group is more than that. We're like-minded friends who have been through much together over the past couple of years, and we continue on our journey of exploration. If you like, come with us tonight, Finn – see what you think.'

'Get as mad as wolves?'

'No, just a taster this time – a little bit of fun.'

'Okay.' I nodded. 'You sell it well.'

His face broke into a smile for the first time and he waved at the twilit glen. 'Look at this place. It sells itself.'

We retraced our steps along the jetty and up the sloping grass. Soft music was coming from somewhere. A dreamy, folky beat. Hope and Madri were clutching their drinks and dancing slowly to the rhythm, their movements sinuous and graceful. I stopped to gawp at their beauty.

Madri beckoned me over and topped up my glass again, then opened a locket around her neck and sprinkled a pinch of dark powder into my drink.

'Just a little something you'll enjoy,' she murmured, her eyes glinting with mischief.

And then I began to dance. It had been years since I had danced. Maybe I had never danced. At that moment, I didn't know, and the only real certainty was that I wanted to join these women in their slow ballet. My legs moved, my hips swung, my arms curved above my head, and I let myself drown in the music.

Fire. A crackle and surge of heat. Magnus and Laurie had lit the pile of timber and we fluttered towards it like moths.

Held by the flames, we continued to dance. All of us. Even Laurie, lumbering about in his outsized jacket, his eyes closed, his limbs swinging in abandon. The firelight played on our grins and the sparks rose to the heavens and something inside me unfurled. Something that had lain dormant for too long.

XII

Later, I lay on the grass watching the embers smoke and pop.

'So where are those lunatics, Laurie?'

He was crouched somewhere back in the shadows, his location revealed only by the spark of a cigarette. 'Didn't you see them pass? Didn't you *feel* them?'

I forced myself to sit up. 'You better explain.'

'He's right,' said Magnus. 'Tell the tale properly.'

I sensed the others shift towards Laurie and then settle.

'Each one of us here tonight shares a common love for the ancient cultures of this wonderful land of Scotland. Celtic, Gaelic, Druidic, animist, pagan, mystic, Pict, Roman, Viking and, yes, Christian. They are all part of the intricate tapestry that makes up our heritage – our *lore*. They are not distinct and separate traditions, instead they wind seamlessly together, merging and correlating, each as valuable as the next.'

A momentary pause as his cigarette flared and then his smooth Highland tones continued. 'First there were the hunter-gatherers, the animists, who worshipped rocks and plants and animals and spirits, and honoured Mother Earth. Then came the farming cultures of the Neolithic Age, with their dolmens, barrows and circles.

'Later came the Gaelic Celts, bringing their Brythonic tongue to this land. Bringing also their own legends. They had heroes like Fingal and Ossian and faerie folk known as *sith*, who lived in faerie hills called *sitheans*. The scholarly elite of the Celts were druids, who worshipped in sacred forest groves. In the far north were the Picts, a people of myth, who left only their carved stones littered enigmatically across our Highland landscape.

'Then the Roman legions arrived in the south below their wall, and though they eradicated the druids in those parts, they did not destroy their intricate lore. Instead they embraced many of the Celtic beliefs. They made offerings at forest shrines and sacred springs and honoured the faeries and the giants and the nymphs of these lands.

'From the darkness that ensued after the Roman departure, new myths emerged. Perhaps the greatest of them all. Arthur and Myrddin Wyllt – the Scottish Merlin. While the Saxons raged across England, the Brythonic Celts still retained Scotland and they protected this intricate web of myths and lore, until a new force arrived from across the waters in Ireland. These came in robes and held crosses before them. St Columba and St Cuthbert and St Aidan. It is often assumed that Christianity swept all before it, but that is incorrect. In fact, the new religion and the old Celtic paganism existed side by side and recognised each other. Churches were located where once pagan shrines had stood. The old sacred springs became holy wells. People's lives were still filled with magic and ritual.

'Finally, from the northern horizons, came the longships, bringing with them Odin and Freyja and Thor, and their own folklore of trows and finfolk and dwarves. In the early years, they pillaged and destroyed, but eventually they settled around the coastlines of Scotland and they interacted with the Christians and the Celts, forging their Kingdom of the Isles over the top of the ancient Gaelic kingdom of Dál Riata.

'I tell you, all these traditions, all these mythologies, need each other. Without the one there cannot be the next. And they have bestowed on Scotland the most intricate and beautiful lore, which we must honour.'

Laurie's voice drifted into silence and the night returned.

'Tell us about this place,' said Hope gravely.

'This is the Fairy Loch,' said Laurie, pointing vaguely into the darkness. 'If we had been here earlier we would have seen that its water is greenish-blue – a colour said to be created by the faeries dying their clothing.'

Beside me, I heard an intake of breath from Hope.

'Further along the bank there is a faerie cave, where they would dance and frolic before disappearing to their underground kingdoms. But we are not just surrounded by faeries. The druids were attracted here because of the faeries and on the island in the loch, they discovered a sacred spring. So they called upon the lunatics of the land to come to this glen and rowed them out to the island. Once they had drunk from the spring, these mad souls were rowed three times around the island and then dunked in the waters of the loch. When they emerged, they were said to be cured.'

Despite the dark, I found myself turning and staring across the water, imagining the priests and their lunatic audience. My skin tingled and my mind seemed at great peace with itself, and I guessed that Madri's powder was working its magic inside me.

Laurie gave a final pull on his cigarette and stubbed it out. 'So there you have it. We sit in a glen that represents the very tapestry I've described, the different threads of the ancient Dál Riata kingdom interweaving.'

'Thank you,' said Magnus eventually, but his was the only voice.

I lay back on the turf and stared at the sky, faeries and lunatics and druids fluttering around me. Eventually, I became aware of Hope's head close to mine. She too was looking at the heavens, and she raised a delicate hand above our eyes. 'I think,' she said, pointing, 'that's the Plough. See? If you move up from the end of it and see the bright light, that should be the North Star.'

I turned my head to her and smelt the perfume of her hair. 'What's your other half?' I whispered.

'What?'

'The half of you that isn't obstreperous American.'

For practically the first time, she smiled and I wished it was light enough to see her features properly.

'Mystical, magical, romantic and Irish.'

XIII

Later still, I lay sleepily on the grass. I had pulled on my overcoat and rolled the blanket under my head. Someone had stoked the fire, and flames once more nuzzled the night. Hope was sitting upright, her legs curled up to her chin. On the other side, I could see Madri smoking a cigarette and Magnus was lying with his head in her lap. Her black fingernails wandered through his curls and I wondered if they were lovers.

Something stirred nearby and Laurie emerged, brandishing his bottle of Scapa. 'Take a swig and pass it on.'

I eased myself up and savoured the liquid burning my throat, then gave the bottle to Hope. She held it solemnly against her chest peering into the fire, then raised it and said in dark tones, 'To the one we lost. May his soul rest forever young in Tír na nÒg.'

I sensed the others stiffen in surprise and saw Madri and Magnus exchange a sharp glance, but Hope ignored them. She drank and gasped and coughed it down, then rose unsteadily and walked the bottle round to the other two.

For a second, Madri refused to take it. She stared up at Hope, her expression rigid.

Hope knocked her with the bottle. 'Say it.'

Madri took the bottle, threw another look at Magnus, then said flatly back at Hope, 'To the one we lost.'

She drank and thrust the bottle towards Magnus. He contemplated the flames for an age, his brows drawn in a tight frown. Finally he sighed and said quietly, 'To Jamie.'

He drank and the world was silent for a long time.

Perhaps it was the drug that eased things. Whatever it was, the tension eventually leaked away into the night and Hope stirred. She rose and walked from the immediate ring of light. Then Madri pulled Magnus into the darkness, and Laurie shifted upright and followed. I got to my feet and wound my way down to the jetty where they were busy untethering the boats.

Hope came beside me, hand on my arm and another pushing a paddle towards me.

'You're with me.'

I followed her into one of the canoes. She teetered up to the front, while I collapsed in the back. We bobbed onto the loch and the murmurs of the others dwindled behind us. Water soaked through the seat of my jeans, but I was past caring. The only thing that mattered to me was the figure of the woman. She was kneeling at the bow, plunging her oar into the loch and banging it clumsily along the side. There was moonlight somewhere and her hands were pale and her hair shimmered.

She was looking around for the other boat. Then she turned. 'Hey, lightweight, get with it. I thought we weren't moving fast.'

I plunged my oar over the side. It swept ineffectually through the water and I almost lost my grip. I realigned and tried again, concentrating hard and eventually getting into a rhythm. I had no idea where we were. Despite the moonlight, nothing could be seen of the shoreline except the beacon of the fire and I had a vague alarming thought about falling overboard and no one being sober enough to find me.

'Are we going to look for the faeries?'

She thought about this, then shook her head. 'Not tonight.'

We didn't get far. The drink sapped my energy and my efforts became little more than a dip into the water. Hope still pulled, but her enthusiasm was ebbing and after a while she just sat still. There were voices over to starboard, followed by a splash.

'Who's Jamie?' I whispered while the others were out of earshot.

'Don't ask. It's not important.'

'I think, perhaps, it's very important. That looked to me like you were commemorating someone, all that stuff about his soul resting forever.'

'Leave it, Finn. Please just leave it.'

I was about to respond when a deep sonorous voice burst into languid song.

'Ah! Finalmente! Nel terror mio stolto Vedea ceffi di birro in ogni volto.'

We stared at each other.

'La pila... la colonna... "A piè della Madonna" mi scrisse mia sorella... Ecco la chiave!... ed ecco la Cappella!'

'Laurie?' Hope called into the night.

'Well, hello, my darling. Where are you?'

'What are you singing?'

'*Tosca*. Angelotti, former consul of the Roman Republic, as he hides in the chapel. Quite wonderful.' He began again.

Despite our tension, she smiled that wonderful infectious smile again and I found myself grinning too and wondering what on earth someone would make of it if they happened to be on the shore at that hour, how they would later describe the scene as Puccini drifted from the Fairy Loch.

XIV

I had hoped to spend the rest of the night curled with Hope in the back of her Volvo, but an invitation was never extended.

At some point, when we had discovered land again, she took herself away and wandered up the track to the vehicles. Not long after, Madri followed hand in hand with Magnus and the pair disappeared inside the VW Camper.

So when I finally stirred in the pale pre-dawn light, I was wrapped in my overcoat and blanket, my face pressed into the damp turf and my bones aching like an old man's. I squinted down to the shore, where Laurie was lying. Somehow he had slept with his back and head on the stones. He had no blanket and lay with his shirt front gaping and his arms spread-eagled like a human crucifix. If it wasn't for the occasional snort, I might have thought he was dead.

I didn't wake him and I didn't dawdle. The strangeness of the night had left me with nothing to say in daylight. I gathered my things, retied my boots and wandered painfully up the track. Behind me the water was flat grey. None of the bluish-green from the faeries washing their laundry.

Hope was waiting for me on the bonnet of her car, legs bent up beside her, cradling a mug of coffee that she had brewed on a camping stove. She held it out and the pungent aroma caught my nostrils.

'God, thank you.' I gulped with relish and savoured the heat in my throat, then handed the rest back to her.

'I didn't think I'd see you for a while,' she said.

'What time is it?'

'Just before six.'

'Christ.'

'You want to go?'

I looked at the silent VW Camper and imagined Madri and Magnus curled inside. 'Yeah, I do.'

She drained her coffee and slung the dregs on the grass, while I stuffed my blanket and coat in the boot.

The journey back to St Andrews was a quiet one. It was too early for anything on the roads and there seemed little to say. Once again, she perched forward and concentrated on her driving, a tiny frown wedged between her brows, and I simply watched the countryside pass us by and sensed the first tendrils of an almighty headache sneaking beneath my skull.

At some point on the lanes towards town, I glanced in the side mirror and saw that a blue van was following us around the bends. I had a vague suspicion that I might have noticed it earlier in the journey, but I dismissed the thought and instead finally discovered speech. 'Did you understand all that stuff Laurie was talking about?'

'Of course. Didn't you?'

'I suppose. But thinking about it now, it just seems a bit – well – weird.'

'Did you believe it at the time?'

I thought about this. 'Yes. The fire, the wine, the night – it was amazing. Magical even.'

'So that should be enough.'

'But I don't feel any of it now.'

'Of course not. Do you think the rest of us wander around all week thinking about faeries? Live in the moment – that's Magnus' mantra. And make it the best moment you can.'

'But you *do* believe in finfolk and trows and sith and all the other things he was coming out with?'

'I'm Californian. We don't have legends over there. Can you imagine what it's like for an American girl to come to Scotland and discover all this? I have Gaelic blood in me and I grew up dreaming of dragons and giants and faeries, and now life has brought me to these magical shores. So you should treasure the heritage you have, Finn. It's wondrous.'

I dropped back into silence and let the journey unwind. I wanted to press her more about the man called Jamie who had been lost, but I guessed this would only antagonise her. I wondered what she knew about Magnus' berserker research, but this too seemed a subject best kept for another occasion.

She dropped me on North Street and drove off without a word of goodbye or a smile. I watched her go and then turned to look back up the street. A blue van was pulled up fifty yards away. I wondered if it was the same vehicle that had been following us, but I dismissed the question and wandered back towards Hall.

I turned left under the arch beside St Salvator's Chapel,

minding I did not step on old Patrick Hamilton's burning spot, and made my way around the quadrangle. Normally I would not think twice about the presence of another human, but the lassitude of the early hour made me conscious of a second set of footsteps following me into the quadrangle. Shoes clicked on the paving, the sound of good footwear, quality leather.

I skirted the university buildings and rounded the front gardens of Sallies, then glanced back and saw a man taking the same route. He was tall and wore a cap and long coat. He seemed too well dressed to be a student, so I told myself he was probably a lecturer or a researcher and there could be dozens of reasons why he was heading to Sallies at such an ungodly hour.

When I reached the marble entrance, I approached the pigeonholes and saw a folded sheet of paper tucked under my name.

Hey Finn. I've baked White Texas Sheet Cake. Call by tomorrow morning and have some! There's a break in lectures at 10. Anna

I refolded the sheet and pushed it into my pocket, then pretended to fuss with other mail to give the man plenty of time to enter. But he did not materialise and I went back to the doorway and stared out at the garden. Nothing. No movement. He was gone.

I mounted the flights to my eyrie. The room was gloomy, so I flicked on the light and threw off my coat, but unease niggled at the back of my mind. I climbed onto the bed and peered out of the tiny window. Beyond the bulk of the fat pigeon who habitually perched on the gutter, I could see the corner by St Salvator's Chapel and there was the man, standing legs apart, hands in pockets, staring straight up at me. Too late, I realised most of the Hall was shrouded in early morning murk and his eyes would have been drawn naturally to my location when I switched on the light. Cursing, I dropped off the bed and snapped the bulb off. Then I returned to my place and held my breath as I watched him, trying to fathom a good reason why someone would just stand motionless on a path at seven in the morning.

The seconds dragged by and I could feel his eyes straining to make me out. Then he swung on his heel and strode back the way he had come.

I sat down on the bed, pulled off my boots and jeans, and lay in my shirt and underpants. *Who the hell was that?*

Forcing myself to forget about it, I shaved at the sink and washed in the shared bathroom down the corridor. I made a pot of tea and lounged on my bed. There was a lecture at nine about the form criticism movement in the late nineteenth century, but my head sure wasn't up for that this morning. So instead I dozed and dreamed of a woman dancing amongst bright sparks of fire.

When ten o'clock arrived and I knew Anna would be returning from St Mary's, I made my way down to her room. She had a filter coffee machine warming and she served me hunks of the sweetest almond and iced cake.

'Do you ever think about the history of Christianity in America?' I asked, licking my fingers.

'Not really.'

'But you're happy to study its development in Israel and Rome.'

'That's different. That's the source. We don't have much history to speak of in Knoxville.'

'You're protestant, aren't you?'

'Baptist. My ancestors were Dutch Presbyterians. Came over sometime after the Pilgrim Fathers.'

'And did they bring any Dutch stories with them?'

'Like what?'

'Like legends, tales. Dragons and that sort of thing.'

She laughed. 'You are funny, Finn.'

I accepted this wordlessly and helped myself to another nugget of sheet cake.

'Are you okay?' she asked, her tone serious. 'You look pretty rough and you missed the lecture.'

'Just a bad night.'

'You need to pace yourself.'

I smiled and sipped my coffee. 'I'm sorry I was in such a mood in yesterday's tutorial.'

'You don't need to apologise, but I think Father Haughton was surprised.'

'Has he set the essay title for this week?'

She reached for a sparkly pink folder on her desk and consulted it. *'How does the division of the Pentateuch into four sources help us understand the development of Israel's religious thought?'*

I sighed and she reached over and tapped a hand on my knee.

'Hey, you want to come with me after lunch to look for the reading-list books?'

I gave her hand a little squeeze, which made her blush. 'I'd like that.'

XV

The knock on the door startled me from my slumber.

It was the sixth Monday of Martinmas term and I had heard nothing more from Magnus' group in the ten days since Fairy Loch. Outside, the trees drooped in autumnal despondency, and on this exposed corner of Fife the first outriders of winter were already gusting across university lawns.

The knock came again, a little more persistent, and I heaved myself upright with a sudden thought that it might be Hope again.

'Coming.' I turned the lock and flung the door open.

Anna's smile dropped and the blood rushed to her cheeks as she saw me in my T-shirt and boxers.

'Oh, Finn,' she stuttered and her eyes jerked to the floor, to the walls, down the corridor, anywhere but on me. 'I thought you'd be up by now.'

Automatically, I hid my wrists and retreated to the sink. 'Yeah, well, there are no lectures and I wasn't expecting visitors.'

Anna took a cautious step into the room and wrinkled her nose at its stale odour. She was wearing a lilac cardigan and a cream blouse tied at the neck with a blue ribbon, over her usual loose jeans and white plimsolls, and she was carrying a plastic bag with weighty contents.

'But it's Raisin Monday,' she exclaimed.

'I already told you I'm not interested.'

'And I already told you I'm taking you with me to Rhiannon's. She's expecting you.'

Rhiannon was a third-year Divinity undergrad and she was Anna's academic mum. Even Charles had got himself an academic father, a short, stocky classicist called Derek, who seemed surprisingly delighted to have someone to mentor.

As for me, apart from Madri's casual enquiry, no one else had even broached the subject of adoption. True to form, I was an orphan amongst a host of academic families, and I was damned if I was going to embrace this stupid event.

Anna stared out of the doorway while I removed my T-shirt, then pulled on jeans and a rumpled shirt. I buttoned the cuffs and pulled them down to cover my scars.

'I'm really not up for this, Anna.'

'But we agreed that we'd go together.'

'It's just not my thing. Why would you want my company?'

'Because it'll be *fun*.'

I doubted this very much, but she said it with such plaintive fervour that I could not help surrendering. 'Okay.'

She spun back to me with a wide grin. 'Besides, I got you this.'

She pulled from her bag a bottle of Sauvignon Blanc.

'What about you?'

She extracted a second bottle. 'Grape juice.'

'So we can pay the toll?'

'We can indeed.'

We were about to exit, when she remembered something and pointed to my bottle of shaving foam beside the sink. 'You'll need that as well.'

'Don't even think about it.'

'*Finn*, stop being such a spoilsport. Just play along. I bet you'll enjoy it.'

I sighed, grabbed the bottle and shoved it in her bag.

'Okay, okay. Shall we go now?'

I walked with her down one flight of stairs and along the corridor on the floor below. Sallies was alive with students milling excitedly in and out of rooms, chattering and laughing. Music drummed from a dozen hi-fis. The air hung heavy with the aroma of coffee and the sweet scent of bacon.

Anna knocked on a door halfway down, eliciting a chorus of cheers from inside, then it was opened a few inches and a stern-faced woman called Debra glared at us.

'Do you have the toll?'

I was sorely tempted to unload a sarcastic response, but I caught Anna's face glowing at the joy of it all. 'What is the toll?'

'The same that it's been for four hundred years. A pound of raisins.'

I glanced at Anna and she grinned.

'I don't have a pound of raisins,' I replied, 'but I do have seventy-five centilitres of another grape product.'

I held up the bottle of plonk and Debra's acerbity collapsed into a smile. 'That'll do nicely.'

She swung the door open and there was another chorus of cheers and catcalls as we were welcomed into the hot, airless embrace of Rhiannon's bedroom. There must have been fifteen people stuffed into the small space, squashed on her bed, perched on her desk and squatting on the floor. Rounds of toast were popping in one corner. Pastries were spread on trays. Mugs were filled with coffee or spiced wine and everyone was talking at once and gesticulating and cackling.

'You snared him,' called Rhiannon, coming to give Anna a hug.

'He took a bit of persuading.'

She released Anna and reached an arm up to my neck to pull me into a light embrace. 'Good to see you, Finn.'

Rhiannon had wild black hair that looked dyed to me, masculine brows and sharp eyes. She habitually wore vintage dresses and looked, I decided, like a frayed Helena Bonham Carter. She guided me through the bodies to a corner table weighted down with refreshments. 'Why don't we eschew the caffeine and go straight for something with more kick?'

She dipped a ladle into a saucepan of mulled wine and poured a generous amount into a mug. 'Get that inside you. It'll lift those clouds.'

I thanked her, uncoupled and picked my way back to Anna. I realised Charles was sprawled across the bed, thin legs stretched out and spine propped against the wall, still in his usual shirt and jacket, a mug of coffee in his hand and a big grin directed towards me. He was squashed against his academic father, Derek, whose own squat legs barely reached beyond the edge of the bed.

Jokes were being told. Derek was ringmaster and he was pointing to individuals and waiting for them to come up with something humorous. Soon I heard him braying my name.

'What about you, Finn? Give us a joke.'

'I don't have any.'

'Oh come on, you must have one stored up there under that lovely hair of yours.'

'I don't.'

They started chanting, 'Joke, joke, joke.'

My face reddened. I opened my mouth and closed it and then Anna came to the rescue.

'I've a game!' she shouted, hand raised, waving their attentions away from me. 'Think of a number between one and ten.'

I released my breath and swallowed. *Thank you, Anna.*

'Everyone got a number between one and ten?'

I realised she was looking at me and I nodded. *Seven.* I can do that, at least.

'Now times it by nine.'

There was a struggled silence and those quick with their maths stared around the circle as though they had triumphed in some Olympian task.

'Okay, now take the two digits and add them together.'

I had never seen Anna so poised and assured. No timidity, no insecurity, just alive in the moment and loving leading her game.

'Now take the sum of those digits and subtract by five.'

The wine was working at me. Or perhaps it was Rhiannon's rum. I felt warm inside and more relaxed now that Anna had stoppered Derek.

'Think of the letter of the alphabet that corresponds with this number, so if you have two then you now think of B. Everyone understand?'

Quiet. Furtive smiles. She could hold an audience when she chose.

'Now think of a country in Europe that begins with that letter.'

I had D in my mind, but could I think of a country? I went round and round, sifting through every east European state I could remember – Hungary, Romania, Bulgaria – not a damn D in sight.

'Vikings,' Anna whispered, leaning into me.

The penny dropped. 'Thanks,' I murmured back.

'Now,' she said back to the room, 'Think of an animal that begins with the second letter of that country's name.' She allowed them time, then smiled archly. 'Is anyone *not* thinking about an elephant from Denmark?'

The room broke into a chorus of exclamations, then laughter and applause.

A thought struck me and I leaned into her ear. 'How did you know I needed a country beginning with D?'

She beamed at me. 'The wonder of mathematics, dear Finn.'

To this day I don't know how her game worked, but those five minutes in Rhiannon's room indelibly consolidated my admiration for my Divinity colleague. She had recognised my embarrassment when Derek had the spotlight firmly aimed at me and she had grabbed it away.

Rhiannon was looking at her watch. 'Time's moving on, folks.'

It was the cue for bedlam. Some of the group danced out

of the room on errands and others started helping Rhiannon pull boxes from beneath her bed.

Anna clapped with joy. 'What fun! You're going to *love* what we've made for you, Finn.'

'Made for me?'

'I've been working evenings with some of the others in our extended academic family to get the costumes ready.'

'*Costumes!*'

'They're wonderful. You wait and see.'

Before I could say more, the boxes were opened to reveal swords, shields and helmets, all made from cardboard and painted grey.

'Arthur and his Knights of the Round Table,' Anna cooed. 'Rhiannon is going to be our Queen Guinevere, and we will carry her through the streets.'

I spluttered laughter at her. 'Yeah, right.'

She ignored my response and rummaged through the clothing, then held aloft a long white tunic with a blood-red cross in the centre.

'I wanted you to have this one, Finn. The cross of Christ. It's the emblem of the very first Knight of Christ, Sir Galahad. Pure, noble and selfless.'

'You want me to wear *that*?' I laughed.

'Not just that,' said Rhiannon, advancing with a cardboard helmet and sword.

'I'm going to be Sir Bors,' exclaimed Anna, forcing me to take the tunic and then returning to the bed to sift through the costumes until she found a red tunic with a golden lion. She pulled it over her head and smoothed it down her front, looking deliriously happy.

'I'm seriously not—'

'Yes, you are,' Rhiannon interrupted flatly, and her tone would brook no argument.

Everyone was changing. Derek pranced about in a helmet with a blue ostrich feather sprouting from it. He was a head shorter than everyone else and kept getting lost in the crowd.

'Our Lancelot,' said Rhiannon, watching me for a reaction, but our glances said it all.

I don't know whether it was a fervent desire not to upset Anna or a genuine thrill at the sheer fun of it all, but I found myself pulling on the tunic and taking the sword and helmet.

'What do you think?' Anna asked earnestly.

I imagined her spending her evenings labouring over the stitching around my cross and all I could say was, 'It's lovely, thank you.'

Rhiannon had transformed. Now she wore an emerald gown over her Doc Martens, resplendent with glass jewels and silk sleeves. 'Well,' she mused in her best Bonham-Carter voice, checking me from head to toe, 'That's my Galahad, if ever I saw one.'

I was pretty sure I resembled something from Monty Python, but I forced a smile and found myself washed out of the room on the tide of the crowd and into town.

'Stick this in your trousers,' gasped Anna from behind her helmet and she nudged me with my shaving foam bottle. I took it and struggled to wedge it into my jeans pocket, then glanced over my shoulder and realised Charles was hurrying behind. He was wearing a black gown and carrying a staff. For a moment I had a vision of him in later years as the abbot of his monastic order.

'Who the hell are you supposed to be?'

'Merlin.'

Honestly, it couldn't get more ludicrous.

As we poured onto North Street, cars slowed and hooted. A van driver wound down his window and yelled something that he thought was hilarious. Tourists turned their cameras on us. Crowds of senior students lined the pavements and chanted. Other academic families appeared from side streets, and I realised we were not alone in our costumed finery. A squadron of bananas raced along the opposite pavement. Fairies danced between the vehicles. Caped superheroes launched themselves from the direction of McIntosh Hall.

I had a sudden fear that Magnus and his group might be standing aloof somewhere, eyeing the proceedings with derision. And I thanked God that my cardboard visor hid my face.

We marched around the town centre, then wound our way back to the main quadrangle, and more and more costumed academic families joined us. A coterie of wizards. A platoon of jogging traffic bollards. Mickey Mouse and his friends. Crowds of senior students were already gathered around the edges, cheering sardonically. We marched onto the grass and jostled in a disorganised mass with all the other Freshers. Heads turned up towards a clock on the chapel's spire and a countdown began. One minute to eleven.

Anna grinned at me and pulled a can of spray-cream from the folds of her tunic. The countdown grew more intense, the hands of the clock reached eleven and the first chimes began.

Pandemonium erupted.

Wizards flung themselves at fairies. Bananas attacked knights. Shaving foam exploded skyward. Limbs contorted and figures grunted and shouted as they struggled.

Anna danced towards me, levelling her can.

'Come on, Galahad, defend yourself!'

She squirted a jet of foam onto my cross and chortled with joy.

'Now you're in trouble,' I declared.

I yanked the can from my jeans, flung off the lid and shimmied towards her. She shrieked and spun, and I sprayed foam over her back.

The exhilaration of it all tugged at me. I grabbed her and we embraced and jumped up and down on the spot. I could feel her body heaving with laughter against my chest and I dipped my head and planted a kiss on the top of hers. Then we danced apart.

'I'll get you next time,' she snickered.

'I'll be ready, Sir Bors.'

She waved and skipped off into a haze of white.

I settled and looked around, wondering if Magnus and Madri and the others could be watching.

At that moment, a guy dressed in blue tights and red pants rushed into my field of vision and unloaded his spray can through the gaps of my visor. I stumbled backwards, snorted with shock and brought my hands up to wipe my eyes, but my helmet stopped me. The foam leaked beneath my lids and stung like hell. I tore the cardboard off and tried to clear my vision, but my opponent was still intent on attack. He sniggered as he flung an arm around my lowered head, his breath hissing in my ear and the spray can coming up towards my mouth. Another volley of froth hit me, and I could feel his chest spasming with laughter.

My emotions shifted and that old dark friend called anger came scampering back into my veins. Before I could control myself, I shouldered him in the chest. He gasped painfully and stumbled.

'Hey, what's your problem, pal?'

He came at me again, but my arm caught him around the neck and flung him over my outstretched leg. Landing hard, he groaned and tried to jerk up, but I was on him, knees pinning his arms, one elbow pressing his throat into the slick grass. With the other hand, I rammed my shaving bottle against one of his flaring nostrils and let him have half the contents.

I've no idea what it must be like to have a whole heap of foam injected into your oesophagus, but I'm sure it can't be good for you. He choked and spluttered and cried and tried to punch me off him, so I stepped away and strode into the surrounding melee. A wizard ran at me, but I side-stepped and clouted him. A fairy turned with a gleeful grin, which creased into fear just before I emptied the rest of the can in her face.

Then I stumbled against a fallen object and the next thing I knew, I had hit the ground. The impact knocked sense back into me. I lay and looked up at the autumnal sky. Figures struggled above me. A strange scent of aloe vera hung in the air, and some tiny part of my brain realised I had slipped on one of the banana squad who sprawled beside me. In other circumstances, this should have been funny.

I got to my feet and stared around. Beyond the contorting bodies, I could see the ranks of older students spectating from the perimeter. Cursing, I escaped the melee and found a step to sit on. My helmet and sword were gone. My hair hung heavy with sludge, and my shirt and jeans were plastered in white stains. I was shocked by the suddenness of my anger. There had been times over the last few years when black fury had grabbed me and I had screamed at the world for what it had taken from me, but this was not the place for such rage. It was supposed to be a day of tradition, of foam and bubbles, of stupid harmless fun. I shook my head and swore at myself under my breath.

Gradually, the action slowed and the teams panted and embraced. The older students grew bored and began to drift away. Still I sat there, even as the foam-soaked ranks meandered back to their Halls.

'Hey, come on, Finn,' came a voice I didn't need to hear. 'No time to hang around.'

It was our very own bedraggled Lancelot. He slumped next to me and eased off his helmet. His spectacles were covered in dried gunk and he spent a few moments cleaning them fastidiously with a tissue.

'Well, what did you think, Finn? I expect you find us ridiculous.'

'It was an experience I shan't forget.'

He pushed his spectacles back on his nose and nudged me good-naturedly. 'It's not over yet.'

'Count me out, Derek. I'm done.'

'No you're not. Come and have a drink with me.'

'I'm fine.'

'Picture the main stairs in Sallies with every drink under

the sun laid out on the steps. A trail of alcohol. A flight to nirvana. Surely you wouldn't want to miss that?'

'Maybe not.'

'It'll be fun, I promise.'

XVI

Derek had not been exaggerating.

When we arrived back at Sallies, it was to find the stairway bristling with shot glasses. Participants were already dotted up it, sprawled in various stages of inebriation.

'Finn's joining,' announced Derek and I saw Rhiannon on the first landing raise a gin bottle in salute. 'I'll be your dice-man.'

'My what?'

'Each Fresher needs a senior to roll the dice for them. Believe me, you won't be capable of doing it yourself soon enough.'

He grabbed a dice from a waiting colleague, knelt at the bottom of the stairway and rolled a four. 'Okay, climb to the fourth step and choose a drink.'

'That's the extent of the rules?'

'Pretty much. First to the top is the winner.'

I shrugged and ascended, picked a tequila and slugged it.

Derek cheered and the game moved up in turns through the other participants.

Eventually it was back with us. I thought the game would be much improved if we just forgot about the dice, and I rumbled my exasperation when Derek only managed a two.

'What's that?' I queried as I stepped up and pointed at a series of glasses containing clear liquor.

'Vodka,' said one of the students on hand with bottles.

I necked it and felt the burn descend through my chest. This time I crouched down on the step and waited as the game moved to others. I looked beyond the first landing and was surprised to see Anna on one of the higher flights. She beamed and waved a plastic bottle of cola at me, and I didn't have the heart to ask her what the heck was the point of the game if she was just drinking that stuff.

Derek rolled a five.

'That's more like it.' I climbed to the first corner, where I helped myself to something disgusting, which I was told was a Martini.

It was not long before I was only three steps from the first-floor landing, and as I closed on the other participants, I felt my competitive spirit consolidating. Derek rolled a five again and I told him he was a star, but as I started to ascend one of the bottle-tenders barred my way.

'Not so fast,' she said. 'He rolled a five. That means three up to the landing, then two down.'

'What?'

'You have to roll the precise number to make the landing successfully.'

Irritated, I descended two steps and drank. When it was my turn again, he rolled a six. Seething, I ascended two to the landing, then descended four and swallowed a gin.

It took five more attempts to get to the landing, and by then my skull seemed to be moving two seconds slower than the rest of me. I found it more comfortable to lie on the steps and Derek became little more than a voice announcing numbers.

I don't know how long the game continued. Eventually, the dice fell well for me and I crawled to the second landing, but when I was urged to attempt the final flight, I waved in surrender.

'No way, pal. I'm out.'

I lay on the landing while the ceiling revolved far above, then my eyelids drooped and I was gone.

'Hey you, wake up.'

Somebody kicked me.

'I said, wake up, you dirty piece of dross.'

I rolled my head forward and opened my eyes. I was sprawled in a chair and three men were standing in front of me. The stairs were wreathed in evening gloom and all the glasses and bottles had been cleared away.

I assumed the men were fellow students, but they all seemed to be dressed in suits and open-neck shirts, and they glared at me as though I was something they had just discovered on the soles of their shiny shoes. One of them leaned forward and examined me.

'Get up,' he said curtly. 'This is the grand staircase of St Salvator's Hall and I don't expect to find an inferior life form like you slouched on it.'

I groaned and sat upright. I was still wearing Galahad's

tunic and I realised there was a piece of paper pinned to it with a note in blue ink.

3.10pm. Tried to move you, but we couldn't. So we found this chair. Hope you're okay. Anna.

Underneath someone else had scrawled in red ink, *4.35pm. You look so lovely when you dribble.*

And beneath that, another hand had added in pencil, *7.28pm. Hello Preach. Living your best life.*

I tore the paper off and stared at it. Only Madri called me Preach.

Before I could move again, a hand grabbed me by the tunic and yanked me upright. 'I said, get up. Didn't you hear me?'

I pushed his hand away and steadied myself.

His face came towards me, blond, handsome and imperious. 'Do you belong to this Hall?'

I nodded. 'Yeah, I'm a student here.'

'They'll let any old rubbish in these days,' said one of the others.

The first man looked me up and down in disgust. 'Get out of here and take that chair with you.'

I was so stupefied by the situation that I found myself taking hold of the chair and complying.

'And one more thing,' he called as I began to ascend. 'Don't let me lay eyes on you like that again. You understand? We have standards at St Salvator's and we expect them to be upheld.'

XVII

Another week passed. A week in which I began to wonder if Magnus and the others had given up on me.

At least Hope had provided her surname, and I made it my business to locate the D'Angelo pigeonhole and check it each day. Her post kept building, suggesting she did not come to Hall often, and I wondered where she was and what she did.

Then, on Thursday, I discovered a formal cream envelope in my own pigeonhole with *Mr Finn Nethercott* inked in letters of the most exquisite calligraphy. Inside was a gold-rimmed invitation card with an intricate symbol of an oak tree in a circle printed above the lines: *Crann Bethadh – Celtic Tree of Life.*

Beneath this, handwritten once more in beautiful calligraphy, was the message:

Clan Dál Riata
invites Mr Finn Nethercott to celebrate
the Feast of Vetrnætr

10pm, Thursday, 31 October
The Undercroft, St John's Garden, Market Street

The date was that very night. My head awhirl and my heart beating, I trotted back up the floors to my room, grabbed my wallet and strode into town. I discovered a little bohemian wine shop on South Street and purchased a Rioja Alta for what seemed a pretty substantial sum, and I was pleased with my choice until I realised that if Magnus brought the good stuff from his own cellars, no one would even bother gargling with my Rioja.

What do you wear to the Feast of Vetrnætr? For some reason this was suddenly important to me and I rummaged around in my wardrobe and took a shirt down to the kitchens to iron it.

I was ready far too early and I paced my room for an hour. Anna called by with some books and cooed when I told her I had a dinner date in St John's. Finally the clock neared ten. I marched out of Sallies and made my way to the corner of Market Street. There, nestled between two residential buildings, was a gated archway in an old stone wall with *St John's Garden* emblazoned in gold and red. A man loitered nearby, wrapped in a big puffer jacket.

I crossed to the gate and peered through. A pathway ran away, lined by boxed hedging and lamps. More lights could be seen from the houses at the other end of the garden, which probably looked onto South Street. I tried the gate, but it did not yield.

'Can I help you, sir?'

'I don't know. Can you open this gate?'

'Do you have an invitation?'

'Er, well, yes.' I extracted the gold-rimmed card and held it out for him to examine.

'Thank you, Mr Nethercott. You are expected.'

He unlocked the gate, then clanged it shut behind me.

My boots crunched on the slate path as I made my way towards the lights of the buildings, but when I reached them, the only access points seemed to be into various apartments. I peered at my invitation. *The Undercroft*. Nothing resembled that description. I began to walk back to the gate, and I realised another finger of path led off across the lawn towards the perimeter wall. I followed it and dipped my head under low-hanging beech branches to discover a set of steps leading down to an old door deep in the wall's foundations.

'Evening,' came a voice, and I jolted with shock.

Hope was sitting on a bench, almost entirely concealed beneath the low branches.

'I was beginning to think I'd gone wrong somewhere. Have you been waiting for me?'

'Not for long.' She rose. 'You're pretty punctual.'

'What is this place?'

'Our little secret away from prying eyes. Follow me.'

She dropped down the steps and pushed open the door. I had expected to exit into the neighbouring garden, but instead we entered a tunnel, lit dimly by a couple of iron wall lamps. She let me squeeze past, then peered back into St John's Garden and closed the door firmly.

'You know,' I joked, 'if you'd wanted to get dark and intimate with me, I think we could have found somewhere less damp.'

If I had hoped for a smile, I was disappointed. Instead

she pushed past me and stared at me with the utmost gravity.

'Have you ever lost anyone special in your life, Finn?'

Her question lanced through me and for several stunned heartbeats I could not formulate an answer. 'Yes,' I breathed.

'So have I. Someone very dear. This is the Feast of Vetrnætr, so take it seriously.'

I followed her wordlessly down the tunnel with my mouth open and my shoulders prickling. We arrived at another door and she paused just long enough to say, 'Tonight marks the very first of the winter nights, a time when the veil between this world and the next is at its most thin. Think on your loved ones, Finn.'

With that, she pushed open the door.

We stepped into a long vault with an arched ceiling and wall lamps flickering. At the far end a fire burned and a door led to rooms beyond. Oak tables and benches had been set in an L-shape beneath vast drapes of purple, silver, gold and orange. The tables were strewn with foliage, vases full of sage and mint and flowers of orange, yellow and russet, the colours of autumn. A scent assailed me, a heady mix of spice and cinnamon, of roasting meats and baking apples.

At the head of the table sat Magnus, wreathed in black with a silver brooch in the shape of a tree pinned to his chest. Laurie was along the other arm of the L-shaped design, his usual tweed jacket and shirt decorated with nothing new. Madri approached us. Her silver-streaked locks were pinned with orange flowers, and this time her fingernails were red like holly berries. She wore a silver dress, long on the arms, high on the throat, pinched at the waist and dropping to nuzzle heeled ankle boots.

Her smile was cool and her voice more reserved. 'Welcome, Preach. Let me take your coat.'

I unpeeled, rolled it into a ball and handed it to her, along with my Rioja. Then Hope removed her own coat. She was wearing a black dress that hugged her figure and made her seem more delicate than ever. A gold pendant hung around her neck and her hair was loose and spilled over her shoulders. She glanced at me, then looked away when she spied my expression of wonder.

'So, what do you think?' asked Madri, waving a hand down the vault.

'It's magnificent.'

'Gold and purple, black and silver, all the colours of Samhain. Orange calendula flowers, nutmeg, rosemary, frankincense and mint, the scents and plants to celebrate the last day of harvest.'

'Madri's really into this stuff,' said Magnus from the table. 'She's our apothecary, ensuring the food and drink, colours and scents all fit with the season.'

'Beautiful,' I said to her. Then added, 'And so are you.'

She dazzled me with a more genuine smile and took my hand to lead me down the vault. I felt gauche in my jeans and grubby boots, but thankful that Laurie too looked as forgettable as ever. Madri handed me a silver goblet of wine. Hope walked silently to the end of Magnus' table and sat down. Iron candelabra lined the surfaces and silver cutlery was already set beside mats of russet red. I noticed the place settings numbered more than five.

'Are we expecting company?'

'No,' replied Magnus darkly. 'The other settings are for

our loved ones in the world beyond. Tonight, they will dine with us.'

I stared at the placemats and for several heartbeats I was rooted to the spot.

Madri saw my expression and put a hand on my spine to steer me round to the bench next to Laurie. I sank down and took a long swallow of the intense wine in my goblet. Madri sat herself beside Magnus and no one spoke.

Then Magnus brandished his goblet. 'To the final harvest and the first nights of winter.'

We raised our drinks.

Then it was Laurie's turn to break the heavy silence. 'Gormánuður.' He rolled the r's and let the word hang on his lips. 'The Slaughter Month. Samhain, the end of summer. Hallowe'en, the Day of All Souls. Vetrnætr, the arrival of winter. Heathen, pagan, Christian, Norse, all celebrating this most significant of nights when the seasons change, the harvest ends and the veil is parted to the netherworld.'

He paused and held us in his net. 'Winter calls. The sun diminishes. We are entering the coldest and darkest time of the year. We must use the daylight hours wisely. Firewood must be cut and the livestock brought inside. The harvest has been reaped and stored, and now the farmers must go over their stock of hay to estimate how many animals they can feed during winter. The rest will be slaughtered. Skins are tanned. Meat is salted and smoked and dried for the long months ahead. As the nights set in, fish-oil lamps are lit. Tools are mended. Needles are bound. Leather sown.

'But it is not all hard work. These are also the times of storytelling around the hearths and of feasting on the slaughtered livestock. We will drink and honour our goddesses and our Norns and our ancestors.'

I felt him shift beside me and rise to his feet. He lifted his goblet above his head and said loudly, 'To our loved ones from across the divide. May they join with us tonight.'

The others were standing now and I joined them. Goblets raised and eyes closed and together we recited the words again. 'May they join with us tonight.'

When I opened my eyes, they were blurred with tears and I would not look at the place settings next to me. I could not think of my loved ones now. Not tonight. Not in this sudden, unexpected way. It would break me.

Thankfully, the door beside the fire swung open and three serving staff appeared carrying plates of food. I was so surprised that I forgot my emotions and watched wide-eyed as platters of roasted meats, potatoes, parsnips and onions were placed before us.

Laurie noticed my expression and leaned towards me. 'Sometimes, when we stay in town, Magnus uses a catering company. He likes to fund these things properly.'

The delicious food warmed not only our stomachs, but also our souls. We began to talk and not of heavy matters now. We chattered about lectures and university, about restaurants and pleasant bars in the town. They teased me about our boat rides on Fairy Loch and pretended they liked my Rioja. But always there was a reverence to this night. The serving staff had placed portions on the empty plates beside me and now this food cooled untouched by any celestial beings. Hope was graver than ever and joined our conversation only rarely. Even Magnus looked sour whenever he thought our eyes were not on him.

The platters were cleared away and, thankfully, the untouched meals of our loved ones too. Then heavenly apple crumbles were produced and the taste made me think of my mum all over again. I had to pause and take a huge ragged breath before I could force a smile and keep eating.

At last, when all the plates had been removed, I reached for a jug of wine and replenished Laurie's goblet, then carried mine to the fireplace and felt the warmth pressing into my jeans. I wondered if the veil to the next world really was at its thinnest this night.

Someone came beside me and looked up to see Madri.

'That was delicious,' I said. 'I've not eaten like that in years.'

'It's a special occasion.'

'Not as much laughter as last time.'

'The right emotions for the right nights.'

'Magnus seems particularly devoid of humour.'

'He's thinking about someone we lost.'

'The person you spoke about at Fairy Loch? Jamie?'

'Don't comment on that tonight, you understand?'

I nodded reluctantly.

Madri eased closer. 'I'd like to ask you something in front of the others.'

'That depends on what it is.'

'I want to ask you about your scars.'

I stared at her, speechless for a moment. Then I coloured and the drink loosened my tongue. 'No you damn well can't. How dare you! *That*… is not your business.'

She faced my anger quietly.

'Why the hell would you even dream of bringing that up?'

'Because of this.' She tugged at her sleeve to reveal the

inside of her left forearm, where an oak tree in a circle, the same design that I had seen on the invitation, was tattooed into her pale skin just below the elbow. 'This is the symbol of Clan Dál Riata. We each have one in the same place. Magnus may ask you to join the Clan tonight. If so, we'll reveal our arms and he'll expect you to do the same. Then he'll see your scars and raise questions.'

'Magnus wants to tattoo me tonight?'

'No, that will be done later at a little establishment we know, but he may well invite you into the Clan.'

'And if I refuse?'

She held me with her gaze. 'I don't think you want to refuse, Finn. I think you want this very much, and you know it.'

I felt her hand take hold of mine and place something in my palm. I looked down and saw another pill.

'What's this for?'

'I thought perhaps it will help give you the words you'll need.'

She left and I remained rooted beside the hearth trying to formulate my thoughts. Magnus and Laurie were leaning together, speaking in low tones. Madri carried a bowl to Hope and ladled dark liquid into a goblet. She offered none to the others and returned the bowl to the kitchens, her face more serious than I had ever seen it.

I placed the pill on my tongue and swallowed, then wandered back to my place just as Madri reappeared with a plate of thick biscuits. She came to each of us and let us take one, then left another at each empty place.

'Cookies?' I asked.

'Soul cakes. Traditionally baked at this time of year as a way to honour our ancestors.'

'Made by Madri,' said Laurie through a mouthful of crumbs.

'Ginger for healing,' she told me. 'Nutmeg for prosperity. Salt for wisdom. And cinnamon to banish negative energies.'

'In ancient times,' Laurie added, 'children and poor people would go from door to door offering prayers in remembrance of the dead and the families would give them cakes in return. The custom was called *souling* and the cakes became known as *souls*.'

Magnus ate his in studious silence, licked his fingers, then turned his attention to me.

'Finn,' he said, 'I'd like to offer you something.'

'Wait,' interrupted Madri, 'I want to ask Finn something else first.'

Magnus scowled but Madri ignored him. 'May I, Finn?'

I wrinkled my nose, chewed my lip and stared malevolently at each of them, then sighed. 'If you must.'

'Will you tell us about the scars on your wrists?'

There was silence and every face turned to me.

XVIII

I was damned if I was going to say anything.

And yet, when the silence was at last broken, I realised it was my own voice that I could hear. Perhaps the pill was doing its stuff. Maybe it lubricated my tongue. All I know is that I was surrounded by people I'd only met a few short weeks ago, and I was opening up to them, telling them my deepest secrets.

'I was just fourteen when I lost my family. I saw them snapped, shattered, pulverised.'

I heard an intake of breath from Hope, but otherwise there was nothing but the crackle of the fire.

'The weeks after their deaths are numbed in my memory. Adults passed me around. Neighbours I'd never really known. Teachers I'd never seen outside the classroom. My nan made the long journey down from Dumfries to Chichester in the south of England.

'People kept coming to the house. Strangers, officials. Their voices seeped up to me in my bedroom. Days merged into nights. Perhaps there was fury in me. Perhaps

I threw expletives at my nan. But mostly I just felt an emptiness.

'Then came the funeral in my dad's old church. Paraded in front of the very people who had complained about him to the bishops, all now busy weeping and squeezing my shoulders. Hymns mouthed. Music that my mum had loved soaring from the organ pipes. One of the bishops standing in the pulpit and telling everyone how special my parents had been. And then the three coffins.'

I think perhaps one of them reacted to that. I sensed a muffled exclamation and felt them all shift and glance at each other. I could have stopped, but the pill was letting the words tumble, and I was lost in my memories.

'I was taken north by Nan. My life in Sussex was over. Not only did I lose my family, I also lost my bearings. Everything I'd known – my bedroom, my school, my southern sun – were taken from me. I was given a new room above my nan's kitchen. The guest bed I'd always used for holidays became my regular resting place. My desk and books and clothes were unloaded against new walls.

'They told me I'd start another school soon. My grief hardened and a different feeling took shape, a conviction that I wasn't supposed to continue like that, that I was meant to be somewhere else with *them*.

'When I look back on this feeling, I can't really explain it. I can't put flesh on the bones of it. I just became convinced that I should have gone with my family to the next world, and something had gone wrong. I wasn't meant to be in my nan's spare room, waiting for a different life to start.

'I don't remember what propelled me out of the door one evening about three weeks after our journey to Scotland.

Maybe I had a furious argument with Nan. I don't know. What I *have* realised though, is that there must have been some reasoned purpose to my actions because I was clear-headed enough to take a small paring knife from a kitchen drawer.'

There was another breathless whisper from one of them and I knew they were already imagining that paring knife biting into my wrists.

'I waited for a bus at the stop near the end of Nan's road and I must have remembered to carry the fare. I don't think I had any idea where I was heading, so I boarded the first bus that arrived and travelled south on the A75 in the gathering gloom. I remember passing through a little village called Creetown and seeing the sea so close to the road, silver under a full moon. I stared at the water as the bus continued and when it next stopped – near some cottages at Carsluith – I propelled myself out and waited until the bus had departed.

'I've been back to Carsluith. I've stood on the embankment beside the road, looking out at the sand at low tide on a bright, blustery day. That critical night, however, the tide was in and there was no wind. I dropped down and walked across the grass to a strip of sand by the water.

'I don't think I had any clear plan. I just assumed that the combination of the blade in my coat and the cold caress of the sea would make doubly sure I would soon be on my way to see my family again.'

'Surely someone saw you?' Madri blurted, her face creased with anxiety.

'I didn't think so then, but afterwards I learned that people in the houses had watched me pacing up and down that beach under the light of the moon for a long time. They had seen I was young, and they had thought my actions unnerving. The emergency services had been called. Police cars came from Newton Stewart. An RNLI boat launched from Kirkcudbright.

'At some point I must have made the fateful decision. The water was terrifyingly cold. I remember jolting with shock. My trainers sank into the sand and my jeans turned heavy as iron. By the time I'd got myself waist deep, my heart was pinballing and my lungs were gasping. My hands were so clumsy that it took me forever to extricate the knife from my pocket.'

'Bloody hell,' Magnus murmured.

'I don't remember the actual action of cutting into my flesh. In all the years of thinking about it since, I can't provide one single reasoned argument why I took that decision. I just kept telling myself that something had gone wrong, and I was supposed to be with my loved ones.

'I don't know what mess I made of my first wrist, nor how I even attempted to change hands and slice the other one. Afterwards the doctors said I managed to cut quite deeply where it didn't really matter and missed the places where my lifeblood waited to be released. They also said my double-whammy of sea and blade had worked against me. The sheer stunning cold of the water had hardened my flesh and forced most of my blood to scamper back into my central organs.'

'Aye,' whispered Laurie, as though he was an expert in such matters.

'Did I go under? Was my last vision supposed to be the moon as the waters of the Solway closed over me?'

My words slithered to a stop and I realised they were all staring at me in shock. Each of them was with me in that moment, under the water, looking up at the moon and waiting for death to arrive. I let them hang.

'Hands came for me. Lights blazed. I was dragged up and then I was speeding somewhere across the water. But these weren't the angels carrying me to the next world, they were dressed in yellow and wore white helmets and they took me to the critical wards of the Dumfries and Galloway Royal Infirmary and then – weeks later – back to my nan and the rest of my life.'

XIX

No one spoke.

A damp log popped in the fireplace. Somewhere a vehicle blared its horn, but in the vault itself, four pairs of eyes watched me.

Finally Laurie stirred and picked up his goblet. 'To the boy who didn't drown, Finn, and the man you've become.'

Magnus' eyes bored into me. 'What happened to your family?'

'Don't be so crass,' hissed Madri.

I held his gaze. 'Don't ever ask me that again.'

Magnus straightened and leaned towards me and for a second I thought he was going to contest my response, but then he pulled up the sleeve of his jumper and held the inside of his forearm towards me. It was white as the moon and hairless, with a tracery of bluish veins curling down to embrace the branches of a great oak in a circle. 'Crann Bethadh. The Celtic Tree of Life and the symbol of Clan Dál Riata, the ancient kingdom of the Gaels. Will you join us Finn?'

One by one, the others eased up their sleeves and placed their forearms for me to see the oak tree. I began to roll up my own shirtsleeve. Then, for the first time in almost five years, I bared the scarred wrist on my left arm and laid it out before them.

'I will,' I replied.

No one commented, though I could feel their eyes dancing over the delicate cuts of that paring knife.

Then Magnus pulled himself together. 'If you do this, you'll need to jump in with both feet. You'll respect what we do and what we share with you, and you won't tell anyone about our times together. Is that a deal?'

'It's a deal.'

Magnus seemed satisfied, but Madri fixed me with a stare. 'You need to understand, Finn, we keep our secrets close. There are people who detest what we do, so keep your lips sealed about joining us. Loose tongues can kill.'

'What's that supposed to mean? Is that why Jamie died?'

I saw their faces darken, but none of them responded.

'Are you in?' Madri demanded, her expression hard as diamond.

I looked at each of them and then nodded sourly. 'Yeah. I'm in.'

Before I could say more, Hope got to her feet, her face tight and haggard. 'Thank you for the food, Madri.'

'You're leaving?' Magnus demanded.

'I am.'

She began to walk down the vault.

'Wait,' called Madri. 'Did you drink it?'

'No, it wasn't the right time.' She pulled on her coat and looked back towards me. 'Too much pain.'

Before anyone could say more, she pushed through the door and we heard her heels tap away along the tunnel.

'What did you give her?' Magnus asked.

'Just a liberty cap in milk, nothing much. It's Vetrnætr, for God's sake. The night when the netherworld is closest. She had a right to want to communicate with him.'

'Well, I'm glad she didn't after what happened at the castle.'

Madri sighed irritably. 'Hope understands these things. She had the sense to realise the emotions weren't right tonight.'

'What's a liberty cap?' I asked.

'A mushroom,' Laurie replied. 'Hope uses them to enhance her visions, so she can communicate better.'

'Who did she want to communicate with?'

'Her betrothed,' answered Madri.

'What?'

'Her *dead* betrothed,' added Magnus ruminating into his wine.

XX

The pain of the needles took me by surprise and I had to clamp my jaw to avoid a gasp.

Madrigal sat just behind me reading a magazine, and I knew she was itching to mock me if I made a fuss. She had escorted me to a little establishment near the museum on the outskirts of town, and I had been underwhelmed by the sight of the bellied, balding Metallica fan who was about to use my flesh as his canvas. The place was cramped and smelt of sweat, and the walls were plastered with images of skulls and knives and serpents, but the man seemed to be an acquaintance of hers and after a quick rummage through cupboards at the back of the shop, he returned clutching a stencil of Crann Bethadh, which he must have used to ink the rest of the Clan.

He swabbed my arm with alcohol, flicked on a powerful lamp and bent to trace the fine details of the oak onto my skin just below the crook of my elbow, and although I'm sure he saw my scars and wondered what terrible circumstances had brought me to tear at my own flesh, he didn't comment. When he was done and I was satisfied with the positioning, the needles whined into motion and he began with the permanent ink.

It was a long ninety minutes of gritting my teeth and feeling Madri's amused eyes running over me. When it was finally done, the tattooist bandaged the area and handed me a tube of antibacterial cream. Madri paid and tipped him extra, then led me out onto the street, where a powerful sea breeze whipped from the east. Over her usual black jeans and ankle boots, she wore a tailored wool coat and cream scarf and I thought she looked every inch the scion of wealthy Perthshire landowners.

'Coffee?' I suggested.

I would rather have gone back to Sallies and collapsed on my bed until the pain subsided, but this was my opportunity to quiz her.

She didn't look best pleased, but she concurred and led me to a discreet café not far from the student union, where we ordered filter coffees, along with two slices of Victoria sponge, because, as she announced to the woman behind the counter, I looked in need of some sugar.

She noticed my hand wandering towards the bandaging as we sat at a window table. 'Keep that on until tomorrow.'

I thought about the commitment I had made. 'So what happens now I'm inked up?'

'We meet to mark a festival, to honour a significant date – be it pagan, Celtic, Norse. And we look for the most amazing ways to celebrate.'

'Don't get me wrong, I love what I've shared so far and I'm on board with it, but *why* do you do it?'

She frowned at this, as though the question had never been posed before. 'Why?'

'Well, it's not the usual student antics.'

I felt her bristle and realised this was delicate ground. The Clan wasn't just Magnus' plaything. Madri was also fiercely passionate about what they did, maybe more so.

'I suppose we're the sum of our parts. Magnus is obsessed by Old Norse culture. His father comes from Uppsala in Sweden, so he likes to believe he has Viking blood in his veins.'

'I thought his father owned most of Argyll.'

'He does. His grandfather founded a paper business in Sweden. The family began looking for opportunities to buy good-quality, well-priced forestry and their searches focused on Scotland. They purchased parcels of land out west and eventually bought a country estate near Strontian, beyond Loch Linnhe. Today they own about sixty thousand acres, mostly in Argyll and some of the islands.'

I whistled. 'That's a lot of trees.'

'You can't make paper without them.'

'So – the Clan, the berserker research – it's all about Magnus honouring his family's roots.'

Madri snorted. 'You'd think so, but it's because of his bloody family that we have to keep our activities so secret.'

'His father doesn't approve?'

She gave me a long enigmatic stare, weighing up what I might already know and what I could deduce.

'It's not his father – it's his mother. She's the power in the family and she'd stop at nothing if she thought Magnus was taking these substances.'

'I'm guessing you don't like his parents.'

'Magnus and I have known each other since we were young. We were part of the same circuit of Highland landowning families, and we quickly realised we shared a mutual derision for it all. When we could, we would meet up and get away. That's when we started exploring our feelings and our beliefs.'

'He called you the Clan's apothecary.'

'I was fourteen when I met an art teacher at my school who opened my eyes to the creativity of different cultures. I was mesmerised. She showed me the pagan calendar and how nature influenced ancient art. She described cultures from distant lands, particularly India, where she had spent a gap year travelling and returned with a love for the gently spiced cuisine of the Mughal north and the yogic practices of the Chola south.

'My parents were convinced she was a bad influence, and they were delighted when she left the school after just a couple of terms. But my fascination in all things heathen remained. I would catch the bus to Perth Library to read more on the symbolism, customs and cuisine of the peoples who celebrated pagan festivals. Then I'd meet up with Magnus and we'd take it from there.'

I got the impression Madri's fascination was fuelled by an urge to break from the strictures of her own family traditions. She was a rebel in expensive clothes.

'So now I bring the colour and the taste and the incense to our little gatherings.'

'Everything that makes them so special.'

She permitted herself a little smile and finished her coffee.

'Then there's Laurie,' I said. 'He brings the stories.'

'Exactly. I think he's been immersed in myths and legends since before he could read. He prides himself on learning extinct languages and devouring the literature of ancient cultures in their source languages. He and Magnus hit it off in their first months at St Andrews and now they're inseparable. You get one, you get the other.'

'And what about Hope?'

She pursed her lips. 'Hope is an American in search of the romance of Scotland. We arrived at St Andrews at the same time to read the same course – MA Hons in Medieval History – and we became friends almost immediately. We would visit each other's rooms and light incense and tell stories. She wanted to learn some of my arts, and I taught her the pagan calendar, the importance of the planet cycles and the basics of alternative medicine. But what she really wanted to explore was how to meditate and how to use this skill to *see*, to communicate with realms beyond this one.'

'You mean with her dead betrothed?'

Madri quietened and refused to be drawn.

'Is that Jamie? Who's Jamie?'

'Hope should be telling you this, not me.'

'What happened to him?'

I could see Madri was irritated that this conversation had gone too far, but she knew I would not let her leave it there now. 'Jamie was one of the Clan,' she continued guardedly. 'He was a friend of Magnus from schooldays and when he met Hope it was like a fire had been lit between them. For a while, they were everything. But like all fires that burn too brightly, the flames died quicker still. Hope soon realised theirs had been a fleeting thing and she called off the engagement. Jamie was bitter, but I think he would have come to accept it in time.'

'How did he die?'

'He was killed in a road accident. Knocked down late one night on North Street by a speeding hit-and-run.'

'My God. And now she uses your mushroom concoctions to communicate with him?'

'She tries. She suffers guilt, Finn. Great voids of guilt. She broke off their engagement just weeks before he died. So she attempts what she can with the medicines I provide, but only she knows if she manages to make any contact.'

I wanted to say more, but her expression wilted my words.

'Come on,' she said, shifting in her seat.

I paid for the coffees and we braved the wind again. We walked in strained silence, and I knew she was angry that she had told me so much.

Eventually we reached a junction and she pointed down a street and announced, 'That's me, Queen's Gardens.'

'Which one?'

She shook her head. 'You don't need to know.'

Her response surprised me and I hovered uncertainly as she prepared to cross the road. 'So how do I contact you?'

'Leave a note in the pigeonholes. Eustace is my surname.'

'And what about Magnus?'

'He has rooms above the History faculty, and if he wants your company, he'll summon you.'

I scowled. 'Seems a hell of a way to run this Clan. Maybe I was too quick getting inked.'

'It's too late for that now, Finn. So keep your mouth shut and concentrate on your study.'

'And that's it? I just hang around and wait to hear from you?'

She turned and marched back to me, and I took an involuntary pace away. 'For reasons I've already explained, we make our plans at very short notice. But, if you must know, Laurie says there's a small Norse festival at the end of next week, something called Einherjar, a commemoration of when those who died in battle were brought to Valhalla by the Valkyries. So Magnus is planning a celebration of autumn and winter, the time between Samhain and Yule when nature closes down, warriors fill Valhalla and winter takes possession of our world. So I suggest you pencil it into your diary.'

With that, she wheeled away again and I watched her receding figure until it disappeared.

XXI

'I don't like the look of those clouds.'

All around us evening was gathering. On a brighter afternoon, the lowering sun would have caught the last autumnal leaves on the slopes of the Ochil Hills and shot them through with gold, but now the woodlands above looked sullen, foreboding and unwelcoming.

Hope was leaning into the steering wheel with her usual anxious posture. 'I don't feel the magic in my bones today.'

'Sod the magic,' I retorted. 'It's the cold in my bones I'm worried about if those clouds decide to give us a soaking all night.'

We were on the lanes above a town called Dollar on the southern side of the Ochils. It had taken us about an hour to cover the thirty-six miles from St Andrews, and Hope had been confident she could find the way, but then she got lost on the run in from the Crook of Devon and so I had to unfold a map on my knees and navigate.

'This doesn't feel right,' I warned.

We had made it through Dollar and were now climbing a very steep lane into the trees.

'I think it is. Magnus said there's a car park up the hillside.'

It had been an awkward journey to share. She seemed graver than ever, and there were moments, especially when we got lost, when I thought she was going to give up on the whole adventure and announce our return to St Andrews.

I wanted to quiz her about Jamie. Words kept forming on my tongue and then dissolving. I wanted to understand how she had fallen for someone so thoroughly. This woman, so reserved. What type of man could have swept her away? And, of course, I was desperate to know more about the accident. What tragic details lay beneath Hope's inscrutability? But I could find neither the courage, nor the language, to broach the subject, and so we puttered along in the old Volvo, and I focused my attentions on the map.

She had the engine in first gear and it was whining in protest as we climbed the steepest section of the lane. It seemed as though we were going to force the car right to the summits of the Ochils, and my nerves shredded further when I realised a dark ravine was opening up through the trees just beside the road.

'The Dollar burn,' she said. 'Magnus said there's a path somewhere deep down the bottom and bridges that criss-cross their way up to the castle, which sits on a promontory where the river splits. The two tributaries above are called the Burn of Care and the Burn of Sorrow.'

'Evocative names.'

'Apparently this is an evocative place. Ah, here we are.'

We came to the end of the lane and turned into a tiny car

park. I recognised Madri's campervan and Laurie's Ducato. Otherwise, the car park was empty. We stepped into the damp caress of low cloud and the drip of moisture on a million leaves.

I followed her up the track that began where the lane ended, then she bore left and dropped down steep steps towards the burn. Night was chasing us and the light beneath the trees was minimal. I trod with care over the leaf-strewn slopes until we came to an old wooden bridge. She crossed expertly and began to ascend stone steps on the other side. I gripped the bridge's handrails and felt the darkness reaching out from the chasm. Only when I was safely over did I realise that I had been holding my breath. I followed her up the steps and around the rock face to easier ground.

She was waiting for me on the path and she raised her eyes to the scene above. Through the trees, I saw crumbling ramparts and a tower caressed by cloud. In my youth, my parents had taken me to magnificent castles in the south of England. Great palaces of state, surrounded by gardens and quadrangles and gatehouses, festooned with colourful standards. But this. This was a real fortress. It stood, brazen and impregnable, high in these wild hills, hemmed by roaring waters, squinting through cloud, broken, austere, frigid and hostile. I felt its violence.

I lowered my eyes and realised Hope had been examining me.

'Castle Gloom,' she said softly and I murmured my agreement.

We continued up to the walls and found a tenuous bridge across the Burn of Sorrow, which led us to the rear of the fortress and a single iron gate. As we neared, the bolts were drawn back and the door opened to reveal Madrigal.

'We watched you from the walls.'

Hope did not reply as she eased past her friend.

Madri peered up the hill. 'I hope you disturbed none of the warlocks or witches who come out when the old grey wanderer wraps his cloak of mist around these hills.'

Instinctively, I checked behind, but there were only the vague forms of sheep cropping the slopes and the cackling of jackdaws in the trees below. She led us across a terrace surrounded by battlements, with the tower looming on our left. We skirted a caged-off well and dropped down uneven steps to a lower terrace that must have once been a significant hall. It was roofless now, and the remains of arched windows ran along those walls that still stood. Beyond them were views of lawns that would once have boasted decorative gardens, then the hazel, beech and willow of the forest, and then – far away – the smudge of the Forth on the horizon and the lights of the road bridge.

In the far corner of the hall, where the two best preserved walls met, there was a bulk in the gloom, and I realised that it was a tent. Magnus was awaiting us, and Laurie was kneeling close by, tending a small fire.

'Welcome,' Magnus said and advanced to shake my hand and give Hope a light hug.

She looked at the fire. 'You better keep that very low.'

'No one's going to be up here on a night like this.'

She seemed to accept this, but dumped her bags and took herself off to inspect the walls and check on the woodlands below.

Magnus made an effort to be positive. 'So what do you think of our Viking lodgings, Finn?'

He ushered me forward, and I saw that the tent was an A-frame, about four metres long and two metres high. At both ends the A-uprights crossed and were topped with an intricately carved dragon's head. One length of the tent had been raised and held as a canopy by angled uprights. Under this protection had been placed furs and low tables.

'It's beautiful.'

'They were known as boat graves back in Norway because they could be erected on the decks of the longships while at sea. Back then the fabric would have been wool or canvas, but this is waterproofed cotton, so it should keep us dry if those clouds decide to unleash.'

'Are you sure about the fire? Hope seemed worried.'

'We're behind the wall and we won't let it burn fiercely. Besides, it's too foul a night for prying eyes.' He clapped me on the back. 'Come on. Let's warm your bones.'

Hope returned from her sortie and we unpacked parcels of food and wines, rolled out our sleeping bags inside the tent and then came to sit on the furs under the canopy. Laurie's fire – made from broken pallets, which they must have laboured to carry up the hill – cast a flickering glow onto the stones, but he tended it carefully and ensured it did not dance up to finger at the low-hanging cloud. Magnus filled my goblet with wine and I sipped gratefully. Hope had squatted next to Laurie, her features lit by the flames, earnest and focused as she stirred ingredients into a large pan and hung it from an iron frame over the heat. Madri joined them and used tongs to pluck a heavy mess tin from the core of the fire. She shook the contents and a heavenly scent crept my way.

I watched the figures around the fire. I hardly knew them, and I could feel their tension, and yet I felt a sense of goodwill towards them. The faces of the women glowed above the flames and even Laurie, at that moment, seemed inexplicably precious.

'We're ready,' Madrigal announced, levering the tin from the fire. She poured the contents into a bowl. 'Roasted hazelnuts, walnuts and chestnuts.'

Magnus refilled my goblet and we clustered together and savoured the tastes of nature's offering. Hope unhooked her pan, stirred it and then poured a thick, creamy liquid into five beakers. She passed them round and came to curl next to me on the furs.

'What's this?' I asked, peering into my beaker and smelling wonderful spices.

'Pumpkin moon milk. It's prepared in autumn when there's enough natural light from the moon to help the plants still grow, but tonight we'll just have to imagine that.'

I took a sip. 'Delicious.'

She gave me one of her fleeting, cherished smiles. 'It actually comes from ancient Indian Ayurvedic traditions and has loads of immune-boosting vitamins. Turmeric, cinnamon, cardamom, coconut oil, black pepper.'

'Just what we need on a night like this.'

After we had finished snacking and drinking, we worked in communal harmony to prepare a chicken stew, then Hope took herself off for another check over the walls. When she returned, she said, 'So Laurie, tell us about this place.'

Laurie was perched on an upturned crate, a whisky in

one hand, a cigarette in the other. He wore his perennial jacket and shirt, and his only concession to the elements was a thick scarf tied at his throat. After some murmured debate, Madri had placed candles in little cups in a wide circle around us and their flames helped to brighten our little gathering.

'Ah,' he purred. 'Gloume. A veritable nest of legends.'

The wine and moon milk had lulled me into a comfortable lethargy, and I was ready for his tales. Now it simmered over the smouldering fire, making our stomachs ooze in anticipation.

'Tonight, we sit upon a frontier, my clansmen and women. Tonight, we perch on the edge of cultures.'

I turned to grin at Hope, but her eyes were locked on Laurie, wide and expectant.

'This southern escarpment is known as the Ochil Fault. In the years before time, seas lapped these slopes. The remains of whales and oyster beds have been found. We are on the true boundary between the Highlands and the Lowlands. A meeting place of cultures – Pict, Gael, Celt, even once a Roman marching camp this far north. It's a place where you will hear the croak of the crow, the burble of the curlew and the scream of the vixen fox. You may, too, hear the distant tunes of the kidnapped piper.'

I heard Hope's intake of breath. Madri was entranced and Magnus was lying back deep in thought.

'Do you know why the burns on either side of these walls are named Care and Sorrow? Because in time immemorial, the beautiful daughter of the most ancient King of the Scots was imprisoned in this very castle. Her crime? To love a man below her station.' He pointed theatrically at the tower, though no such structure would have existed all that time ago. 'Imagine her face at those windows, crying for her love and lamenting her destiny.

'There is a track outside this castle. It winds east along a narrow pass and eventually, even today, you will come to a spring known as the Maiden's Well. It's named thus because the king's daughter was occasionally permitted to walk that track and bathe in the spring. It was to be her only experience of life beyond these fortress walls.'

I could sense the heaviness of Hope's emotions. Was she imagining her own life and the loss of the man she had once thought she loved?

'The story does not end there. Many centuries later, the son of the Chief of the Clan McCallum was celebrating his birthday in this very hall and the conversation turned to legends. The young prince listened to the story of the Maiden's Well and was told that a spirit in the form of a beautiful woman would rise from the spring. Drunk, the prince boasted that he would seduce this spirit and he set off along the pass at midnight. They say he encountered the beautiful woman and went for his sword, but we will never know the detail because he was found face down beside the spring, clutching his blade, quite dead.'

Madri rose and checked the stew, giving it a careful stir and declaring it was almost ready.

'What about the piper?' Hope asked.

Laurie mulled over his whisky with a sad smile. 'It's said that the hill directly above this castle is a faerie fortress.'

Hope shifted and stared longingly into the night sky, though none of the landscape could be made out through the cloud.

'One night long, long ago, a piper set out from an inn in the valley below to cross these hills, when he spied a great castle up there, filled with lights and music. As he gaped, the faeries came out and took him into their hall. They promised they would release him if he played for them. So he did. He piped every tune he knew and when he had finished, the grateful faeries kept their promise, and he found himself back on the track in the darkness. Shaken, he returned to the inn. There he found the innkeeper was dead and his son an old man. The piper had been in the faerie castle for a hundred years.'

Magnus chuckled and Hope sighed, and I couldn't help admiring Laurie's skills at storytelling.

We dined on stew and thick crunchy bread warmed in foil on the embers, and at one point I turned to Hope and asked softly, 'Are you planning to See tonight?'

She frowned and shook her head. 'You shouldn't be asking me that.'

XXII

When we had cleared away the bowls, Hope and Madri tended the candles, then disappeared into the tent, and I assumed they must be preparing their sleeping bags. Laurie was fussing with the fire's embers, and Magnus was squatting next to him retrieving small jars from his kitbag.

I took the remnants of my wine across to the edge of the lower terrace and looked over the lawns to the forest beyond. The clouds still lay so thick that I thought I could reach them. The forest was silent. I wondered if the jackdaws and crows slept or simply had nothing to say at this hour. The constant rush of the burns was the only sound. I thought about the warlocks that were supposed to walk these hills and the faeries in their castle high above. If I was brave enough to take the track to the Maiden's Well, would the beautiful woman rise for me and would the others find me dead when the sun came up?

I turned back and something flashed in the corner of my eye. On the hillside above, a light had flicked on. I watched it sweep across the grass, then rise in our direction.

'Magnus,' I called quietly.

He must have sensed the edge in my voice as he rose and walked over.

'Someone's above us.'

Just as he reached me, the light extinguished.

'There was a torch,' I declared in frustration. 'About halfway up the slope and coming our way.'

We stared for an age, and I could feel the tension in his bones.

'Are you sure?'

'Of course I am. It was a bloody great light in the middle of the hill. Why would someone be up here at this hour?'

'And why switch the torch off?' He looked back at the fire, then answered his own question. 'Because he could see us looking at him.'

We waited for a long time, but the darkness was not disturbed again.

'How do you know it was a man?'

'They're all men.'

I was about to demand what he meant, but he put a heavy hand on my shoulder and pulled me close. 'Don't tell the others, you understand? This is just between us.'

'Are we going to abort?'

'Too late for that. Madri would go spare.'

I peered up at the hill again. 'I suppose it could just be a walker. Or a shepherd.'

'Perhaps.'

We both knew we were doing a poor job of reassuring each other.

'Anyway,' he concluded, 'if someone's up there, they'll be a damn sight more miserable than we are.'

He stalked back to his jars as the women emerged from the tent, and I forgot everything.

Madrigal came first, sheathed in silver. She had removed her fleece and now, above her jeans and boots, she wore a coat of chain mail that flickered and shone even in the minimal light. Protecting her head and the top half of her face was an iron helmet of perfect Viking design, and hanging from a thick belt around her waist was a broadsword in a leather and bronze scabbard. Her silver-streaked hair cascaded over a woollen cloak that dropped to her calves.

'A Valkyrie has come,' said Laurie breathlessly, making Magnus stop what he was doing with the jars.

She was magnificent, but my eyes were already shifting beyond her. Hope stepped out in a floor-length gown of russet brown and simply decorated with braids on her wrists and at the neck. A single golden locket hung down her front and her waist was bound by a cord belt. From her shoulders flowed a hooded cloak of the deepest blue, held by a brooch at her throat.

'Brown like the roots' bed,' she said of her dress, her eyes on me. 'Blue as the boats' road.'

'You look astounding,' I replied. 'You both do.'

Madri shot me a sparkling grin and went to Magnus, who stood and embraced her.

Hope hovered close to me, but now her attention was on the jars that Magnus had been checking, and her expression grew dark.

'You intend to search for your berserkers again tonight?' she snapped.

'Do you have a problem?' replied Magnus, releasing Madri.

'There are raging burns either side of us and a chasm

below. The hills are steep, the walls high. Yet you're prepared to lose your mind again.'

'We're safe on this terrace, and we've prepared only minimal quantities.'

Hope blew out her cheeks and shook her head. 'My God, Magnus, you really have lost your mind. Haven't you learned your lesson? Isn't one tragedy enough? You'll not stop until someone else is hurt.'

She slumped onto the furs and glared at the fire, and my eyes shifted between them.

'What is it?' I asked. 'Another mushroom?'

'Yes,' said Madri. 'But not our usual one. This is *amanita muscaria*, from the fly agaric mushroom. It gives a darker hallucinogenic experience, but we're only using two grams.'

'I'm doing it as a tea,' said Magnus testily.

'We've tried that before,' Laurie commented with a frown.

'I know, but I've powdered it more finely this time to see if it makes any difference.'

'Seems like we're running out of ideas.' Laurie's tone was sour.

'Well I don't see you coming up with any new ones. Besides, I want to see how it makes Finn feel. We all agreed after his performance at the foam party that he might react differently.'

'Wait,' I declared, stepping towards them. 'What's that supposed to mean? You watched me at the foam party?'

'Of course we did, and we took great interest in how angrily you reacted to something so innocuous.'

'You have violence in you,' Madri interposed. 'And that's a fine quality.'

I tried to sort my thoughts. 'So, let me get this right, you've invited me into this Clan because you think I'm a violent person who might show more natural berserker qualities once I've downed a few of your mushrooms? I'm just here as part of your experiments? A human guinea pig?'

'Of course not.' Madri raised her hands to appease me. 'We wanted you to join us because you think like us, because you get what we're all about.'

'But there's no denying some of what you've just said, Finn.' Magnus approached me. 'Those Viking troops who took the berserker drug must have been immersed in violence already. They were warriors used to battle. So it's possible their natural fighting qualities were simply enhanced by the drugs.' He swept an arm in a circle at all those gathered. 'The trouble is, these days, warrior instincts are damned hard to find.'

'So you've tried this stuff before without success, but you think I may react differently?'

Magnus shrugged. 'It's a working hypothesis.'

I glanced at Hope, but she refused to look at me.

'Is it safe?'

Hope snorted, but held her tongue.

'Well, technically, it's poisonous,' answered Madri, and that teasing smile returned. 'But what's a little poison between friends?' She waited to gauge my reaction, then added with a wink, 'Just two grams, a very moderate trip. No big deal.'

I nodded slowly and tried to ignore Hope. 'Well, okay then.'

Magnus fingered careful teaspoons of powder from one of the jars into four beakers and Laurie poured hot water into each. They took turns to stir and stare down at the mixture. Then Madri carried one over to me. It was steaming and warm in my hands, but the scent was like rotting vegetables and I wrinkled my nose.

'All of it?' I asked and she nodded.

'It's not too hot, so best get it inside you.'

I drank. The taste was revolting, so I decided it was better to gulp the lot and get it past my taste buds as fast as possible. I drained the beaker and watched as the others did similarly. All except Hope, who sat wrapped in furs, still not looking at me.

'Now what?'

'It'll take a while for you to feel anything,' said Madri. 'So just relax and prepare yourself.'

I'd no idea what that meant, so I sank onto the furs near Hope and tried throwing her a fleeting smile.

Magnus and Laurie rose and stalked into the tent, while Madri took one of the stools over to the edge of the terrace and sat there contemplating the forest.

'Come with me,' Hope said unexpectedly. She picked up a heap of the furs and walked over to one of the far walls. I followed and watched her as she arranged them as a bed. 'Settle down here, with your back against the wall.'

I did as she bid and then she put more furs over me and tucked me in as best she could.

'This is dangerous ground for a trip,' she said, as if scolding me for partaking. 'So you need to lie back and get as comfortable as possible and just stay here as your journey begins. Don't get up. Don't wander away. The others are fools.'

'Will you stay with me?'

She considered this, then stretched out a couple of the furs and knelt beside me. 'Yes, I will. I will be right next to you.'

She took my hand and held it, and I felt a rush of emotion and squeezed her fingers.

After a few minutes, the two men emerged also wearing chain mail, helms and swords. Laurie looked absurd with his shirt hanging out underneath, but Magnus was magnificent.

'Are those real?'

'They're made by true craftsmen, but their edges are blunted. You can give someone a good clout, but nothing else.'

Hope spoke up with authority. 'No blades tonight. No weapons now you've drunk that stuff.' Magnus was about to protest, but Hope cut him off. 'I'm adamant. You do this without a sword.'

He heaved a sigh, sheathed his weapon and unbuckled it. Laurie did too and Madri eventually rose from her stool and unstrapped her own.

My hands were getting clammy and I knew Hope could feel the damp between our fingers. My stomach gurgled and rolled with nausea.

'I don't think anything good is happening,' I told her anxiously. 'I just feel sick.'

She pressed my hand. 'Don't worry. Anxiety about the trip is actually a sign that the dose is starting its work. Just sit back and relax.'

For a while I tried to follow her instructions, even though my stomach continued to complain. Magnus and Laurie had found themselves separate perches and were huddled down under their cloaks. Then I thought the moon must have broken through the clouds, because the sills of the windows behind them began to glitter and the stonework, so dark before, now seem rich with texture. I smiled. It really was very beautiful.

The jackdaws started to argue again, a chorus of sound that harmonised and rose and fell. They came to perch on the walls one by one and croaked at me. They beat their wings and jabbered and danced, and I tried pointing them out to the others, but no one seemed to notice.

Madri rose from her stool and walked across the horizon of my vision. She shone like Galadriel and raised her arms to the heavens. I wanted to dance over to her, but I found I could not move because the terrace beneath me was shifting. It rose gently, then fell back, then rose again. I gasped aloud and tried to change position. The stone surged and this time I felt water droplets hit my face. At long last, the rain had started. Down we rolled, then the terrace climbed again and the water hit me harder.

But this was not rain. I ran my tongue over my cheek and tasted salt. Someone was shouting at me, yelling curses and urging me to pull. The sound of the burns on either side crescendoed until they roared like ocean waves. I squeezed Hope's hand, but it would not give under my pressure. It was cold and unyielding and I stared down at it. I was gripping an oar. Of course I was. I had always been gripping an oar.

I pulled back, forcing the paddle through the thick black waves as spray soaked me. There were figures in front. Helmeted, their hair braided, dragging on their own oars. Beyond them, stood a giant of a man, staring ahead, a spear held in his outstretched arm, and the other hand resting on the dragon-headed prow of our longship. Above me, canvas and rope strained and squealed against the wind. The boat reeked of damp leather, mouldering wood, sweat and urine, and even the unmistakable tang of fresh blood.

I heard a whimper from lips that were too young for this company. Stowed at the front, beneath the tall warrior, was a girl, white with fear, arms bound. One of our prizes from the first raid on these islands. We would collect more before the night was done.

The man next to me shoved me with his shoulder. He stank and was covered in grime. His eyes glittered malignantly beneath his helmet and I discovered the source of the blood scent. He was spattered in gore. He cursed me and told me to pull harder, then stared ahead at the girl and licked his lips.

I turned my attention back to her and my heart jerked. Oh no, surely not! How could it be her? I knew those eyes so well, and that little mouth and fair hair, jostling in the wind. Caitlin. My beautiful Caitlin. What are you doing here? How can we have captured you? Go away, flee from us!

Panic rose in me. Horror so complete that I released my oar and struggled to stand. 'Caitlin,' I yelled. 'I'll save you.'

Hands came for me. The man next to me, stood and hurled such obscenities at me that his spittle washed over me as much as the seawater. I struggled to free myself from his grip, but his fingers were around my throat and the other hand grabbed one of mine and squeezed it. I struggled and managed to get his fingers from my neck, but his other hand would not stop squeezing.

Squeeze, squeeze, squeeze.

'Hey, Finn. Come back to me.'

The sea receded. The boat dropped away.

Forlornly I watched as Hope's face materialised and, for another lifetime, I lost Caitlin again.

'You're fine,' Hope whispered, her hand rhythmically pressing mine. 'Everything is fine.'

I was sweating and my heart was convulsing, but her words soothed me and I knew I was back in the castle.

'Can you hear me?'

I nodded. 'Yes, I can.'

My voice was ragged, but my heart relaxed and my body felt heavy against the furs.

I lay quietly, content to feel her body warmth next to mine. Laurie was prancing about, swishing his cloak and singing. Madri leaned against a far wall, her face upturned to the skies. Magnus was low on his haunches, head down, rocking and chuckling.

I lifted my own eyes to the clouds and smiled as they twinkled with lights. The lights multiplied and I realised they were windows in a giant castle and there were figures looking out the windows and calling to me.

'Play,' they shouted. 'Play, piper.'

I answered that I could not play anything, they must have mistaken me for someone else, but they just laughed. My fingers were moving now and although I had no instrument, I could hear the most wonderful tunes rising from me. The figures at the windows clapped and hurrahed and began to dance. They floated out onto the night sky and jigged their Highland reels and the lights came with them and spun around their heads.

My chest swelled with awe and wonder at the sheer beauty of the castle on its mountain and the movements of this throng. The music swelled, the dancing reached a climax and the figures rushed to congratulate me. I was surrounded by them, carried up into the night sky to sing and dance again with them.

But, too soon, they grew bored with me and began to jig their way back to their windows. I looked down to see Castle Gloom laid out below me. I could see the others. Madri was spinning and twirling alone. Laurie had folded himself into the furs. Magnus stood tall, hands before him as if in prayer.

And Hope sat there far below me, still holding my hand.

I came down to her gently and the furs greeted me. I sank against the stone and leaned into her and watched as the last of the faeries slipped back through their windows and extinguished their lights.

I don't know how long I lay there. It could have been minutes. It could have been hours. I felt cocooned and safe. I was content to watch the fire die and to witness the clouds shift. I think there might have been a fine rain, but I welcomed its caress on my cheeks. I nuzzled towards the woman next to me and my heart ached with such love for her. I felt a fathomless connection to her, soul to soul.

Perhaps I slept. I know my eyelids became heavy. If I did, it was dreamless and I woke to find her hand still in mine and her eyes closed in sleep herself. I leaned towards her and bestowed a single kiss on her cheek, soft enough to ensure she did not wake. From the others there was no movement. They were lumps under the furs. The fire had died. The sky was clear and there was even the first hint of light in the east.

With a deep, blissful sigh, I relaxed against the wall and allowed myself to slip back into unconsciousness.

XXIII

The Clan wasn't good at after-party conversation.

We broke camp in the morning twilight without a murmur, rolling sleeping bags that had not been used, folding the tent into squares and dismantling the frame. Hope used a small brush to sweep the remains of the fire into saucepans, then Madri and I discarded the contents in long grass outside the castle walls and clambered cautiously down to the Burn of Care to wash the pans.

Laurie leaned over a pot of coffee on the gas burner, raining ash into it with his first cigarette of the day. Despite the assiduous preparation for our night of celebration, no one had thought to bring anything for breakfast. So we glugged the hot liquid gratefully and prayed for the caffeine spike.

I was as sluggish as the daylight. My head was clear, but my limbs responded to the commands of my brain only after a pause, as if deliberating whether they could be bothered. Madri looked paler than ever, a sickly cream rather than her normal shining self. Laurie shook and twitched and his eyes settled on no one. Magnus was surly and kept glancing at me.

Hope was silent thunder. Her brows were drawn in a steadfast scowl and her jaw set so hard that I could see a tendon twitching. She looked ready to explode and, sensibly, no one tested her fuse. When everything was shipshape, she shouldered her bags and stacked several boxes in her arms, then fixed me with a glare. 'You can catch a lift with Magnus and Laurie. They're desperate to interrogate you.'

Madri had gathered her things as well. The two women took a moment to check that they were leaving Castle Gloom just as we had found it, then walked solemnly to the gate and abandoned us.

Magnus ignored their departure and came to crouch in front of where I hunched with my coffee. 'Tell me what you felt.'

'It was good.'

His face fell. 'That's what I was afraid you would say.'

'Did you see lights?' Laurie asked, though he would not turn to look at me.

'Yeah and those damn faeries with their piper.'

He laughed. 'At least they brought you back before a hundred years passed.'

'Was there anything nasty?' Magnus demanded.

I thought of the longship and the warriors on their way to pillage. 'Not nasty, but unexpected.'

'Nothing that made you angry?'

I did not want to be reminded of Caitlin. 'Perhaps. But only for a few moments. Mostly I remember laughing and dancing and thinking this place was a damn sight more beautiful than it looks now.'

Magnus harrumphed and started gathering his bags. 'Well, that was a complete waste of time then.'

Laden with belongings, we left Castle Gloom and descended on the path beside Dollar Burn. I glanced back up the hillside and wondered if someone had really spent the hours of darkness watching us. I considered raising the incident again with Magnus, but the set of his shoulders on the path below was enough to warn me to hold my tongue.

It was only when we were an hour into our journey in the Ducato and heading back to Fife, windows down, Laurie at the wheel, on his fourth smoke of the morning, that I finally found my voice from where I was squashed between bags in the back.

'Why was Hope so angry?'

'You'll have to ask her,' replied Magnus tetchily.

Laurie kept his eyes on the road and refused to glance at either of us. He sucked on yet another cigarette and flicked the ash through a crack in his window and it was a surprise when he spoke. 'Hope limits herself to a milder hallucinogen and selects the timings of her trips carefully and only when everything feels right. She wasn't at all happy about the circumstances last night.'

There was a heavy silence, and then I clambered forward to the gap between the front seats. 'If you think you're going to keep *experimenting* on me, then I expect a better account of everything you've been up to.'

Magnus snorted. 'We gave you nothing we haven't tried ourselves enough times. Two grams of *amanita muscaria* from the fly agaric mushroom. A fairly normal hallucinogen that should give you a moderate, if darker, trip. What are you getting hot about? If you didn't want to drink the stuff, you could have refused.'

'My problem isn't about drinking the stuff, it's about you not giving me a fuller explanation. If you want me to be a guinea pig, you better damn well start talking.'

'He's got a point,' said Laurie.

Magnus rained daggers at the man next to him. The first suburbs of St Andrews could be seen over the hedgerows.

'Okay, I'll give you the background when we get back to town, but only on the condition that you tell me *why* you're happy to be – as you insist on calling it – a guinea pig? Because most sane people would run a mile.'

His question took me by surprise. I leaned back against the bags and pondered my motivations. 'I guess because these nights with you are so different. And because I'm interested in the academic nature of this quest. You're seeking the answer to a real historical conundrum and the right drug might actually take us back across the centuries to feel first-hand what berserkers themselves felt. And, well, that beats essay writing every time.'

The men glanced at each other and I think they appreciated the response.

Laurie took us to South Street and then pulled up opposite St Mary's. We alighted and he left us. Magnus led me to a blue-painted door beneath a colonnaded portico with a sign beside it bearing the university's coat of arms and the words *School of History*.

We stepped into a foyer with doors breaking off each side and a stairway winding to the floors above. The place was quiet on a Sunday morning, but these rooms would usually have been filled with the hum of students awaiting seminars.

I followed him up to the first-floor landing, then higher still into the eaves of the building, up to a central landing, richly carpeted and hung with gold-framed depictions of smoke-filled battles. Two doors led off and Magnus took the one on the right.

I entered a place of beauty.

The room extended through the eaves of the house. It was floored in polished oak and scattered with opulent rugs of crimson and cream. Recessed windows ran down both sides, framed by plush curtains and cushioned sills. Morning sun streamed through skylights and bounced off polished surfaces of antique mahogany. In pride of place was a magnificent desk with paperwork piled across its surface and surrounded by a sprinkling of armchairs.

'This is yours?'

'Just for the duration of my studies. The space belongs to the School of History.'

'But how do you get something right above the teaching rooms?'

'Friends of friends.' Magnus led me to the armchairs. 'Have a seat. Tea? I have Earl Grey or breakfast.'

'However it comes.'

A workbench ran down the southern wall, replete with glass apparatuses that would not have looked out of place in a chemistry laboratory. Rows of bottles stretched along the surface, some containing liquids and others what looked like herbs, roots and seeds. At the far end was a compact kitchen.

'Where do you sleep?'

'Across the landing.'

'That's yours too?'

'I suppose it *is* rather extravagant, but as you can see, I fill it up with odds and ends. The place suffers from noise when the students are moving between lectures, but otherwise my privacy is undisturbed.'

He brought over the teas and I eyed the bottles. 'I'm guessing you think the answer lies in one of those?'

'I wish it did, but if there's an answer in one of those, I'm damned if I can find it. I've scoured the libraries in St Andrews. I've spent hours in the national library and gone south to the British Library too. I've discovered historical accounts, mastered modern botanical theses and made a few useful contacts in other universities, but nothing emerges as an obvious solution. I've even got in touch with a few *dealers* in these parts to get their take on the substances they sell, but they're mostly focused on the chemical stuff these days – acid, ecstasy – and there's no way the Vikings were getting their hands on any of that.'

'So it's a natural substance.'

'Either that, or it's ancient magic and if that's the case, then we're stuffed. No, it has to be natural, something that grows: root, seed, leaf, bark. Or something that was cultivated back then: grain, vegetable, fruit.'

'That's a lot of options.'

'Aye, but most things can be discounted because there's been over a thousand years of experimenting since the Vikings. Mankind knows well enough what can be fermented and distilled, what can be smoked and consumed, and if there's a way to get off our heads, we've usually discovered it.'

'You're sure it's not drink? The Norse enjoyed plenty of ale, and I guess they also had cider and mead.'

'The answer isn't alcohol – or, at least, alcohol isn't the

only ingredient. We all know the effects of drink and they don't fit the descriptions of the berserkers.'

'What about cannabis?'

'I originally thought that might be a contender. We smoked it in the green dried form. We crumbled the black resin blocks and baked it in cookies. We boiled it, we fermented it in alcohol, we dropped it into stews.'

'We?'

'Me and Laurie. Sometimes Hope and Madri too.'

'And Jamie?'

He looked at me sharply but didn't respond.

I shrugged and said, 'Madri told me about him.'

I could see he wasn't happy about that, but he lowered his eyes and nodded. 'Yes, Jamie tried things too.'

'But with no success?'

'Some of us experienced paranoia, even physical fear, but the effects seemed to be dependent on mood. Mostly, we felt giggly, euphoric and very in need of food.'

'Hm. Not very warrior-like.'

'And then we realised what fools we'd been. I think it was Hope who said one day *didn't cannabis originate in China?* She was right, of course. It had been used in those parts for thousands of years as a stimulant and for its healing properties, but there is not a single historical source that suggests the plant could have found its way into the hands of Norse Vikings.'

I smiled to myself. I could imagine Hope's expression of utter condescension as she made that remark.

'It was a lightbulb moment,' Magnus continued. 'Whatever the source of the berserkers trance-like behaviour, it surely had to be something that grew in Scandinavia or could be easily imported in large quantities in the ninth century. If it was the latter, then there should be documented evidence of other contemporary societies displaying similar behaviour. But these warlike trances seem to be unique to Norse culture, so it's likely that the stimulant is gathered or cultivated from plants that grow in the cold climate of Scandinavia. And that limits the candidates.'

He put down his mug and extricated a parcel of tissue paper from a drawer under the workbench, then beckoned me closer. 'Look at this little beauty.'

He unfolded the layers of tissue to reveal a single mushroom, withered and beginning to rot, but its bright red cap and white gills still easily discernible. 'Fly agaric.'

'A magic mushroom.'

'Not technically. That name is usually given to the hundred or more species of mushroom worldwide that contain a compound called psilocybin. We came across psilocybin after we had discounted cannabis. Madri put me on to it. She knew of psilocybin's therapeutic properties and had seen it used for cluster headaches, anxiety and depression. Some of those mushroom varieties grow in Scandinavia and here in Scotland, so we got really excited. But when we started testing them, we found the psilocybin also gave us a sense of wonder. Sometimes there was nausea and tremors and mild paranoia, even arousal, but mostly we agreed we had positive trips, followed by calm and detachment.'

'So you gave up on those?'

'Hope still uses them for her Seeing, but rarely now. For a time, I was at a loss and then we came across references to this.' He touched the withered mushroom with a delicate finger. 'I know this one looks worse for wear, but fly agaric is actually a gorgeous-looking fungi.

'The active compound is *amanita muscaria*, a hallucinogen that is a deliriant rather than a psychedelic because of the way it affects our neurotransmitter systems. And the key is that this stuff is acknowledged to bring on negative hallucinogenic experiences.'

He looked at me. 'Hallucinogenic, trance-like and negative. The description fitted. A bit of further research and I realised this grows well in woodland and heathland, on light soils, amongst birch, pine or spruce.'

'In other words, Scandinavian forest.'

'Exactly. And British too. This thing is indigenous and can be collected in both Norway and Scotland if you know where to look.'

'This is what you put in my tea last night.'

He pulled a rueful face. 'Madri's tried fly agaric a couple of times, but Hope won't touch it. So it's been left to Laurie and me to keep testing. We've eaten it, fresh and dried, and – believe me, the damn things are disgusting. We've boiled them, powdered them, tried to smoke them. We've smeared their juices on our skin. We've soaked them in alcohol. Consumed them with mead and ale. Anything and everything a Viking might have done.'

'And what have you found?'

He reached down and folded the mushroom into its paper and returned it to the drawer. 'Pretty much what you experienced at Gloom. Lights, visions, some fear and paranoia, lots of dreams, but mostly euphoria.'

'Not the strength of bears and oxen, or the madness of wolves, like old Snorri Sturluson said?'

'Not even a whiff.'

'So, you're stuck.'

He didn't like that, but he swallowed a retort. 'Like I said, we hoped you might experience something different. We thought perhaps it's down to the personality of each individual and maybe *amanita muscaria* only stimulates aggression in those who are naturally warlike.'

I refused to rise to that comment. 'So what next?'

Magnus ran a hand through his curls. 'I don't know. Keep toying with ideas. There must be something we're missing. Perhaps an extra ingredient or a method of preparation we haven't considered.'

'Or perhaps it's not fly agaric at all.'

'If it's not fly agaric and it's not psilocybin, then I'm as far away as ever. I'm lost. Everything I've tried, everything we've experienced, has been leading us in the wrong direction.'

XXIV

A fter all the revelations of the weekend, I tried hard to get myself back into the academic week and focus on my studies. Tuesday evening found me working late with Anna in the St James Library and we were both steeped in mythology.

How have the writers of Genesis adapted stories borrowed from the mythologies of the Ancient Near East?

As soon as Father Haughton had given us the title of that week's essay, I felt something stir in me. Here was a question that went right to the heart of my interest in divinity. You see, I always liked the God of the Old Testament. The one who fought chaos and dished out righteous punishments like they were going out of fashion. There was something unsavoury about him, something unchristian. I pictured him with his flowing beard and his deep-set eyes and his bellowing voice, and if he had clutched a war hammer in his fist, it would not have seemed amiss. He was Odin, Fingal and Arthur, all rolled into one.

That night Anna and I were settled in neighbouring desks.

History crept from the rows of leather-bound books and tiptoed over to embrace us. Even the worn surfaces of the desks spoke of the passing of ages. Ink splats and tiny nicks made me wonder who had sat there before. What had their lives been like? What type of god had they sought amongst these books and manuscripts?

'Listen,' I whispered, leaning in to Anna. 'This is from Enūma Eliš, the Babylonian creation epic: *What Osiris said to Atum: 'What does it mean that I must go to the desert of the kingdom of the dead? It has no water, it has no air, it is so deep, so dark, so endless.*

'Now listen to this from Genesis 1:2. *The earth was without form and void, and darkness was upon the face of the deep, and the spirit of God was moving over the face of the waters.*'

'They're similar,' said Anna quietly.

'More than similar. They both use the same qualities to describe the chaos before creation – lightless, boundless and deep. The Genesis writers must have known about or even had direct access to Enūma Eliš.'

Anna's expression exhibited none of the passion burning in my own eyes, and I realised that stuff like this was hard for her to consider. Her entire Christian faith was based around the concept that the Bible was the direct word of God – inviolate, irreproachable, sacred – not a second-hand set of stories pinched from other writers and cobbled together from a patchwork of earlier religions.

'Except that,' she mused with her brow furrowed, 'these Babylonian tales feature many gods, whereas the Yahwist and Priestly writers of Genesis are recording the actions of the one God.'

We continued debating in hushed tones, but it was getting late and I could see she was tired.

'Enough for tonight?' I asked eventually.

She looked relieved. 'I think so.'

We packed up our books and wandered back through a steady drizzle to Sallies. I bid her goodnight, then headed up to my eyrie thinking a whisky was calling from the bottle I had brought with me from nan's.

The second I opened my door, I knew something was amiss. Instead of the usual mouldering fug, cold air and the scents of the night rushed to embrace me. I groped for the light switch and saw that the room was just as I had left it, except my little window was open.

Swearing, I jumped onto the bed and slammed it closed. It was only then that logic caught up with me and I paused and looked more closely at the window, running a finger along its frame. I had never opened it before. In fact, I thought the catch was stuck after years of neglect. For a moment, I assumed the wind must have forced it, but I quickly realised the nonsense in that. The window opened outwards. I had just *pulled* it closed. Whatever force had done this, had come from inside my room.

I got down from the bed and checked around the little space. Nothing else seemed untoward. I returned to the door and examined the lock. I was sure I had secured it before departure and there were no signs of forced entry. I hovered for several long seconds, trying to make sense of the situation, then forced myself to accept that there must be some simple explanation that would come to me in the light of a new day.

I was no longer tempted by a whisky. The room was too

cold for a languorous nightcap, so I ensured the door was locked, stripped down to my undies, flipped off the light and flung myself under the bedclothes. Shivering, I pulled them up to my throat and squirmed down the mattress.

That's when my toes touched something.

Something alien. Something that should never be encountered down a bed.

Instinctively, I yelped and whipped my legs up, then thrust an exploratory arm back down. What my fingers met was soft, cold, heavy and sticky.

Yipping again, I leapt out and struggled to find the light switch. I raised my hand to examine the stickiness and sucked in a lungful of air. Blood covered my fingers. Blood and shreds of flesh. I stared at the mess, turning my hand to and fro, then grabbed a corner of bedclothes and dragged them off.

My knees buckled.

There at the bottom of my bed, in the centre of the mattress, was the carcass of the fat pigeon who always perched on my gutter. Blood and feathers were scattered in a confused mess around it. Slick, dark horror oozed from a hole in its breast and its head lay discarded.

I stumbled to the sink and twisted on the hot tap.

'Come on!' I shouted as the water took an age to splutter and arrive.

Not waiting for it to warm, I scrubbed at my hands. I soaped and rinsed and only relented when the water turned too hot.

How could this have happened? My brain struggled to find a solution. The rain had somehow dislodged the catch. The window had come open, startling the bird. It had flown inside, then thrust itself around the room in such a panic that it had decapitated itself. Then it had collapsed on the bed and thrown the covers over its corpse.

Yeah, right.

I sank onto the chair once more, my eyes not leaving the carcass.

Bloody hell. Bloody hell. Someone had broken into my room, grabbed the pigeon and left it mutilated in my bed as a warning.

Well, warning duly delivered.

I was Clan Dál Riata's newly inked-up recruit. And somebody was seriously pissed off about that.

XXV

I wrapped the carcass, the head and all the loose globules of gore and feather in two plastic bags, then decided I could not endure having the thing in my room until morning. So I dressed, slipped out the door, locked it ever so carefully and padded downstairs. My heart was in my mouth. I peered around every corner, I scanned each shadow, I jumped at the faintest noise.

I exited the building and made my way round the back of the kitchens to the rubbish bins. The area was lit only minimally and I almost faltered and dumped the carcass where I stood. But, stealing myself, I padded over to the nearest bin, forced the lid up and dropped the bloody thing into the interior.

When I got back to my door, I had to screw up courage to enter again. I studied the lock and waited for an age, listening for any movement. Only when I was inside and the door secured and the room checked, did I force myself to calm. I stripped the bedding and rolled it into a ball for washing. Then I pulled on a dressing gown over my clothing and curled onto the bare mattress and waited for dawn.

The next day, I forced myself to lectures, but God knows what they were about. If my ears heard the words, they did not register them. My mind was elsewhere.

Anna joined me for a sandwich lunch on the bench outside St Mary's.

'Finn, you look dreadful.'

I batted her concerns away and she had the sense to cover my silences with light chat about her plans for the weekend, though I could feel her gaze on me.

Towards the end, when I was shifting and saying I might head back to Sallies, she said solemnly, 'Finn, you know I'm always here if you need a friend? You don't need to tell me things, if you don't wish. I'm not someone who pries. But whenever you need quiet company, you know where I am.'

I thanked her brusquely and stalked away, though, in truth, her words touched me more than she would ever know.

I spent the afternoon washing the blazes out of my bedding. I scrubbed the sheets in the sink. I put them through two full cycles in the machine. I whacked the temperature up as high as it would go. But nothing would obliterate the bloodstains. I flung the whole lot in a dryer and sat in moody silence while other students came and went with their own piles of laundry.

That evening I was tetchy with Charles over dinner and retired to my room to glug a couple of whiskies. As the night deepened, I finally decided enough was enough and I was damn well due some answers. I marched out of Sallies and back to the School of History.

'You again,' said Magnus when he opened the door. He looked far from pleased to see me, but at least I had not brought him from his bed. He was dressed in black trousers and a white shirt, complemented by a smart pair of grey wool slippers.

'I've come to get answers.'

Grudgingly, he let me enter. 'Have a seat. I'm drinking Oloroso.'

He ferreted in a cabinet of polished chestnut and filled a second crystal glass with a deep amber sherry, while I slumped into one of the chairs.

Once he had seated himself, I told him about the dead bird and I saw his face blanch.

I jabbed a finger at him. 'Ever since I met you lot, there's been little comments here and there about people who don't like the Clan. So you'd better start explaining things properly, because I'm not used to finding avian carcasses in my bed.'

Magnus closed his eyes and rubbed his scalp, then said in a tired voice, 'Does 1746 mean anything to you?'

'Enlighten me.'

'It's the name of a group in St Andrews.'

'Never heard of them.'

'They're one of the university's private clubs. Invitation only and incredibly exclusive. They like to think they're the elite, though there are other clubs amongst the more affluent of St Andrews students who also vie for that prestige. The red, green and white ties of the Kensington Club, full of male members with – allegedly – endless virility. The secret interviews and ceremonies to be admitted to the Kate Kennedy Club. The Lumsden Club, the Strafford Club and so on. Barbours, balls and Bollinger, you probably get the picture.'

'Hmm, I think I probably do.'

'And then there's the 1746 Club. Members can only come from public schools and must already belong to one of London's exclusive clubs. They guard their secrets closely and you are only considered for membership if you demonstrate – in their words – *the appropriate historical and political perspectives*. Anyone who joins must sign a non-disclosure agreement with a penalty of a hundred thousand pounds.'

I whistled.

'I was a member,' Magnus added.

'Somehow, that doesn't surprise me.' I glanced at him. 'But you're not now?'

'I left quite some time ago – and they really weren't happy about it.'

'Did you have to pay up?'

'Not so far.'

'So why'd you leave? Wasn't their endless virility enough for you?'

He took a few moments considering his reply. 'I hated their ways. Most of what they did was indulgent foolery. They hung out in the most prestigious establishments and drank the most expensive wines, and gorged themselves and fornicated and wrecked things. Meaningless and stupid.' His dark eyes examined me. 'I didn't want to be a part of it, Finn. I needed more. I wanted meaning and beauty and wonder and awe. Do you get it? I wanted to find something way beyond all their nastiness.'

'Are you saying these guys are responsible for the pigeon?

Why do they care that you left? Students leave clubs all the time.'

'Not this one.'

'Oh yes, there's the small matter of a hundred-grand penalty. But I guess you have access to that sort of money or they wouldn't have invited you to join in the first place.'

'It's not about the money. It's more calculated than that. They're putting me in my place.'

'And I seem to be collateral.'

Magnus glared at me for long heartbeats, then he dropped his eyes to his Oloroso. Somewhere the grandfather clock chimed the half-hour.

'It's better if you're not involved.'

'I already am. Those bastards just stuffed a dead pigeon down my bed.'

I let him have a few moments, then he took a breath. 'No one ever leaves the 46ers. The current membership numbers only about a dozen, but it's been going for decades and is incredibly prestigious amongst certain circles. Members come from families with money and influence in Scotland. If your background fits the criteria, you'll be invited to join when you arrive at St Andrews and you're expected to embrace the privilege. Posh boys together, forging networks of power that will last lifetimes. For many, membership is expected. Their fathers will have been 46ers and, no doubt, their unborn sons will join one day as well.'

'Was your father?'

Magnus inclined his head. 'Yes, and now he's not happy about my departure.'

'Why call the club 1746? What happened then?'

'Culloden happened. The destruction of the Jacobite

Army of Bonnie Prince Charlie by the Duke of Cumberland and the end of the glorious 1745 Rebellion. There followed months of suppression in the Highlands and untold numbers of atrocities, while the Jacobite leaders, including Charles, fled to France with their dreams in tatters.'

'Why would Scottish posh boys celebrate an English victory?'

'Because Culloden was never a simple fight between the Scots and the English. In truth, there were more Scots fighting for Cumberland than for the Jacobites. It was also a fight between the Establishment and the rebels. Since the club's inception, they've twisted the politics more and more. They glory in Culloden as the symbolic and violent moment when the Establishment ensured its privileges were never challenged again. They treat fellow Scottish students with disdain and they style themselves as the rightful masters of this land. They know full well that, even today, celebrating the Battle of Culloden is offensive to many Scots and so they flaunt it all the more.'

'And Clan Dál Riata is your answer to this?'

'It's a damn sight better than what they represent.'

I lapsed into silence and gulped my sherry. The liquor warmed my throat and helped to soothe the adrenaline that was still pumping through my system, but it couldn't dispel my unease. 'Why are these 46ers setting their sights on me?'

'You're our new recruit. I don't know how they've worked that out, but they use younger students to be their eyes and ears, and they make it their business to know what we do.'

I stared at my empty glass and tried to get my head around this information. Something wasn't stacking up.

'I still don't get it, Magnus. Why would these guys *care* what you do? Shouldn't they just be into themselves?'

'You can't underestimate the insult they perceived by my departure.'

I blew out my cheeks in exasperation. I'd already had two whiskies that evening and I wondered if the alcohol was blunting my perception.

Magnus examined me. 'Does this news change things?'

I shook my head. 'Not really. Posh wankers don't scare me, but I do expect you to be totally honest with me. Have you told me everything?'

'I have.'

I could see from his expression that I would get nothing more. I rose and thanked him stiffly for the drink, then made my way out. I wandered back to Sallies lost in my thoughts. Something was wrong. Something wasn't adding up.

And I hated being taken for a fool.

XXVI

It was a wet, black, wretched evening when Hope sallied back into my life and then, almost as suddenly, stalked out of it again.

I was sitting with Anna in a corner of the main library and we had been scribbling notes for a couple of hours, but I was getting hungry.

'I'm calling it a day. You coming?'

'I think I will.' She wrapped a long scarf around her and packed her books carefully so they would not get wet.

We descended to the main entrance, where people were arriving drenched and dishevelled and shaking umbrellas.

'Oh, Scotland, how I love thee,' Anna said and smiled.

'You missing Tennessee?'

'We have our fair share of wet, but it's the wind here that gets me. It feels like it blows straight from Siberia.'

'At least Sallies isn't far. If we run, we'll be there in five minutes.'

'If we run, I'll be flat on my back on the sidewalk!'

I laughed, but the sound died in my throat when my eyes

alighted on Hope. She was just pushing through the library doors, so engulfed in hat, scarf, gloves and coat, that barely anything of her was visible.

'Hello, stranger.'

I startled her and she took a moment to adjust. 'Oh, Finn. You made me jump.'

She removed her hat and unwound her scarf, shaking them and frowning at their sodden state.

'How have you been?' I asked.

'Fine, I suppose. Although I could have done without getting caught in this weather.'

Anna was waiting just behind me and Hope threw her a quick smile. 'Hello again.'

'Hi there. Rotten night.'

'Are you here for a while?' I asked.

'Probably. I've an essay to complete by tomorrow.'

'I'm going for dinner in Hall, but maybe we could get a coffee later?'

I could see in her expression that she was tempted, but her face fell. 'I've too much to get done.'

'Maybe another time?'

'That sounds good. I'll leave you a note in your pigeonhole.'

I accepted this vague proposal, but as she was about to climb the stairs, I asked, 'Are you still angry with me for doing what Magnus wanted?'

'Of course not. You decided to do it and you're fine, so no harm done.'

'It's just that you seem distant.'

I knew as soon as the words left my lips that I was only making matters worse. She opened her mouth to remonstrate, then decided better. 'This is not the time nor place to talk about such things. I've a busy evening ahead and I need to concentrate. So I'll leave you a message in your pigeonhole. Okay?'

'Of course. Happy reading.'

I murmured an apology to Anna, pulled up my hood and strode into the elements.

Half an hour later, I joined her and Charles for dinner. The hall was candlelit and warm and the scents of the food made my stomach gurgle. Once we were served, I tried to make small talk, but I was deflated. After the experiences I had shared with Hope, I thought we were friends, perhaps even more than friends. She had held my hand all through my drug trip. She had brought me back to my senses and comforted me. Yet, each time I saw her, I had to tap away at her tough exterior.

'I assume you have a ticket for tomorrow evening?' asked Charles, breaking into my contemplation as the main course plates were cleared away.

'Oh, hush,' scolded Anna. 'Finn won't be interested.'

'Interested in what?'

'Anna will be singing in St Salvator's Chapel.'

I turned my gaze on Anna. 'You will?'

'Rhiannon persuaded me to join the University Chamber Choir and we're performing tomorrow night. All proceeds to WaterAid's work in east Africa.' She dropped her eyes sheepishly. 'I didn't tell you because I assumed you wouldn't be interested.'

'Nonsense,' said Charles. 'Finn would want to support a fellow Divinity colleague as much as I do – isn't that right, Finn?'

'I don't really know that kind of music.'

'It's a wonderful selection of early choral. Palestrina, William Byrd, a seasonal Bach and a dash of the modern with "Ubi Caritas". I've sat in on the rehearsals and the acoustics in the chapel are simply glorious.'

'I said hush, Charles. I'm sure Finn has better things to do.'

'I'm sorry, Anna. You never said you'd been rehearsing. Of course I'd love to come.'

She blushed at this and retrieved her rucksack from beneath the table. 'In that case, there are still some seats.' She pulled out a wad of numbered raffle tickets. 'They're three pounds – I hope that's not too steep?'

She was about to tear the first one off and write my details on the stub, when she paused and shot me an enigmatic glance. Then she began rifling through the pack until she came to a particular stub and checked the details penned on it. With a nod, she selected the next numbered ticket, tore it off and handed it to me.

'Thanks. I'll settle up with you tomorrow.'

'It starts at eight. Only ninety minutes' duration, so hopefully we won't bore you for too long.'

I waved her silent.

'I'll meet you by the pigeonholes at seven forty-five,' suggested Charles. 'And we can walk over together.'

'It's a date.'

XXVII

Charles was waiting in the entrance hall when I hurried down the stairs a few minutes after our assigned meeting time.

'Chop, chop, Finn. Never good to be late for a performance.'

His tie was back in place and his shoes buffed beneath his charcoal suit.

'Heck, is this a smart affair?'

He inspected my jeans and chequered shirt and rather less buffed boots. 'I don't believe a dress code was stated.'

As we walked into another wet evening, he opened a black umbrella and held it so I could dip under. We arrived at the buttresses running along the north side of St Salvator's Chapel and approached a couple of students checking tickets.

'Right down to the end of the choir stalls, second row on the right,' said one of the checkers and I followed Charles inside.

'Lucky you,' he commented. 'Seems I'm seated further back.'

'You can swap if you'd like.'

'Wouldn't dream of it. The acoustics will be better back here and I suspect Anna will be dying to see you right up at the front.'

We were standing at the western end of a long nave, tiled in black and white marble. Above us, a ceiling of oak and gold leafing rested on the shoulders of Gothic arches. Facing each other across the nave were rows of tiered choir stalls and, at the far end, three magnificent stained-glass windows looked down upon a stone altar, surrounded by chairs and music stands. Reverential whispers hummed around the stonework. This was the type of place where no one raised their voices except in song. Memories of my visits to country churches washed through me, and I was rooted to the spot until Charles nudged me.

'Better get down to your prestigious position before the musicians arrive. I'll see you later.'

I continued along the nave and whispered thanks to a couple in the second stall on the right as they pulled their legs in to let me stumble past. Two raffle tickets were placed on the only vacant cushions remaining and one matched my number. Programmes lined the pews and I studied one by candlelight.

Missa Nigra sum – Giovanni Palestrina, 1590
Ave Verum Corpus – William Byrd, 1605
Cantata 140 (Wachet auf) – J S Bach, 1731
Ubi Caritas – Ola Gjeilo, 1999

I was so engrossed that I failed to realise the couple were shifting again and a final arrival was coming to occupy the place next me. A scent of something floral alerted me – a hint of delicate rose curling over the deeper aroma of the candles – and I looked up to discover Hope.

'Well, this is a surprise,' she whispered with an edge of consternation.

I discarded my programme and stood to give her room. 'It really is.'

She removed her coat and wrapped it into a ball, and when we both lowered ourselves, we were so close that her arm pressed against mine and our thighs nuzzled.

'Did you arrange this?' she demanded.

'No, I swear I didn't. My friend Anna just gave me this seat number.'

'Ah, Anna. I met her when I bought my ticket. Lovely person. I suspect she had a hand in putting us together.'

She looked at me – so close – and when her lips widened unexpectedly with a glimmer of a smile, I wanted to kiss her. St Salvator's be damned. I didn't care if the whole audience saw. But, of course, I didn't. Instead I just grinned stupidly and failed to come up with any words.

The moment was broken by the bustle of the chamber orchestra arriving to take their places. Hope's attention drifted away, and I watched as the choir lined themselves in two rows in front of the altar. There was Anna, dressed in a white blouse and long black skirt, unmistakable, her cheeks already glistening in the candlelight. She peered towards our stall and broke into an animated smile. For a moment, I thought she was actually going to wave, but then the conductor rattled his baton, and she drew herself back into the solemnity of the moment.

I wanted to say more to Hope. I wanted to whisper her questions, but the silence was heavy now and her eyes were fixed on the performers. Gritting my teeth, I settled in for a long ninety minutes.

I might have been a heathen when it came to music, but I recognised beauty when I heard it. My God, those voices were angelic. There were moments in that music when I even forgot about the woman next to me, seconds when my eyes rose to the gold-leaf ceiling and I sensed something divine.

We came to a pause and I found myself wiping watery eyes. Hope tipped her face towards my ear and said, 'It's ethereal, isn't it?'

'Did you know it would be so moving?'

'I like concerts, especially early music like this, and it always finds a way to my heart.'

I felt her hand seek mine in the gloom and my pulse spiked, but then the soft texture of a tissue was pushed into my palm.

'It's the Bach next, and it gets even more emotional.'

I laughed quietly and accepted her gift.

As the music soared again, I watched Anna singing with earnest passion and I thanked her. In the library the previous evening, she had obviously noticed the way I had fluttered around Hope, and she had realised it was in her power to bring us together. She was, I decided yet again, a special friend.

Eventually, the final note extinguished and the chapel

embraced a heartbeat of silence, as though mourning the sounds that had been lost. Then applause erupted, and I clapped as hard as anyone. Anna really did wave this time, and I waved back. Then she trooped off with the rest of the choir, and I watched Hope sit forward and unwrap her coat.

'Are you going?'

'We have to. It's the end of the concert.'

'You know what I mean.'

'Yes.' She played with the buttons on her coat. 'But I wondered if you'd like to keep me company?'

She could see my answer written across my face. We rose and filed silently out of the stalls. I wondered if Charles would be waiting under the buttresses but, when we exited, I felt Hope's hand take mine. 'This way.'

We came out on North Street. In the darkness, she had marched right over old Patrick Hamilton's burning spot, but I kept my lips sealed. We went east towards the cathedral, and then Hope ushered me into a wine bar. She removed her coat and hoisted herself onto a stool. It was the first time I had ever seen her wearing a short skirt, and I could not stop my eyes from dropping to her long thin legs encased in black tights.

The barman seemed to know her. They passed pleasantries and she ordered a bottle of white, which I suspected came with an astronomical price tag.

'My dad's a surgeon back in California. So don't worry, he provides me with a more than adequate allowance.'

'Sometimes I feel like I'm the only pauper in town.'

'You're no pauper.' She stared at me as she chose her words. 'You're thoughtful and sensitive, wise about some things and stubborn when you believe you're right – and those are riches lost on many.'

I felt my cheeks blushing and my tongue tying, so I raised my glass and gulped at the Chardonnay. We were silent. I had spent weeks praying for an opportunity like this, but now it had arrived I could think of nothing to say.

A memory came to me of the last time we had been in each other's company. 'I've been wanting to thank you for keeping watch over me at Gloom.'

'It was a stupid place to play with hallucinogens, and Magnus should have known better.'

'You seemed pretty angry, and yet you use those drugs to See.'

She arched her brows. 'People have been talking.'

'Maybe a little. Just Madri and Magnus.'

She wasn't pleased. 'I don't use the same drugs. Very occasionally, when the mood and the place is right, I use psilocybin from liberty cap mushrooms to help me meditate. In the early days, the rest of the Clan used it too, but Magnus' research propelled him onto fly agaric.'

'Magnus told me they've boiled it, powdered it, oiled it over their skin – him and Laurie and sometimes Madri.' I knew I was heading onto very treacherous terrain, but I pushed ahead anyway. 'And Jamie, too... before the accident.'

Her eyes flared, and she turned her face away and glared into a mirror behind the bar. 'Is that what Magnus said?'

'I don't remember who said it, but I know Jamie was in the Clan until last year, when he was killed on North Street by a hit-and-run. And...'

My words dried up, and she swung back to me. 'And what?'

I looked down at my hands. 'And I know he was your betrothed.'

I half expected her to hit me or to hear her stool lurch back as she departed, but there was just a deathly silence, and when I looked up, she was drinking from her glass and staring into the mirror again.

'You need to be wary of Magnus. He's obsessed. And obsession does strange things to people. He doesn't see things like we do. He doesn't want to listen. He's convinced there are people out to get him, out to stop his research. And he refuses to see the ramifications of what he's doing.'

She examined me with a dark expression. 'Jamie wasn't just killed in a tragic accident. He was stuffed with fly agaric at the time. His veins popping with *amanita muscaria*. He'd been taking it with Magnus up in the rooms above History and he was out of his head when he walked into the road.'

'Bloody hell.'

'Bloody hell indeed. Those are the real ramifications of what Magnus is doing and *that's* why I have every right to be angry – every God-given right.'

XXVIII

It was getting late and we were amongst the last people in the bar, but Hope refilled our glasses and angled her body towards me.

'Okay,' she said. 'You're inked now. And that means you're mixed up in it. So there's no point you hearing things in dribs and drabs from the others. I came up to St Andrews three years ago and met Madri. We were on the same course and shared the same interests, so we hung out.

'She introduced me to Magnus who was a friend from her younger days. He was in his final year of an MA and intending to continue into postgrad research. He was gentlemanly and attentive and showed us around town. Occasionally he mentioned a club he belonged to – some all-boys thing.'

'The 46ers. Magnus told me about them.'

'Exactly. He obviously thought it was all very prestigious and would drop it into conversation to impress me. It had the opposite effect on Madri. She loathed the club. The two of them were both from influential families, and I got the impression this club was something many of the young men from such families were expected to join if they applied to St Andrews. When it came to her own background, Madri never had anything good to say about her parents, and she used her pagan passions as a means to distance herself from that whole circle. So the existence of this club wound her up big time, and Magnus' membership was a constant thorn in their relationship.

'One night towards the end of that first Martinmas term, I was surprised to be invited to join them both at the club's pre-Christmas celebration held at the Old Course Hotel. I expected Madri to reject the proposal out of hand, but she was all ice and steel in her acceptance. She wanted me to witness it for myself. So we went into town and hired gowns. When Magnus picked us up in an Aston Martin, he was dressed in a scarlet military jacket, a kilt of green and yellow, a leather sporran and a silver dagger in his knee socks.'

I could imagine Magnus arriving at the Old Course Hotel in all his pomp, and I tried to picture Hope in a ballgown. I wished I could have seen her.

'There were fifteen of them. Some had brought female companions, but most were alone. They were dressed in similar regalia, and we were escorted into one of the more intimate rooms and seated around tables heavy with silverware. Madri was as cold and emotionless as I've seen her, but as the drink flowed and the food arrived, I began to think it was okay.'

'But you were wrong?'

She pursed her lips. 'It became the most disgusting night of my life. The whole thing descended into chaos.

The men were repulsive. They were full of themselves. Bragging and honking and posturing. The women were treated like decoration. I lost count of how many times I was propositioned and how many times they would not accept no for an answer. As the drink flowed, they seemed to lose touch with reality. Food was thrown. Serving staff physically manhandled. Plates and silverware ended up on the floor. Champagne was sprayed on everyone. There was chanting and shouting and drunken dancing. And none of the hotel management intervened. It was as if these men were beyond the rules of normal society, beyond sanction, beyond the law itself.

'I don't know how we stayed there as long as we did. Madri seemed to take perverse pleasure in it, as though the bedlam proved she had been right all along. She watched everything with a vicious gleam in her eyes. Just when I thought it couldn't get any worse, Magnus stumbled to a corner table and prepared a line of coke. I was shocked to see him being so blatant, but it seemed no worse than everything else that was going on. But others felt differently.

'There was a blond man present, who I guessed was one of the more senior in the club by the way he had been seated at the centre of the room, and everyone deferred to him. He was as obnoxious as the rest. In the early part of the evening, he had approached me with sneering conceit and spoken as though I was a piece of meat. By the later stages, he was inebriated like everyone else, singing and drinking and breaking things. But when he saw Magnus preparing his coke, he went berserk. I mean, apoplectic. He raged at Magnus and launched himself over the tables to grab him. They went down in a mad tussle, with the others crowding round and cheering. Honestly, I couldn't believe it. I'd hired a gown for the night and come to the poshest hotel in town, and it was like witnessing a school fight. The blond man, it seemed, was more than happy to embrace alcohol, debauchery, ransacking and even sexual violence, but drugs were beyond the pale.

'Somehow Madri intervened. She pushed through the crowd and got between the fists of the two men. Together, we dragged Magnus from the room and led him to a taxi. He was inebriated, filthy and utterly shocked by the assault.'

Hope paused and frowned in consternation. 'Looking back, I've realised that evening was fundamental to a lot of things. The assault on Magnus set him on a path to leaving the club, but I also think it focused his own obsession. This fixation he has with hallucinogens and berserker drugs is driven by his rage at how he was treated. I think perhaps he uses the drugs to antagonise the 46ers.'

I blew out my cheeks and was about to make some facetious comment, when I caught her expression. She was lost somewhere in her memories.

'The evening was fundamental for another reason. It's when I met Jamie.'

'Jamie was a 46er?'

She inclined her head. 'Indeed he was. Of course, I didn't think he was anything special at the time. Term ended and I flew back to Corte Madera. Then one evening, soon after I returned for Candlemas, I took myself to Madri's room and discovered Magnus and Jamie both there, lounging in armchairs, listening to Madri talking about the forthcoming festival of Imbolc.

'It was a special evening. The start of something. We

shared tea and cake and chatted until late about the festival of light, the coming of spring, the burning of candles to symbolise the strengthening sun. And Jamie was... well... nothing like the man I thought he was, nothing like those men in the hotel.

'We met on many more evenings and when the night of Imbolc approached, we all drove to a lake nestled between the Lomond Hills and lit a fire and celebrated with candles and poppyseed cakes. That's when Laurie joined us and regaled us with stories of ancient Scotland.'

Her wine was forgotten. She was lost in her recollections.

'The five of us spent many similar nights during that Candlemas term and then – after the long summer break – into the next Martinmas term. Jamie loved them as much as the rest of us. We started talking about being a clan together and Laurie came up with the name Dál Riata. It was innocent fun. We revelled in ancient traditions. We ate wonderful foods from the past and drank fine wines. We travelled to places of wonder and danced and worshipped and listened to Laurie tell his stories.'

Hope stopped speaking and her eyes were glazed. She was lost somewhere far away from that bar.

'Oronsay,' she said with melancholy. 'One afternoon a little over a year ago, the five of us waited until the tide had retreated enough for us to cross the sands from the island of Colonsay to its tiny neighbour. As night cloaked us and the sea returned to cut us off from the world, I stood with Jamie under a starlit sky, between the walls of a crumbling priory, on the Isle of Oronsay and he proposed to me.'

She closed her eyes and screwed them tight. I dropped off my stool and tried to put my arms around her.

'No,' she said and pushed me away. 'No, don't.'

I retreated and she composed herself and took a tissue from her pocket to dab her nose. 'It was just a brief thing. A spark that cooled between us. But it was special at the time.

'Soon after that the Clan began experimenting with drugs. Just a few pills to start with, enough to add new dimensions to our celebrations. But Magnus was getting more and more interested in the Viking berserkers. Laurie had got him into them with his tales of ferocity and immunity to pain.

'We focused on naturally occurring hallucinogens – cannabis and psilocybin mushrooms. We brewed them up, powdered them, snorted them. And we had some weird times. But I don't think I realised how serious Magnus was becoming. He spent half his waking hours researching everything he could find on the berserkers and he got Laurie and Jamie involved as well.

'One night, not much over a year ago, Madri and I went up to Magnus' lodgings to find him and Jamie in a real state.'

'Overdosed?'

'No, not this time. Instead, they told us they had left the 1746 Club. Apparently they had been planning it for quite some weeks. I was shocked, but Madri was exultant and I suspected she had been working to this end for some time, picking away at it whenever she had Magnus alone. His departure was her victory. I noticed the raw fear in Jamie's eyes. He was pale, clammy, trying to smile, but shaking, and when I glanced at Magnus, he too was rigid with adrenaline. I had never seen him so uncertain, so anxious about his actions.

'For a time, nothing happened. We neared the end of

Martinmas and we decided to celebrate Yule amongst the dunes of West Sand beach, just beyond the golf course. We had our fire going and Magnus prepared the psilocybin. I think Laurie had just started on one of his stories and that's when they came for us.'

'The 46ers came for you?'

She nodded. 'Ten of them, at least. It was difficult to tell in the dark. They'd probably been observing from the dunes. They ringed us and charged. They kicked the fire out. They scattered our things. Laurie was thrown off his perch and I heard Madri yelp. I saw Jamie and Magnus wade into them with fists flying, but then someone grabbed me and dragged me into the grasses. I remember a body on top of me. I remember his breath hissing between teeth and the stink of wine. There was a fist in my hair and a weight forcing my legs apart. I screamed, but it made no difference. Then I heard a voice yell and my attacker was manhandled off me. Someone crouched by our mugs of psilocybin. He threw threats at Jamie and Magnus while he tipped the contents of each mug into the sand. Then they retreated and it was over.'

'Bloody hell. Did you report them?'

'Of course not. We had no evidence to pin on anyone and, besides, there was no way Magnus and Jamie were going to start telling tales.'

'Not even to protect you?'

She ignored my pointed question.

'Christmas arrived and I flew back to California, where I spent my days soul-searching because my feelings for Jamie had changed. I'd been trying to ignore them, but since the joy of the proposal, my love for him had consolidated into a deep companionship, rather than the passion of lovers. So I returned for the start of Candlemas and broke off the engagement.'

'How did he take that?'

'Pretty well, I think. He told me he understood and said he never wanted our friendship to undermine my happiness. So he gave me space and time, and I saw little of him for a few weeks. In truth, I hoped he would come back soon and we could be friends and life might get back to some kind of normality, but I learned afterwards that the boys had got into a new mushroom – fly agaric.'

Hope closed her eyes and I could see her battling her inner demons.

'Sometimes I wonder if Magnus took advantage of Jamie's vulnerability at that time to encourage him into taking more risks with the drugs. On the final Wednesday of last January, Jamie left Magnus' lodgings in the early hours of the morning and walked onto North Street. A witness said he was behaving strangely and meandered into the path of a blue van. He was mown down and died in an ambulance at the scene. Later, it was confirmed that his bloodstream was loaded with toxic substances. The verdict was death by misadventure. I tore into Magnus. I screamed and punched him. I swore I would never speak to him again.

'Jamie's body was taken to his family's private estates in the north and he was buried in their family chapel. I was not invited. I could not stay in this country. I fled to California and remained there for two months. I thought my life at St Andrews was over. I believed I could never look on this place again. But time brings perspective. I began to communicate with the university authorities and they agreed that I could return, although I'd need to catch up on what I had missed once my third year began.

'I came back in April, and Madri was there to support me. One evening in early summer, I brought the Clan together – even Magnus – and we planned a first outing into the forests of Perthshire. It was a subdued affair. We found a clearing amongst the trees and honoured Jamie's memory with incense and posies of purple primrose, white garlic, pink dog rose and yellow gorse, which we wandered far and wide to collect. We raised our eyes to the pale sky and sent Jamie on his way to Tír na nÒg, the Otherworld of the Celts, an island paradise of youth and health and joy. We were careful. We lit no fire and sang no songs, and we stayed sober and clear-headed.

'Over the coming weeks, we shared more outings. Still we kept our profile low, made sure we were not seen together in the university, selected locations outside St Andrews, never drew unwanted eyes. But since Jamie's death, the bastards have left us alone.'

'I'm… I'm sorry,' I said softly.

She did not acknowledge my words. She must have heard them so many times and they had become meaningless.

'No wonder you hate the drugs Magnus keeps using.'

'I don't hate the drugs, but I fear Magnus' obsession, because he's seeking something dark and dangerous, and I don't think he's in control. I know in my bones that it cost Jamie his life. I also think – though I'm saying this to you in the utmost confidence – that Madri makes it worse. She adores what we do in the Clan. She lives for it. And she holds such contempt for the 46ers. So she encourages his obsession, she plays on it. In her eyes, it separates him from his past and makes the Clan what we are.'

'If you feel like that,' I said, 'why do you stay in the group?'

'I don't know. I suppose because there's too much water under the bridge. I've been through such highs and lows with them and I just don't see myself walking away. Not yet anyway.'

She speared me with her eyes. 'But you need to be careful, Finn. You're new. You don't owe them anything. Magnus will keep taking risks and he'll keep asking you to help. He sees you as some kind of replacement for Jamie. Someone prepared to go deeper with the experiments and someone who could be useful extra muscle if the 46ers ever come back.'

I thought about the pigeon. 'Why *would* they ever come back? It makes no sense. Why would they care what drugs Magnus puts down his throat, especially now he's not in their damn club?'

I noticed Hope waver and pause before she answered. 'Maybe they won't come back. Maybe they're gone. But you must be careful because the 46ers took Magnus' departure really *personally*. And they're not forgiving types.'

Once again I sensed I was getting only a half-answer. There was something the Clan wasn't telling me and it rankled.

When we finally left the bar, Hope gave me a light hug and walked off in the direction of the Botanic Gardens. I offered to escort her home, but she said she was fine.

With a heavy heart, I strode back to Sallies.

XXIX

After lectures the next day, I spent the afternoon trying to focus on that week's essay: *Did Mark impose a Messianic secret on his material?*

Every time I got a bit further through the notes strewn across my desk, images of Hope and Magnus kept popping into my head. By dinner my essay comprised just two opening sentences:

During the nineteenth century, most synoptic critics looked towards Mark for historical accuracy because his was the first gospel written. So they took one of the more noticeable characteristics of this gospel – the wishes of Jesus to keep his messiahship a secret – and approached it from the wrong end.

I joined Charles for food and listened to his interpretation of the Messianic secret, then returned to my room to make more progress. But the two sentences stared back at me, taunting and infuriating.

I was jolted out of my despondency by a tap on the door. 'Finn?'

It was Hope's voice, and all cares about Mark evaporated.

'Have I disturbed you?' she asked as I let her in and her eyes ran over my papers.

'Not really. I'm getting nowhere.' I turned the chair for her to sit.

'Writer's block?'

'Pretty much. I know what I want to say, but the actual words are stuck somewhere. Like they're piled up along some central nerve, beeping at the ones in front to get a bloody move on.'

She smiled faintly at this, but her eyes were as sombre as the previous night, so I perched on the bed and quietened. Eventually, as the silence extended, I ask if she'd like a drink and she nodded. I poured a finger of Lagavulin into two glasses and she spluttered over her first sip.

'Whoa, that burns.'

'From the islands. Smoky as hell.'

She didn't reply and our conversation stuttered to a halt. I could sense indecision behind her stern expression. She had things to say, but had no more idea where to start than I did with my essay.

'It's funny,' she said at last, toying with her dram. 'It's funny how things sometimes happen all at once. After we talked last night, I barely slept and did a lot of thinking. Then I made my way to lectures this morning, and I saw someone I'd not come across for a long time. It was as if he'd walked right out of my thoughts from last night.'

'Who was it?'

'The blond man. The 46er.'

'The guy who had a fist fight with Magnus?'

'The same one. I had the misfortune to run into him a few times last year, but I'd not seen him for a long time. And then, there he is, coming towards me along Market Street this morning.'

'Jeez. Did he say anything?'

'No, but I thought he was going to. His eyes locked on to me from fifteen yards and he recognised me. We just stared at each other as we passed. There was a momentary break in his pace when I thought he was going to speak, but I was damned if I was going to slow and maybe that stalled him. But his expression, Finn. He stared at me with such intensity. I got his message clearly enough.'

'He was threatening you?'

'It felt that way. It was like he knew we were gathering again. Like he knew Magnus was still taking drugs. There's trouble ahead. That's what his eyes told me. Right to the moment we passed and I could breathe again.'

'Do you know his name?'

'He's called Justus.'

'Bloody hell, do these 46ers all have weird names?'

'Some of them.'

She drained her whisky and gasped as she swallowed. 'I don't think it's over yet, Finn, and that scares me.'

'It's just a coincidence. St Andrews is a small place. You're going to bump into people you don't want to sometimes.'

'It's more than that. He knew what he was doing when he locked on to me. He was telling me that nothing was forgiven and nothing was over. And now I'm frightened.'

'Then leave the Clan. If you leave, I'll leave too. We can step away from it all. His beef's with Magnus, not us.'

She shook her head. 'No, I'm too in it to walk away that simply. That's not the way to go. I said I did a lot of thinking last night, and this encounter has consolidated the conclusion I'd already come to. I realised I've been taking the wrong approach with Magnus. I was so furious with him after Jamie's death, and since then I've been blanking out his experiments. I keep telling myself, just ignore what he's doing and it will go away. Just stay quiet and everything will be okay.

'But that's stupid. Magnus is never going to stop voluntarily. He's more obsessed than ever. Now he thinks you're going to help him. Madri's encouraging him and Laurie's too lost in his myths to recognise any real problems. So he's just going to keep going and get deeper and deeper into it until something happens to change everything. I don't know if it's academic success that drives him, the prestige that comes from a major discovery, or whether he actually thinks this berserker drug could be some kind of magic potion to protect us.'

'One swig and we bash the 46ers to kingdom come.'

'Something like that. But probably Magnus doesn't even know himself. He's just caught by the need to keep trying. The lure of the next trip.'

'But if we're not going to step away, then I don't know how we stop him.'

'I think we help him.'

'What?'

'Every time he tries some new method, he puts all of us at risk. Not just from the 46ers, but because we never know how our bodies will react to these substances. Whatever the truth behind Jamie's death, the one thing that's proven is that he had fly agaric in his bloodstream. He must have been dosing up in Magnus' rooms. But maybe, if Magnus had already discovered the berserker secret, they wouldn't have been taking anything that night, and Jamie might still be alive.'

She looked at me gravely. 'So I'm here to ask for your help, Finn.'

'What do you want me to do?'

'Help me find the answer to Magnus' obsession. It's not fly agaric. He's done that enough, so it's got to be something else, and I want you and me to put our heads together.'

'I don't really know where to look.'

She put her glass down on the desk. 'I suppose I don't either. I hoped we could visit the libraries, try out all the relevant sections, find any references to historic hallucinogens.'

'It's a long shot.'

'I know, but it's better than sitting around waiting for events to spiral out of control. If we can solve the puzzle and convince him he's found the berserker drug, then maybe he'll stop. He can write up his findings. Justus can go back down his hole. And we can all move forward.' She opened her palms towards me. 'It's the only way ahead that I can think of, but I don't know if I can do it alone. So, will you help me?'

Of course I would. We both knew that.

She smiled gratefully and rose. 'Then get your essay crisis sorted and we'll make a start on Saturday morning. I'll meet you outside the library at ten.'

XXX

The sun was shining when the weekend arrived, and I strode out to meet Hope at the library. It was a pale, watery December light that fired the dew on the quadrangle and made it sparkle. My breath plumed in the moisture-rich sea air, and thousands of spiders webs glinted from nooks in the ancient walls.

I had little faith that our library plans would reveal anything new about the berserker drugs, but I was haunted by Hope's revelations and keen to spend more time with her. She was right about fly agaric. It didn't matter how many different ways the cookie crumbled, *amanita muscaria* was the wrong hallucinogen. Magnus could keep powdering it, oiling it, boiling it, baking it, but no amount of coaxing could lend the taker a berserker rage.

There she was, waiting outside the main entrance, ensnared in a scarf the size of a python.

'I've brought cake,' she announced, as though that was the answer to all our problems.

The place was quiet on a Saturday morning, and we

settled around a table in a discreet corner on the second floor, discarded our coats and took ourselves over to the catalogues.

'You try the card files,' she instructed. 'And I'll search the electronic system.'

She sat herself at the single big computer and fired it up. We began searching on specific terms like *berserker, hallucinogen* and *battle rage*, but it was useless. The catalogues were designed around titles or author names, and so we only discovered a couple of periodical papers.

We broadened our criteria, looking instead for more general information about Viking culture, Viking war tactics, and the use of hallucinogens in modern alternative medicine. We slipped into sections of the stacks that were alien to both of us: Botany, Biology, Medicine, Psychology and Biochemistry. I felt like a trespasser, fingering through articles that meant nothing to me, so incomprehensible that I might as well have been trying out the foreign language shelves. Gradually we accumulated books and papers, and arranged them on our table.

The morning slipped away and shadows slid across the floor. We read and we noted, but both of us knew we were finding little of value. At lunchtime we took a break and bought coffees, then wandered outside to the bench around the back where Laurie and I had talked. She peeled the foil off her cake and we ate quietly, watching the robins on the grass and the sea glittering lazily in the distance.

When we were done, we returned to our search. Though our task was proving unproductive, her proximity was exhilarating. When she was engrossed in one of the books, I would watch her and wonder at how life had brought us together. I listened for her breathing and the way she would clear her throat softly as she started each new page. I grew to know that she liked to stretch her arms back and tighten her hair in its ponytail, yet the strands at the front refused to obey and would soon fall back across her eyes as she bent over the books. Her fingers were long and elegant, and the forefinger of her left hand tapped out a Morse code whenever she became engaged with her reading.

The sun sank and our stomachs growled, and we agreed to adjourn and meet again on Tuesday evening and then the following Thursday. Tuesday came and we kept reading, but our progress was minimal. By the time Thursday arrived, I made my way to the library for the pleasure of seeing her, rather than any belief that we could achieve something. So I was surprised when she greeted me with more purpose and ushered me inside.

'I want to show you something.'

She led me past the book-return desks to a small room and flicked on the light to reveal two computer terminals. I had noticed people in there, but had no use for the things myself. She pulled up a pair of chairs and began tapping the terminal keys. The screen lit up with code, and she typed in letters and pressed enter several times until she had got to where she wanted to be, then she sat back and pointed at a message that had appeared.

'I have a friend in the States and after we gave up on Tuesday, I sent her an email.'

'An email?'

'You *do* know what an email is?'

'Of course.' I did, but I'd never used one.

'Well, she's a senior researcher at Yale, a geographer,

specialising in the concentrations and migrations of populations in Europe during the first millennium. It was a long shot, but I thought she might be able to help us. I didn't tell her specifically about the berserkers, I asked her more broadly about the movement and settlements of populations in the colder climes of Scandinavia and Scotland and what crops they would have cultivated that would have shaped their settlement patterns.

'Her first reply was too broad, so we exchanged a few messages and I focused her down on whether there are records of wild plants or cultivated crops that were being used for medicinal or ceremonial purposes because of their perceived psychedelic effects. This is her response.'

She clicked to enlarge the message and pushed her chair back so I could see.

Hi again, Hope.

This is not really my area of expertise. You say you've already considered the usual suspects – psilocybin, mandrake, datura and – much later – coca and marijuana – so I'm struggling.

There are records of something called 'St Anthony's fire' – or ergot – which is a fungus that infects and replaces the cereal grain on rye and barley. Accounts describe convulsions and hallucinations when eaten, though it would normally have been ingested by mistake rather than given ceremonially or for medicinal reasons.

It's been around a long time. Caesar's legions in Gaul

were supposed to have been invalided by an outbreak. Historians also think that during the Dark Ages many of the witch trials were due to the effects of ergot making the victims seem possessed.

Barley was the staple crop in Scandinavia and Scotland for many centuries, so it seems more than likely that psychedelic behaviour due to accidental ergot ingestion would have occurred. It could have been as simple as eating bread baked with infected barley or drinking beer brewed with it.

Not sure if this helps and not even sure why you're looking for this information! But let me know if you need anything more.

I hope St Andrews is going well and Scotland is not too cold. Call me when you're back in California and we'll get together.

Katie

P.S. Weirdly, a Swiss chemist was playing around with the health benefits of ergot in the 1930s when he accidentally synthesised it into LSD. So perhaps this little-known fungus has actually had an unsurpassed psychedelic influence on mankind.

'Half the Vikings' diet would have been barley,' Hope said when she saw I had finished reading. 'They'd have been packing it away every day. They're bound to have blundered across a bad batch and discovered the psychedelic properties.'

'It's a contender.' I nodded. 'What do you want to do?'

'Let's do some further digging.'

So we started searching on *ergot* and *St Anthony's fire* and *barley cultivation in the first century*. I thought it all seemed a bit desperate, so I was surprised when the results began bouncing back and we gathered several articles on ergot outbreaks through the centuries.

We read quietly and made notes and then exchanged papers so each could see what the other had been digesting. Eventually we sat back and looked at each other.

'I don't like the sound of it,' said Hope.

'It's pretty serious stuff.'

Ergot ingestion, it seemed, was not something to be trifled with.

Convulsions, vomiting, muscle spasms and hallucinations were just some of the symptoms. Fantastical names had been given to it in the past: 'the burning disease', 'hell fire'. In some forms it caused gangrenous pain in fingers and toes, '*eaten up by the holy fire that blackened like charcoal*'. Caesar had lost legions to the infection. In Viking times, thousands had died across Europe. There was even an outbreak in the 1950s in a small French village when three hundred people needed medical care after delirious experiences.

'We'd be fools to toy with this,' Hope stated emphatically.

I nodded slowly, but was less convinced. 'It's dangerous, no doubt, but it also seems to come down to how much is taken. In a lot of these cases the ingestion was by accident. People probably consumed infected barley in significant quantity before they even realised there was a problem.

They could have been drinking it in ale or eating it in their bread. Then when they fell ill, they suffered badly.'

'It kills,' Hope said. 'Let's not kid ourselves.'

'But it also says that if taken carefully, ergot – like many medicinal plants – is a poison that heals. It's given to help migraines. Midwives fed it to mothers to induce labour. It's used in rituals to create delirium at levels carefully measured to avoid the burning and gangrene. And, most important of all, these historical accounts tell us that the hallucinations were unpleasant experiences. Unlike psilocybin and fly agaric, ergot brings dark, painful and frightening visions. Doesn't that sound more like the sort of thing berserkers would ingest to prepare for violence?'

Hope pursed her lips. 'This is a dangerous path to take, and you know I've already lost too much to bear any more tragedy.'

'I'm not suggesting we start taking bellyfuls of the stuff. But we've spent a lot of time going round in circles these last few days and now we've found something interesting, so I don't think we can discount it.'

Hope sighed and nodded reluctantly. 'Okay. I just worry about telling Magnus. What if he gets carried away?'

'Then we have to keep him reined in. We brief him and we tell him that if we take this any further, we work on it together. Step by careful step. And we stop at the first sign of trouble. How about that? Do we have a deal?'

I proffered my hand, but she would not shake it. Instead she deliberated, then took just my thumb in her fingers and squeezed gently.

'Deal.'

XXXI

It was late when we left the library, but we decided to take our findings straight to Magnus.

He offered us wine and listened without interruption, though I could see resistance in his expression. He didn't appreciate us getting involved with his research, especially when he had asked for no help. But when the details of ergotism were unveiled, they began to work their charm. His gaze intensified and he scribbled notes on a pad. He might have wanted to stick with fly agaric, but there was no disputing that this ergot fungus threw a whole new light on everything.

The weekend passed and I heard no more from Hope. I swung between lethargy and restlessness, dozing at odd hours, then striding into town just for something to do. It was time wasted, time I wished away. My life in a holding pattern. I had become accustomed to the silence of the Clan, but this time I felt their quiet in every pore of my body.

Hope. Hope Finola D'Angelo floated with me through

my squandered hours. I could smell her scent, feel her hair, hear her breathing.

Finally Monday came and I headed with Anna and Charles to our last tutorial of Martinmas. We settled and poured teas, then Father Haughton began a conversation about the final scenes in each of the three synoptic gospels. He said that we had spent much of this first term focusing on Mark – the earliest gospel to be written – and now he wanted us to broaden our thinking to consider Luke and Matthew. There would be no essay this week. Instead he proposed we spend the Christmas break reading and thinking about why these three synoptic gospels had such different endings. If they were faithful histories of the life of Christ, how could Mark end with the discovery of the empty tomb and say absolutely nothing about the resurrection of Jesus?

Despite my restless mind, I still found myself intrigued by this conundrum. Mark was the original evangelist, so why would he ignore the single most vital event? It was a powerful mystery. Perhaps the most powerful in the history of the world. If there had been no resurrection, if it had been dreamed up in the decades after Mark wrote his work, surely that destroyed the entire Christian mandate? Surely it meant that two thousand years of religion was based on a myth with no more credibility than that of a piper abducted by faeries?

At the end of the hour, Father Haughton gave us our final reading list and bid us a good Christmas. We wandered up to the St James' Library to discover the books and we asked each other about our Christmas plans.

'The family is gathering for a few days at my grandparents'

house in the Borders,' said Charles. 'Aunts, uncles, cousins, the whole tribe. It's our annual tradition and my grandma would have it no other way.'

Silently, I wondered how big his grandma's house must be to accommodate all that lot. My nan's house was going to feel crowded with just the two of us.

Anna was quieter. She said she would be spending the festive period with her mother and sister in Knoxville. They would bake and host friends, and she would help decorate the church as she did every Christmas. She was looking forward to it, but I also saw in her glances a regret to be leaving this place of academia even for just a few weeks.

Monday slunk into Tuesday, and Tuesday sped away. Panic rose in me like a tide breaking over my dejection. Term was ending. Some students could already have departed. What if Hope flew off to her New World without making contact? I could hardly bear the thought.

I forced myself into town and bought a card showing a herd of reindeer hemmed in by snowdrifts.

Dear Hope,

There may be no finfolk and faeries and dolmens and barrows in California, but I still wish you a wonderful Yule.

I am leaving town on Thursday on the 11.48 bus to Leuchars. Please come round before that if you can. I would love to see you.

Below is my address in Dumfries. If you get a chance, write to me.

Take care. I will miss you.

Finn

I sealed the envelope and left it in her pigeonhole and hoped she was not already halfway across the Atlantic.

By Wednesday evening, the card was still there and I paced around Sallies, unable to settle. In the end, I could bear it no more and I threw on a coat and plunged into the drizzle to walk to the only address I knew.

'Have you heard from Hope?' I demanded as soon as Magnus opened the door.

His appearance startled me. For the first time, he looked unkempt. The curls that usually piled artfully on top of his head were a neglected mess. His complexion was so sallow it accentuated the dark rings around his eyes. He still wore a white shirt, but this one looked as though it had not lost contact with his armpits in several days. When he beckoned me inside, the air in his palatial room was stale and heavy with the smell of takeaways.

'Not a thing,' he said in reply to my question. 'I expect she's long gone by now. She doesn't like to hang around when lectures finish.'

My heart sank. I hovered by the door, not sure what else there was to say.

'Do you... do you think she'll come back?'

'What makes you ask that?'

'I don't know, just a feeling.'

He ignored my response and changed the subject.

'Seeing as you're here, let me show you something.' He unlocked a drawer and held up a small sealed bag of black powder. 'Dried ergot alkaline, capable of remaining dormant for long periods.'

'Jeez, how did you get hold of that?'

'It's taken a lot of work. I started with my usual supplier

through the drug routes. We knew ergot can be synthesised into LSD, but he couldn't get far enough back in the supply chain to find anything of the fungus in its natural form. Instead, we got lost in a quagmire of chemical derivatives like ergotamine and ergocryptine. Modern confections. Useless to us.

'Then we tried the medical route. Apparently this stuff is used for Parkinson's disease, but again, only in some chemically altered state. Lysergic acid or something or other.

'Finally, we realised there was a simpler way. We needed to go directly to the grain industry. My supplier worked his contacts amongst the barley distributors for the whisky distilleries. Seems ergot is a pretty rare thing now, what with modern harvesting and storage techniques. They do, however, have to sift and remove some contaminated grains, especially during the drying stage. These are usually discarded, but my supplier pulled in some favours and this is what came through.'

'Why's it black?'

'That's the colour of the fungal body on the barley stem.' He passed the bag to me so I could study the contents more closely. It looked like a fine tea from Assam.

'Pure, unadulterated ergot fungus,' he continued. 'Just as the Vikings would have known it.'

'Don't get carried away, Magnus. Not now.'

His expression hardened and he took the bag back from me. 'I'm not getting carried away.' He stuffed the bag back into the drawer and locked it again.

'That stuff's dangerous,' I warned.

He harrumphed, but did not respond. For want of

anything better to say, I asked if he was heading home for Christmas.

'I haven't been home in a long time. I told you, Finn, my family's pretty disappointed in me.'

'Well, whatever you do, try to have a good Yule.' I didn't want to be there anymore. The news that Hope might already have left the country had sapped me.

'You too, Preacher. You too. See you in Candlemas.'

I strode back to Sallies in a mood blacker than the ergot. But when I passed the pigeonholes, my blood surged. The card was gone.

My elation lasted until dinner, when I sat alone in the old dining hall and gazed around at the few remaining faces. No Madri. No Clan. No Hope. Afterwards, I hovered in the Common Room until I could find no valid reason to remain away from my eyrie in the roof for one final night.

Anna was waiting outside my door.

'Oh hi, Finn. I'm off early tomorrow and I didn't want to miss you.' She waved a notepad and pencil. 'If you give me your address, we can correspond. I'd love to hear from you.'

I found a scrap of paper on the desk and wrote out my nan's address. She grinned and hovered uncertainly, reddening with embarrassment. 'Well, I guess this is it.'

I took her in a hug, and I felt her arms come up and squeeze around my neck. 'You take care, Anna, and have a safe flight. I'm going to miss you.'

She released me and bobbed back. 'You too.' Her timid smile faded as she saw the despondence behind my eyes. 'Look after yourself. Rest and recuperate. And come back revived.'

Once she was gone, I locked the door and half-heartedly

packed my rucksack. There were a few fingers of *Lagavulin* left in the bottle, and I decided there was no point leaving them until next semester. I emptied the contents into a mug and drank it down while I finished my packing.

It was a big mistake. Perhaps if I'd resisted the temptation, I wouldn't have been so dead to the world in the small hours.

I might have heard them come for me.

XXXII

The first I knew that I was not alone was when my jaw was forced back and something stuffed into my mouth.

I woke with a start and found myself lying on my back on the bed, where I must have drifted into oblivion still fully clothed. It was pitch-dark, but there were bodies all around me. Hands clamped my forehead, my shoulders and my wrists to the bed. More had hold of my ankles. Someone had a knee on my chest and someone else was still forcing a sock down my throat.

I roared in defiance and thrashed to free myself, but it was no good. I was going nowhere, and my roar came out as a muffled moan. I tried to rear up and headbutt the figure looming over my face, but they had me too tight. Someone swore softy, but then – much worse than that – someone giggled. The bastards thought this was funny.

Jokers, they might have been, but they trussed me expertly enough. Once the sock was in place, they rolled me onto my side and gagged me, then whipped my hands behind my back and bound my wrists. Others worked on my ankles and then they levered my shoulders up and shoved a linen bag over my head. I bucked and wriggled and forced noise from my lungs, but it was pointless. They were even confident enough to stand back and let me test my bonds. I could hear them breathing hard from the exertion, and I could smell the heat of many bodies in my tiny room.

'Check the corridor,' someone whispered curtly.

Someone else moaned in pain. 'Hurt my shoulder doing that. The tosser wouldn't stay still.'

But then the giggle again. A hushed joke and a snigger. This was a game to them.

I heard my door open, followed by a soft debate about how best to lift me. Then I was up in their arms and being carried down the corridor. Still I bucked and twisted, and I blunted their humour. They cursed quietly and dug me in the ribs and told me to stop or I was for it.

I felt my body inclining and knew I was being carried down the stairs. Then night air rushed to embrace me. I thought I could see streetlights through the weave of the bag. I tried to kick again, but within moments I was manhandled into the boot of a vehicle and the rear door slammed. I heard some of them clamber into the seats in front.

'Keep an eye on him,' came the same voice.

The one who had hurt his shoulder complained about the pain again, but someone else swore back at him, 'Keep your fucking knickers on, you fanny.'

Somehow through my fear, I sensed I was in a good-quality vehicle, powerful and smooth and smelling of leather. But then, of course, it would be.

The drive was short. Soon I was being carried through the

night again. The air smelt saltier and heavier with foliage. We dropped down steps and into a space that seemed colder than outside, like a garage or a cellar.

There was debate about where to put me.

'Line him up with it.'

The jokes had stopped and there was hissed exertion as they levered me onto some kind of beam on the floor. I arched my back, but a knee came down on my ribs and forced me in place, pinning my bound arms painfully behind me.

'Let's do his legs.'

'Don't be an idiot. We need to get his hands sorted first.'

They rolled me half off the beam and struggled to untie my wrists. My left arm was squashed under me, but the moment my right arm was free, I balled my fist and launched it up towards the sound of breathing. I connected with a cheek and there was a ferocious yelp and then a hubbub of voices arguing and swearing. Wherever we were, they didn't care about being overheard.

I tried to keep swinging, but they grabbed my arm easily enough and pushed me back onto the beam. Gripping my right wrist, they yanked it out level with my shoulder and tied it to a crossbeam. For a second my left arm was freed from the weight of my torso and I tested a punch again, but they were wise to me this time and caught it and tied it off as well. Then bodies pressed down on my knees while my ankles were secured.

Finally they stood back and there were seconds of silence as everyone regained their breath. The point of a shoe kicked painfully into my ribs.

'I won't forget that, you little prick.'

'Leave him be, Rodders. We need to get this thing upright.'

I sensed them arrange themselves around me again and then felt the end above my head begin to rise.

'That's it, keep going.'

'Christ,' someone swore with exertion.

There was another snigger. 'Isn't he just, old boy.'

They squabbled and panted and heaved, but seemed stuck. They were attempting to lever me vertical, but they couldn't get the beam high enough. Instead, they got it leaned as far up a wall as they could and left me hanging at an odd angle, sort of forwards, but probably looking at the ceiling.

'He's coming,' came a new voice with a hint of warning.

There was a general murmur and then the noise ceased. A long silence ensued, broken at last by the immaculate tones of the newcomer.

'Well, that wasn't what I was expecting.'

'It's the best we can do. The ceiling's too low.'

'I suppose it will have to do. There's a certain artistic flair to it.'

I sensed the man approach. I didn't know how far off the floor I was, but his voice seemed close. 'Well, Divinity boy, what do you think of our little tableaux? Your very own crucifixion. Call it research.'

I hurled muffled snarls at him.

'Well, get the bloody thing out of his mouth,' the man demanded. 'I want to converse with him.'

Hands came under the bag and yanked at my gag, then pulled the sock out. I gasped in relief and felt my tongue unfurl painfully. 'Ah, God. You bastards.'

'Now, now, less of the colourful words from a man of

Divinity. A *fascinating* subject I've always thought, but I'm afraid I'm stuck with a patrician's brain. Law and governance and policy are my fortes.'

I swore again, but he chose to ignore me.

'Do you know why you're here?'

His tone was like Madri's. Elegant, cut-glass, pleasant and yet mocking. He had said he wanted to converse, so I decided I was damned if I was going to give him the pleasure. I snaked my tongue around the inside of my mouth, testing for cuts, but refused to utter another sound.

He moved, and I felt his hands on my left arm. His touch was gentler than the others. He fingered my cuff and rolled it up above my elbow.

'That's why. See it everyone? Magnus' mark. His little tree. Isn't it quaint?'

His mouth came near my face and I thought I could smell a cologne sneaking under the bag and drifting up my nostrils.

'Now why would you go and get that inked onto your skin? You've only been here one term and already he's had such an effect on you. I can only assume you're an impressionable young theologian.'

I wondered if I could snap my head forward and butt him, but he probably wasn't as close as he sounded, and the ambition faded.

'Tell me,' he continued quietly, 'what's with all this dancing around fires and telling stories? I get the drinking and the girls. I just don't know why Magnus wants to do it in the dark in the middle of nowhere, when he could be having the same fun in a fine dining establishment. It all seems... well, rather heathen.'

He waited for a response, then sighed when I refused to rise to his questions and stepped away. 'So we're not going to converse. Okay, so be it. In that case you'll just have to listen to things from my perspective. To be frank, Finn Nethercott, I don't care what you do. I don't give a toss if you addle your brain with drugs. You can puncture every vein in your body with heroin needles. You can kill yourself for all I care. Your untimely death wouldn't perturb me for a second.'

There were a few snorts of agreement and more sniggers.

'But...' the man said loudly to silence them. 'But, you have to understand that *Magnus* must stop... playing... with drugs.' He spoke slowly, enunciating each word as if I was a child. 'He... must... stop.'

'What's it to you?'

'Ah, the boy speaks. Hallelujah.' He laughed, but his next words crackled with ice. 'It's everything to me, Finn. If Magnus fucks up again with the drugs, I can't be held responsible for what I'll have to do. Do you understand?'

Once more, I held my tongue.

He sighed and altered tack. 'I thought I was going to tell you to scrub your arm until it bleeds and your flesh peels and that tree of Magnus' disappears. I thought I was going to demand you leave his Clan...'

'Dál Riata,' said someone. 'Whatever the fuck that means.'

'His Clan Dál Riata,' intoned the man. 'But I'm not going to. Instead, this is what I expect you to do. You're going to head away for the Christmas break – back to, I believe, Newton Stewart – and you're going to spend the time working out how you call a halt to Magnus researching his drugs. You understand? He can drink himself into a stupor. He can fornicate until his cock falls off. He can break things. He can have his fires and his dancing. You all can. But the drugs stop. You make that message clear to him.'

'Why should I? You don't scare me.'

'You know, Finn, the boys wanted to use nails. You get what I mean? One in each palm and one through the ankles. Just for historical realism. I felt it was a bit radical on this occasion, when we're just introducing ourselves. But if there needs to be a next time – I'll let them go the whole hog. Perhaps a crown of thorns and a sponge of vinegar wine. Who knows? Maybe we'll even leave you up there for three days and nights.'

He let his threats hang in the air. For once the others were absolutely silent.

'Okay,' he announced more loudly and turned away. 'I think he gets the message. What's the time?'

'Two-thirty.'

'We'll let him mull things for a couple of hours. Merry Christmas, Finn. Sallies 'til we die. I hope very much that you and I don't need to meet again.'

With that there was a general movement. Someone checked my bonds and forced the gag back around my mouth, though thankfully without the sock. Then they exited and I heard a door close and there was silence.

XXXIII

They left me alone for what seemed an eternity.

My limbs began to moan. My muscles throbbed. The beam pushed hard into my skull. My hands tingled with pins and needles, then lost feeling altogether and I wondered if the blood flow had stopped. I grimaced and gasped. There was a metallic tang of blood in my mouth and I was desperate for water. I faded in and out of strange visions. I imagined what it must have been like to be nailed to a fully vertical cross for days and I realised it would have been torture in the extreme.

They took me down less roughly. They could see the fight had gone from me and when they stood me up, they left my legs unbound and actually allowed me to walk unsteadily from that cellar. When we finally returned to St Salvator's they had to ease me up the stairs with hands on my shoulders. I heard my door being opened and felt the proximity of their bodies in my tiny room.

'Sleep tight, Finn.'

Most beat a hasty retreat, then a pair of hands released

my gag, untied my wrists and hurried from the room, leaving me to pull the hood off.

It was still dark and the Hall still slept. It was as though nothing had happened.

I sank onto the bed and drew my knees up and stared at the shape of my desk and the outlines of the papers on it. Then the last vestiges of strength collapsed, my adrenaline reserves flooded away, and I wept. Deep, quiet sobs. Salty tears. Heaving chest. Snot in my nose. Like a kid who's been kicked at primary school.

Morning arrived slowly. There was no breakfast scheduled in Hall, so I brewed a mug of tea in my room and then washed and changed. Morosely, I packed the last things into my kitbag and waited for the time to tick away until I could catch the bus. I locked up, then carried my bag down to the ground floor and left the key on hook number 138.

Rain had come and gone. A wind buffeted the bare trees and jostled around the buttresses of St Salvator's Chapel. I walked down North Street to the bus stop and checked my watch. Just a couple of minutes until the bus was due and then the short journey to Leuchars to catch the train to Edinburgh.

There was a small crowd of students laden with luggage, wrapped in coats and trying to shield from the elements. I slipped into the back of the group and waited with my head down, as though I feared someone would recognise me or start a conversation. At last the bus arrived. I let the others jostle for position, then made my way down the aisle to a seat near the back and threw my bag down next to me. The doors clanked shut. The driver looked in his side mirrors and indicated to pull out.

I sighed with relief. I needed to leave that place. I needed to go home and work out what the hell I was going to do next. I couldn't even begin to think about the Clan, nor even Hope. For once, I was thankful she was gone.

The driver's head swung back towards the pavement. The doors opened again and he conversed with someone outside. After a few moments, he nodded and a final person alighted and peered down the bus.

It was Hope.

Dazed, I stood and she came to me. She wore no scarf. Her hair was loose beneath a wool hat, but her face was flushed, as though she had been running.

Without uttering a word, she reached for me and took me in a hug. I wrapped my arms around her waist and squeezed her tight. A few catcalls and whistles started up, but I didn't care. I needed that hug. Her squeeze almost brought tears to my eyes again. I breathed in the scent of her hair and thought that this woman could have been my whole world if only the world had let me.

Finally, she stepped back with a solemn expression and that little dip between her brows. Only then did she see the state of me. For a moment, it stoppered what she had planned to say. Then, with renewed effort, she whispered, 'The obstreperous American half of me desperately needs time under Californian skies. The magical, romantic Irish side of me will miss you.'

I nodded, but could not reply.

She frowned and took my hand. 'Are you okay?'

'Like you, I just need some time away from here.'

She gave me an uncertain smile, then turned and strode back down the aisle. With a nod of thanks to the driver and a chorus of cheers from the other passengers, she was gone.

The bus pulled out into the traffic and I sank back into my seat and watched her marching back into that ancient university town. I watched her until she was just a dot in the distance.

'I'm sorry, Hope,' I whispered, my breath steaming the glass. 'I don't know if I can do this anymore.'

PART TWO

CANDLEMAS

XXXIV

What is it about Christmas that makes it such a global obsession? Tinsel and turkey, paper hats and jingle bells. A fat man dressed in Coca-Cola colours.

How can that even begin to compare to the festivals of the old calendars? The fires of Imbolc as the sun intensifies after a terrifying winter. The darkness of Yule as King Oak returns to kill his brother King Holly. The feasts of fertility to mark the coming of Ostara, the goddess of spring. The joy of Beltane as summer's promise finally arrives. The slaughter days of Lughnasadh to nourish for the cruel months to come.

Perhaps, when I was young, Christmas had been a good time. Perhaps there was love and warmth and joy. But I blotted out those memories in my fourteenth year. Since then, Christmas has always been – and still is – silent desolation.

That year of 1992, I was supposed to spend the weeks between Martinmas and Candlemas semesters with my nan in Newton Stewart. Nan baked and cooked and hung a few decorations and arranged cards on the sideboard and did her best to mark the occasion in some small way. On Christmas Day itself Nan prepared a small roast dinner and we ate off trays while watching Christmas shows. The food was good and the company easy. We didn't need to talk about emotions or memories, so we just enjoyed the fare and stared at the TV.

'*Slàinte Mhath*,' my nan said, raising her dram and smiling at me.

'*Slàinte Mhath*.'

I thought of Hope and wondered what her Christmas was like. I imagined her sitting amongst friends and family in a garden surrounded by exotic ferns and looking out over the azure waters of the Golden Gate towards the sparkling towers of San Francisco.

My mind went to Madri as well. Was she somewhere on her estate in Perthshire, riding horses to avoid her parents? And what of Laurie? I pictured him in an old pub beside a winter fire, regaling the locals with stories of St Nicolas and the Yuletides of old.

Then there was Magnus. The son who could not go home. Rejected. Deplored. Did he spend those festive days in his rooms above the History faculty drinking Oloroso and fuelling his pain with dreams of berserker fury?

I needed those weeks with Nan to process the shock of what had happened to me. I woke at night convinced there were men around me. Over and over I relived the hours alone on my cross, bound, blinded and defenceless, while I waited for them to return. I had told the leader that he did not scare me, but I had lied. The adrenaline at the time had kept the fear at bay, but ever since then I trembled at the audacity of their ambush and the ease with which they had reduced me to a lesser life form.

My weeks with the Clan had seemed so visceral and empowering within the strictures of university life, but now – away from the context of St Andrews – they seemed rather ludicrous. I had worked hard to gain a place in the School of Divinity against the odds, yet I had spent my first term deviating from my study and obsessing about a set of new friends, whose influence was far from healthy. How in hell had I managed to chart a course that washed me up in a cellar, afraid and confused, tied to a cross?

I told myself, dejectedly, that Candlemas must be different. I must detach myself from the dangerous circle of the Clan, and focus once more on obtaining a good degree and making a life for myself.

On the Saturday after New Year, a letter dropped through our door addressed to me and postmarked from the United States. I tore it open and I was six lines into it before I realised the script was not the elegant hand of Hope, but the voluptuous loops of Anna.

I tossed the pages on the sofa and stared out of the window, but then my heat cooled and I reconsidered. Perhaps it was better that it was not Hope. If she had written to tell me she missed me, I would have found myself being reeled straight back into the Clan's net.

Retrieving the pages, I escaped to my room and perched on my bed. Sweet Anna. Her news was not scintillating – she had been baking with her mother for the church fête, taking walks in the park, reading all the books Father Haughton

C.F. BARRINGTON

had highlighted and singing in her Baptist choir – but I was nevertheless touched that she had bothered to write from so far away.

I found myself realising that Anna was perhaps the best influence in my life at that moment. Her cheerful smile and gentle understanding and work ethic were things I should make more time for in Candlemas. It was towards her that I should orientate when I returned.

XXXV

A week after Anna's letter, I was reading in my bedroom when the phone rang downstairs. I heard my nan asking – *and who shall I say is calling?* – in a tone she didn't use with her friends. When I came out my room, she was halfway up the stairs.

'It's a *girl* for you,' she said, looking almost as surprised as me. 'A Maggie, I think.'

'Hello?' I said once I was down and the receiver to my ear.

'Finn, it's Madrigal.'

'*Madri.* How did you get this number?'

'That's not important.' Her tone was taut. 'Listen, it's Magnus. He's really ill. He's dying, I'm sure of it.'

'What?' I crumpled onto the chair beside the telephone table. 'What's happened?'

'I don't know, but he sounds on his last breaths.'

'Are you with him?'

'I'm stuck on some estate north of Ullapool at a stupid function we got invited to. So I'm hours away.' I could feel her desperation flowing down the phone line. 'You're closest, Finn. *You've got to go to him.*'

I shook my head in bewilderment. 'Madri, it's Sunday morning. There'll barely be a train running.'

'Then get a taxi, I'll give you the money.'

'It'll cost a fortune...'

'*Finn*, he *needs* you.'

This wasn't supposed to be happening. I had convinced myself that when I returned to St Andrews in a couple of weeks, I would maintain a healthy distance from the neurotic activities of the Clan. I squeezed the bridge of my nose with two fingers and screwed my eyes shut.

'Finn, are you still there?'

'Yeah, I'm just...'

'Bloody hell, Finn, we haven't got *time* for this.'

'Okay, okay. I'll get something booked and I'll... er... be there in about four hours, maybe five.'

'You know where his rooms are?'

'Above History.'

'I'll join you as soon as I can. And Finn...'

'What?'

'Keep him alive. Promise me that.'

'Of course.'

She clicked off and I stood up and stared blankly at the front door as I tried to gather my wits.

'Nan,' I called. 'I need to book a taxi and get back to uni.'

She came to the door of the kitchen. 'Is there a problem?'

'There might be, I don't know. Can I... I mean, is there any way I can borrow the fare off you?'

'Is she a friend?'

Her question flummoxed me. 'Yeah, I think so. Someone's in trouble.'

Nan pierced me with an assessing look. 'You don't have to be the one that goes, you know that? You have your own troubles to consider.'

'I know. But I need to do this.'

Nan nodded. 'Then you'd better call the taxi firm, and I'll find you the money.'

'It's going to be a lot, but I'll pay you back, I promise.'

'Just you focus on the important things.'

The car was with us in half an hour, and Nan pressed a wad of notes into my palm. 'You go do what you have to, but you also take care of yourself. We've lost too many already and that makes you even more precious.'

I hugged her and found my tears welling up as I sat in the back of the car. I had not even thought to tell her how grateful I was for the days we had spent together.

XXXVI

The taxi got me to St Andrews mid-afternoon and dropped me outside the School of History.

I had a moment of horror when I thought that between semesters the door would be robustly locked, but it yielded and I wondered if Magnus ensured they kept the whole building running just for him. I loped up the flights and tapped on his door. Nothing. I turned the handle and found it locked. Swearing, I stepped back and was about to start calling his name, when a thought struck me.

I stalked to the door on the other side and rapped on this. Again there was no answer, but when I tried the handle, it opened. A noxious stink of vomit and urine and excrement rushed out to grab me, and I gasped in distaste. Pressing my sleeve against my nose, I dropped my kitbag and entered. The curtains were drawn and the place was dark. I stumbled over something heavy and hoped to God it wasn't a body.

'Magnus?'

I made it to the window and flung back the curtains. Yanking open a pane, I managed to get some air into the place, then turned to see his curls protruding from a heap of blankets on the bed. I hurried over and pulled back the coverings.

He was alive, but his breathing was so shallow that it was inaudible. His face was paler than ever, except for great red blotches on his cheeks. Heat pulsed from him and a slick sheen of sweat bedraggled his hair. Despite the quiver of his lungs, a stink came from his lips.

'Magnus,' I whispered, shaking a shoulder gently. 'It's me, Finn.'

He breathed something and may have said my name.

'Yes, it's me.' I shook him more and his eyes fluttered open. The pupils were as dark as always, but the whites were mottled red.

'Finn?'

'My God, Magnus, what have you done? I'll go downstairs and ring for an ambulance.'

'No,' he protested weakly.

'You can't stay like this.'

I made to move away, but his hand came up and caught me with more strength than I anticipated. 'Not an ambulance...'

'You need medical help.'

'No... go to...' He was struggling to speak. He licked his lips and took a ragged breath. 'Go to house on... The Scores. It's called The Pres...'

'The what?'

'The Presbytery. Near... a church. Tell them...'

'What Magnus? Tell them what?'

'I need help.'

Madri and Hope would have known what to do. They

would have given him water and got flannels to cool his skin and rung for an ambulance regardless of his wishes. But I dumbly agreed to the demand and said that I'd be back as soon as I could.

I tumbled down the stairs again and flew onto South Street. By the time I'd made it to North Street and was running along an empty Butts Wynd, the whole escapade seemed ridiculous. What the hell was I doing? The man needed urgent medical attention. When I broke onto The Scores, I stopped and realised that I had no idea where the damn place was. I stared up and down the road and glimpsed a modest church spire, down towards the golf course.

I jogged that way and came to a place of worship with a plaque saying *St James Catholic Church*. I backtracked and examined the property next to it. It was a stately sandstone villa behind a high garden wall and set on the edge of the cliffs. Beneath magnificent Edwardian windows was a modern lobby of glass and wood. The name *St James* was painted in gold lettering on the front door, but when I ran my gaze along the façade, I spied older words engraved into the sandstone. *The Presbytery*.

Bingo. As I walked up the drive, the garden looked windburned and devastated by winter, but I guessed that come summer, this might well be the most beautiful place in all of St Andrews. The lawn meandered around the side of the house where there was another glass extension and a patio arranged with furniture for *al fresco* dining despite the season.

I climbed the steps and yanked on the doorbell, conscious that I was still in the clothes that I had been wearing to lounge on my bed in Newton Stewart. A man appeared from the main house and crossed the lobby. Smartly dressed in tweed, he was younger than I had expected for the occupant of such a property. I wondered if he was some kind of private physician called upon by those in the higher echelons of St Andrews society. Certainly he had expensive tastes.

'I'm here with a message from Magnus. He said to tell you he needs help. Does that make any sense?'

The man displayed no emotion, but stood back and said grudgingly, 'You'd better come in.'

He led me through the lobby and into the hallway of the main house, redolent in porcelain and marble and portraiture. I followed him through an opulent drawing room rich in purple seating and heavy curtains. I started to suspect that my companion was not actually the owner of this establishment and he was simply leading me to meet someone else. If he was just the doorman, who on earth was the intended recipient of Magnus' message?

I was escorted into a breathtaking conservatory. Cream sofas and pale rugs were sprinkled over a flagstone floor. But it was the view through the glass that bewitched. The rear of the house reached daringly towards the cliff edge, and all I could see were endless waves stretching away to a stormy horizon. They were grey-and-white-foamed in the dying light, but on another day, with the sun shining and the blue sky reflecting in the water, it could have been heaven.

It was a moment of calm, before someone spoke behind me and my world fell through my stomach.

'Well, hello.'

I didn't need to turn. I would recognise that voice

anywhere. With a ragged gasp, I braced myself and swung on my heels to face him.

'My God. It's *you*.' I balled my fists by my sides. 'I might have been wearing a hood, but I know a bastard when I hear one.'

He was tall and disarmingly handsome. His hair was neatly cut and tawny blond. Even in the dull January light, his complexion was smooth and healthy, coloured with the vitality of outdoor pursuits. He wore a navy wool jumper over a white shirt and cream chinos. But now that I wasn't tied to a cross and he didn't have a bunch of rich tossers at his back, he didn't seem like such a hotshot.

'Well that's quite a greeting.'

I thought I'd encountered him more than once. Not just the disembodied voice in the cellar, but the face too. A memory tiptoed to me of waking on Sallies' stairs after a night of drinking games and finding him examining me, arrogant and affronted.

'Are you Justus?'

'You're well informed.'

'And this place is yours?'

'Alas, only for the rest of this term. The house is owned by the Honourable 1746 Club, and they make it available each year to the Club's most senior member.'

I didn't really care what he was saying. I faced him and held my gaze until his words faltered. Then I said evenly, 'I swore to myself that you'd regret the next time we met.'

'I don't think this is the time or the place for follow-ups, do you, Finn? I understand you have a message for me.'

'Not for you. There's been a mistake.'

'Magnus needs help.'

'Well, yes… those were his words.'

'Then let's not dally.'

'But…'

Justus was already striding back through the drawing room, and by the time I caught up with him, he was being helped into his raincoat by the doorman.

We marched down the drive and along The Scores and Butts Wynd, my legs barely keeping pace with him. I wanted to fling my arm around his neck and throw him to the ground and hurl questions at him. But all I could do was call, 'There's got to be a mistake. Why would he seek your help? You and Magnus hate each other.'

'Hate is rather a strong word, don't you think? We have our differences, that's all.'

'But, why would he ask for you now?'

Justus snapped to a stop and faced me with a sudden glare. 'Because, Finn, I am his *brother*.'

He began moving again and must have taken a dozen paces before I could make my legs respond.

What? My brain was exploding. *What did he just say?*

For the rest of the way, I skittered along behind him, like a lamb following its shepherd, and I did not catch up with him until he was sitting by Magnus' bed, holding his hand and wiping his forehead.

'What's the bloody sod been doing?' he demanded.

'I think he's taken something.'

'Do you know what?'

'A type of fungus that grows on barley. We thought the Vikings may have consumed it to make themselves mad.'

'My God, you lot get more stupid by the day.'

He released Magnus and stood to remove his coat. I could

see he was furious, but he mastered himself and focused on urgent matters. 'Get me a bowl of water and flannels. And then go downstairs and call this number.' He rummaged in his jacket pocket and produced a card. 'She's the finest physician in St Andrews. She'll know what to do.'

I took the card and stood gaping.

'Well, get to it, you idiot. There's no time to waste.'

XXXVII

Justus' physician proved to be a woman in her fifties who spoke like a master of foxhounds and lectured me like the head of a primary school, but she knew how to take charge of an emergency. Even Justus wilted in her presence. She checked Magnus' temperature, blood pressure and pulse, examined his limbs, and listened, appalled, as Justus made me explain what ergot was and why Magnus had probably ingested an unknown quantity.

The good news, she said, was that he had already gone through the worst of it. The bad was that he must have suffered alone in his room for many hours, writhing in agony, blood boiling, heart ready to explode. I should be thankful, she said in derisory tones, that he had survived.

Although the patient quite obviously needed hospitalisation, she seemed to understand Justus' wish for discretion and made no proposals about calling paramedics. Instead, she handed him several packs of pills and wrote out a prescription, which she said I should collect from the nearest pharmacy as soon as it opened in the morning. With a final few whispered words to Justus and another series of tuts in my direction, she departed.

Justus spent the night beside his brother's bedside and banished me to the room opposite. The last image I saw as I departed was him holding Magnus' head to help him wash down pills with a glass of water, murmuring encouragement and leaning close, as though the two men had never had a disagreement in their lives.

I awoke suddenly the next morning, thrown from turbulent dreams by a sharp cry. I was sprawled in one of Magnus' armchairs, legs akimbo, head angled upwards and my mouth hanging open. Groaning, I leaned forward and rolled my shoulders. Through the southern windows, pale shards were fingering across the sky, attempting to kick-start another fleeting December day.

The shout came again. I recognised the voice and mumbled a curse, because I knew things were about to get worse. I stood and listened to angry denunciations and heated replies, then the door across the hall slammed and moments later Madri stormed in.

'What the hell is *he* doing here?'

She looked aghast. Her expression was one of horror, fury and grief, all rolled into one. As she marched around the antique tables, tears sprouted from the corners of her eyes.

'Magnus asked me to get him.'

She punched me on the shoulder. 'And *I* asked you to help. Just *you*. Not anyone else. I trusted you, Finn. I believed you could tend to him while I was making my way down. Instead you… you…' Her words caught in her throat as she waved again towards the door. 'You run to him. To *him*, of all people.'

'I didn't know it would be him. Magnus just gave me an address and told me to go there. I was more shocked than anyone. Did you know they're brothers?'

'Of course I did.'

'Well, when was anyone going to tell me?'

Madri smothered an angry response and broke her glare to peer at the bottles along the workbench. 'What's he saying about Magnus trying a new drug?'

'We'd been researching something else because the mushrooms weren't getting us anywhere.'

'We?'

Something in the way she expressed the word told me to leave Hope's name out of this. 'Me. I found a compound called ergot that may cause symptoms similar to those displayed by berserkers.'

'You told Magnus about this stuff and then you left him to look into it and you didn't think he'd cram it down his throat at the first opportunity?'

'He said he'd wait. He knew we needed to play safe.'

'You idiot.' She spat the word angrily, but there was a crack in her voice as well.

'Are you okay?'

'No, I'm not okay. I've driven all night to be here on roads that went on forever, the constant threat of deer in my headlights. I've worried myself stupid because I knew in my heart that this time Magnus must have taken a toxin that was too much for his system. And I've arrived to find I can't even care for him because *that* man is there.'

'I'm sorry, I didn't think it would come to this.'

'It's too late to be sorry now.'

I was about to object when Justus strode through the open door.

'I wondered when you'd show up,' he said icily to Madri. 'You're never far from him for long.'

'Thank God I'm not, if he falls into your hands the moment I'm gone.'

'Can't wait to get your talons into him, can you? Always whispering in his ear. Always leading him to the next stupid thing.' He advanced and stood legs astride. 'You were like that right from the start. The idiot teenage bad child who thought she'd take my brother down with her.'

'Rot in hell, Justus.'

He nodded grimly. 'The problem is, Madrigal, that with your potions and brews and ointments and poisons, you're taking Magnus to hell much quicker than I'll get there.'

I could feel her shaking with anger, but before she could find a response, he angled his head towards me. 'The pharmacy on Market Street will open at eight just for us. So get down there.'

'He's not your messenger boy,' Madri snarled.

'He's responsible for this whole mess, and he's going to help me clear it up.'

'I won't leave Magnus in your hands.'

'Magnus is in the best possible hands. I wish to see him returned to health as much as you do and – just for the record – I won't be feeding him toxic fungus.'

With a final glare at me, he returned to his patient.

We waited until the door across the hall had closed and then I glanced cautiously at Madri. 'What do we do?'

She looked broken. Her body shook and her lips trembled. She jabbed angrily at her tears. 'I don't know. I can't even think at the moment. You get the prescription sorted if that's what Magnus needs. Then you'd better come to my rooms on Queen's Gardens. Number 17. I won't stay here when that man hovers so close.'

XXXVIII

The pharmacist was as good as his word. At exactly eight, he appeared at the door, peered through the glass at me loitering outside and unlocked. I expected him to demand some identification, but he simply checked up and down the road, scowled, pushed a paper bag into my hands and then barricaded himself back into his shop.

When I returned, Magnus was asleep and Justus was perched on the windowsill, a cup of tea in his hands. He stood to examine the contents of the bag. 'Right, I suggest you make yourself scarce.'

'Is he okay?'

'He's stable, no thanks to you.'

I retreated to the door, then looked back to see Justus popping out a series of pills according to the dosage instructions. He sensed my stillness and glanced up.

'It's not over between us,' I said.

'Is that a threat?'

'It's a fact.'

He put the pills aside. 'You know, the questions I asked you while you were up on that stupid cross were genuine ones. What's the point of all this dancing around fires and getting wasted? What do you see in my younger brother? I mean, look at him. He's a bloody junkie, destroying all the privileges life laid at his door.'

'I could turn the question round and ask you why you have such a problem?'

He considered this. 'Magnus and I have always had differences of opinion. Christ knows, we used to go up a hill near our old school where no housemaster could see us and punch the lights out of each other. Sometimes I stuffed him into a gully in the rocks and forced him to stay inside all night. It was the place we always settled things.'

'What schoolkids do is one thing, but you're supposed to be adults now.'

'Now his misdemeanours are more serious. Unlike my brother, I'm very aware of the privileges life has gifted me, and I make the most of them. I'm about to graduate with a PhD in European Politics. I'm President of the St Andrews Debating Society, and I've been offered a post as parliamentary assistant to a senior MP at Westminster, a position that should lead me to a fast-track in politics.'

'Well, bravo. But what's that got to do with anything?'

'Because the government of the United Kingdom, in all its wisdom, doesn't force too many limitations on its citizens when it comes to enjoying themselves. We can drink ourselves under the tables. We can smoke. We can eat pretty much anything. We can party until we drop. But what we can't do – what's against the law of this land – is take drugs. Drugs are illegal.'

'Only *some* drugs,' I countered, beginning to understand.

'They're all the same once the papers get hold of them. Imagine the headlines when they find out my brother can't stop popping every pill, every flower, petal, every goddamn root, if it gives him a high.'

'So this has all been about *your* career?' I stepped towards him, my temper rising. 'You take me hostage, you tie me to a *cross*. You terrorise my friends. And just because you're worried about a job offer?' I jabbed a fist at him. 'And are you even prepared to kill? It's so easy to make a hit-and-run look like an accident.'

A weight dropped in his expression. 'That's the sort of accusation that could put someone on very, very dangerous ground.'

I bit my tongue and lowered my fist. He was right, it was a dangerous question and I had nothing to back it up. I made for the door. 'Like I said, it's not over between us.'

Justus called after me, 'When I had you up on that cross I told you to go away and work out how to *stop* him taking more drugs, but I discover you right here helping him reach for death's door.'

'If you must know, I thought ergot could be the answer to his research. I thought, maybe, once he found a solution, he might give up.'

'Well, you were wrong.'

'My point is that some of us in the Clan have reached the same conclusion as you, Justus. We use different means, but we're also trying to stop Magnus falling down a hole he can't crawl out of.'

Justus guffawed at this, but he didn't come back at me. Instead, he looked down at his sleeping brother and pondered what I had said.

I took my cue to leave.

XXXIX

I found number 17 near the southern end of an extensive Edwardian terrace and thumbed the buzzer labelled *Eustace*.

'Top floor,' came Madri's voice over the intercom.

She answered in a bath robe, her silver-streaked hair pinned in a bun and her face wiped clean of make-up. Without it, she seemed younger and more fragile, an impression exaggerated by the pink of eyes that had shed many tears.

'I'm taking a shower. I'll be out shortly.'

She left me to discover a galley kitchen where recipe books sprouted on every surface and herb jars lined shelves. I peered around a door and found a spare bedroom with a fold-up bed, a yoga mat and a small shrine where incense sticks drooped over heaps of ash. Her sitting room was brightly furnished in creams, with a sash window looking out over the southern suburbs of St Andrews. On one wall was a poster of the Norse Wheel of the Year and on another, framed in gold, an enormous map of Scotland. In the north, the artist had embellished the highland landmass with the name Moravia and down the eastern coast he had inked the word Picts. And there, running up the length of Kintyre and over the western lochs to Mull, was a phrase of poignance: Scots of Dál Riata.

There was a sudden thud against the sash window and I jumped out my skin as a figure loomed against the glass.

'What the…?'

It was Laurie, cigarette hanging from his lips, still in his scruffy shirt and jacket.

'Whoa there, lad,' he warned as I approached. 'Open up slowly, there's not much room for error out here.'

I grasped the bottom of the sash and eased it up to permit a cloud of fag smoke to blow in and smother me.

'What the hell are you doing?'

'Taking the air while Madri showers. Make a cuppa and join me.'

He edged away along the angle of the roof, and I stuck my head out and watched as he reached a section in the lee of a large chimney where the gradient eased and there was room to sit.

'You're not serious.'

'I wouldn't advise it in damp weather, but we've sat out here on many mornings like this.'

While Madri's shower hummed through the kitchen wall, I boiled the kettle and brewed tea, then balanced the mugs on the sill and clambered cautiously onto the rooftiles.

'You lot are bloody mad,' I said as I carried the drinks to Laurie and sank beside him.

'Aye, lunacy is a requirement in this Clan.'

He offered me a cigarette, and I drew hungrily as I squinted out at the parklands and the farmland to the south.

'If you'd brought me into your confidence,' he said eventually, 'I could have warned you about ergot. St Anthony's fire. Convulsions, vomiting, fever and gangrenous pain.'

'Yeah, we were pretty stupid.'

'The stupidity was giving Magnus the space to try it alone.'

I raised my head and blew smoke above us. 'You know Justus is with him now?'

'I picked that up as soon as Madri answered her intercom with a list of expletives. She and Justus have history.'

'What? Like romantic history?'

'Are you kidding? Can you imagine those two getting it together? No, I mean they genuinely detest each other. They're from the same circles, so they've been meeting up for years. But Madri was always determined to break the mould. I think Magnus was probably enthralled by her from an early age and ever since she's given him a pretty crazy ride.'

'And Justus hates her for that?'

'Justus is the older brother. The heir to the estates. He blames Madri for corrupting Magnus. Turning him into an eccentric, a subversive, a junkie. And he blames her for persuading Magnus to leave the 46ers. Unforgivable sins in his book.' Laurie sucked on his cigarette and thought for a moment. 'And he's probably right. But don't ever repeat that.'

Madri clambered through the window and joined us, her

hair still damp and a rug around her shoulders. She slumped beside me and stared grimly at the horizon.

'There's some warmth in the air,' she said at last. 'Imbolc is coming. The time when Mother Earth's womb shows the first signs of spring and life begins to return.'

'When Magnus is better we should mark it,' said Laurie, but he got no response.

Instead she just kept peering out over the town.

'Are you okay?' I asked.

'How can I be when Magnus is so ill and I should be with him?'

'He'll recover. He has the best medicines now.'

'I don't trust those sort of medicines.' She would not look at me. 'You were such a fool to leave him with something new and untested.'

'I thought it might be the answer to his research. I thought you'd support that.'

'Not if it *kills* him.' She spat the word at me. 'And now you've brought Justus sniffing around again. Right to his bedside, whispering things into his ears and claiming him.' She rose and brushed down her skirt. 'I won't forget your part in this, Finn.' She moved cautiously back to the window. 'Don't ask me why, but I'm going to cook. I need to do something to take my mind off things or I'll go crazy.'

She levered herself back over the sill, then stuck her head out. 'And you two can get off your backsides and go shopping.'

So we did. Laurie and I wandered around a supermarket, searching for each item on Madri's list, more lost and confused than we had ever been amongst the ruins of Castle

Gloom. When we finally returned, she was decorating her living room with seasonal sights and scents. She filled a bowl with pine cones, fir sprigs, cinnamon sticks and cloves. She lit candles scented with cedar and frankincense, and arranged bloodstone crystals on a glass dining table. It should have felt pleasant, but she did all this with a severe intensity, her lips clamped and her eyes fiery and vengeful.

When she was done, she threw chickpeas, butterbeans, sweet potato, tomatoes and dumplings into a stewing pot, while Laurie and I mulled cider. My eyes wandered over the rows of herb, spice and seed jars, all with handwritten labels. Some I recognised, like rosemary, coriander and thyme. Others had rarer, wilder names, such as burdock, mugwort and hibiscus.

'A real chef's larder,' I commented.

'An apothecary's,' Madri replied dryly. 'There's plenty of them I could put in this stew if I wanted you writhing in pain.'

We ate solemnly around the glass table. I thought of Hope in California, but mostly I imagined Magnus lying under the ministrations of his brother.

'Have they always fought?'

'They've been rivals since birth. Nurtured to compete,' she said.

'Justus said they used to knock hell's bells out of each other on a hill when they were at school.'

'It was a boarding school south of Edinburgh. The sort of place where rich families pay fortunes to have their kids ruined. It was a tinderbox for those two. They took their arguments away from the school and sorted them out in private. Magnus told me of a gully they found amongst the rocks, which Justus decided should be a *judgement cell*. On occasions he'd force his younger brother into it and leave him trapped inside as a punishment.'

'He told me about that. He also said something strange. He seemed to think the papers could find out about Magnus taking drugs and blow it across their front pages. Why would they do that?'

I noticed Laurie's eyes flicker to Madri, and she wiped at a small stain on the glass table. 'I've no idea,' she answered eventually. 'Justus has always assumed his life is a media sensation.'

I didn't want to accept this, but Madri was sounding less vindictive now and the blaze in her eyes had been replaced by a colder, more implacable steel. So I decided not to shake the wasps' nest again.

'We'll get Magnus back,' I promised her. 'And sod his brother.'

She looked at me and I had the distinct impression I had just made a promise she would hold me to.

That should have been it. I should have held my damn tongue and focused on the stew. But, instead, I thought I'd add something else to reassure her. 'And we'll make sure he stops playing with the drugs.'

She stared at me. '*What* did you say?'

'We'll stop the drugs. I thought you'd agree, seeing as how he almost died.'

'Magnus' sudden proximity to the next life was *your* fault. You showed him ergot without checking with me, without running it past any of us.'

'So isn't it better to stop using any of these chemicals? We can still be the Clan. We can still celebrate festivals and honour the old ways. And Justus will lose interest and piss off.'

'Who the hell do you think you are, Preacher? You've been part of this Clan for less than a term and you think you can dictate what we do? If that's how you feel, you can walk right out of here and not look back. Magnus and I built this Clan and we're *never* going to stop doing what makes it so special.'

Later, as the other two cleared the dishes in the kitchen, I blew out the candles and cajoled myself for being such an idiot. Only the previous morning I had still been at home, convinced that I must distance myself from the Clan for my own wellbeing. And yet here I was, right back stuck in it deeper than ever. I was losing control, falling foul of events that I was powerless to shape.

And that frightened me.

XL

I spent the next few nights forced to kip in Madri's spare bedroom.

I really didn't want to, but my eyrie in Sallies was not available until term started, so I assembled Madri's fold-up bed and she gave me the sleeping bag she had used at Gloom. The room smelt of incense and the bag cocooned me, but I felt vulnerable in the darkness of her flat, wondering if she was asleep or if she moved furtively through the rooms beyond my door.

In the mornings I discovered she had well-honed routines. She started each day with yoga, stretching and holding postures in front of the living room window. When she was done, she showered, dressed and breakfasted on green tea and pastries. Then she spent a short time with her books on pagan cuisine, scribbling notes in pencil and making the occasional foray to the kitchen to check ingredients. After that, she attempted to settle into her History reading list, but she fidgeted and found excuses to find other tasks, and I knew her mind was elsewhere.

Though she did not raise it, my words at the dinner table had broken something between us. I would catch her looking at me when I thought she was reading, and there was no mistaking the resentment and suspicion in her eyes. She didn't want me in her Clan, any more than she wanted me in her flat.

So I took to wandering the town. I had no purpose except to keep out of her way, but luckily the weather was considerate and there was something liberating about roaming without ambition. If there was an undiscovered alley, I took it. If there was an open gate, I stepped inside. If there was a lost parkland, I crossed it. I found a café squatting furtively down a walkway and stopped each day for a pot of tea.

I let the days pass like this, because I knew a storm was coming.

One evening I met Laurie in The Keys Bar on Market Street and we grabbed a table near the fire and drank whiskies. I encouraged him into tales of dark deeds in St Andrews, but he smiled little and his eyes flitted more nervously than ever.

'Everything seems to be a mess,' I said.

'Aye,' Laurie nodded, swirling his dram. 'We need Hope back.'

I reflected on this as I walked back to Madri's, head bowed against a frigid easterly, and I realised Laurie was right. It was not the coming storm I was waiting for, it was the return of Hope.

On the third day, the Divinity library reopened and I sought some of the books on Father Haughton's reading list. Being once more amongst the desks, the lamps and the rows of leather tomes, fortified me. I settled into my usual place and spent the evening in the company of Mark, Luke and Matthew.

The next morning, Madri was just completing her yoga and I was avoiding her in the kitchen, when there was a knock on the door. She glanced at me in surprise because there had been no buzz on the intercom. Whoever was on the other side must have stolen through the main entrance when another occupant left.

She slipped the chain on the door and leaned her ear against it. 'Who is it?'

'Me,' came a low voice and she removed the chain, stepped back and opened up.

It was Magnus.

Perhaps I should say, the ghost of Magnus.

He hovered where he stood, as though the climb to her apartment had spent his last reserves. His complexion was the colour of white gloss paint that had yellowed over time, like milk gone sour. His eyes were coals, but their fire was extinguished. His cheeks were hollowed and his hair wilted. He had thrown a long coat over a dishevelled T-shirt, as though he had escaped from his sickbed and fled his captors. He did not smile and his hands remained thrust into the pockets of his coat.

'Does *he* know you're here?' Madri asked.

'Aye. He said I'm yours for now.'

His voice scratched weakly over the words, but it was enough to break the spell. Madri opened her arms and took him in an embrace. He wrapped himself around her and they held each other tight for long seconds.

'I thought I'd lost you,' she whispered.

He raised his face from her shoulder and sized me up. 'There were moments when I thought that myself.'

'I'm sorry,' I said, ashamed. 'I should never have told you about the stupid stuff.'

He cracked a weak grin. 'It was a contender, so someone had to try it. And there were moments when it was a hell of a ride.'

'Don't talk such utter rubbish,' Madri said fiercely.

'I'm wondering if it was just the method that was wrong. Maybe next time we can try smoking it or eating it.'

Madri yanked his head round to face her. 'Listen, you obstinate cuss, I'm going to get you well and then we're going to do all the things we love doing and we're going to keep taking extraordinary mind trips and keep working on your berserker mystery – but that *stuff* you took, that stuff is history. You understand me?'

I did not need to see his expression to know they had much to talk about, so I excused myself.

'I'll go get a morning cuppa somewhere.'

The town was beginning to fill as I made my way to my usual café. Candlemas was approaching and more students were returning, bringing life and vitality back to the old buildings. I drank my tea at a corner table and watched people passing up and down the alley. There were more comings and goings now. A steady stream of customers entered to order breakfast takeaways and the old bell above the door announced each new arrival.

I was lost somewhere when I became aware of someone standing over my table and I knew it was her before I even looked. Don't ask me how, I just knew.

'Hello again, Finn.'

'You're back,' I breathed and clinked my cup onto its saucer.

'Arrived last night. Madri told me you'd be here.' She gestured to the chair opposite. 'May I?'

'Of course.'

She sank into it, removed her woolly hat and unwound her giant scarf. I thought she looked sun-kissed – a Christmas spent under blue skies – and somehow more captivating than ever. My heart thumped and colour rose to my own cheeks and I barely knew what to say. The last time I had seen her, she had chased down a bus and held me like a lover and I had been surly and unresponsive.

'Thank you for not telling Madri about my part in the ergot hunt,' she said.

'You know what it did to Magnus?'

'She called me in the States and told me everything.'

'So you also know about Justus?'

She nodded grimly.

'Why didn't you tell me they were brothers?'

'I thought it didn't matter. I thought he'd moved on from us.'

'He's been watching us at least since Gloom.'

Her eyes sharpened. 'What makes you say that?'

I squirmed in discomfort. 'Magnus and I saw a light on the hill that night. We think he sent someone to spy on us.'

'Nice of you to bring the rest of us in on that.'

'And… you mentioned a blue van when we talked after the concert. I think a similar vehicle may have followed us back from Fairy Loch all those weeks ago.'

I could see her shock and I wondered what revelation hit her more – the van or my silence on the matter.

'Why's the man rearing his head again?' she asked herself.

'Me, that's why. Magnus recruited me. He actively reinforced the Clan. And that's irked Justus into action.' I dropped my eyes. 'Over Christmas I thought maybe I shouldn't come back. Maybe I needed to steer clear of you all and let the situation return to some kind of status quo.'

'I'm not sure Madri would miss you.'

'Yeah, I'm Mr Popular all round.'

She looked out at the alley and up at the sky. 'You know, there's still a couple of days until terms starts. Are you doing much?'

'I guess not.'

'Then meet me tomorrow morning at ten at the Old Course car park. Bring warm clothing and borrow Madri's sleeping bag.'

'What shall I tell her?'

'Whatever you want, she'll be delighted to get rid of you.'

'And where are we going?'

She pulled her hat back on and began to wrap her scarf. 'Somewhere you don't have to be popular.'

XLI

If there is a God, what persuaded him to make the world so damn beautiful?

There are moments in our lives when light and season and place come together to create something too ethereal for mere mortals to comprehend.

This was one of them.

I grasped the handrail along the side of the small black and white ferry and felt the vibrations of the engine tingling up my legs. On the western horizon, a winter sun began its *adieus*, the first tendrils of pink tickling the water and stretching for the clouds. The air had been still when we walked down the concrete pier and boarded, but a breeze whipped up the moment the ferry committed itself to the crossing, snapping at the flag beside the funnel and hoisting the gulls that soared above us.

She had brought me to a place my dad had always wanted to see. She stood beside me, elbows on the handrail, hair given up to the wind, eyes alight either side of that tiny frown. The timetable said it took just ten minutes on this stretch of water, but the crossing felt like a pilgrimage.

'The edge of Britain,' I said and she smiled.

There it was. *I Chaluim Chille*. The isle of Columcille. Columba's island. Iona.

The engine changed cadence as we approached and the ferry turned, then backed smoothly up to the sloping pier and ropes were cast and caught. We disembarked and carried our bags up the slipway. Two cars came ashore and were replaced by a few vehicles heading back to Mull for the night. Then the ferry's engines crescendoed, the ramp came up and it edged into the channel.

Peace descended. Absolute silence. No breeze, no birds, not even the lapping of the waves. The sun bled across the horizon and silhouetted a church tower further along the shore beyond the houses. Iona Abbey.

I looked to Hope and smiled. 'Wow.'

'Your first time on a Scottish island?'

'My first on any island.'

'You either get it or you don't. Ninety per cent of people back on the mainland would hate this. They'd think it's the middle of bloody nowhere. But ten per cent are like us. They understand the magic.'

She turned and checked the sunset. 'We must hurry. I know a good spot, but we're going to lose the light.'

I shouldered my bag and followed her along a lane heading inland, past crofts and farmsteads and empty fields. As we breasted a rise, the sea opened before us again and I realised how small Iona was. We could be on the opposite shore in fifteen minutes. But Hope changed direction where the lane ended and took me south on a track that rose into low hills. We left the fields behind and climbed over tougher terrain.

As the day disappeared, she stopped beside a small reservoir nestled amongst the slopes and ferreted in her kitbag for a headtorch. On we went. I tucked in behind her and followed the beam. It was our own fragile star, imitating those already beginning to sparkle above.

The ground dropped gently and just as the dark was pressing on all sides, I caught sight of a pale mass. Sand. A hidden beach. We stumbled over hummocks of pebbles, then down onto the sand itself and stopped to listen to the sea slurping somewhere ahead.

'We're here,' Hope announced. 'This is the spot I wanted to get us to. Columba's Bay.'

I peered into the murk. 'I read about this. Port a' Churaich.'

She laughed at my pronunciation. 'I don't know my Gaelic, but I'm pretty sure you don't either.' She pointed her headtorch towards one end of the beach. 'Come on, if I remember, the spot's over here.'

We crossed the beach and climbed rocks to a knoll of grass and heather.

'Here.' She pointed and let her light play over a circular stone enclosure that might have been the foundations of an old hut. 'Madri called this the Hermit's Cell and it's as good a place as any to shelter on a dry night.'

'Did the Clan come here?'

'Just the two of us in my first term, when I was only just starting to get to know the others. Call it a girlie weekend.'

We opened our bags and retrieved a ground sheet, which we spread over the floor of the enclosure, then unrolled the sleeping bags. A deep chill was descending, so we pulled on coats and hats. Hope had brought an old lamp, and after several attempts we managed to light a thick candle and closet it away behind the protection of the glass. I balanced this on the wall and it gave us just enough ambient light to complement the headtorch.

Next we cleared an area beyond the groundsheet and fired up a camping stove. We did not have the capacity to prepare hot food, but at least we could warm soup and teas, and we were both thankful for the bellyful of fish and chips on the ferry to Mull. Hope produced several packs of meat and I examined them in the lamplight.

'Tonight is Þorrablót,' she said.

'And what's that?'

'The Icelandic festival of midwinter, named after Thor.' She shrugged. 'I didn't want you getting too Christian on me.'

I peered at the packs. 'Dried lamb, blood sausage and smoked herring.'

We settled in and washed the meats down with hot soup. The sausage and herring were pretty good, but I thought the lamb was like something I could have found shrivelled on the beach.

I reached into my sack and pulled out a bottle. 'Islay fire. I hope you still like your whisky.'

She rummaged in her own bag, then pulled out another bottle. 'The last mulled wine in the shops.'

'No wonder the bags were so heavy.'

We warmed the wine on the stove and slopped drams into it, then snuggled against each other and sipped the heat into us.

'They say this is the spot Columba first set foot on Iona,' I murmured. 'He came from Ireland with twelve companions and landed on the Kintyre peninsula to meet with Conall, the ruler of that kingdom. Then he journeyed up the coast to Colonsay, but he could still see Ireland across the water, so he wanted to find somewhere further before he would settle. He continued to Iona and they say the tides here would have naturally guided him to this beach, where it's relatively easy to scrape a wicker currach ashore.'

'Oronsay,' Hope corrected me. 'Oronsay is the smaller sister of Colonsay and the priory there marks where Columba first landed.'

We lapsed into silence. It also marked where Jamie had proposed to her and I wanted to change the subject.

'This was a place my dad dreamed about. He had this little booklet and I can still remember the photos.' I drew in a lungful of night air. 'I wish he could have come here. I think he believed it represented the ultimate location in Britain's early Christian history. A time when we were all closer to the Christian God. My mum had visited here with her own dad, and she really wanted to bring mine. But... they didn't get around to it.'

'Do you want to tell me what happened?'

I shook my head slowly. 'I don't think so.'

We drank our wine and listened to the tide eating up the beach.

'I also wish I could bring my Divinity colleagues here. They're good people and I think they'd find this place captivating. Anna especially. She's American too, and I suspect places like this only live in her imagination. I wish I could bring her.'

'Then you should.'

'Maybe.'

Hope raised her mug. 'To Anna.'

We clinked china. 'To Anna.'

Later, I was slumped against the stone wall of the enclosure, half asleep, when I realised Hope was staring towards some unseen spot over the sea.

I sat up. 'Oronsay's somewhere out there.'

'It'll still be there in the morning,' she replied, but I knew what she had been contemplating.

I chose my words carefully. 'If you want to communicate with him – if you want to See – then I can give you some privacy.'

'No. If I See, I want you right here with me.' She deliberated and then looked at me. 'Are you sure?'

'I'm sure.'

XLII

Hope reached into her pocket and retrieved a small plastic bag. 'Just a pinch of psilocybin.' She scattered some into the wine warming on her stove. 'You want some?'

'This island is wonderful enough. I don't need to trip this time.'

She stirred the concoction and waited for it to steam, then poured it into her mug and cradled it near her lips.

'Would you move the stove out the way and arrange the sleeping bags?'

I busied myself preparing an area for her, while she drank the wine and studied the stars. 'The weather is so kind to us.'

When she was ready, she crawled to the space and lay with her head resting on her rucksack. I pulled a sleeping bag over her and settled back against the wall, but she beckoned me.

'Will you hold my hand?'

My fingers entwined with hers and my other hand rested on her hair.

'Keep watch on me. Last time I did this it went wrong.'

I remembered when I had first seen the Clan together, gathered around a fire in the castle ruins at St Andrews. I remembered witnessing their fear and the arguments as Hope thrashed around on the ground.

'Please be careful.'

'It'll be okay tonight. I'm in a beautiful place with good company and my dreams will come gently.'

Such bittersweet moments.

As the night held its breath around us and the water sighed languorously across the beach, I held the woman I maybe loved. I clasped her hand and stroked her hair and lay close enough to give her warmth. Sometimes she woke and reached for my neck and thanked me and cried lightly into my shoulder. Sometimes she clutched me so tight that I thought we might never let go.

But as her lids fluttered and her arms trembled, she was with another man.

There were moments when she whispered his name over and over. Then others when she shouted it, in warning perhaps or exasperation. Her face creased with anger, her fingernails bit into my hand, her legs flailed up and down as though running, but whether she was fleeing from some danger or racing to save him, I could not know.

Her eyes snapped open and I thought she was back with me, but her gaze was fixed on the heavens and I knew her mind was still somewhere far away. She began to jerk and the hand that wasn't holding mine pounded against the stone enclosure, so I had to reach over and grab it before she skinned her knuckles.

'Bastard,' she exclaimed, but it wasn't directed at me.

After several minutes of grappling, I found myself atop her, pinning her limbs, and I realised how bad this would look if she woke. But gradually, the tension in her muscles escaped and her breathing regulated. I studied her features and brought my face so close that the oxygen from her lungs went straight into mine. It would have been simple to kiss her. I'll admit I considered it.

But at that moment she whispered, 'Finn.'

I was so shocked, I released hold of her arms and slid off her to gabble an apology, but when she didn't respond, I realised she was still somewhere else.

I quietened and examined her.

She had said my name in her dreams. Wherever she was and whatever she was experiencing, I had come to her. And that was enough for me.

XLIII

It must have been nearing the middle of the night by the time she was completely back with me. I brewed up tea and fed her the leftovers of the sausage. I wished she would tell me what she had experienced, but she lay wordlessly in her bag, drinking the tea and mulling her thoughts.

The candle had burned down in the lantern and it would not be long before we were deprived of its light. I guessed the tide might have turned because I could see pale sand again and the slither of the water seemed further away. I removed my boots and got into my own bag, zipping it up so that just my arms and head were free. I pillowed my rucksack and lay beside her, both cradling mugs and watching rogue clouds extinguish the stars.

My eyelids were growing heavy when she spoke. 'Thank you for being here.'

'Did you reach him?'

'A little.'

I took my time weighing my next words. 'Did you do it because you still love him?'

She gave no response, and I thought I'd offended her. Then she murmured, 'He was someone I once thought I loved, and his life should never have been cut short by a headful of hallucinogens.'

'By discovering ergot, we almost condemned Magnus to the same fate. Maybe our plan to help was flawed.'

'Ergot was wrong, but that doesn't make our plan flawed. Madri and Magnus are becoming dangers to themselves and to everyone around them. She sees them both as some sort of Bonnie and Clyde. The pair of them against the world. And she's damned if she's going to lose him. As for him, he's lost sight of everything except the riddle of the berserkers, a mystery he'll go through hell to solve.'

'If they're so dangerous, then why don't you just walk away? If you walk, I will too.'

She pushed herself up, balanced her mug on the wall and looked at me. 'Do you think that's fair?'

'It might not be fair, but it's the most sane thing to do.'

She reached out and squeezed my hand. 'Don't go anywhere, Finn. You were caught in a web of Madri's making last term and recruited into the Clan under false pretences, but that doesn't mean you haven't become a valuable part of us since. We need you now. *I* need you. God knows, there could be a hard path ahead, but sometimes it takes pain to help us get to a better place.'

Our words dried up and we lay in heavy silence. Her final statement circled inside my skull. *Sometimes it takes pain to help us get to a better place.* I toyed with the words. I flipped them over, folded them, stretched them out, let them hang in the air.

And a new conviction germinated inside me.

'Are you awake?'

'Yes,' she mumbled.

'Can I tell you a story?'

'Is it a good one?'

I stared at the dying candle. 'No, it's a terrible one.'

I felt her raise herself up against the stone wall. 'Are you ready to tell it?'

'Only to you.'

XLIV

1987. February half-term in the English Lake District.

We had abandoned Sussex for a week and come north, though not this time merely as a stopover before continuing to my mum's parents in Dumfries. Instead, we had hired a self-catering cottage outside Keswick and used it as a base for family hiking excursions.

We had never before seen the Lakeland landscape in winter. The hills were spotted with snow. The lower slopes were bare of the usual summer bracken and the roads just as empty. The Herdwick sheep, which we usually found spread far and wide, were marshalled into enclosures to protect them from winter's bite. The trees were naked and the tarns edged with ice.

Looking back, I can see that we were stupidly unprepared for winter in the hills, but the weather that week smiled on us, handed us dry days and crisp cold air. We treated the Lakeland countryside as an old familiar friend, fully at one with its pleasant summer guise, but not comprehending how it changed in the cold months.

On Friday morning of that week, we were pulling on our hiking boots in a car park at the end of Langdale valley and the sky was a canopy of blue. We would go high. We all knew that. Days like this should not be wasted in the lowlands.

As we ascended, we fell into a pattern of quiet concentration. Breathing became laboured and sweat blossomed. Seven-year-old Caitlin came to walk beside me, her boots pounding on the stones, her head down, her small backpack bouncing.

'Hold on, you two,' Mum called after us. 'There's a track off to the right somewhere around here, called the Climber's Traverse. I went along it when I first climbed this fell, and it's a more interesting route than this haul up to the col.'

'Dear, do you think it's wise?' Outside of his church, Dad was always the more cautious one.

'The path's obvious enough. Look, you can see most of it.' She pointed up to the right. 'It runs under the great buttress, across the face of the mountain and then loops back on itself, bringing us towards the summit from the other side.'

We abandoned the main path and made our way across sloping ground, littered with stones and tufts of grass crisped by frost. Over a rise we saw the buttress, an uncompromising shaft of rock, clawing skywards, but the track itself was simple enough and we strode along, swivelling our gaze between the obstacles under foot and the views.

'Let's slow down a bit,' Mum said. 'All keep together. It gets a bit steeper around the corner.'

I heard Dad mutter something irritably, but although the way did get steeper, it was manageable enough. We perched on a large boulder and waited for Dad to catch up. I remember looking at Caitlin next to me. She was wearing a climbing hat with ear pieces pulled down for warmth, and her nose and cheeks glowed red.

We continued over the rocks and skirted steep drops. Caitlin was humming a tune and Mum dropped back to keep with Dad. The air was calm and fresh and there was such a silence beyond the immediacy of our footfalls.

And then I heard a first tell-tale crunch beneath my boot – that first light tinkle like someone treading on glass.

I knew the sound. Ice. I stopped and bent to investigate. It was only a small patch, little more than the size of my boot, and I didn't think about the implications.

Christ, I didn't think about the *implications*.

'Look, Caitlin. Is that the first time you've seen ice on the mountains?'

'Yeah, cool.' She stepped in it, further breaking the remains, and grinned devilishly.

We pulled ourselves higher and, as we did, larger and more frequent patches of ice appeared, some on the path, some amongst the rocks on either side. Then there were glimpses of snow on the stones, hardened by the altitude. At one point we came to a patch that extended for over three feet and required a jump to clear. It was after this that Mum called up to us and told us to wait. She was obviously taken aback by the conditions, and so we gathered to assess the situation.

With hindsight, that was the point when the future was still there for the changing. We could have turned around. Dad wanted to, but Mum was reluctant. She knew we were close to the top. We could see the track rising up and then looping back on itself to a crest, which she said marked the end of the serious gradient. After that it was a gentle walk to the summit.

Easy enough. The dice were thrown, the gamble accepted. We would continue.

There was, however, one proviso that Mum required. She reached into her rucksack and withdrew a small length of rope. She always carried this, but I could only remember one other occasion when we had used it.

'Right, Caitlin,' Mum said. 'Come here and let's tie you on.'

Caitlin thought it was even more of an adventure and happily allowed the rope around her waist.

'And you too, Finn.'

'No, I'm okay.'

'Finn, come on, I want you tied on like everyone else.'

'Jeez, Mum. How old do you think I am? I'm fine.'

I took several strides up the path and when I looked again, Mum had tied Dad on at the back and herself in the middle, and they were all following.

I must surely have been aware of the rock feature to my left, sheering down at a sloping angle, smooth and devoid of any stone. It must have nagged at my brain, must have demanded that I notice it. I would soon come to know it well enough. It was called the Great Slab. A section of rock about the size of a tennis court, running at a gentle angle and uncannily smooth, as though a giant knife had sliced off the top of an otherwise normal rocky section of mountain.

I should have stopped. I should have looked at it. If God had been watching, he should have made me weigh up the dangers. But he wasn't, and I didn't.

I just kept walking up that easy path.

Finally, I paused and looked back. I will remember the snapshot forever.

The other three had reached the crest and were resting, pleased to have made it. Mum, dressed in her blue windproof top and wool hat, was looking back at the view and pointing at something across the valley. Dad, bare-headed and rucksack slung over one shoulder was nodding. Caitlin, still tied to Dad, wearing her red winter coat and with her hat pulled almost over her eyes, was staring up at me, smiling and wanting to be with me. I waved at her, and she raised her hand in return and laughed.

Then I took another few steps, and they were my last few moments of happiness.

It was Dad's surprised exclamation that caught my attention. There was something about the tone, the urgency, that stopped me mid-stride and made him spin round. Dad was on his back, a few feet onto the smooth rock of the Great Slab, sliding over what must have been black ice. Mum was stumbling, caught by his legs as he passed her. She fell to her knees and tried to arrest her momentum. Then, in that dreadful split second, even as the images seemed to slow before my eyes, I knew with terrible certainty what was about to happen. The rope. As Dad continued to slide, the slack on the rope tightened. Mum was whipped from her knees and dragged backwards.

And then that one crushing moment. That one briefest blip in history, when my eyes met those of my young sister. Caitlin knew as well. She knew exactly what would happen next. She stared at me, imploring, eyes wide, mouth open, hands grasping at the rope around her and then she was thrown backwards.

Time came back to reality. The slow movements of the second before surged into frantic commotion. Dad reached the edge and disappeared. Mum's legs hid her face, scrabbling at the air as she was dragged backwards. I thought I heard her call, but it may have been the wind. And then there was only the red-coated blur of Caitlin, torn to the edge, held for the briefest of seconds, just long enough to see her face, and then gone.

I stood rooted to the spot for what seemed an eternity – alone on the mountain.

Then I charged back down to the crest, slipping and stumbling out across the Slab, screaming their names. I dropped onto my knees, then pushed forward until I could peer over. They were lying like rag dolls about fifty feet below, strangely peaceful, yet their splayed limbs evidence enough of the violence.

I knew Dad was dead. There was something about the way his arms hung back across the rocks in an abandon that only comes after life has left the body. But there was a low whimper coming from the tiny form of Caitlin, and Mum coughed slightly as scarlet trickled from her mouth.

I dragged my eyes away, crawled up the Slab and started to head over the crest and back down the track, tears streaming across my cheeks, terror locked in my throat. Checking my momentum, I forced my scrambled brain to think. So much rested on making the right choice. Every fibre of me wanted to find them and hold them and tell them it would be okay, but a voice was warning this was foolish. The priority was to get help.

With a cry of despair, I hauled myself around, pulled back over the crest and began to run for the summit. The main path would be there and this would drop to the south, towards the col and perhaps to other hikers.

I had to descend a long way before I came across a lone walker making his way up. I managed to blurt out the basics and, thankfully, the man took charge. He decided that he would be the quickest to get to a phone in one of the farms. So he gave me a whistle to blow and sent me back to the Slab.

It took fifteen minutes of hard scrambling and climbing to get to the crest again and then I dropped down the path we had ascended, calling their names, scrabbling amongst the boulders. As I lost height, I also lost perspective. I could see the uncompromising edge of the Slab above, but could not place where they must have landed. I yelled and blew the whistle. For one joyous moment, I thought they must have got to their feet and started the descent. And then, just as this image took shape, I caught a glimpse of blue in the rocks.

They were lying as I had last seen them, spread-eagled, facing away from each other like a three-pointed star or perhaps a giant flower – for the colours were so bright amongst the stone – and the rope snaked innocently between them. There was no evidence of impact on Dad, and he could just have been resting. Only his wide eyes told a different story as he stared up to his Christian God in his Christian heaven.

Caitlin was curled on her side, head tucked towards her chest. But now she was making no sound, and I knew implicitly that she had died in the intervening half an hour. A coroner was later to decree that it was a combination of internal bleeding and shock. I could not bring myself to go near her and just hovered in horror.

Then I realised Mum was still showing small signs of life. I flung myself beside her and wiped the blood from the edges of her mouth. I talked to her, told her everything would be okay, pleaded with her not to leave. I did not feel the cold. I was unaware of the stones stabbing into my knees. I did not even register the helicopter until it was directly above. I just whispered and prayed she would open her eyes.

Yet, this time, she did not heed me. As the winchman began to lower himself towards the mountain, I felt her leave.

One by one, we were carried into the sky. And then we travelled together as a family for a final time, swept over the floor of the Langdale valley and onwards to Furness hospital and the new ordeals of my life.

XLV

When my words finally dried, Hope reached out and wrapped her arms around my shoulders and held me like a vice.

'I'm sorry,' she whispered in my ear. 'I'm so, so sorry.'

The candle had died, and all we had were the stars and the wash of the ocean and the press of our bodies. Her hair fell over my face, her cheek pressed against mine and her fingers squeezed the flesh of my upper arm. The core cold of the night had descended, and I shifted in my bag so that my pelvis nestled into her. For a moment, she paused her ministrations while she pushed the rucksacks together to pillow both our heads and then we settled.

I think she slept. Her brow was heavy against my ear and her fingers stopped working. For my part, I seemed to be in some sort of wakeful daze. I lay utterly still, simply gazing at the sky and imbibing the salt-scents of the coast.

Dawn arrived so subtly that it took me by surprise. No blushing eastern sky, just a dissolving of black to grey and a realisation that the stars had gone. I had not moved for hours for fear of disturbing her, and I was so stiff that I suspected she would have to prise herself from my embrace. I tested a leg and grimaced.

The movement woke her. She mumbled and nestled further into my neck, then there was a pregnant pause as though she were gathering her wits and she lifted her head and frowned at me.

'Morning,' I said.

Her frown broke and she smiled.

'Did you sleep?' she asked.

'Maybe for a moment.'

She eased herself up with a groan and I stretched my limbs.

'I think there's just enough water left for a brew.'

'You know the way to a woman's heart.'

I got the stove going and we drank coffee and ate biscuits that I had discovered in my pack. When we were finally done, we packed everything and walked back down to the village. The ferry had just arrived and a gaggle of tourists were hovering around a minibus called 'Robbie's Tours', their boisterous American accents slicing through the island silence. They watched us as we approached, intrigued by these two rough-looking figures who had emerged seemingly from nowhere.

'Hey there,' called Hope, releasing her own accent.

This fascinated them even more and they waved and greeted a fellow countrywoman.

We walked along the pier to the waiting craft, but then I slowed and stopped.

'What?' asked Hope over her shoulder.

'Thank you.'

'You're welcome.'

'Seriously. Thank you for bringing me here. I needed to unload.'

She stopped too. 'I know. Come on. That skipper's not waiting.'

I did not realise it at the time, as the ferry rumbled and swung away from the arms of Iona, but a blackness was waiting for our return, a dark storm of devastation. It lurked just beyond the horizon, but it would come fast. It would rush us and grab us and spin us and take us down into its depths.

And worst of all, it was probably me who brought it upon us. I've spent thirty years trying to deny this to myself, but I can't maintain the lie.

It was my idiocy that called the darkness, my stupid actions that beckoned it and let it run amok.

XLVI

So into Candlemas.

The town revived. The pavements once again bustled with young people on their way to lectures. The libraries hummed. My room in Sallies reopened to me, and I packed my things at Madri's and happily departed.

She resented Hope taking me to Iona. She kept referring to it as our 'secret trip' and suggested our timing was inconsiderate with Magnus in such poor health and the threats from Justus hanging over us all. It was as if she distrusted us, suspected we were making plans behind her back.

But Magnus strengthened. He took to walking through the grounds of the ruined cathedral each afternoon, and I joined him when I could.

'Justus would have everyone believe I've given him my word,' he announced on one such walk.

'To stop playing with dodgy drugs?'

'To cease being disruptive.'

'And have you?'

'Of course not.'

We were winding between ancient gravestones, a wind blowing hard off the sea.

'Then it's unfortunate that Justus seems to think differently.'

'He can think what he likes. What happened over Christmas changes nothing.'

Silently, I thought it perhaps changed everything, but I did not comment.

Anna was back. Radiant and jolly and flushed with embarrassment when I gave her a hug.

'Did you get my letter?'

'I did. Thank you for writing and I'm sorry I didn't reply. Christmas turned out to be surprisingly busy.'

'Don't apologise, I don't mind at all.'

She beamed at me, but her eyes told a different story. She had probably checked the mailbox every single day and hoped I might make a tiny effort to reciprocate her feelings.

On the morning of our first tutorial, Father Haughton was hunched in his usual armchair. He looked as if he had been there all Christmas. Perhaps he had lost the strength to stand and no one had noticed. He steepled his bony fingers as he watched us pour tea, one eye on me and one on Charles. Rhiannon had told me he was blind in one of them, but even after all these weeks, I still didn't know which.

He led us in a review of our work in Michaelmas, then moved on to the four New Testament evangelists and asked us to discuss what we had gleaned from our holiday reading. I engaged where I could, but I struggled to add much of value. In truth, I'd not had time to sink deep into the reading material, because my mind had been filled with more immediate matters of life and death.

Afterwards, the three of us huddled outside St James' Library while Charles elaborated about his Christmas. When he was done and he had sidled off to the library desks, Anna touched my arm.

'Are you okay?'

'Shouldn't I be?'

She raised her shoulders. 'You look really drained. Maybe you need a friend to talk to. Would you like to get a drink somewhere?'

'Don't you have study you want to do?'

'Nothing that can't wait.'

I was about to bat the idea away, but I found myself agreeing. Perhaps her company really would do me some good.

'There's a pub out of town,' she suggested. 'It looked nice when I went past the other day.'

'Out of town?'

She beamed. 'I've got myself a little car. I figured it would be such a waste not to see more of Scotland while I'm over here. And I'm intending to follow the routes of some of the Scottish saints. Find the places that were special to them.'

'You can drive over here?'

'Sure, a US licence allows me to drive in the UK with suitable insurance, but only for the first year after I arrived. So I've a lot to pack in before next September.'

'Well, okay then. Take me to this pub.'

Anna's purchase turned out to be a tiny Fiat Uno with 60,000 on the clock and painted lurid green. She said it was all she could afford and hoped, if she didn't put too many miles on it, she could get a fair whack back as a resale in a year. We trundled along the lanes, our arms brushing as she changed gears, and at every junction Anna reminded herself aloud to *drive on the left*, which did little to settle my discomfort.

We arrived at a quaint stone inn called The Forge resting on the banks Kinness Burn and entered a smoky bar, cluttered with so many oddities hanging from the ceiling that I had to dip my head. Fires smouldered at both ends. Candles guttered on tables. Portraits of irritated people hung from the walls.

Anna turned on the spot and grinned from ear to ear. 'I just love these sorts of places. We don't have anything like them in the States.'

I ordered a glass of red wine and looked at her. 'Orange juice, I'm guessing?'

'Actually, grape juice this time. Red.'

We took the drinks to a window table and sat opposite each other. Her cheeks were the colour of her juice and she wouldn't raise her eyes to me.

'You know,' I said, pointing to our glasses. 'They're almost the same things. Mine's just been left around a bit longer.'

'Now, now, naughty. Don't try to tempt me.'

'Have you ever indulged?'

'Not socially.'

I didn't know what she meant, but I took a different tack. 'Jesus drank wine at the Last Supper. The gospels are explicit about that.'

'Just table wine, and in those days it was watered down.

They consumed it that way because water alone was usually foul.'

'But he never explicitly said his followers shouldn't drink alcohol.'

'Luke records him saying, *I will not drink of the vine from now on until the kingdom of God comes*.'

'But there's debate about whether he broke his own vow when he accepted a sponge of sour wine to drink on the cross.'

She pulled a grimace, and I feared I had pushed the subject too hard. I looked out at the burn and I could feel her eyes roving over me. To my surprise, she continued the theme.

'At my church, most of us drink grape juice at communion.'

'It's supposed to be the blood of Christ.'

'But we see drinking alcohol as a sin.'

I blew out my cheeks and swallowed a further comment.

'Not me though,' she said. 'I drink wine at communion.'

'Oh. Why?'

'Because, like you said, it's a representation of his blood. It's so central to everything. Other than the cross, the holy wine is probably the most important symbol in Christianity.

'I have a theory,' she continued. 'Today we view wine as a luxury. It's marketed as a premium product and we pay extra for the best grape or the right vineyard. And that's why I refuse to drink it socially. My lifestyle choices are not made to impress others.

'But back at the time of Jesus wine was the drink of the masses. It was as central to life as bread and water. In fact, for the common person, wine was symbolic not only of their way of life, but also of their death, because its blood-like qualities were a metaphor for regeneration and immortality. Tell me, when ancient graves are unearthed, what item is most often found alongside the remains?'

'Er, wine?'

'Well, not wine, that would be long gone. But the flagons or cups that would have contained wine. Throughout Europe, priests of lowly orders were habitually buried with replica chalices. In Orthodox communities, wine was poured into the grave in the shape of a cross. Common Egyptians were buried with amphoras filled with wine. In Roman society, wine was drunk in honour of the deceased and then the flagons broken into pieces and placed beside the body. Heck, even that Viking grave discovered in Scotland had a drinking horn that once contained wine.'

My brain clicked stop and rewind.

'Viking grave? What grave?'

'It was on the news last term. They found the remains of a Norse woman on one of the islands. It got coverage because she was buried with an axe, a pouch of henbane seeds and what may have been a bearskin, so this could be evidence that women were warriors in Viking society. Anyway, my point is that they also discovered a drinking horn containing traces of wine.'

I held up my hands to halt her flow, and she gazed at me, bemused.

'I'm sorry, let me get this straight. The woman was buried with a bearskin?'

'Well, there probably wasn't much of that left after a thousand years, but that's what the article said.'

'A bearskin, an axe and some *henbane* seeds?'

'Is this important to you?'

'What's henbane?'

Anna shrugged. 'Some kind of herb, I think.'

'You're sure about this?'

She looked startled and replied more sheepishly. 'Well, not totally. If you really need to know, I guess the library should have the relevant cuttings.'

'You're right, they will.' I was shaking my head as though trying to clear a brain fog. 'A Viking grave on a Scottish island. I can't believe we all missed it.'

'Are you okay?' She glanced at my almost empty glass. 'That wine playing tricks?'

'No, I just find it fascinating. Everything you said was so interesting. Thank you, Anna.'

'My pleasure. Would you – er – like another?'

'One's probably enough in the middle of the day, and I should be getting back.'

'Right, well okay, I guess. This has been fun. Thanks for the invite.'

'Anytime. Thanks for the ride out.'

I was already pulling on my coat and rising. She gulped the rest of her juice and stood too.

'Fun and weird,' she said under her breath.

XLVII

Henbane. *Hyoscyamus niger*. One metre tall. Hairy, sticky, with striking yellow and purple veined flowers. Native to temperate Europe, Scandinavia and Siberia, naturalised and common in Great Britain and Ireland.

My God, my God, my God.

I'd already found the relevant media articles about the Viking burial. The university library paid a cuttings service to identify and catalogue any story in Scotland of academic interest, and I discovered a clutch of them from October when the Council for Scottish Archaeology announced the excavation of a gravesite in sand dunes on the Atlantic coast of South Uist.

Anna had been wrong about the wine. The drinking horn found beside the woman's bones was thought to have contained some kind of mead. But all the articles agreed that there had also been a pouch of henbane seeds, which had somehow failed to decompose over the last millennium. No one seemed much interested in these seeds. Instead, the excitement was all about the remains of the bearskin, the quality of the sword blade and a few rusty rings of iron that suggested she had worn a coat of chain mail. This was *fascinating*, declared various experts. A woman, honoured in death with the trappings of a warrior. It corroborated earlier finds in Scandinavia that pointed to those raping, pillaging and burning Viking hordes of common legend containing their fair share of female fighters.

And there, in just one of the cuttings, was the word that spellbound me: *berserker*. Could the bearskin and the mail, the reporter asked, quoting a source, possibly suggest this woman was a member of the most elite fighters: the spitting, cursing, crazed berserkers, who threw themselves first at every foe?

The day had extinguished and dinner would soon be served in Sallies, but I barely registered. I sat glistening-eyed, wondering why in hell no one was asking about the henbane? The finds in the grave weren't just random objects that happened to be on this woman's person when she died. These were carefully considered items placed in her grave by fellow Vikings as symbols of what she had once been in life.

The pouch of henbane mattered. It meant something. And, just possibly, it meant something long ago to a real living, breathing berserker.

I disappeared to the catalogues and then the stacks, searching references that led me to the botany and natural sciences sections, then early medieval history, and finally medicine. What I found reminded me very much of my ergot research with Hope. Like ergot, henbane was historically well used for its medicinal properties. It could help ailments like toothache, rheumatism and asthma. Mixed with oil to make an ointment, it was often smothered onto bandages to cover wounds because it acted as an anaesthetic.

Anaesthetic. I pondered this. The berserkers were said to feel no pain.

So much for henbane's nicer qualities. The bad stuff didn't make easy reading. The name may have originated from an ancient Saxon word *hen*, meaning death. Well, that made me pause.

Hallucinations, convulsions, narcosis and hypertension were less fatal effects, but not much more attractive. In the Middle Ages, henbane was closely associated with witchcraft. It could be boiled with oil to make potions. Or its leaves were dried and then smoked or brewed into tea, beer or even wine. It all came down to dosage. I found a reference stating under three grams was non-fatal and that sounded a worryingly tiny amount. Was the difference between life and death literally an extra seed in your tea?

The evening was drawing on, and I had exhausted all the references I could find, when I came across one new revelation that stalled me. Henbane, apparently, was also known as stinking nightshade.

I sat back in my chair and stared unseeing across the library desks. I knew that name. I had seen it only recently.

My God, it had been right in front of me.

XLVIII

'What?'

I had tried the intercom three times before Magnus at last drawled into it. He sounded strange and his presence rattled my plan.

I had left the library at a jog and headed back to Sallies where I still had Madri's borrowed sleeping bag from my Iona trip. Using the return of this as a pretext, I had intended to talk my way inside and then hoped I could find a few moments when she wasn't watching. But I hadn't accounted for Magnus.

When I reached the top floor, he was standing in the open doorway half-clothed and looking like a broken man.

'Are you still unwell?' I asked.

There were fingernail scratches on his chest and his eyes were bloodshot and vacant.

'Hey, Finn,' he mumbled. 'We're just sort of… getting back into old times.'

He stepped aside and I walked into a smog of hashish.

'Who is it?' Madri's voice came from a darkened living room.

'Just Finn.'

There was no response, but I guessed she wasn't jumping for joy.

'I only came round to return Madri's sleeping bag. I don't want to interrupt.'

He waved weakly towards the room. 'We're chilling with some mushrooms and some weed. You want some?'

'No, no. You just keep doing whatever you're doing.'

'Stay. Get yourself a cuppa.'

He slapped me on the shoulder and wandered unsteadily back to the living room, and I realised a golden opportunity had opened up. Popping the sleeping bag in Madri's spare room, I switched on the kitchen light and gazed at her rows of apothecary jars. Milk thistle. Neem leaves. Hemp seed. Meadow sweet. Comfrey. *Stinking nightshade*.

My pulse pumping in my throat, I turned back to the landing and listened. Some sort of chanting was coming from the living room. I took the jar and turned it in my hands. On the reverse she had written: *For incense only*. I tried to consider my actions logically, but the moment was too filled with adrenaline. I took a deep breath, shoved the jar into a pocket in my jeans and pushed the others together so she hopefully wouldn't notice the absence.

'Hey, you two, I won't hang around. Enjoy your chilling. I'll see you soon.'

Magnus answered unintelligibly, and I took that as my farewell cue, closed the door and rushed down the stairs.

XLIX

It took me four days to summon the courage.

Four evenings of staring at the little jar, opening the lid to sniff the contents, pouring a sample onto my palm and fingering it fearfully. They weren't seeds, and I worried that this might matter. Instead, they were the leaves of the plant, dried and flaked like so many other more innocent herbs.

I wanted to tell the others. I thought I should bring them in on my discovery and get a group decision. But everything was so messed up that I knew it would end up in accusations and squabbles. It was Madri's advice I really needed, and that was never going to work out well. She had noted that the flakes were for incense use only, so how would she suggest I ingested them? Smoke alone surely wouldn't do the trick. Should I oil them into an ointment or stir them into hot liquid? Would they dissolve or sit at the bottom of a cup like tea leaves? In that scenario, would it matter if I only drank the brew and not the leaves themselves?

I didn't even have a measure to gauge three grams. Would that be a teaspoon? Half a teaspoon? I imagined doctors poring over my corpse, shaking their heads and tutting, appalled that I had ingested an entire teaspoon of stinking nightshade.

On the second day, I went into town and toured three off-licences until I found one that sold mead. It came in a delicate, feminine bottle, and the burly man behind the counter looked at me as if I was weird. I found myself declaring it was a gift for my girlfriend and that seemed to satisfy him.

The mead only added to my confusion. The presence of it in the Viking's grave suggested it was an important possession for berserkers, but it might have had a ceremonial purpose entirely separate from the henbane. I opened the bottle, sniffed it and then took a cautious sip. It was syrupy and pleasant and not at all the sort of tipple I would normally associate with crazed warriors. I imagined them standing around holding tiny glasses of the stuff with their little fingers raised, murmuring pleasantries and waiting for the canapés.

I tested some serving ideas. I poured a slosh of mead into a glass and sprinkled a few flakes into this, then watched them sink to the bottom and do nothing in particular. When I thought everyone was asleep, I tiptoed down the corridor to the shared kitchens and heated a small amount, then dropped a few more flakes into this and stirred. The drink might have changed colour, but it was hard to tell, and it smelt no different. In the end, I poured it down the sink and took myself to bed in a foul mood.

The next morning I was convinced that I needed Hope's wisdom. If I could have found her, I would have gone straightaway and spilled everything about my discovery and my little theft. But – maddeningly – I still knew nothing about where she lived and had no direct way to contact her. I scribbled a note – *Hi Hope. Come up and see me urgently. I've something to show you* – and left it in her pigeonhole, but it was still there by the fourth evening and it was probably this silence that finally tipped me into action.

As the night deepened and the corridor quietened, I sat on my bed and stared at the jar. Then I boiled my kettle and poured water into a mug. I shook flakes onto a teaspoon until I had covered half, considered this and then sprinkled some back into the jar. I tipped the little remaining into the water and stirred until the liquid was a murky green like a stagnant pond. Then I poured a slug of mead into a glass and placed this beside the mug.

I considered leaving a note to be found next to my body, and I briefly toyed with how my epitaph should read.

'Oh, for bloody hell's sake,' I swore and launched myself off the bed.

I grabbed the mug and took several gulps, leaving the swollen leaves piled at the bottom. Then I ran my arm over my lips and threw the mead down my throat. That was it. Done.

I stared in the mirror over the sink and thought I looked a confused idiot. I considered the door and decided to leave it unlocked. Then I sat on the bed with my back against the wall and my legs crossed under me, took a ragged breath and waited.

The minutes ticked by. Nothing. My stomach rumbled and grew gassy. I burped and left a noxious taste in my mouth. My breathing shallowed, and I thought perhaps my limbs grew heavy, though conversely my pulse accelerated.

Of course, it was Hope who stole into my mind first.

I remembered us on Iona, curled together against the cold, her hair tickling my cheek. I could feel the delicate vibrations of her lungs against my chest and the murmur of her breath on my throat. My heart swelled. I loved her. She was so precious, so delicate. How could anyone dream of threatening her?

The voice of Justus whispered to me. *You know, Finn, the boys wanted to use nails.*

My breathing slowed even more. My face creased and my hands tightened into fists. I imagined Justus sprawled below me, fear scrawled across his features. His eyes were swollen, his lips bleeding and he looked imploringly up at me.

The vision passed. I was swept up into the night, floating over Sallies. Magnus was with me – and Laurie. We were pumped. Yelling and gesturing and dancing. We joined hands and whirled in a Highland fling above the chapel. Somewhere there were bagpipes playing and perhaps faerie lights. Magnus embraced me and slapped my back. *Yes, Finn. Yes. You've done it. Nothing can stop us now.*

He released me and I began to fall. The sky would not hold me. Down I went, down towards the quadrangle, but it wasn't there. I kept falling. There was a great cold now. Sleet, wind, hail. I fell past mountains. Crags lurched at me and missed. They rose around me and I was disappearing into the deepest ravine, falling and falling. I should have broken into a thousand pieces on impact, but I landed lightly on my feet.

I stood on granite, slick with ice.

I looked around. To the east the valley of Langdale

stretched away. A summer landscape, green and lush, sheep frolicking, trees stooping beneath the weight of their foliage. Yet still I stood on ice. Behind me a path rose to a summit and I saw figures lost in the clouds, wraiths. Three of them. They held each other and one of them waved to me. *Come, Finn. Come join us. We have been waiting for you for so long.*

I spluttered with relief and shouted *yes* back to them and started up the track. Tears poured from me, tears of joy. Dad's hand was extended and I reached for it. So close, our fingers touched. But I could not get a proper grip and we lost contact. The earth's axis tilted and now I was above them and there was terror on their faces. They were falling, Dad's hand still stretching for me. *Save us, Finn. Please save us.*

I was on the ice platform again, and Mum and Dad slid over the edge in slow motion. Then there was just Caitlin, holding the rope and watching me in disappointment. *Why didn't you stop this, Finn? I don't want to go.*

I shouted to her and lunged. My arms came around her and I gripped her to me, holding her with all my strength and weighting her down on the rock. I had her so tight, yet she still slipped through my arms. She tutted at me and shook her head as she was pulled away, then her expression widened into a look of such abject fear and misery that my heart broke. I stood on the Great Slab and screamed to the heavens. Obscenities poured from me. Fury at God and all his angels, fury at religion, hatred for everything that still had the temerity to live and breathe.

I howled until my lungs hurt, then I choked back the sounds and sobbed. When I looked again, a man was loitering on the ledge, considering me. I had never seen him before, but I knew he was Jamie. He approached and placed his hand on my shoulder and regarded me solemnly. *You must protect her. I am relying on you, Finn. Protect her for me.*

I hated him then. I loathed this handsome, strong, gentle man who looked at me with such gravity. How the hell could she love him?

Violence came to me. I struck his hand from my shoulder and smashed my forehead against his nose. Bone splintered, blood exploded. He staggered back, groaning and holding his face. My first punch took him in the stomach, my second in the side of the skull. He gasped and curled into himself and pleaded because he already knew his fate. I shouldered him to the edge until he teetered above the precipice. I studied his features and tried to imagine Hope in his embrace. It sickened me. I kicked him. My boot hit his hip bone and he was thrown back over the edge. As he screamed his last, I raised my head and howled again, drowning out his final sounds.

There was blood between my teeth, salty and metallic. It quietened me and I wiped at it and gagged at the taste.

Who the hell do you think you are, Preacher? I spun to find Madri approaching across the rocks. She looked at me with such reproof that it pacified me. I thought she was castigating me for killing Jamie, but now she held up the jar of stinking nightshade and shook her head. *I could have you writhing in pain.*

Behind her stood another figure. It was Hope, exactly as I had first encountered her over the memorial to old Patrick Hamilton. The same coat and scarf, the same books clutched in her arms. The same look of opprobrium, eyes indignant, brow furrowed.

You can't stand there. You need to get off right now.

Why?

This is the spot where Jamie died and it's bad luck to stand on it.

I tried to make sense of her words. Blood still flooded my mouth and I was shaking with cold. Her tone was so stiff.

Everyone knows that.

Don't say those words. Indignation flared through me and I sucked in air to throw an obscenity back at her, but she was gone. I spun on the spot. Where was she? I staggered around the ledge, peering into a growing cloud bank, sensing the ice beneath my boots.

Hope. I sobbed and called for her and was about to call again, when a vast weight landed on me and knocked me down. I hit the ground so hard that all the air in my lungs was flung out and my face smashed into the rock. Pain rippled through me, but I was barely aware of it.

Someone was on top of me. They were astride my body and trying to tie me to a crossbeam. They seemed confident enough in their strength and yet I could barely feel their exertions. They were like a fly on a lion. With a roar, I rose and swatted them away. I sensed them thrown from me and turned to see a 46er rolling across the rock, winded and broken. Despite the mountain conditions, he was wearing a blazer and tie and chinos. He rolled to a stop and held his stomach, then forced his head up to gaze at me in wonder. *Who are you?*

Justus was behind him, cloud swirling around as he signalled the attack. Figures launched themselves. They flew at me, fists and feet striking, but I was past caring. Nothing hurt. I roared in exaltation and battered them back like a cricket captain smashing every attack for six. They collapsed into the rocks, rose and charged again, and I hit them once more. I laughed; I sobbed. It was all too easy, too bloody. And yet it was also so meaningless. *Why am I hitting these people? What am I proving?*

I swatted a final assailant, then turned from them and began to run. The edge of the mountain shot towards me and I grinned wildly. Now I would join my family. Now I would be with them. I launched myself into the abyss and waited for the almighty thump of my bones breaking, but instead my boots landed on sand and I was running along a beach at night.

There were flames ahead. Twin rows of 46ers holding burning torches. I screamed defiance at them, I screamed bereavement because I should have been joining my family. I opened my arms wide as I ran and they collapsed on either side like dominoes.

No, Finn, no. It was Justus again, backtracking across the sand. I chased him and he fell into the waves. I waded out to where he was floating, but he sank beneath the surface and I continued wading into a channel towards a distant horizon. Towards an island. Towards an abbey bathed in moonlight. Wading and wading. Further from the shore, ever further.

'What's going on? What are you doing?'

The island dissolved. The sea dried up. I tried to control my breathing.

Someone was standing in my open doorway. Some guy from down the hall who usually said nothing and kept his distance.

'You're mad. I can't take the noise anymore.'

My mind returned. I was crouched on the floor of my room beneath the window. My bed was hauled out from the wall and my chair overturned. Books and papers lay scattered. I could still taste blood, and I ran an exploratory hand across my chin that came away crimson.

'What the hell do you want?' I rasped angrily.

'You've been yelling and bashing things. So I'm telling the wardens.'

I hurled something insulting in his direction and told him to give that message to the wardens, but another figure hove into view and I forced my eyes to focus properly. Hope was there, clutching my note in her hand. She was speaking urgently to the guy.

'Just forget it. I'll sort him out. Get back to your room and stay there. Everything will be fine.'

He surrendered and pranced away, then she closed the door and stared around in utter shock. She took in the state of the place. She saw the bottle of mead and the empty mug and the jar. At last, reluctantly, her attention settled on me, her face bloodless and flabbergasted.

'You idiot, Finn. You absolute stupid idiot.'

L

Hope cleaned the blood from me.

I could see she was furious, but there was also such concern in her eyes, such diligence in her touch, that these soothed me more than her ministrations. She crouched beside me and used tissues from her bag to dab the worst of the blood, then wetted more at the sink and wiped stains from my lips.

She righted the furniture and collected the books and papers. Then she found my kitbag and threw a few clothes into it, as well as the mead and the henbane jar.

'Stay put,' she ordered. 'Don't you dare move. I'll go and ring for a taxi.'

She closed the door and I sat alone, running my tongue gingerly around my gums to find the source of the blood and trying to remember where my brain had taken me. Figures jostled at the edges of my mind, but I could put no faces to them. I had an uneasy impression that violence lurked somewhere close, that it had been playing hard and wasn't quite ready to be boxed away. But that may simply have been the metallic taste still lingering in my throat.

Hope returned, business-like and abrupt.

'Can you stand?'

'I think so.'

She knelt beside me and placed her hands under my arms, then together we levered upright. I leaned against the wall as she unhooked my coat from the back of the door and helped me into it.

'Are we going somewhere?'

'You bet we are. I lost one man to drugs because he was alone and I'm not about to lose another.'

She was so strong that night. I mean, physically strong. Perhaps it was the anger pulsing through her. For someone so slight, she held my weight all the way along the corridor and down the stairs and out across the gardens.

'Good riddance. At least we'll get some peace,' said the guy from his bedroom doorway as we passed.

'Piss off,' she hissed and I found myself grinning.

Somehow she got me to North Street, my arm over her shoulders, my kitbag in her hands, and a taxi was waiting at the kerbside beyond the bulk of St Salvator's Chapel.

I had no sense of where it took us. The night was wet and I just remember the grate of the wipers and the wash of the streetlights.

'Where are we?' I asked as we pulled up on a quiet road.

'Somewhere safe.'

She eased me through a small gate and along a garden path into the shadow of an imposing house. I got the impression we were still in town, but everywhere seemed so leafy, silent and suburban. We reached steps, but instead of helping me ascend, she steered me around the edge of the property, past shrubs and lawns and darkened windows, until we came to a set of French doors.

My mind seemed able to grasp details clearly, without comprehending the broader canvas. While she unlocked the doors, I studied the peeling paintwork and the antique handles. I saw the brown winter stems of climbing plants – ivy and clematis – looping and winding their way over the doors with a promise of luxuriant greens and flowering colours in spring. Bird feeders decorated branches, filled with seeds and fat balls. Wind chimes hung beside them, silent that night. A rickety bench was tucked into the bushes, and a mug with forgotten coffee rested on one arm. I wondered if this was her spot, the peaceful place where she drank her morning caffeine and felt the sun and enjoyed the birds and tended to her memories.

She ushered me inside and flicked on a lamp, then watched me inspect her private space. Her anger had dissolved. Now she seemed coy and uncertain, wondering what I would make of the things I saw. Everywhere there was foliage. It was as if she had left the doors open by mistake and the garden had launched a successful offensive. Leaves ran along bookshelves. Greenery drooped from baskets. Vast stems towered in corners.

She switched on little white lights, which wound themselves along her bookshelves, making the room sparkle. Footwear was wedged in uneven lines beside the doors. An old wooden bed stood along one wall, its flowery bedspread competing with the petalled wallpaper to dazzle the senses. Candles populated each surface. Books and clothes jostled for space on the carpet.

It was clutter. But it was *her* clutter and I loved it.

She removed my coat and sat me in a fraying armchair, then removed her own outer layers and lit incense sticks.

'How are you feeling?'

'Like I'm home after a hell of a trip.'

She smiled fleetingly at this, then examined me fiercely again. 'Do you need a doctor?'

'There's nothing wrong with me.'

'Hm. That's a matter of opinion.' She extracted the henbane and mead from my kitbag and made a space for them on her desk. 'Right, I'm going to make green tea and you're going to drink it. And then you're going to explain to me exactly what you've been up to.'

She left the room and I guessed there must be a shared kitchen somewhere further into the house. I sat quietly and savoured her living space. Perhaps it was the after-effects of the henbane, but I felt fathomlessly relaxed, soothed by the incense and the quiet and the evidence of her life around me.

'Where are we?' I asked when she returned and handed me a steaming mug.

'South-west limits of the town, beyond the Botanic Gardens. I like it out here. There's a peace and a proximity to nature that nourishes me.'

I drank my tea and I knew she was waiting for me to explain. 'I've spent most of last term trying to imagine where you live.'

'Sorry it's a mess. I wasn't expecting to bring anyone back.'

'It's beautiful. It's a room with so much personality. I love it. It's, well, *you*.'

She accepted this without comment, but then added, 'I feel safe here.'

'Have you brought the others here?'

'Yes, but mostly Jamie and Madri.'

I glanced at the bed and imagined Jamie lounging on it and I had some strange memory of punching him. I shook my head and frowned because that made no sense.

'So,' she said with a change of tone, reaching for the little jar. '*Stinking nightshade*,' she read aloud, 'And *for incense only* written in Madri's hand. I think you'd better start talking.'

'I've solved the mystery. It's the real thing, I know it.'

I told her about the Viking grave on South Uist. I described the items found beside the corpse and the academic consensus that it could be the resting place of a female berserker and, despite her better judgement, I could see the fascination deepening in her.

I winced as I spoke. My tongue burned with pain where I must have bitten it, yet when Hope had been cleaning the blood from me, I had felt nothing. I supposed the drug must have been numbing me, and I remembered the observation that berserkers were immune to pain.

'So you just thought you'd help yourself to Madri's stinking nightshade.'

'It's another name for henbane, and it was right there in front of me.'

'Does she know?'

'Of course not. If I'd asked her, then Magnus would know too and I needed to keep it secret, at least until I'd found out more.'

'What you mean is, until you'd thrown it down your

throat and found out if you died or turned into a blood-crazed maniac.'

'Something like that.'

She took a moment to swallow her frustration and compose herself. 'So, tell me what you felt.'

'It's the genuine thing, Hope, I know it. Everything stacks up. Where it was found, what I read in the library. And then the experience itself.'

'What was it like?'

'I can't remember it really. There were lots of visions and memories, but I've lost them now, like dreams when you wake. But I do know that I felt… supreme. Unstoppable. Angry. Vengeful. Violent. Powerful.'

'Your room looked pretty beaten up. I wouldn't have liked to be on the end of that.'

I nodded. 'I may have been a little out of control.'

'It's a poison, you fool!' Hope erupted. 'Fatal. The slightest wrong calculation and I would have been discovering your corpse. It's just the same stupidity as Magnus and his ergot.'

'But look at me,' I responded forcefully. 'I'm okay. The trip was short. An hour tops. And now I'm back to normal. Magnus was ill for weeks. If the Vikings had been taking ergot, they'd have been useless for anything. The Celts and the Gaels would have kicked them from our shores and sent them packing back to Norway. The berserkers weren't taking ergot.' I held her gaze in the lamplight. 'They were taking henbane. Simple henbane, whether dried or seeds. Found growing in much of Scandinavia and northern Britain. Already known for its medicinal properties. They drank it as a tea. They used it to fire themselves into a frenzy. They fought like gods for an hour or two, fearless, ferocious and immune to pain. And then they came down from it and recovered. And they valued it so much that they buried their berserker dead with mead and seeds and bearskins.'

She brooded over my words, then she rose and opened the patio doors. After pulling on a pair of wellies, she stepped into the garden and stood on the lawn and examined the night sky. I followed her out. The rain had stopped and the silence was broken by a million droplets filtering through the shrubs.

'If you tell Magnus,' she murmured, 'nothing will stop him attempting to take the stuff himself, and we could have another crisis on our hands.'

'But if I don't tell him, he's going to get deeper and deeper into his wild theories and keep finding other ways to addle his mind. And all the time Justus will be watching.'

She was silent for an age and I waited. At last she blew out her cheeks. 'Then you have to tell him, and God forgive us if it goes wrong.'

LI

The rain was still with us in the early hours before dawn. I had spent the night wrapped in a blanket on her floor, listening to the soft sounds of her slumber from the bed above. I rose before six and padded about, finding my boots and coat.

'Where are you going?' Hope whispered from the bed.

'I've something to do.' I wanted to bend and kiss her on the forehead like a husband departing for an early shift. 'And will you stick to our plan?'

'Yes,' she said through the darkness.

I eased open the doors and made my way through the rain to the front of the house, tacking from side to side to avoid puddles. It was a long walk back into town, and it was nearly seven o'clock when I broke out on The Scores and headed for the spire of St James. The others would be aghast at my intentions, but in my frazzled head this seemed to be the only option that avoided escalation.

I strode up the drive of the Presbytery and rang the bell. This time it was a different man who answered. He looked rumpled and surprised, but he still wore a suit even at this ungodly hour.

'I need to speak to Justus.'

'I'm afraid he doesn't hold audiences at this time in the morning. Are you here on matters of the 1746 Club?'

'Tell him Divinity boy called. I've an important proposal for him.'

'Perhaps if you'd return at nine—'

I'd not expected this obstacle and petulance flared in me. 'If he wants to hear this proposal he can find me in the quadrangle of St Mary's college at nine. Please pass that on.'

I took myself to my room in Sallies and was surprised to see the state we'd left it in. I made coffee and pushed the furnishings back in place, then bolted an early breakfast in hall.

By the time I reached St Mary's, it was gone eight and I decided to pass the time up in the Divinity library. The place was empty at that hour, and I sat in my favourite desk and pulled out a notepad. The silence hung like hill fog. Rows and rows of books peered down, and I wondered at the incredible insights they must contain. I wished I could read them all, but even a lifetime devoted to study would not begin to break the back of such a task.

The door clicked behind me and someone entered and selected a desk in the periphery of my vision. We nodded to each other. He was a big lad with groomed chestnut hair and stout features. He was wearing a jacket and open-neck shirt, and I tagged him as one of those sports-mad jocks, probably handy on the rugby field, and cocky off it. Not the type you usually bumped into in the Divinity library.

I tried to block him out and rummaged in my bag for a book from my reading list.

The door clicked again and someone else slipped past and sat directly across the table. I looked up irritably and met Justus' eyes. He stood and removed a long raincoat and arranged it on the back of his seat.

'You're early,' I said once he had settled.

'I assumed I would find you here.'

I glanced behind at the door. 'You're not even supposed to have access.'

To my surprise, he reached over and picked the book from my fingers. '*Searching for the Divine: 1,500–500 BCE.*' He turned it around in his hands and made a show of reading the text on the back. 'Fascinating.'

He handed it back and his tone grew serious. 'You have a proposal?'

He wasn't meant to be here yet, and I'd not got my thoughts in order.

I glanced at the other man. 'Are you two together?'

'Rodders, are we together?'

'Rarely apart.'

I'd heard that name the night I was kidnapped. 'Do you remember me?' I asked the man malevolently.

He made a show of rubbing his jaw where my fist had made contact. 'Oh, I remember you.'

'Save the banter, boys,' Justus interrupted. 'What's the proposal?'

'I've found a new drug.'

His brow furrowed and any insouciance evaporated.

'I've checked the historical records,' I ploughed on. 'And

I've found everything I can in the libraries. And I'm sure it's the berserker drug your brother's looking for.'

'What part of this am I supposed to like?'

'If Magnus has the answer to his search, he doesn't need to look anymore.'

Justus sat back with his elbows on the chair arms and studied me over steepled fingers. 'Go on.'

'I intend to tell Magnus about my find and then to arrange a night away when he can try it for himself.'

'Have you tried it?'

'I have and it doesn't have the terrible effects of ergot.'

'And you genuinely think it's the berserker stimulant?'

I nodded. 'I wouldn't be telling you if I didn't.'

He peered at me, trying to read my motivations. 'Why *are* you telling me?'

'Because you seem to know what we're up to most of the time and if you discover we've been off on another drug-filled extravaganza, I worry we're all going to get caught up in a bitter circle of retribution. And none of us want that, especially when we have nice careers lined up.'

His expression tightened at this dig, but he didn't rise to it. 'So I'm just supposed to turn a blind eye to more disgraceful – and *disreputable* – behaviour by my brother?'

'Magnus has become an obsessive and a mess – perhaps even an addict – but he still clings to the belief that what he's doing has academic merit. If he has the chance to find the answer, he might realise he doesn't need to keep filling his head with toxins. He might even write his findings up and achieve something more *reputable*. There seems to be a gap in academic knowledge about this peculiar Viking behaviour. He might be able to fill that gap and then break out of the bad place he's got himself into.'

'That's a lot of positive sentiments, Finn, but I think you're placing too much confidence in my brother. Especially when he has that witch beside him goading him on.'

'Then look at it another way. Magnus and Madrigal have no intention of stopping and you have no intention of letting them continue. So there's going to be an impact. And impacts tend to draw unwanted attention. Lots of attention. The sort you really don't want after the mystery of Jamie's accident.'

I hit a nerve, and he had to calm himself by running his eyes over the stacks of books behind me. Finally he came to a decision. 'Okay, one night away. One chance to give Magnus what he wants. But I'll send someone along. I want eyes on the ground. Where are you going?'

'I don't know yet. It's the festival of Imbolc the weekend after this, an important occasion in the pagan calendar and one the Clan won't want to miss. I will lay the ground for an overnight trip that Saturday. If you ensure the car park by the Old Course is watched all that day, at some point you'll see us depart.' I shrugged. 'Then your "eyes on the ground" will have to follow and keep out of the way.'

Justus considered this, then stood abruptly and gathered his coat. 'I hope you know what you're doing Finn. I suggest you send a few prayers to the big guy up above. I look forward to hearing the reports.'

He marched away and Rodders followed with a final sullen scowl in my direction.

LII

I stayed where I was for a long time, letting the silence descend again.

The plan had worked so far. Justus had taken the bait. I should be pleased with myself, but I actually felt deeply despondent. It had struck me at some point during that conversation that all of us – the Clan, the 46ers – were just caught up in some pathetic psycho-drama between two pig-headed brothers who had been punching each other's lights out since they were toddlers.

And I was bang in the middle of them. How the hell had I managed that? After all my efforts to overcome a past far more tragic than anything those pampered prats had ever endured and to win myself a place at a great university, I was standing dead centre between their flying fists, taking blows from both sides and thinking it was my responsibility to be peacemaker.

I swore more profusely than that venerable holy library had probably ever witnessed and took myself outside for a cigarette. I sat on the bench near the holm oak and watched students begin to troop past for the first Divinity seminars of the day. It wasn't even nine and I'd had my fill of one brother, so I really didn't need the second showing up.

'There you are.'

Magnus was standing before me in a long coat very similar to the one Justus had been wearing. His features were still haggard. Blotches prowled at the corners of his eyes. A tracery of delicate lines wove across his forehead. Pink still stole around his irises. His dark polo neck and chinos looked slack on him and unkempt. But his gaze was steady enough, and I couldn't miss an indignant fire burning deep in them.

'Come with me.'

Without further ado, he walked back under the arch of St Mary's and disappeared onto South Street.

'What?' I yelled, making heads turn. Swearing, I stamped out my cigarette and jogged after him.

He had crossed the road and rounded the corner into Baker Lane by the time I caught up with him.

'You can't just turn up and order me to—'

He swung on me and pushed me up against a door. 'Did you tell anyone about our Feast of Vetrnætr?'

'In the vault? Of course not.'

'Did you say anything to anyone – like your theologian friend that you hang around with?'

I forced myself to swallow my own rising indignation. 'You shouldn't even have to ask.'

He rumbled in the back of his throat and let go of me. I followed him down the lane onto Market Street and strode the few yards to the gate into St John's Garden. This time there was no keeper, but Magnus produced a key. He waited for a group of students to pass, then clicked the lock and opened the gate just wide enough for us to slip through.

'What's all this about?' I asked again as we stalked across the lawn and ducked under the boughs of the beech tree.

He stopped dead, and it was so sudden that I almost crashed into him. There, below us, the door to the tunnel stood open and the old lock smashed.

'Shit,' I whispered, and I sensed a cold, hard fury seeping from the pores of the man next to me.

'So it's true,' he said quietly. 'My service company called me and said I needed to get down here.'

We descended the steps and made our way cautiously into the tunnel. The lamps had been broken too, but there was just enough afternoon light to permeate the gloom and reveal the other end of the tunnel where the second door also stood open.

'Shit,' I said again as we stepped into the vault.

The place had been wrecked. Tables were upended. Oak benches and candelabra broken like cardboard. Crockery had been brought from the kitchen and diligently smashed across the flagstones and the silver goblets hammered flat.

Madri was there amongst the wreckage, and she laid raging eyes on me.

'What happened?' I demanded.

She sneered. 'Isn't it obvious?'

'Well, nothing about this place escaped my lips.'

They didn't dispute this, but neither did they accept it. Magnus walked through the debris, touching pieces, sifting with his toes.

'That bastard helps you get better,' Madri said in a

malignant hiss. 'Then he thinks he can send a message like this.'

Magnus continued prodding shards, and I could feel the black fury still leaking from him.

'Well, nothing changes,' Madri almost shrieked, as though trying to force a reaction from him. 'The man has no power over us.'

At last Magnus broke from his reverie. 'He's goading me.'

'Not just him, your whole family is.' She went to him and thrust herself around him. 'It's because they hate the two of us together, they hate everything we stand for. But they're powerless if we stick together. They can't make us do anything we don't want to.'

I caught him glancing at me over the mass of her silvered hair, and I almost thought he looked apologetic for getting me caught up in all this.

'How do we answer him?'

He had been asking me, but Madri pushed herself away. 'We raise the rest of the Clan and we arrange the best, wildest, most magnificent night we've ever spent together. That's how we answer him.'

'Imbolc,' I suggested.

She spun on me and fixed me with a shrewd stare, then raised a nail at me. 'Imbolc, yes, of course. The coming of spring. The most perfect celebration.'

'Saturday week,' I offered. 'We find a place and we have that perfect night you've described.'

A glitter of suspicion crept into her eyes. 'That's quite a change of attitude, Finn. Not long ago you wanted to stop, you wanted us to behave like normal people.'

'I never wanted to stop, but after Magnus' ergot

poisoning, I want us to be much more careful about the substances we experiment with. We can't take any more risks like that.'

Madri jutted her chin at me. 'We've been doing this a long time before you came on board.'

I dragged my attention to Magnus. 'I've found something.'

'What's that supposed to mean?' Madri demanded.

I had discussed my next words with Hope the previous evening. She had told me that Magnus would be resentful if he thought I had solved his long search without any input from him. So now I described everything about the Viking grave and the contents laid beside the corpse. I informed them of my reading in the library and my beliefs about how the berserkers ingested henbane as a tea with mead. But I said nothing about actually testing this hypothesis. Magnus need not know of my trip, of my violence, of the emotions that had ripped through me.

This – Hope and I had agreed – should be left for Magnus to discover himself.

I saw his eyes fire as I described the gravesite and explained the importance of the pouch of henbane seeds.

'I have stinking nightshade in my kitchen,' said Madri despite her irritation, when I gave this alternative name.

And she should again soon. Because Hope was supposed to be surreptitiously returning the jar to her shelves that morning.

'You really think this is the answer?' Magnus asked cautiously.

'Nothing's certain until we've tried it, but the evidence suggests it is.'

'How did we miss the news about this burial site?' he

mused. I knew he would head to the libraries and pull up all the information I had already found.

Madri was suspicious again. She circled me and eyed me slyly. 'And how do you know it's simply stinking nightshade and some mead?'

'I just do,' I replied. 'I've checked the options. Mix the henbane leaves into hot water and drink mead alongside. That's the method. That's the Viking way.'

I said this with such authority, that they did not think to tug at the holes in my logic.

Magnus was caught in the excitement of the discovery, the wreckage around him almost forgotten. 'If we're going to do this, we have to do it well.'

'Yes,' declared Madri, now also enthusiastic. 'It has to be the best of us, the best of the Clan. Just as I said. We will have the wildest, most magnificent night. And we must find somewhere suitably special.'

'Then it should be the seat of the Lord of the Isles,' Magnus rumbled, his face alight. 'The home of Dál Riata. Finlaggan.' He rolled the word around his tongue.

Madri grabbed him again and stared heatedly into his eyes. 'Yes, my dear, Finlaggan. A place of wonder and atmosphere and power. You promised you'd take me.'

He glanced at me. 'A place to go berserk, Finn.'

A place to go berserk.

I thought about these words and then my mind was filled with the voice of Justus.

I hope you know what you're doing.

LIII

Finlaggan.

Even now – thirty years later – I still can't think of that name without a shiver. My memories mourn for a time when I didn't know a place called Finlaggan.

We gathered just after first light and I shot agitated looks around the Old Course car park, hoping that if Justus' watcher was there too, he would ensure he was well concealed. Magnus and Madri joined Laurie in his Ducato, while I commandeered my usual seat in the Volvo, furtively studying Hope's profile as the town slipped behind. On my knees was a map, and I would occasionally announce directions, but the roads were long and the route straightforward, so mostly we travelled in silence.

I should have been excited to go to Islay. It was the island of whisky. Six of the world's best distilleries on just one small isle off Kintyre in south-west Scotland. Intense, complex, smoky drams, which I had first encountered in my grandad's drinks cabinet, and which still entranced me. But now there was a heavy stone in my stomach, weighing me down into the seat.

I wished I could tell Hope about my secret encounter with Justus. I thought she would see the sense in it, but I couldn't be entirely confident. Informing Magnus' brother of our plans was like showing him all our cards and that just might be the stupidest thing I'd ever done.

The journey was much longer than I had expected and I was surprised to find we were not travelling north. I had always imagined Islay lying somewhere far up the wild Atlantic coast of Scotland, but – as I traced the route with my finger – I realised we were going a hundred miles due west, then turning *south* for another sixty, to a tiny ferry port called Kennacraig halfway down the long peninsula of Kintyre.

Over those hours, we crossed through the boundless country of the southern Highlands. Nothing on either side. No proper towns. Just legions of hills, fighting for space and hemming us in. Past the never-ending shore of Lochearnhead. Onwards through tiny places called Crianlarich, Auchtertyre and Stronmilchan. Names to get your tongue around.

To begin with, the morning blossomed blue, but as we went west, a vast wall of cloud awaited. It just hung there, motionless and foreboding, whispering that the islands would greet us with a cold embrace. Looking back, I still remember that cloud bank. Perhaps it was a warning. Perhaps it was trying to tell us that we should turn around and flee, because the five of us were chasing a storm and if we caught it, we would be blown away.

We arrived at Kennacraig at midday, in good time for the

timetabled crossing to Islay, and there, at the end of the pier, waited the giant red funnels of a CalMac ferry.

I often think about that journey across the water.

Today everyone lives in a world of surveillance. If we made that crossing now, we would book our tickets online. We would type in our names and addresses and our vehicle registrations. We would pay with Visa cards. On board would be cameras logging the cars, filming the passengers. Our every last movement recorded. And yet, in that February of 1993, we rocked up without a booking. We paid in cash without needing to give our names. We drove on board and were guided to parking spots by waving staff, who then took our paper tickets. No cameras. No bank records.

In fact, no evidence at all that the five of us ever set foot on Islay.

We lunched in the ferry restaurant. We all knew the night would be long, so we gathered at a table beside a salt-encrusted window and ordered battered cod and piles of chips. There was something intoxicating about being at sea and the others laughed and greased their lips with oily food. But I had no appetite and could only pick at my chips and wonder if there was another passenger on board on the orders of Justus. Outside, the blanket of cloud opened to embrace us, tucking us under, drawing us into the darkening shores of Islay.

We docked at Port Ellen, an elegant curve of beach and houses. Lights already twinkled from windows even though it was barely mid-afternoon. I climbed to the upper deck to watch the skipper navigate the final approach and the air was scented with peat smoke and barley. When we rolled onto shore, Hope followed Laurie's Ducato out of the town.

The land opened around us, wide, flat, featureless. A place of heather and bog and sea beyond. The ribbon of tarmac undulated as though it floated on the bog and might sink under the weight of our vehicles. The cloud hung above us and a few spits of rain rattled the windscreen.

'So much for the first days of spring,' grumbled Hope. 'The festival of light.'

'This place is winter,' I replied.

Finally, Laurie's brake lights came on, and he took a careful turn onto a walled track that sloped into a hollow of land. We bumped after him, and I could see a metallic disc of water at the heart of the valley, a lost loch with islands breaking its surface. The track came to an abrupt end and Laurie parked up beside a stile over a sheep fence. Hope pulled in alongside, doused the lights, and we all stepped into the twilight.

The silence hit us. It was like the whole world had stopped.

Then it was broken by the click of a lighter and a cigarette fired between Laurie's teeth.

'*This* was the seat of the Lord of the Isles?' queried Madri, peering dubiously over the fence.

'Aye,' purred Laurie through a cloud of smoke. 'It feels remote by car, but this spot is central to the realm of the ancient lordship of the Isles. The local leaders and council members would have come in their boats. They would have found safe harbours to the south and west and north. An easy place to congregate. A good place to meet and feast and officiate, away from prying eyes.'

'I had been expecting something more inspiring,' said Madri flatly.

The rain toyed with us. Madri shivered and pulled on her coat. Hope did likewise, zipping hers tight and yanking up the hood, so only her eyes blinked at me from the shadows.

'Well, we better get this festival started,' she said. 'Where do we go?'

'To the islands,' answered Laurie and he pointed towards the loch. 'Can you see them? Eilean Mor, the Great Isle, and Eilean na Comhairle, the Isle of the Council. We will make camp on those.'

'I'm not rowing anywhere in this light,' stated Madri.

'No rowing. There's a boardwalk,' answered Magnus gruffly. 'But we'll have to do a few runs to get all our stuff down there. In this weather we're going to need the tents and we've brought firewood, wrapped against the elements.'

'The festival of fire and light,' said Laurie and we tried to smile at this, reassured by the prospect of warmth.

We shouldered bags and filled our arms with essentials, then climbed over the stile and followed Magnus down the muddy track to the water's edge. Sure enough, a boardwalk reached out across the loch to the first of the islands, but it was thin and far from well maintained. The wood was sodden and slimy and a layer of rusting chicken wire had been nailed across it to provide a modicum of grip. The whole structure creaked alarmingly when Magnus placed his weight on it, and I heard Madri swear quietly.

'If I end up in that water,' she said more loudly in Magnus' direction, 'there'll be hell to pay.'

Cautiously we made our way out over the loch. The walkway bobbed beneath us and the water slopped softly against the edges. For some reason the loch's stillness was disquieting, as if something lurked below, waiting for one of us to fall.

'Home sweet home,' said Laurie, stepping onto dry land and following Magnus towards the centre of the little island.

We wound between remnants of stone, some still high enough to give us a sense of what might once have stood there, others mere protuberances, ready to trip us if we lost concentration. Laurie said there had been a castle built by Somerled in 1130 and grand enough for subsequent kings of the Isles, men whose rule extended over Argyll, Arran, Bute, Kintyre, Ardnamurchan, Knoydart and the Hebrides. But I could not imagine it. To my eye, the ruins were a disconnected jumble, sprouting randomly from the soil as though the island itself had grown them.

We made the perilous return across the boardwalk and back to the vehicles for more armloads of kit.

'Are we really going to need all this?' I moaned.

'If tonight we discover the riddle of the berserkers,' said Magnus, following me down to the shoreline again, 'then we need to do it in style.'

In truth, I respected the thoroughness of their packing. We had groundsheets to protect us from the damp. We had two tents, with large canopies under which we could spread furs and blankets. Madri set up her mobile kitchen. Sleeping bags were unrolled inside the tents and candles placed in lanterns to ensure the rain could not get to them. I helped Laurie arrange a stack of firewood on top of a flat gravestone, then covered it with plastic sheeting while the rain still played with us.

Our preparations were time-consuming, and the darkness assembled. But when we were finally done, it felt good to sit on dry furs beneath the canopies and to watch Madri warming a saucepan of hot mulled wine in the light of a dozen candlelit lamps. Spirits rose, despite the gentle patter of rain on the canvas above our heads.

The wine tasted different from the usual fare and Madri saw me pause.

'This is Imbolc, so I've used honey, vanilla and spring jasmine for flavour. What do you think?'

'I think it's the sort of divine taste I've come to expect from our apothecary.'

I knew she still distrusted me, but this response elicited a brief smile. I was about to say more when something caught my attention and my heart rate spiked.

'What is it?' asked Hope, but the others had seen it too.

'We have company,' murmured Magnus darkly.

Away up the slope, twin headlights were jolting down the track. They slowed, and the vehicle pulled in alongside Hope's Volvo. None of us moved or uttered a sound as it manoeuvred itself around to face back the way it had come, and the lights angled up onto the verge and extinguished. There was an interminable pause and then, in the last glimmer of day, a figure emerged and the soft thump of a door came to us.

'Who the hell is that?' Magnus whispered.

I placed my cup of wine aside, my pulse banging in my skull. 'I'll go and see.'

'Aye, I'll come too.'

'No. Just me. They don't need a welcoming committee.'

Without waiting for an answer, I left the shelter of the canvas and strode back across the grass. The boardwalk was almost invisible now, but I made it to the other side safely.

Behind me, four white faces, lit by the candles, watched as I tramped up the field. The vehicle was a campervan like Madri's. It's rear door was still open, and I could see blankets and bags and a small kitchenette. The figure – a man – was fussing with a bag on the ground, and he did not notice me climb the stile and emerge from between our vehicles.

'Hi,' I said, stopping just a few yards from him.

He spun round. 'Hey, pal, you made me jump.'

He was young – young enough to be a student, young enough to be one of Justus' eyes and ears – but he didn't sound like one.

'I came up from the loch,' I said, thumbing in the direction of the lamps.

He regained his composure and nodded. 'Aye, I didn't notice you until I'd parked. Looks a good spot you've made for yourselves. Are you set in for the night?'

'That's the plan.' I peered at him through the darkness. If he was nervous, he was hiding it well now, so I tried to elicit more. 'You come far?'

'Arran and Kintyre. Going north after this. Colonsay, Mull, Skye. See where I get to.'

I wasn't sure of my geography, but his answer sounded plausible.

There was an awkward silence and then he said, 'Do you mind if I hang around? Light's gone now, so I don't want to be looking for somewhere else. I'll keep out of your way up here. I've a tent and a stove, and I can sleep in the van if the sky takes a proper piss on us.'

I didn't know how to respond. If he wasn't Justus' man, then

I wished he'd get lost and leave us alone. If he was, then his arrival had hardly been subtle.

All I could do was shrug and say, 'Sure.' Then I added, 'What's your name?'

'Blaine. And yours?'

'Finn.'

Just for a second I thought I saw him pause and reassess me, and I was so close to testing Justus' name on him.

But then he seemed to come to his own decision and said simply, 'You have a good night, Finn.'

'Yeah, you too.'

The others were all eyes and open mouths when I returned.

'He's okay,' I assured them, retaking my place under the canopy. 'He's just some camper.'

'So what's he doing?' Magnus pressed.

'Says he's going to spend the night up there.'

'Sit and watch us more like.'

'Perhaps.'

They exchanged glances and Hope nestled closer to me. 'You sure about this?'

'Just forget about him.'

She looked dubious, and I reached under cover of the dark and squeezed her hand.

'Right,' announced Madri. 'Let's focus again.'

She busied herself heating water in a pan and placing a smaller pan in this to warm. Then she handed four glass bowls to Laurie and told him to pass them round. We watched Madri spoon thick honey into the pan and warm it gently in the water until it was fluid as syrup.

'Fill your bowl and pass it on.'

She passed the pan to Laurie, who quickly dribbled honey onto his trousers. When he wiped the mess, he got it on his hand and then onto the cigarette between his lips, which annoyed him most. He shoved the pan to Hope and she filled her bowl more carefully. Magnus and I, however, were just as useless and the circle descended into swearing and licking sweetened hands.

Next Madri produced a Tupperware box filled with petals.

'Violets, one of the first splashes of spring colour.'

'Not in these parts,' Magnus murmured, but she ignored him.

I pictured her wandering fields collecting the flowers, but this was Scotland in early February, so I decided they must have been purchased.

'Take some,' she said. 'And stir them into your cups.'

I was in no mood to appreciate the delicacies of Madri's Imbolc cuisine and barely bothered with the petals, but then Hope took my wrist and guided one of my glazed fingers between her lips. Softly, intimately, she sucked the mixture from my skin and time stood still. My heart thumped in my mouth and my breath came in gasps.

LIV

The night matured.

The rain relented and Laurie and Magnus got the fire going. Soon it was crackling and spitting and the flames reached high. We leaned close and drank mulled wine. Madri laid stones in a double row beside the fire and balanced seeded loaves on these. When they were warmed, we broke them into hunks and lathered them with violet-scented goo. They were heaven on the taste buds even though my stomach was still knotted.

Laurie began to stir himself into storytelling mood. His voice purred in our ears, telling us that Imbolc meant 'navel' and it symbolised the womb of Mother Earth as new spring life emerged from it. The whole world, he said, was giving birth. Animals were calving and lactating, trees and plants budding. For some, this was a time of plenty, but others still suffered the cruelty of hunger after a long winter.

'The lamps,' he said, waving his cup of wine around the circle, 'And the fire are so important tonight. Their heat thaws winter, fights the dark, strengthens the sun and speeds the coming of spring. We honour our fires because they bring help to those who have suffered the terrors of the lean months.'

He toasted the flames and flung his wine onto the wood, making it sizzle and hiss. I think we were supposed to do the same, but I was too busy snatching glances back to the car park, wondering what the hell the newcomer was doing and why he was up there.

The rain returned, hammering our canvas roof and spilling over the edges. The fire spluttered and surged. Madri and Magnus knelt beside the camping stove and opened plastic boxes to mix ready-cooked ingredients into a pan, like an old married couple.

I proffered more wine to Hope, but she was contemplating the elements and waved the ladle away. Then she stood and pulled her coat around her and retrieved a torch from one pocket.

'What are you doing?'

'Would you want to be out there in this?'

'Hope, don't...'

Before I could say more, she launched herself into the deluge and disappeared. I had removed my boots to sit on the furs, so it took a few moments of frantic swearing to get them back on and hurry after her. By the time I reached the boardwalk, it was empty. She was either safely on the other side or at the bottom of the loch.

I stomped back to the shelter of the canvas and glared at the others. Magnus shook his head, and I swallowed an angry oath and slumped on the fur to await her return.

It seemed an age. God knows what she was doing up there. Eventually we saw her torch beam bobbing towards us, and she arrived back into the firelight, sodden but smiling.

'Hey, everyone, this is Blaine.'

Oh Christ, no.

He came behind her with a strained smile from beneath his hood. 'Hi there. Kind of you to come find me.'

Hope made me shunt along, and she took his coat and got him seated next to her. He was stiff with tension, and I wondered if this could get any worse. She gave him a cup of wine, and he sipped the warmth and tried to be grateful.

'Madri's special mix,' said Hope, and Blaine squinted at the other woman and nodded his thanks.

She acknowledged the compliment, but I could see suspicion in her eyes. She passed bread and honey to him, but she watched him like a hawk. And then, unexpectedly, her eyes swivelled to me, and my breath snagged in my throat because I was sure she knew.

The newcomer gnawed at his bread and attempted to find words. 'You know how to camp in style. You do this often?'

'Just when there's something to celebrate,' said Hope.

'What's to celebrate?'

'The coming of spring.'

The stew was ready and Madri piled it into six bowls and passed them round. She was playing the good host, but she maintained her sly examination of Blaine. The others didn't notice and the food fortified their generosity. Laurie explained to him about Imbolc and, over spoonfuls of violet honey, Magnus even said a bit about the Clan.

'You know your history,' Blaine observed.

I sat rigid and silent, my wine forgotten and my food

barely digested. At some point, Hope disappeared into the tent, and she emerged wearing the russet-brown gown she had worn at Gloom. A simple cord bound her waist, and a gold locket hung between her breasts. Over her shoulders was a cloak of deep blue, clasped by a brooch at her throat.

'Brown like the roots' bed,' I whispered.

She smiled at me. 'Blue as the boats' road.'

Madri went next and she returned magnificent in silver chain mail, silver helmet, silver-streaked hair over a woollen cloak. At her waist was a broadsword scabbarded in leather and bronze. Eventually, Magnus and Laurie changed too. More mail, more helmets, more weaponry, though one looked the part far more than the other.

'Are those blades real?' Blaine asked.

Madri speared him with a stare. 'Their edges are blunt, but I reckon they could still do some serious damage if we felt inclined.'

'Don't you have something to wear?' Blaine asked me, and I shook my head.

'Yes you do,' said Madri unexpectedly. 'But I've left it in the van, I'll go and get it.'

I rose and stepped towards her. 'You don't need to do that.'

'I think I do.'

I placed my hand on her arm. 'You really don't. It's wet and dark, and you shouldn't go across the boardwalk in those conditions.'

Her expression was belligerent, but there was no denying the weather was horrid, and so she relented with a scowl. I waited until she had sat down and then returned to my place.

Hope squeezed next to me and whispered, 'Are we still going to do this?'

I cocked a finger at Blaine. 'Not with him.'

She acknowledged the situation, then peered at the sky and announced, 'The rain seems to be easing, Blaine. Perhaps it's now more comfortable back at your van?'

He glanced at me and obviously wasn't sure how to respond.

Hope deployed a disarming smile. 'There are things we would like to do in privacy.'

He stood and flashed a reluctant smile. 'Okay, that's my cue to leave.'

'Your coat,' said Madri, advancing with it.

'Thanks for the food,' he replied stiffly. 'Enjoy the rest of your night.'

He shot me another look as he passed, and for a heartbeat I spied something rougher in his expression. He marched away across the island and disappeared, and I exhaled with relief.

LV

'Are we all taking this little journey?' asked Magnus, eyeing each of us.

We had gathered in a circle around Madri's camping stove. On a napkin she had placed Laurie's bottle of mead and her jar of stinking nightshade. If she had noticed the contents were half a teaspoonful lighter, she did not comment.

'No,' I said emphatically and they looked at me in surprise.

'You're not coming?' Magnus pulled a face. 'After all your research into henbane, you don't want to experience it first-hand?'

'If it's really what I think it is, some of us need to keep clear heads.'

Hope agreed. 'Count me out as well.'

'Perhaps someone else should also sit this out.'

'What?' Magnus was indignant. 'You're suggesting only two of us take the bloody stuff?'

'I'm suggesting that this bloody stuff has the potential to

induce fighting hysteria and God knows what else, so we need three clear heads.'

Magnus rumbled his annoyance and then turned to Madri. 'Will you do me the honour of being my partner in crime?'

To his surprise she shook her head. 'Not this time, my dear.'

'Why ever not?'

She peered at me over the fire. 'Tonight I want to be one of those with a clear head.'

This seemed to mollify him. 'Well, Laurie, it looks like it's you and me.'

'Aye, it does. I'll have one last smoke and then you can take me to the land where warriors are as mad as wolves.'

He lit up while Madri got a pan of water on the boil.

I examined the men in their chain mail and helmets. 'No weapons.'

'They're not edged,' Magnus countered with an exasperated gesture.

'No weapons,' I repeated in a tone that brooked no argument.

He heaved a sigh of dismay and unbuckled his belt. 'Anyone would think we haven't done this before.'

Laurie removed his belt and blade too, cigarette hanging from his lips.

The water in the pan began to bubble and Madri picked up her jar. 'How much, Finn?'

'Half a teaspoon. Do you have a teaspoon?'

She rummaged in one of her bags and produced one. 'So a whole teaspoon if two are drinking.'

She unscrewed the jar and tapped flakes onto the spoon until it was neatly heaped.

'Wait,' I directed. I was determined the dosage should match what I'd taken as exactly as possible. 'Better do each cup separately. Drop a conservative half spoon into both and stir.'

'How are you so certain?' Magnus demanded suspiciously. 'You been trying some?'

'Of course not. This is *your* research and that might make you the first person to experience a berserker trip since the tenth century.'

We watched as Madri dosed each cup and stirred the brew. Then she opened the bottle of mead and held it ready.

'Okay,' said Magnus, steeling himself. 'Let's not put this off any longer. You with me, Laurie?'

The other man stamped on his cigarette and came to kneel next to him. 'Ready, aye.'

Madri handed them the cups.

'Drink the tea,' I said, 'but not the leaves in the bottom. Then take a swig of mead.'

They clinked cups.

'See you in Valhalla,' Laurie quipped.

'In Valhalla.'

They drank and Madri gave the mead to each of them to gulp, then took the cups and threw the dregs into the grass.

'It's going to take a few minutes to get into your systems, so I suggest you find somewhere comfortable to wait.'

The circle widened as they went off to perch on a fur or a stool, and Madri wandered over to me.

'The rain's lighter. I'll go and get your robe.'

'It doesn't matter, I don't need it.'

'Oh, I insist.'

I almost grabbed her arm again, but she swung away to get her coat and find Laurie's Ducato keys. Short of manhandling her, there was nothing I could do.

'I'll be back before the henbane kicks in.' She disappeared into the night.

It was an interminable wait, and I kept staring so much in the direction of the vehicles that Hope asked if I was okay. After about fifteen minutes, we noticed the first signs of change in the men, and I forced myself to focus on them. Magnus emitted a long, heavy sigh. Laurie walked slowly from under the canvas to find a rock at the edge of the firelight, where he slumped with his back to us. A few heartbeats later, Magnus yanked off his helmet and started rubbing his hair vigorously. He sighed again, and this time his breath vibrated out of his lungs. Laurie stood and took a few faltering steps down slope.

'Keep an eye on that idiot,' I murmured to Hope. 'No one gets near the water tonight.'

She rose wordlessly and circled Laurie so she could shepherd him back to the fire. Laurie turned to her and said something. I did not catch the words, but I heard the snarl. Hope took a faltering pace backwards and looked to me in shock.

A bang wrenched my attention back to Magnus. He had picked up one of the ceramic cups and hurled it onto the gravestone beneath our fire. It smashed into tiny pieces, and he strode over to examine it and then contemplate the flames. *Don't start toying with the fire, you fool.* I inched closer to him and glanced at Hope. Both of us were realising that ingesting Viking drugs at this lonely spot with fire and water, darkness and cold, was a hell of a different proposition from my initial experiment in the comfort of Sallies.

A long keening moan came from Laurie, and he lowered his face into his hands. His shoulders shook and his body swayed.

'Careful,' I warned as Hope approached him with a comforting hand.

In the second before she touched him, he swung on her, howled in fear and fled down the slope into the dark. Hope ran after him, but then she returned to the firelight.

'You can't leave him,' I protested.

'I'm not going after him in this light. I can't see anything.'

I swallowed a response because she was right. Laurie was in no state to look after himself, but it would be even more dangerous to go chasing after him.

'Bloody hell,' I swore.

Magnus had collapsed onto his knees and was moaning at the fire. He extended his arms and his hands clenched into fists. He was staring at something in the flames. Something visible only to him, and something he hated.

He reached out and grabbed a branch from the blaze.

'Christ,' I cursed again and bounded forwards.

He sensed me coming, leapt to his feet and swept the burning branch in an arc to make me dance a retreat. I was terrified that his hand would scorch and the agony would only hit like a freight train after the henbane deserted him.

'Magnus, it's me.'

He was beyond hearing. He cursed and prodded the branch until I was back at the edge of the firelight. Then he glared at Hope and flung the stick far into the night. It missed the tents by a whisker and landed in sodden grass where it smoked and guttered.

And that was the moment Madri returned.

She came fast and her expression was taut. 'He's not up there.'

'Blaine? Has he left?'

She shook her head and her eyes glittered more wildly than the fire. 'Oh, he's still here, have no doubt about that. I checked his tent, and I peered in the windows of his van.' She advanced and squared up to me. 'And do you know what I saw in his dashboard?'

'Madri, we've got more important things to worry about.'

'A university permit for central St Andrews.'

Hope came up behind me. 'Blaine's from St Andrews? Why wouldn't he say?'

Madri looked at her as though she was a fool. 'Because he's a 46er, of course.'

Hope drew an intake of breath, and I held up my hand to try to calm things. 'Wait, we've got no proof.'

'Who else would come here to watch us?' Madri hissed. 'Blaine's a 46er and you know it just as much as I do. He's out there spying on us right now, watching Magnus take the berserker drug that you so conveniently discovered.'

She spoke loudly. Too much so. Her words skipped over our heads and danced across the furs and stools and pots to where Magnus stood. A noise came from him, guttural and animal.

'A 46er,' he repeated in a voice deep as Hades.

There was a last moment of relative control and then all hell broke loose.

Magnus sprang across the campsite, lunged to grab his

sword and charged into the darkness with the howl of a hunter.

'Magnus,' yelled Madri and she started running too.

'Wait,' I shouted, but it was too late. She was swallowed by the night.

'Oh my God, Finn.' Hope had a hand over her mouth.

'Stay here,' I ordered. 'Don't stray from the fire.'

I grabbed a lantern and followed the others. Somewhere down by the shoreline Magnus roared again, and it was answered by a further cry by Laurie.

The boardwalk. It was the only way off that damn island and I forced myself to change direction. In the corner of my eye, I thought I saw Hope holding a lantern and running into the dark. *Goddammit*.

The candle gave me just enough light to twist through the ruins and judge where we had crossed. I saw water ahead and angled left until I could make out the shape of the boardwalk lurking on the surface. *Far enough*. I ground to a halt, held my lantern high and peered back into the night. Someone was yipping like a hound on scent. There were muffled gasps of exertion and the thud of heavy impact. A woman's voice cried in alarm and my pulse surged.

I wanted to hurl myself towards the cry, but I knew I must hold fast because they would surely come this way. They had to.

There were more shouts. A bellow that sounded like Magnus came from my left, followed by the baying of a chase. They were somewhere along the shoreline and coming round it. I could see nothing, but I could feel the terror and the violence and the emotions rolling towards me.

I hunched. No one must leave this island. Blood boiled with berserker rage, and I must stop them here.

The assault came far quicker than I could imagine. For a split second my lamplight illuminated a figure hurling itself at me.

'Get the fuck out of my way.'

It was Blaine, fast, furious and powerful.

He shouldered into me with such force that I was thrown backwards. The lantern flew from my hand, and my lungs emptied as I hit the ground. Pain surged through my bones, and I felt him pass above me, a rush of air and limbs.

I struggled to my knees, but a roar came from the night, and Magnus lunged past without a pause. He didn't even bother to find the end of the boardwalk. He just charged into the water, and his momentum propelled him within reach of the bridge. In a flurry of legs, arms and water, he hauled himself up and across it.

Cursing, I followed them, but I had to slow my speed on the wet wood or I would be headfirst into the loch. I skittered and stumbled and finally saw the shore ahead. I made it to the bank and struggled up the field, then forced myself to a stop and strained my ears. The land above me was undisturbed, the car park quiet, but muffled exertions were coming from below and further along the bank. They must be running around the outer edge of the loch.

I angled back down and onto the mud of the shoreline. The night was almost impenetrable, but our fire across the water was just enough to illuminate two rushing shapes ahead of me. My legs carried me fast, although the soft surface toyed with my ankles and splayed them left and right. In the corner of my eye, a lantern was bobbing on the island, heading towards the boardwalk, and I guessed it might be Hope.

The shapes converged and went down in a heap. They began thrashing and writhing in silence, as if they had lost the energy for words. I yelled and redoubled my efforts. Rocks reared at me, then came a stretch of open sandy shore, and I was upon them.

Magnus was astride the other man, and he was just raising his sword for the killer strike, so I flung myself at his outstretched arm. He cursed in surprise as I wrenched him off Blaine and dragged him several yards away, until my heels caught and we both collapsed.

'Finn?' he hissed in surprise.

'Yes, it's me Magnus. Can you see me? Can you hear me?'

A few feet away, Blaine began crawling along the shore. Magnus tensed at the sound, but he did not summon a fresh assault. Instead he let out a long breath and sagged onto the mud next to me.

I felt for his face. 'Magnus, it's okay. You don't need to hunt.'

His breathing regulated, and I hoped the heat of battle was deserting him. Lanterns approached, and Blaine continued dragging himself along the shore. *Thank God*, I thought. *At least the bastard is alive*. Somehow I had paused the berserker fury just in time.

And then Laurie arrived.

He leapt from the field above and stumbled across the few yards of sand towards the fallen figure. In his hand he brandished his iron helmet, and he wrenched Blaine over so that the man stared up at his assailant. Without a sound – no words, no cries, no snarls – Laurie smashed his helmet into Blaine's face. There was a whimper like a puppy, then the helmet came down again. And again.

'*No*,' I shouted and shoved my way from Magnus to flounder over the mud, but those few yards seemed to last forever. All I could see was Laurie punching his helm down again and again and the splintering of the skull beneath. Bone and teeth and sinew and hair disintegrated. Pulp clung to armour. Blood sprayed. And still Laurie pummelled, his mind utterly given up to the rage of the Norse.

Somewhere – maybe when I was one pace from the fight – Blaine died. I sensed it, rather than saw it. I *felt* him go, a physical sensation, as though his spirit whipped past me and ran a trailing hand across my face before it flew out over the loch.

No, no, no. The knowledge broke me, and I fell beside the figures and coughed on a mouthful of grit. *God, no.*

Laurie also seemed to realise that death had come. His movements slowed until he held the helmet stationary above his head. Then he struggled unsteadily to his feet.

'Laurie, it's me, Finn. Can you hear me?'

He made no acknowledgement. He simply stared at me wordlessly, took a deep breath and walked away along the shore.

A cry broke from behind. Madri and Hope had reached us. They gripped lanterns, but their other hands were clamped to their lips. Shock shuddered through them. Madri sank to her knees near Magnus, her eyes on the body of Blaine. Hope lurched backwards and gazed at me. She began shaking her head and murmuring to herself.

For a few moments, the whole world was still. Magnus

trembled where he knelt. Hope and Madri were frozen. Laurie receded into the dark. And Blaine lay limp beside me.

Then the silence was broken by a sound more shocking than everything that had passed so far that night.

An engine spluttered into life. Headlights came on and lit the track above us where the vehicles were parked.

'What's happening?' Hope cried.

I staggered upright. Blaine's van was revving away along the track as fast as it would go.

'Oh my God, oh my God, oh my God.'

There had been two of them.

LVI

'We should have known,' Madri said bitterly. 'They always hunt in pairs.'

I sat with the two women amongst rocks on the shoreline with a single lantern still attempting to provide light. Across the water, the embers of our fire glowed on the island.

To begin with, when the van disappeared, emotions had overflowed. The three of us had yelled at each other and garbled accusations. We had stalked the shoreline, throwing out useless thoughts, adrenaline running uncontrolled. Noise for the sake of noise, but nothing of any value.

'Get after him,' Madri had shrieked, as though we could give chase across a darkened island we didn't know and somehow corner him and beat him to pulp too.

'We have to get out of here,' Hope had declared, and we panicked at the thought of blue lights appearing over the rise. She had run back to camp and begun packing things, but she soon gave up. Would he really go to the police? Was there even law enforcement on the island? We were too confused to forge a plan.

And there was another issue. Magnus and Laurie had both fallen into a deep lethargy and were in no state for an escape.

'It's the descent from the henbane. I felt calm afterwards too,' I said thoughtlessly.

Madri pierced me with a stare. 'You've taken it before?'

'Well, I was going to tell—'

'You bloody cretin,' she hissed. 'You knew what it could do and you didn't say?'

She had advanced to punch me, and I was forced to stumble into the water to avoid her attack. She jabbed a finger at me from the shoreline. 'This death's on you.'

Since then the adrenaline had leaked from us and despondency set in. We brooded. We avoided each other and wandered with black thoughts. Eventually we gathered and collapsed amongst the rocks. We could see Magnus still sitting on the sand and we knew Laurie was perched on the bank further along. Though we did not voice it, we wanted to hate them. We wanted to curse them and kick them where they sat, but we knew that they bore no blame for the effects of the drug. As Madri had announced, this death was on me. And in so many ways.

I trembled and swore under my breath and screwed up my face when I thought they weren't looking. I had told Justus about our plans. I had agreed that he should send a watcher. Then I'd let Magnus and Laurie drink the berserker drug that I'd discovered. And now there was a corpse lying just yards from us and God knows what trouble ahead. How in hell had I thought I could control the situation?

Hope broke my soul-searching. 'When's the next ferry?'

Neither of us knew, and she shook her head in exasperation. 'Doesn't anyone have a timetable?'

'I think there are departures from Port Ellen and from Port Askaig in the north,' Madri answered.

'So the other 46er could leave from either of those.'

'What are you suggesting?' I demanded sourly. 'Do you think we can find him before he departs the island? We don't know what he looks like. We haven't got his number plate, and it was too dark to tell the colour of the van. We don't even know if it's a *he* we're looking for.'

'He's a 46er,' Madri interrupted. 'He's a he.'

'We must find him,' Hope affirmed.

'And do what?' I countered. 'Follow him onto the ferry and throw him overboard before he can report us to the police?'

Madri's head, silhouetted by the embers from the island, turned to me. 'If he gets away, reporting us to the police will be nothing compared to what awaits us in St Andrews.'

From further along the shore, Magnus shifted and groaned. None of us had been to check on him and even Madri shied from getting too close. Logic told us that Magnus was still our friend, but logic had been in short supply over the past half hour and the images of his aggression were seared onto our minds.

As for Laurie, no one had spoken of him. It was as though we were trying to pretend he wasn't out there in the dark. What could we say to him when his mind returned? How could we tell him what he had done? The vision of him bludgeoning Blaine to a gory death played over and over in my head.

Hope stood and peered down the shore past Magnus. When she spoke it was with the desolation of someone who had never imagined they would utter these words. 'We need to get rid of that body.'

I came beside her. 'That's easier said than done.'

'We have to hide it before daylight. If we're still on the island when someone finds it, we'll be trapped. They'll close the ferry ports, even turn the ships around.'

It, I thought. Blaine had become an *it*. Death makes objects of us.

I toed the ground. 'We've no shovels. The shoreline's a mix of mud and sand and silt, but it's solid enough. Without tools to dig, we won't be able to bury him.'

'What about upslope? Do you remember seeing any long grass?'

'Nothing that wouldn't look trampled by the time we'd finished and that could hide a body in daylight.'

'It's got to be the loch,' said Madri from behind.

We all looked at the water and I shivered. Not because it would be cold, but because it lurked there so still and silent, so menacing. To me, that loch already spoke of death, and I tried to imagine Blaine rotting beneath its surface for eternity.

'Corpses float,' Hope stated.

'Then we weight it down. Put stones in the pockets, tie rocks.'

I pondered this. 'It's shallow round the edges. We'd need to get the body out into the middle.'

This information robbed us of momentum and we stood wordless for long minutes.

'How long have we got?' Hope asked.

Despite being dressed as a Valkyrie, Madri still wore her wristwatch. 'It's just after three. Four hours until dawn.'

'We have to be gone long before then. No one must see our vehicles leave this place.'

Hope began to pace along the shore and we followed. As we rounded Magnus, I paused to check him. He was staring at Blaine's body, and I could tell from his solemn expression that his mind was back with us.

'You okay?'

He nodded and I thought I saw a film of tears. I was robbed of words and all I could do was grunt and continue the few yards to where the women had gathered around the corpse.

It seems strange to describe a body as inanimate, but that was my first thought. It might as well have been a fallen log or debris washed ashore. There was nothing of Blaine left. The hands were so pale in the dark that they seemed to glow, but the face was a black wound.

'Rigor mortis sets in after two hours,' said Hope. 'So we need to get on with this.'

'How do you know?'

'I was raised by a surgeon father.'

She crouched and scooped up a handful of pebbles, then prodded his coat to locate the pockets.

'That's not going to be enough,' I stated dismissively.

She ignited and threw the pebbles away. 'Then what the hell do you suggest?'

'We need rocks, then we need to tie them somehow. I don't know. Just split up and look for rocks.'

We began to circulate, eyes down, straining to discover stones light enough to pick up, but heavy enough to sink a corpse, and it was a few moments before we realised Magnus was among us. We stopped and watched him in silence. Even Madri seemed unable to communicate with the man with whom she had shared so much intimacy.

He began undressing. He unbuckled his sword belt and let it drop, then hauled his chain mail coat over his head.

'What are you doing?' I demanded.

He threw the mail down next to the corpse. 'Through the centuries, many a warrior will have met their death in water, taken down by the weight of their armour.'

Of course. The chain mail.

'And yours,' said Magnus pointing a finger at Madri.

She began wriggling to rid herself of her own Valkyrie protection and Hope had to help her get it over her head.

Magnus stooped and picked up his belt again. 'Wrap both coats round the body and bind them with this.'

He threw the belt to me, then started to walk further along the shore.

'Where are you going?'

'To get Laurie's.'

'Hey,' I called and trotted after him. 'Did you see what happened?'

'Some.'

'Do you understand?'

He nodded grimly. 'Enough to know we played a dangerous game. And lost.'

I let him go and returned to the others. We knelt and wrapped the chain mail coats around Blaine's torso, then struggled to get the belts under him.

'It's so heavy,' gasped Madri.

'Blood's pooled under him,' said Hope. 'But he's still flexible, thank God.'

Silently, I thought there was nothing to thank God about this night.

After a few minutes, Magnus returned and he had his hand on Laurie's shoulder. Laurie stared mutely at Blaine. Unbelievably, he still held his helmet. No one moved or knew what to say. Then Laurie emitted a low sob and walked to the waterline. Kicking one leg back, he braced and flung the helmet far into the night. We heard a splash and then hush and we knew it was gone.

'Get your mail off,' Magnus ordered.

Laurie unbuckled his belt and struggled with the mail. He was shaking and unsteady, and we had to step in and help him. Something about this shared action brought us back together. No matter the gravity of what had occurred, no single person was to blame. We had all sought the secret of the berserkers. We had all been dazzled by the quest. That night we had discovered our answers and now we would face the consequences together.

We fastened the third coat of mail to the corpse with Laurie's belt and then stood back to peer at our handiwork.

'No good just dragging it into the water,' I explained. 'It's too shallow. The loch might look black enough now, but the first person who walks along here in daylight is going to see that thing under the surface. We have to get it into the middle, but now we've weighed it down, we can't float it out.'

Magnus was still slow and heavy with his movements, but he was our Jarl and his mind was firing properly again.

'Get back to the camp. Dismantle the tents. Cut all the ropes and bring them here.'

I scuttled off with Hope and Madri to do his bidding, while Laurie and Magnus loitered on the shore, standing vigil over the man they had hunted.

The ropes were more cords, but they were thick and strong enough. Our sword blades were uselessly blunt, so Madri rummaged through her cooking utensils and found a knife. It seemed to take an age to roll the sleeping bags and clear all our belongings from inside the tents, then we collapsed them and started cutting at each length of cord. At last we had them all, and I wound them into loops and carried them back across the boardwalk, leaving the other two to continue breaking camp.

The three men laid the cords out and tied them together into one long length, grimacing as we yanked each knot as tight as we could.

'Is it enough?' I asked.

Magnus grunted. 'Not to cross the boardwalk and keep our feet dry. One of us will have to swim.'

I looked again at the black water and refused to volunteer, but Laurie was already removing his shirt and trousers. His body was so thin, so flimsy. He looked more skeletal than the corpse at his feet. We said nothing. It seemed Laurie was taking the burden for what he had done. It was his way of trying to atone.

Magnus knelt and knotted one end of the cord to the belts on Blaine, tugging and wrenching to ensure everything was secure. Then he took the other end to Laurie and tied it in a loop on his wrist.

'We'll have blankets ready for you on the other side.'

I collected Laurie's shirt, trousers, socks and brogue leather shoes, then watched as he inched into the loch in his underpants. God knows what was underfoot, but he waded up to his thighs with only a couple of stumbles. Then he took a deep breath, and his white flesh tumbled into the water, and he began to doggy-paddle towards the island.

The channel was no more than thirty yards wide, but he seemed a long way out as we made our way back across the boardwalk. The silence of the night was broken only by splashing and the occasional gasp. We made it to the island and paced around the shore to a point directly opposite where Blaine must still lie. We could hear Laurie coming and the women stopped their packing and watched beyond the embers of the fire.

'Is this really going to work?' I murmured to Magnus.

'Never going to know without trying.'

Laurie rose from the loch like some malnourished mermaid and staggered towards us. Hope came forward to meet him with blankets, but he made no acknowledgement as she placed one over his shoulders and rubbed his back dry. He handed the end of the cord to Magnus, then took his clothes from me and shakily began to dress again.

The cord was only just long enough and Magnus had to walk a couple of paces into the water to ensure there was sufficient for Laurie to grab behind him and then for me to loop around my waist.

'Okay,' said Magnus. 'Let's see if this bugger shifts. On three. One… two… three.'

We heaved in unison, and the cord whipped tight. For a moment there was no give at all at the other end and then we pulled again and we felt ourselves inch backwards.

'And again. Heave.'

We could not see the opposite shore. We did not know what was happening to Blaine. We could only tell that the cord was coming with us and we were gradually retreating onto the island.

He must be in the water, I thought. He couldn't float with the weight of the mail, so we must be dragging him along the bottom, down the sloping shallows. I reversed into a segment of ruined castle and placed my legs against it for purchase. The others joined me and we yanked and gasped and swore, but the cord kept coming.

'It's working,' I panted.

'Aye,' replied Magnus.

After an age, he raised his hand and we stopped our exertions. He examined the cord on the ground beside us. 'That looks about half to me.'

'So he should be in the middle of the channel.'

Magnus bent and retrieved a large flat stone from beside the ruins. He wound the cord around this and tied it off, then advanced to the water's edge again and threw the stone far into the night. The cord went with it and, we prayed, sank without trace.

'Go and take a look on the other side.'

I crossed the boardwalk and walked along the shore with my heart in my mouth. For some reason, I feared Blaine would still be there. He had seemed so immovable. The fact of his death had felt so absolute that I could barely believe he might have vanished. I slowed and slunk forward, straining my eyes into the dark.

The shore was empty.

I could see drag marks and our footprints, but otherwise

there was nothing. I circled and examined every last section of embankment for anything we might have dropped, because nothing must ever connect us to this spot. Then I went to the water's edge and scuffed at the drag marks as best I could.

'It's done,' I called softly into the night and heard a rumbled acknowledgement from Magnus.

Blaine was gone.

LVII

We abandoned Finlaggan an hour before dawn.

We had cleared every trace of our presence as best we could, though doing this in the dark unnerved us. What if one of us had left an item that could connect us to the place? What if Blaine had not actually sunk and was bobbing in the middle of the loch for the first pair of eyes to see as soon as the sun was up? Everything we did as we cleared the camp, every movement we made, our heads always turned to the water, as if we might see him floating back to us.

Madri said we should wait and check again in daylight, but Hope was categoric that our vehicles should not be witnessed on the roads from Finlaggan.

Laurie was a mute wraith. He wandered around performing tasks, smoking like his life depended on it, but never speaking and rarely showing any sign that he was even aware of the situation. At one point I wondered if all the cigarette butts he cast away were going to be a problem. Could police specialists isolate saliva traces and identify the culprit? If they could, it was too late to fuss about it. The island was littered with butts and we were never going to find them all.

Laurie did achieve one useful task. In his van he had stowed a printout of ferry timetables and he passed these to Hope. Sundays saw fewer sailing times, but there was a departure from Port Ellen at nine forty-five and one from Port Askaig just after midday. Madri decided we must not travel together. I said Magnus and Laurie should get off the island first, but Magnus disagreed. According to him, Port Askaig was a much quieter departure point with fewer prying eyes. So Hope and I should take the Volvo back to Port Ellen and board the earlier sailing. The others would travel north towards Port Askaig and wait up somewhere until midday.

In fact, remaining separate seemed to be the general plan.

'When we get back to St Andrews,' stated Magnus as we stood in a circle in the car park in light rain, 'we split up. Get to your rooms and keep low profiles.'

'Isn't there safety in numbers?' I countered.

'Stay apart. Lock your doors and remain inside. When you must, walk with colleagues and friends to lectures. Don't navigate the town alone. And don't contact each other unless it's an emergency. Understood?'

I didn't see how sitting in my room with the door locked was going to help the situation. 'For how long?'

'Until this blows over,' said Hope.

'This isn't going to blow over,' snapped Madri.

I stared at the loch as we drove up the track. I watched it until a fold of the valley finally masked it. A black hole in the landscape. The burial site of kings and lords and now the resting place of one final body. At the end of the track, we indicated right and headed south to Port Ellen and in our mirrors we saw the headlights of the Ducato swing north. I bid them a silent farewell. No turning back now. We'd rolled the dice, but we had yet to see how they landed.

We passed no other vehicles on the road at that early hour, and we were grateful for small mercies. When we reached Port Ellen, Hope found a lay-by with a good view over the little town and the ferry terminal. A few lights twinkled along the crescent of houses and we could see the pale curve of the beach. Slowly, the sky diluted and dawn was upon us. Now we could make out an area beside the pier where vehicles habitually queued for the ferry, and we scanned it for any hint of a van. There was nothing but a minibus left for the night, but it got me wondering what we would do if such a van arrived during the next two hours. Could we imagine approaching it? Was there anything we could realistically do to change the future, to unravel the consequences of what we had done?

Secretly, I think we both knew it was already too late. That 46er would have found a phone box and made the incriminating call. As we watched the sun rise over the eastern horizon, someone would be waking Justus from his slumber at the Presbytery and sealing our fate.

I was desperate for caffeine and I knew Hope felt the same, but even if that crescent of cottages had been ablaze with coffee outlets, she would never have allowed me to make a purchase.

'Except to buy the tickets, we stay in the car until we are on board. No one sees us.'

And that's exactly what we did.

We sat in that lay-by, with the windows sealed and the engine off, as day arose around us. I thought about the others probably waiting somewhere similar at the other end of the island, and I did not envy the extra hours they needed to kill before their sailing. I wondered if the first dog-walkers were already marching down the fields to the loch. What would confront them? I had an irrational fear that our efforts last night were miscalculated and Blaine would be washed back up on the shore. I remembered seeing films where bodies bloat after death. I didn't know the science, but I was suddenly convinced he'd be so full of gases that the chain mail could no longer hold him down. I felt my heart pumping and the stirrings of a panic attack. *Christ, where is that bloody ferry?*

It appeared just after nine, steaming sedately around the corner of the coastline, white and black and crimson, dwarfing the houses. It approached the jetty at a measured pace, smooth and easy, like there was nothing untoward, like we hadn't just murdered someone. Hope started the car and we drove into the village in silence and joined a few other vehicles waiting to board. She sent me out with a fistful of notes, and I scampered across the parking area to a tiny office where a bored-looking man sorted me tickets for one car and two passengers. Thankfully he showed no interest in small talk, and I escaped with little more than an invocation to have a good trip.

There was only one van and that had the British Telecom logo plastered along its sides. We watched a few foot passengers board. We had no idea what our 46er looked like, but he sure wasn't one of them, with their rucksacks and waterproofs and whisky carrier bags. Finally, it was our turn, and we were waved onto the boarding ramps. Relief flooded through me as we bumped over and entered the bowels of the ship, and I knew Hope felt the same.

We parked and alighted, then climbed the stairwells to higher decks. We didn't need to speak. Instinctively, we made our way to the outside deck at the aft of the vessel, where we could look down on the jetty. Would this be the moment a police car appeared? Or would the man in the ticket office spring from his warm seat, gesticulating towards the crew to cut the engines?

'I'm so sorry,' I said without looking at her. 'It's my fault. I should never ever have started reading about henbane. I wish to god I'd never heard of the stuff.'

If I had hoped she would reassure me, I was disappointed. She greeted my apology with a stony silence.

It seemed to take forever to get the final vehicles on board. *Come on!* At last, the bow rose and sealed the car deck, ropes were hauled in and the engine crescendoed. To my surprise I felt Hope's hand reach for me. Since we had left Finlaggan, she had been so taciturn. She had removed herself from any intimacy. Yet now she found my fingers and we both squeezed as the first yards of seawater separated us from the jetty.

Goodbye, Islay. We won't be back.

LVIII

When we arrived in St Andrews six hours later, the town was just as it always was on a Sunday afternoon. I don't know what I had expected – sirens, mobs, a vengeful gathering of 46ers – but it wasn't sleepy mundanity.

Hope took me to St Salvator's. She pulled up beside the spot where we had first met, and she didn't kill the engine.

'I don't think we should stay apart,' I reiterated.

'No, we should. Get back to your rooms and go to ground. Magnus is right.'

'But is he? Don't you think Justus knows where we live? I don't know if Blaine was a 46er or just some acolyte they liked to use. Either way, Justus isn't going to forgive us. So if we stay separate we'll be no help to each other. Seems a pretty suspect plan to me.'

'We have to stay low. Laurie committed *murder*. Magnus aided him. And *we* helped them. We're all killers now. So keep your door locked and curtains drawn.'

Locks don't hold them, I thought, but I didn't want to

worry her more. I stared miserably out of the window and my heart thumped slowly, like a bell at a funeral.

She spoke again. 'Blaine was the *second* victim of Clan Dál Riata and this has to be an end to it.'

Just a few yards from where we sat were the *PH* initials engraved in the paving stone, where old Patrick Hamilton had sizzled and popped his last. I had the distinct impression that, after all we had been through, our relationship was right back to where it had started. *You can't stand there. Everyone knows that.*

'I'll miss you.'

'I know.' She tapped lightly on my arm. 'Go, Finn, before we're seen.'

I felt as if I'd been dismissed. I grabbed my bag from the boot and stood on the pavement watching her do a three-point turn and head back towards the Botanic Gardens. I waited until her car had disappeared, then shouldered my bag and wandered through to the quad.

In Sallies, a smattering of students milled around the Common Room, and I kept my eyes down. I mounted the stairs, but as I approached my corner room, I could feel the dread rising again. What if they were inside? A 46er welcoming committee ready to carry me away?

I studied the lock, then turned the handle and eased open. The room was empty. No window hanging off its hinges. No bird carcass under the bedclothes. No posh twats sniggering as they sprung their trap. I sealed myself in and shifted my bed so that it blocked the door. Then I sat and listened to the bangs and creaks and voices of normal Sallies life, alert for anything out of place.

By evening, I was even more of a nervous wreck, but

the scent of hot food licking its way up from the dining hall made my stomach groan. I dared not head down. Too many eyes. Eventually, I was driven to the only course of action I could get my head around. I pulled on my boots and dropped one floor to Anna's.

'Finn,' she exclaimed in obvious delight, then stiffened when she saw my pallor. 'Good Lord, you look awful. What fun and games have you been up to now?'

'Just stupid stuff. Nothing you'd be interested in.'

'Well, try me. Are you coming to dinner?'

'I'm too exhausted to go to Hall. Could you possibly bring something up to my room?'

I saw a flicker of surprise in her face, but then she covered it with another smile. 'Sure.'

'Anything would do. Just some bread. I don't want to put you to trouble.'

'It's no trouble, Finn. And you look as though you need a lot more than bread.'

Blessed Anna. When I returned to my room, I assumed I would have to wait until she had eaten her own meal, but after just a few minutes, she arrived carrying a tray of beef and potatoes.

'Do you want company?'

'I'm fine. Go and have your own.' I sat in my chair and wedged the tray on my knees. 'And Anna?'

She turned back from the door.

'Thank you. I mean it. Not just for this food, but everything. I don't know what I'd do without you.'

She reddened and beamed so wide that any response she hoped to make got caught in her throat. With a nod and a little rush of air, she left me.

I spent a night of terrible sleep and worse interludes, listening for the slightest noise in the corridor. I dreamed of violence. Of impacts and cries and bodies falling from great heights. The next morning, I heard rustling just beyond my door and lay frozen under the bedclothes. At last, when the corridor bustled with the normal activity of students leaving for lectures, I peeked out and discovered a tray of pastries and a pot of tea. I was too worked up to eat, but I thanked her again nonetheless.

That morning lasted forever. I paced the room. I stared out of the window. I dozed fitfully. I wrote notes to Hope then screwed them up. I thought about Anna and Charles in the libraries. I tried to picture the rest of the Clan locked in their rooms and wondered if they were scared like me. And then I imagined Blaine, sunk in the mud of Finlaggan, weighed down by our coats of mail, fish weaving into his mouth and out of his eye sockets.

Just after one there was a knock.

'I brought you a sandwich,' announced Anna. 'And I've one for me too, if you're happy to eat together. How are you feeling?'

'Still rubbish.'

'Do you need a doctor?'

'No, I'll throw it off soon.'

She passed me a sandwich and I ate perched on the edge of my bed, while she sat in the chair.

'What shall I tell Father Haughton?'

'Tell him I'm unwell. Surely God allows for that sometimes.'

I knew my response had irritated her and we ate the rest

of our lunch in silence. Afterwards, she said, 'I think it's about time you told me what's really wrong.'

The question bumped me from my contemplation. 'What do you mean?'

'Back home, I do a lot of voluntary work for my church. I help those in need. So I know when someone's scared. I can see it in their faces. And, let me tell you Finn, it's written all over yours.'

I lowered my face and when the words came, they were easier than I expected.

'I've got caught in something stupid, Anna, something really stupid. I got into deep stuff with some friends and now I can't get out and we've ended up hurting someone.'

'Is this person hurt bad?'

'Yes,' I replied weakly.

'Do they need medical help?'

'No.'

'Do they need urgent care of any kind?'

'No.'

It was a truthful reply, if not an honest one and it seemed enough to satisfy her.

Most people would have demanded more, but not Anna. She simply stood and came to sit beside me, then put her hand gently on my cheek. 'Oh, Finn, you're an idiot.' She traced the structure of my face. 'I've seen you getting into trouble for a long time and I've known it's your friends who've led you there. It's easy enough to tell, but it's not always easy to know what to do when you're in the middle of it.'

She looked around my stagnant room. 'It seems to me

that when bad things happen, you shouldn't hide and let them fester. You have to face up to your actions. You have to talk to your friends and to those you hurt. Find common understanding and forgiveness. *The words of the reckless pierce like swords, but the tongue of the wise brings healing.* Proverbs 12.'

I wasn't in the mood for Proverbs, but her words struck a chord. She was right, of course. She was always damn right.

I found tears welling unexpectedly and tried to cover my face, but she placed her arms around me. I let the tears flow more freely and when they were over, a deep weariness blossomed through my bones. We leaned together for a long time and at last I drifted into nothingness.

LIX

I was thrown from my nightmares by a pounding on the door.

Anna spasmed beside me. She had dozed too and we were still bound together, her arm around my neck and my head slumped on her chest. I squinted at my watch and saw it was after two. The door reverberated again, and I sprang upright and pulled her behind me.

I put my finger to my lips and held her hand. 'Just stay quiet,' I mouthed.

Then a voice, pressed right against the hinges. 'Finn.'

I took a juddering gulp of oxygen.

'It's okay,' I said to Anna and reached forward to unlock the door.

Hope's eyes widened. 'Anna?'

I let go of Anna's hand. 'She was keeping me company.'

Anna smiled weakly. 'Hi, Hope. I'll get back to my room, Finn.'

'Thanks for the advice. I'll come see you soon.'

Hope waited until the door was closed and only then I realised how white she was and how shallow her breathing.

'What is it?'

'Justus has got Madri.'

My mouth opened and I stared at her. 'No, there's got to be a—'

'She's *gone*, Finn.'

'She's probably with Magnus.'

'It's Magnus who told me. He came banging on my doors an hour ago, heaving from running all the way, gasping to find out if she was with me.'

'She must have gone out.'

'Oh, come on… you know we're all staying low. Magnus went to her flat late morning and let himself in when she didn't answer. He saw her bag and coat were still there and her bed had been slept in, but the sheets had been left thrown back, which is really unlike her. He panicked. His only hope was that she might have come to me. When I told him I'd not been disturbed, I saw the light go out in his eyes.'

I slumped on the bed and ran my hand through my hair. 'Justus hates Madri. He blames her for everything.'

'She's in trouble. I feel it in my bones, Finn.' Hope stared imploringly at me. 'What do we do?'

'Where's Magnus?'

'I don't know. He ran off, garbling nonsense.'

'Was he doped up?'

She shrugged in exasperation. 'Maybe he was or maybe he's just feeling like everyone would in this situation.'

I mouthed a silent oath and tried to gather my wits. 'Perhaps he went to Laurie.'

Hope shook her head. 'He's gone for her – I know it.'

'But where is she? The Presbytery?'

'He doesn't think so. He stood by my garden doors looking devastated and groaned, *He's taken her to be judged*. Then he burst back into the garden shouting, *Oh, St Mungo. He's going to give her up to the winds*.' She took a ragged breath. 'Something terrible's going to happen. I know it.'

I stood and tried to gather my wits. 'There must be a way to stop this. Justus isn't stupid enough to harm her, even after what we've done. Why the *hell* won't he just leave us alone?'

'Finn.' Hope came towards me, her hand outstretched. 'Finn, listen to me. There's something you don't know.'

She waited for me to calm and take several breaths.

'It's not only Justus. It's his mum. It's *Magnus*' mum. She's the driver of all this.'

I stared at her as if she was a halfwit, but somewhere I remembered Madri once saying Magnus' mother was the real problem. 'I don't understand…'

'Do you know Magnus' surname? It's Engstrom, his father's Swedish family name. Have you heard of Mairi Engstrom?'

I scowled at her, trying to drag up strange names at a time like this. 'She's… there's someone called that in government…'

Hope watched me, her eyes moon-wide. 'She's the Home Secretary. The person in charge of the UK's policy on drugs.'

My hands went to my head. 'Oh my God.'

'Can you imagine what would happen to her career if the papers found out what her younger son was doing?'

'So it wasn't all about Justus and his bloody job offer?'

'Justus only thinks about himself, and he wants Magnus stopped as much as anyone, but he'll be desperate to keep his mum from learning that Magnus got mixed up in murder while out of his head on hallucinogens.'

'What if he's already told her? What if that's why Madri's been taken? It could be secret-service shit.'

'Justus won't do that yet. But he's going to end it today, I feel it inside. Something awful is going to happen.'

I took a shuddering breath and tried to think. Then I came to a conclusion. 'I want you safe.'

'I'm coming with you, whatever happens. We're in this together.'

'*No*, I need you safe. If these are the stakes, you have to promise me to lie low. You can't go back to yours and you can't stay here because we don't yet know if he's grabbing all of us. He could be sending people to your address already or they could be on their way here.' I swore and banged my head with my fist. 'Madri's – go to Madri's.'

'Why?'

'Because they've been there already. They won't go back. Get inside, and if anyone presses the intercom, don't answer. Do you know her hiding place on the roof?'

'No.'

'Good, that means she keeps it close. If anything happens, climb out of the window in her living room and wait on the space by the chimney. If it's me, I'll press the buzzer four times. You understand?'

'Yes, but what about you?'

I grabbed my coat. 'I've got to find out about St Mungo.'

LX

St Mungo. In God's name, who the hell was St Mungo?
There was only one place I could think of that might hold the answer. I ran to the Divinity library. The book-encrusted space was tomb-quiet, and as I creaked across the floorboards, I felt the ghosts of scholars past looking down on me. A pale sun illuminated dust motes in front of the Greek Testament shelves.

I began to flip through the card files, searching the M's for Mungo and the themed sections under S for Saints. Puffing my cheeks with relief, I discovered several references to Mungo, and I slipped off to the shelves to find each volume.

The next hour was an agony of frustration. St Mungo, it seemed, was born sometime around 530AD at Culross on the banks of the Forth, but by age twenty-five, he moved to the Clyde to begin his missionary work. He was welcomed by the people and he built a church, which now formed part of Glasgow cathedral. Mungo was driven away from the Clyde by an anti-Christian king and he journeyed through Cumbria to Wales and then may have made a pilgrimage to Rome. I screwed up my face. Glasgow, Cumbria, Wales, Rome. *Where the hell has Justus taken Madri?*

My mind returned to Culross. I knew of the village about an hour's drive from St Andrews. Culross. I ruminated over this name. Perhaps it was the key. But what did Magnus mean about *given up to the winds?*

I marched outside and prowled around the holm oak, sucking smoke into my lungs. A fresh idea blossomed, and I mounted the stairs to Father Haughton's room. There was no answer to my insistent knocks and the door was locked. A final-year Divinity student whom I vaguely knew walked by.

'Do you know where Father Haughton is?'

'At a conference in Inverness.'

'Really?' I'd always assumed Father Haughton had difficulty just getting down the stairs. 'Hey,' I called after the student again. 'Do you know anything about St Mungo?'

'Mungo? Sure. St Kentigern.'

'Kentigern?'

'The other name for him.'

'Listen, do you know of any really special places in the life of Mungo or Kentigern? Where he may have had a judgement or something?'

The man shrugged. 'Not really, sorry.'

I wandered forlornly back down to St Mary's quad. Each hour that passed gave Magnus and Justus more time to make things much worse.

I'd barely stopped to think about why I was so desperate to find the answer, but deep inside I knew it was because everything that had happened was my fault. It was me who discovered the secret of henbane. I coaxed Magnus into a final outing. I blabbed to Justus. I knew about his watcher. And I let things get so out of hand that Blaine was killed and now Madri kidnapped. All because of me.

Forlornly, I decided I must try the main library. I began to run along South Street and then cut through Market Street and North Street and onto Butts Wynd. I sprang up the steps to the glass entrance.

'Finn!' It was Anna, waving at me from the steps on the other side, a wedge of books under each arm. 'I never thought I'd see you so eager to get into the library.' Then she saw my expression and her face fell. 'Are things still bad?'

'A bit. I'm sorry about earlier.'

'Don't worry, I guessed you needed time with your friend.'

'Listen, Anna, I don't suppose in a million years you know anything about St Mungo and someone being given up to the winds?'

'Oh yes, sure,' she replied breezily. 'That'll be Mungo's mother, Denw, daughter of Loth.'

I gripped her shoulders so hard that she was momentarily alarmed. 'I'm serious, Anna. You know about this?'

'I like to learn about the saints of Scotland. That's why I got the car, so I could potter around the countryside and follow in their steps.'

'And you followed St Mungo?'

'Sure. St Mungo, St Cuthbert, St Margaret, St Giles.'

'You went to some of the places that were special to Mungo?'

'I drove down to Culross. Even took the train to Glasgow last term.'

I was still gripping her, as if she might slip my grasp and

escape. 'What about this Denw, his mother? Was she given up to the winds and, if so, *where?*'

'Oh yes, that's easy. That's Traprain Law.'

My knees felt as if they were going to give way. 'You know where that is?'

Gently, she removed my hands. 'Finn, I don't just know where that is. I've been there.'

LXI

There were moments that afternoon when I was convinced I was in more danger than Madri.

For the first hour, we trundled south through the rolling farmland of central Fife, Anna at the wheel of the little Fiat Uno. But then we joined heavier traffic over the Forth Road Bridge and around the capital's ring road, and the lorries tore up so close behind us that they almost nudged the rear bumper. Anna was clearly terrified, and she sat rigid and perspiring, her elbow bumping mine.

I wanted to yell at her to speed things up, but I bit my lip because she had so readily forsaken her study plans and her evening choir rehearsal just so she could drive me to some damn hill in the middle of nowhere. That was Anna through and through. Always putting herself out for others, always doing the Christian thing. She had probably been exasperated when I'd told her I must meet my friends at the top of Traprain Law, but she had recognised the distress in my eyes and the urgency in my body language and she had offered to take me simply because it was in her power to help.

We swung off the ring road and followed signs for a village called Haddington. The countryside swelled around us again and the lanes quietened, and I breathed more easily. Time, however, was still slipping away, and we had lost the muted sun of St Andrews behind a cloud bank that slunk from the west, low and laden.

'Tell me about Mungo's mother,' I said to keep my head from going crazy.

'It's just a legend really, but that's what appeals to me. We have in this story an example of early Christian history combining with ancient Arthurian lore. This whole area of Lothian is named after King Lot, the ruler of these lands in the first century. It's said that Traprain Law was the site of his capital, a rocky volcanic hill from where he could see his entire realm.

'Denw was his stepdaughter. She was seduced by a young prince and fell pregnant. A furious King Lot accused her of adultery and condemned her to be given up to the winds. She was taken to the precipitous cliffs on the southern side of Traprain and thrown off. Somehow she survived the fall and was smuggled away from Lot's wrath and cast adrift on the Forth in a coracle. The story goes that she washed up on the further shore at Culross and gave birth to Kentigern.'

'Who grew up to become St Mungo,' I added, seeing how the story fitted neatly with what I had already learned.

'And are you going to tell me why this legend's so important to you?'

I had been waiting for her to ask and to be honest I had no bloody idea. Why would Justus take Madri to this place, and why would Magnus know about it? What did this hill mean to them?

And then, quite suddenly, the fog in my brain lifted and the solution came to me.

'We're south of Edinburgh now, aren't we?'

'Yes, just a bit below the ring road.'

I remembered both Madri and Justus telling me separately that the brothers had gone to a boarding school south of Edinburgh and they used to go up a hill where no one could see them and punch the lights out of each other. It was their secret place to settle arguments. A place of judgement.

'Well?' prompted Anna. 'Why do you need to meet your friends up this hill?'

'It's a place that is important to some of them, and they want me to see it.'

She gave me a sidelong glance. 'They're trouble, Finn. You've already admitted that someone has been seriously hurt.'

'And that's why I need to get up there. It's our chance to resolve matters.'

'Up a hill in the middle of nowhere with evening coming on? It's a silly place to resolve matters.'

We drove quietly for ten minutes until she turned off the road for Haddington and took a small lane between thorny hedgerows. As we came over a rise, a hill appeared before us, barren and unwelcoming beneath the leaden sky, but much smaller than I had been expecting.

'There's your destination,' Anna announced coolly.

'It doesn't look much.'

'It's no great height, but the land around is so open that you can see for miles from the top.'

'Traprain Law,' I said to myself. 'I feel as if I know that name.'

'A hoard of Viking silver was discovered up there not that long ago.'

'Of course. The Traprain treasure. I remember reading about it. It was Roman hack silver, probably carried by Viking mercenaries to sell in Scotland.'

I studied the hill and thought of Hope back in St Andrews. I wished I had found the time to tell her where I was going. But then she would have insisted on coming and I couldn't allow that. Not after what she'd told me about Mairi Engstrom. I still couldn't really get my head around that revelation. Thinking about it took my breath away.

'Is there a school near here?'

Anna pointed across the fields in the other direction. 'See those turrets? That's a school. St Kentigern's.'

I laughed emptily. 'Of course.'

We passed a stile and a track leading over the first folds of the hill, then came to a small empty car park. Anna pulled in and killed the engine.

'Seems you've beaten your friends.'

'Is this the only car park?'

Anna looked dubious. 'Well, there are other approaches, so I suppose they could be there, but usually people start from here.'

'Where's the best way to the top?'

'Just follow the track. It winds past a couple of old barns, then rises to the summit. You can't get lost.' She looked around the car park. 'Wouldn't you be better to wait and see if they turn up?'

'No, I'll make a start. I'll go up and see if I'm first.'

'I can come with you, although I have to warn you I'm rather a slow climber.'

She started to unbuckle her seatbelt.

'Please don't. I wouldn't dream of asking you to come up. You've already done so much.'

As if to help persuade her, a few drops of rain pattered on the windscreen. 'I'll just wait here then.'

During all the time I had sat next to her in the car, I had never considered that she would insist on waiting for me, and I was momentarily at a loss. 'Absolutely not, Anna. You must get yourself back to St Andrews before it grows too late. My friends will drive me back.'

'But what if none of them solve the puzzle and get here tonight?'

'Some of them are bound to. They're good at this sort of thing. I'll probably discover them already up there enjoying that bottle.'

She wanted to say more, so I cranked open the door and climbed out. Closing it, I walked around to her side and waited for her to wind down the window, then gave her as broad a smile as I could. 'We'll only be a little behind you on the way back.'

'I still don't like it.'

'Anna, I'm serious. You should go. I'll see you at Sallies soon enough. What's the essay this week?'

She had to think about this. Her brow furrowed and then brightened. '*If the existence of evil points against God, does the existence of good count in His favour?* Father Haughton seems to be moving us on to more philosophical ground.'

'Indeed he does. In that case, I'm going to need your help more than ever. Will you take me round the library stacks tomorrow?'

She flushed and smiled happily. 'Of course. I've already got most of the reading list, so I can give you some of those. And I've baked a buttermilk and pecan waltz cake, so we can indulge over afternoon coffee.'

I reached into the car and squeezed her hand. 'Thank you, Anna. Thank you for everything. You're so special to me.'

I heard her exhale and felt a tremor in her palm, so I released her and backed away. Buoyed by my words, she started the engine and smiled from ear to ear as she waved and pulled out of the car park. I watched her lights come on and weave away along the lane until they were lost behind the hedgerows and the gathering gloom.

I was alone.

LXII

I leapt the stile and began to stalk up the track.

To my right, a grand view opened. Folds of land rolled away past the lights of Haddington until they reached the metallic glimmer of the Forth. On a clearer day, King Lot would indeed have been able to survey his realm.

The path continued on a simple circuitous contour, but I didn't have time to waste, so I left the track and began to climb hard straight up the incline. My lungs pumped and sweat blossomed across my spine. I bent into the work and drove from my knees with each stride. Gradually the slope eased, and I saw the broad summit ahead, crowned with rocky outcrops.

The place seemed to be deserted, so I stopped and turned in a circle. Daylight was fading fast and the rain still pattered gently, but nothing stirred across the entire hill. Had I made a mistake? Had I jumped to the wrong conclusions and forced Anna all the way here for nothing? A sickening thought swept through me. Perhaps they were all still in St Andrews settling their differences right now.

I forced myself to calm and think straight. No, this had to be the judgement place. St Kentigern's school was down in the valley. St Mungo's mother was given up to the winds on this summit. It had to be correct.

I stumbled on, and as I closed on the circle of rocks, I spied an outline of someone lying against one. It was Magnus, and I rushed to him. His eyes were closed and his mouth open. His curls hung lank, blasted by wind and rain. He was wearing a black polo neck and chinos, as though he had dressed that morning for an outing in town, not a journey to such a wild place.

'Magnus?' I placed a hand under his chin. 'Can you hear me?'

He quivered and made a noise in the back of his throat. I realised there was sticky blood in his hair and his lips were badly cut. I tried to shift his shoulders against the rock, but he cried out in pain and his eyes flickered open.

'Magnus, it's me. Are you hurt?'

'I'm not hurt,' he slurred. 'I'm judged.'

He raised an arm with a grimace and gingerly touched his face and lips. I wished I had something to revive him. A nip of whisky, a slurp of hot tea, even just some spare clothing. I unzipped my coat and spread it across him as best I could.

'This is not your business, Finn Nethercott,' came a voice surprisingly close, and I twisted to find Justus crouched against another contortion of rocks. In my haste, and in the fading light, I had not noticed him. 'This is between brothers.'

Awkwardly, he raised himself and I saw pain ripple across his features and knew he was also injured.

'Is it done?' I asked.

Justus sighed. 'It should be. We've shared our disagreements and our judgements with words and fists, just as we always used to on this spot. But this time, my little brother is proving remarkably belligerent.'

I squared up to him. 'I know who your mum is.'

He tensed, but he kept his voice even. 'Then you should understand why I have such strong feelings about my brother's fixations and why none of us are getting off this hill until this situation is sorted.'

'What does Magnus need to do?'

'He needs to swear that he's done with the drugs. All over, once and for all.' He stabbed a finger at me. 'And this time it's final.'

He looked down at his brother. 'Hey, Mags, did you know that Finn here took it upon himself to meet with me? He had the effrontery to ask me to give you one more chance. One last blowout. He thought he could persuade you to finish with the drugs after a final hit.'

Magnus raised accusing eyes to me.

'Oh yes, I knew all about your jaunt to Finlaggan,' Justus continued. 'That's why I sent Blaine to keep tabs on you. Finn actually had me believing he might bring you to your senses without my input. But, boy, did you blow it.'

Quite suddenly, he crouched and his tone became almost plaintive. '*Magnus*,' he hissed. 'You *must* swear tonight. Give me your oath that you'll stop the drugs. Otherwise you'll leave me with no choice but to escalate the situation and tell *her*.'

'Then tell her,' Magnus answered. 'See if I care.'

'Don't you get it, Mags? You're at least an accessory

to murder now and a junkie. She'll come down on you so hard, you won't know what hit you. She'll use every power of the state to shut this situation up.'

Magnus laughed emptily. 'It'll be the first attention she's shown me for a very long time.' He raised himself against the rock and pointed his own shaky finger towards his brother. 'But you're not going to tell her, because you're more scared of the repercussions than I am. She's lavished so much faith in you. Sorted you such a smooth, easy future. A nice fast-track into Parliament for her wonderful elder son. And you'll not risk that by telling her anything about this little mess. *You* sent Blaine to spy on us and *you* allowed events at Finlaggan to unravel – and in her eyes that compromises you as much as the rest of us and undermines her own position. So, don't hold that threat over me, because you're not going to tell her anything.'

When Justus had sunk to his knees and beseeched Magnus, I thought perhaps the brothers were going to work things out. But now I felt the anger surge through him. He stepped back and his fists balled.

'Are you staying, Finn?' he demanded.

I glanced at Magnus and nodded. 'I am.'

'Then this is no longer an issue between two brothers. I'll give you a short opportunity to reconsider, and then I'll come back up here with my friends and they'll do whatever they have to do until I'm certain we've concluded our business once and for all.' He peered one final time at his brother and said regretfully, 'We shouldn't have got to this point, Mags.'

'It's been coming for years,' Magnus replied.

With that, Justus left us and limped down the slope to where I could just make out the two barns Anna had mentioned. Light was coming from one of them and I could see four or five figures loitering by the doors.

Magnus levered himself painfully upright.

'Where's Madri?' I demanded.

He pointed towards a jumble of rocks that marked the summit. 'She's over there, in the judgement cell that we used when we were kids.'

I stalked to the boulders and examined them in the dim light. What did he mean? There was no one there, just the rocks piled on each other for millennia. I crouched and prodded at each, then lay on the ground and tried to see into the spaces underneath. I clambered up and balanced on the top and stared around, but there was still no movement.

I was about to give up when something came to me on the air. It was a heavy, sweet scent and it had no earthly reason to be up on this hill. I lowered my face to the rocks and sniffed, and there it was again. *My God, she's inside.*

'Madri?'

There was no answer. Shunting back on my knees, I began to push and tug at each stone and one moved a fraction. It was as broad as my shoulders and heavy as hell, but I wrapped my arms around it and braced my legs and yelled as I heaved. I managed to lever enough to reveal an opening, so I gripped it again and swore as I dragged it another few inches until the hole was large enough to allow a person to drop in.

She rose like a serpent.

I don't know how long she'd been in there, but she should

have come out shaking and tearful, cold and frightened. Not Madrigal.

She rose from that cell with expressionless steel. Her face was a rigid death mask. Ferocity glistened in her eyes. If she'd had a forked tongue, it would have slipped out to test the air. It was as if I'd just opened a crate and released an animal back to the wild.

She jumped down from the boulders and approached Magnus, running gentle hands over his cheeks. 'My love, my love,' I heard her whispering. 'He will pay for this.'

'Madri,' I called from behind. 'We have to get off this hill.'

She turned on me and the anger rippled through her. 'We're not leaving. Not after what he's done to us. I heard everything that was said, and we're finishing it tonight.'

'We've got a window while Justus recovers. We can't just wait. He's got 46ers down there, and they'll come up this slope soon enough.'

'And we'll be here. Magnus and me, just as we've always been. Us against the world.'

I swore and told her she was mad, but then movement caught my eye on the hill from the car park. I moved in front of the others and clenched my knuckles.

Here they come.

'Finn?'

A voice carried to us, high and desperate and feminine.

My hands unclenched, and I straightened. 'What... what are *you* doing here?'

Running towards me was the last person I ever wanted to see on this god-forsaken hill. It was Hope.

I could barely compute what was happening. 'How can you be...?'

Laurie lumbered behind her. 'You're not the only one who can solve riddles.'

Then they were amongst us. Hope ran to Madri and checked on her. The two women came together, and I heard them converse in low tones. Madri smiled fiercely and embraced Hope, then took the other woman's bag and searched in it.

'How did you solve the riddle?' I asked Laurie, who had lit a cigarette next to me.

'I already knew about this place and the name of their school, so once I heard what Magnus had said, it was obvious.'

I sighed. 'I wish you'd been around when I needed you.'

I saw Madri retrieve a thermos from Hope's bag, unscrew the top and drink from it. Unease flickered up my spine. 'What's that?'

Madri ignored me. Instead she walked to the outer edge of the boulders, raised her arms and began to call to the heavens.

Hope approached me.

'What's that?' I demanded again more forcefully.

'You know what it is.'

I stared at her open-mouthed. My heart rose into my throat and thumped like a bass drum. 'No, Hope. Why in heaven's name would you bring that?'

'I told you already. I *know* these 46ers. They're bullies. They think they can get away with violence. I witnessed their antics at the Old Course hotel the first time. Then they

attacked us on West Sands. I saw them beat Jamie and
Magnus, and I felt the crush of one of them on top of
me. I thought he was going to assault me. I thought
he would rape me right there amongst the dunes and nobody
would care. *That's* why, Finn. That's why I've brought the
berserker wrath. Because they killed Jamie and got away
with it. Because we've now killed one of them and they'll
never forgive us.'

'Hope, this isn't right.'

'We can't solve this with words, Finn. As soon as Blaine's
heart stopped beating, the time for words was over. So I've
brought the drug *you* discovered, the one we always knew
we might need to save ourselves.'

Madri was singing to herself now and wringing her
hands. Hope twisted the top of the thermos and poured a
slug into the cup. 'Hot water, honey mead and a pinch of
henbane from Madri's kitchen. Just like you said.'

She raised the cup to her lips.

'Hope, don't.'

Perhaps I should have leapt at her and flung the contents
into the wind, but I was frozen to the spot. I watched her
drink and her eyes never left mine.

There was a heavy silence when she was done, then she
poured more and took it to Magnus. 'You always suspected
that one day we'd need to defend ourselves. I guess you
were right.'

He nodded grimly and threw it down his throat. Then
Hope approached Laurie, but he halted her with his hands
and shook his head. 'Not me. I can't. Not after Finlaggan.'

She accepted this without argument.

'I'll watch over you instead,' he explained. 'It's my

responsibility to keep a clear head and ensure no one else does what I did.'

'This is so stupid,' I remonstrated. 'We could still get out of here.'

'Right off this hill without Justus pursuing us?' she countered. 'I think not. That man is responsible for Jamie's death and there's no forgiveness for that. So this fight is coming whether it's up here or in the car park.'

She filled a final cup.

'Will you join us? This is the time we always knew we needed you.'

I could not answer, but neither could I refuse. The drug already ran in their veins and it was too late to change anything. Grudgingly, I took the cup from her, gazed into the pools of her eyes, and imbibed the wrath of the Vikings.

LXIII

I don't know when it began.

I'm not sure what was real and what were the imaginings of my fevered brain.

I remember I still couldn't accept that we needed to stand and fight. So I took myself off in a southerly direction through more rock outcrops. I felt the slope begin to curve away and then had to brake hard because I'd run out of ground. Inches from my front foot was nothing but darkness, a deep black chasm. I had found the Traprain cliffs. They were not high, and I could just make out clefts and stones perhaps thirty feet below, but they were sheer enough. Once over, there was no coming back. I wondered if this was the spot where Denw had taken a last hateful look at her stepfather.

I circled round to the east of the summit and discovered even steeper drops where they fell away into a modern quarry. I returned to the northern side and squinted towards the glimmer of the Forth. The incline here was much more gentle. It dropped and then rose over a lower slope and found its way to the car park.

'We can still get off here,' I cried hoarsely as I staggered back to the others.

But they were beyond listening.

Madri had completed her salutations and now she was crouching like a fox ready to jump on its unsuspecting prey.

Magnus strode to the edge of the circle and looked down at the barns. I thought he was weak, but I heard him howl his defiance. The whole valley heard him. And I was just sane enough to imagine Justus recognising his brother's voice and realising it was not the sound of a beaten man.

Madri approached and ran fingers across my cheeks. Perhaps I was already deep in the henbane because I couldn't get the image of the fox out of my mind. It was as though she had transformed into a vixen. When I next looked at Magnus, he had the face of a wolf – and even Laurie, clear-headed and free of the effects of the berserker drug, perched on the rocks behind us like a vulture.

Hope came beside me and I gasped in surprise. Her long hair was unbound, cascading over the St Andrews' crest on her university sweatshirt, and her delicate features had sharpened into those of an eagle.

Had my face changed too? Perhaps I came at the 46ers as a raging bear or a snarling lion, my breath stinking of henbane.

'He's not forgiven for Jamie.'

Those words of Hope's were the last I recall. After that the bloodlust rose in me and the sky exploded.

I remember the stars.

Maybe the rainclouds really did retreat and reveal the

bright heavens above. But these stars hung in a sky of tortured orange and their pinpricks mirrored the 46er torches coming towards us. There had been five of them – I could just remember that. But now I counted forty, no a hundred, no thousands, swinging to the rhythm of massed troops as they climbed the slope. They closed on us and flowed seamlessly around us. Then the torches were extinguished and there was just the swell of voices.

I saw Madri standing in the centre of the circle, her fox snout turned to the sky, her arms held high as she implored the gods to ride from Valhalla. Winds buffeted her, thrashed her black cloak, tossed her silver-streaked hair. The air sparked, little explosions crackled down her arms. The elements coalesced around her into a whirlwind. Then she dropped her hands and thrust them down the slope and a storm tore from her fingers and broke upon the advancing columns.

A wolf rushed past me, tall and yelling incoherently. The animal ran agilely into the night and I heard cries of fear down the hill. Then, just for a moment, I saw an eagle on a giant outcrop. She was resplendent, so poised and focused. Her arms opened, her wings spread and she flew from her perch. But something was reaching for her from below. Arms came up, missiles were thrown and I watched her tumble.

That's when the anger arrived. I had never experienced anything like it, not when I waded into the Solway with a knife at my wrists, not even when I watched my family shatter on the ledges of the Lakes. It rose from my core, up to my lungs. It bubbled down my arms and folded my fingers into fists. It ignited through my throat and burst into the night in the wildest scream of defiance. My legs began pistoning, carrying me forward to save my eagle.

Someone came at me. Just a shape with limbs and torso. There was a huge crack against my head. I staggered and my vision swam. Fireworks exploded inside my skull and my ears hummed, but I felt no pain. I lurched to a stop and brought my hands up to check my face. Some sane voice inside me was telling me I had been hit hard, yet the fireworks receded and my vision stabilised and I sensed no discomfort.

I advanced on the figure and this time I saw the stick swinging for my head again. It came in an arc, but I tore it from the man's grasp, then thrust it end first into his gut. I heard his squeal and he collapsed in front of me and I raised my pole for another strike when I realised new shapes were flooding past me in search of the summit.

I must not let them. Suddenly that was all I knew. I could not permit them to take the high ground. From there they would be able to comprehend the struggle, they would be able to assess their attack options, how many to risk, which point on the battlefield to send reinforcements. I don't know where this conviction came from. I'd never been a military man. I can only imagine that all my years of reading about ancient warfare, about long-lost fields of conflict, coalesced in my brain at that moment and lent me the foresight of a battle-hardened jarl.

I roared to my Clan. *Back, back. Come together.*

The vulture was already there at the top. Perhaps he had never left. He spun and parried as his attackers probed. Madri came in answer to my call. She strode across the grass with sparks hissing at her fingertips, her expression grim and her eyes on me. She knew the sense in what I was shouting and she levelled beside me, her shoulder pressed against my bicep, extending her arms and daring them to approach.

I swung my stick at every shadow, feeling the impacts through my arms as wood hit bone. The vulture joined us and we stood our ground as a threesome.

Shields, I yelled. We had no shields, but I shouted the command again.

We wedged together and hunkered against the coming assault. Something bumped against my arm and I realised Madri *was* holding a shield, a great round one of limewood, with an iron boss and a leather handle. Across the front stretched a painted oak tree, *Crann Bethadh*, the symbol of our Clan. I tried to move closer to her, but I was impeded by the shield on my own arm, and I had to jerk it free and realign it against hers. The vulture did likewise on her other side, and I sensed our foe pausing and debating in the dark as they saw this rudimentary wall waiting for them.

My stick was heavy. I rested it on top of my shield and realised it shimmered in the moonlight like sharpened steel. I snarled in exultation. We were armed and crazed. *Mad like wolves.*

I yearned to see my eagle. Where was she? I yelled for her, but she would not fly to me. I thought I saw her briefly, just a glimpse of claw and feather rushing across the ring of stones, then disappearing into the gloom. A different yell answered me and the great wolf was back with us. He came charging up the hill, yipping with excitement and his tail high. He rushed straight to my side and thrust his great fur body against mine and it felt good to lean against his muscle, like a wall of sinew protecting the end of our line. He rose on his hind legs and grabbed a shield of his own and there was new steel in the moonlight, slipping into place over the rim of each shield.

We were four. I wished desperately that we were five, but it was enough. We screamed our Clan challenge and sang our songs of war and the enemy broke upon us.

Did we really fight? Or was everything that night just the drug in our veins?

I remember the press of the shield wall, the sheer weight of our foe. I rammed my shoulder against my shield and gasped with the exertion of holding them back, but my boots still slipped on the grass and I could not keep the line. Steel shot across our defences to jab at us. Blades arced underneath, cutting for our calves, striking up like cobras for our vitals. Axes smashed iron-rims, crunched into limewood.

All that mattered was the ground we stood on, the blood and sinew of each friend beside us. Madri was our Valkyrie, wild and untamed. Her sword carved into them, her song stretched over their lines, and I would have followed her into the mouth of Hades. The wolf growled beside me. His head was down, his blade stabbing as each new face appeared over our defence. Blood glistened on his fangs and a stink came from him, the deep corpse-heavy stink of a predator.

We knew our rhythm. Brace against the assault. Shove back with our shields. One step forward. Then stab across the iron-rims. Brace. Shove. Step. Stab. Together we inched forward and regained the summit. Madri sang of violence and loss and her voice synchronised with our movements; each note was another action.

With the music of war in our ears, the Clan Dál Riata advanced in line and sowed death around us.

And then we stopped. Or at least I did.

LXIV

The sky was no longer orange and my friends had scattered. I carried no shield, I brandished no blade. In my hand I still clutched a stout stick, but it did not glimmer of steel. I seemed to be alone. I thought there might be voices out there, but they were scattered and uncoordinated. Short cries of alarm broke the night. Then a long howl. Someone cursed and a woman answered.

The stars were gone. I felt the world swim, so I spread my legs and bent my knees to stay upright. I peered at my hands and expected to see them coated in blood and lacerated by blades, but other than some grazing on the knuckles, they seemed untouched.

There was still heat in me. I could feel it seething through my veins. Hot anger. Then the image of my beautiful eagle flew into my mind. Where was she?

Hope!

I think I yelled her name again and again. I lurched across the hilltop looking for her. I dipped my head under rocky outcrops, I marched into the ring of stones, I peered down the slope to the barns. I circled back and found myself closer to the cliffs. Even through the drug's stranglehold, I sensed the steep drops and a small sane voice inside me warned me to keep away. That way lay death.

Someone rushed me. I think it might have been Justus or Jamie. I lunged at them. My fist made contact with the side of their skull and they crumpled. I stumbled over rocks, still aware of the chasm somewhere just to my left. Magnus appeared. He was laughing and swiping at the empty air. Laurie was atop a boulder, sitting cross-legged in his oversized tweed jacket. He held an iron helmet, the one he had used to bludgeon Blaine to death. Surely I had seen him throw it into the loch at Finlaggan? He stared at it in fascination and mumbled over and over: *We reap what we sow.*

Music tumbled around me again, but this time vast chords of splendour. A light came on across the summit and there was Charles sitting at a great organ, smiling manically and dishing out Elgar's Sonata, first movement, all the stops out. His fingers stretched over the keys, his legs parted across the pedals and his lips pulled back in a rictus grin.

I wanted to shove him off his damn stool, but Anna wouldn't let me. She lurched into my field of view and hurried to me. I could see mud on her clothes and rain in her hair. Her cheeks were flushed with exertion and terror shone in her eyes. She closed on me and pushed against me, with her hands gripping at the collar of my shirt. *Oh, Finn, I've known for a long time that your friends are leading you into trouble.*

Despite the violence in me, I was gentle as I unpinned her hands. *It's fine. Don't worry about me.*

She sniffled and placed her head against my chest as though attempting to stop me advancing. *Not on a hill in the middle of nowhere, with evening coming on. Such a silly place to meet.*

I pushed her gently backwards and was going to say more when another figure materialised behind her and my heart jerked.

Hope.

Where had she been all this time? Was she hurt? She loitered between the rocks, meeting my gaze with an expression of such devastation.

I tried to get to her, but Anna was still herding me in the other direction. *Oh, Finn, she's trouble.*

I'd had enough. Hope was backing away and I was terrified I would lose her again. The cliffs were there. They yawned somewhere behind her and I thought of frail Denw being cast from them.

Get out of my way. I shoved Anna hard and she tumbled from me with a single gasp of surprise and disappeared.

I rushed towards Hope with a hand outstretched, but she was still retreating.

What are you doing?

There was defeat in her eyes. *Going to Jamie.*

No! No! No!

Even though I ran like the wind, I still never reached her. The night sought her out and wrapped its cloak around her until she was lost from view.

And she left me.

Stones caught at my feet and I tumbled. I hit the ground and my skull cracked against something hard. Lights blazed across my brain and then everything went dark.

LXV

There was rain.

That was my first thought. Hard, persistent rain, pummelling the rocks and hitting my upturned face like thousands of tiny pebbles. I opened my eyes and let the deluge soak me. Even if I had wanted to find cover, my body would not allow it. I was exhausted. Tired to my bones.

I lay on the grass summit, and I realised there must be the first hint of light in the morning sky. I liked the rain. Or, at least, I was too lethargic to register any discomfort. I blinked and moved my eyeballs and thought I could see someone else relaxing in the downpour. It was Madri, sitting cross-legged in the centre of her circle with her hands upturned on her knees in some sort of yogic pose. She was still as stone, her eyes closed, just a few strands of sodden hair shifting in the breeze.

I probably slept again, because when I next looked at the sky it was pale and the rain was thinner. I turned my head and saw that the world was just waking in the grey light before dawn. Madri was still in her circle, but as I watched she raised her arms and stretched her torso. A scent came to me. Cigarette smoke. Groaning, I shifted onto my side and spied Laurie sat against a rock, holding up one side of his shirt in an attempt to shield his cigarette from the fine rain. He nodded a silent acknowledgement to me and blew smoke.

I patted down my body. No gaping wound in the chest. Two legs, both still attached. In fact, I seemed in pretty good shape. My shirt front was rumpled and soaked, and my knuckles hurt, but I had the strangest suspicion that I'd stood in a Viking shield wall, dishing out death to every face that reared in front of me. I forced myself to sit up, certain that the ground would be littered with the dead and dying. But there was nothing. A crow landed and eyed Madri and rasped at her, but otherwise nothing moved. No Vikings, Picts or Gaels. No 46ers.

Magnus came slowly over the rise. He was sluggish and imperturbable, but he too looked unharmed. Or, at least, no worse than I had found him last sundown. But as he drew closer, I saw that his eyes were haunted and he would not look at me.

'Where are they?' I croaked.

'They're all gone. The barns seem empty.'

'Did they attack?'

He shrugged in bewilderment.

I rolled my neck and let out a low groan. 'Christ, I ache. One thing's for sure, my body's telling me it was thrown around last night.'

'So's my voice box. It kills to say anything above a whisper.'

Madri stood and stepped gingerly from the circle. I looked at her fingers and remembered sparks exploding from them. She saw my expression and inclined her head.

'You had powers,' I said limply. 'There was magic coming from you.'

'Is that what you saw?'

'You harnessed the winds last night and conjured up storms.'

She smiled thinly. 'Lots of men have told me that.'

She had made a joke of it, but her eyes told me something different. She wandered slowly past and went towards the cliffs to find a rock to sit on and take in the views.

I noticed a stick lying near me and I wondered if I may have been grasping it for much of the night. I twisted round to Laurie. 'Hey, what happened? Did you see much?'

He flicked his cigarette away and came over to us. 'Aye.'

He sat down and we waited for him to say more.

'Well?' I prompted.

'Justus brought his mob up. Five of them in total. A couple of them carried batons and they looked like they meant business. But they were dismayed by all the howling and shouting coming from you lot. Your blood was well and truly up and they hesitated.

'Then one of them went for you, Finn. He cracked your skull with his stick and I thought you'd go down like a stone. But you barely seemed to notice. You tore back into him and grappled the weapon from him, then gave him an almighty blow in return. He collapsed. I thought you'd killed him. I thought, oh God not again. I managed to avoid getting in your way and went to check on him. Thankfully he was breathing, but was out cold. Must have been fifteen minutes before he moved. Then he hauled himself up and just staggered away down the hill.'

'What about my brother?' Magnus asked quietly.

Laurie examined him. 'You don't remember?'

Magnus shook his head.

'He made a beeline for you. I guess he thought he could beat you into submission and the whole thing could be called off. Except he'd not calculated for berserker wrath. You took him down with a tackle that would have made the headlines at Murrayfield and you both grappled on the ground for an age while the rest of the action flowed around you. At last you pinned him down and punched him into submission. I think you knocked him unconscious. When he came to, he had no fight left in him.'

'Wow,' I said softly. 'The power of plants.'

'And did we solve anything with all this violence?' Magnus asked.

'That depends if you'll keep your word,' Laurie replied.

Magnus and I exchanged glances. 'What did I say?'

'At the moment of your victory, when you had him pinned and he'd submitted, you grasped him by the collar and leaned down over his face and shouted: *This is what it feels like to fight a berserker, brother. Yes, I've discovered what I was searching for. The elixir of the Vikings' most elite warriors is flowing through my veins and now you've felt their fury.*

'Fine words, Magnus. Fine words indeed. You straightened above him and added more solemnly: *So you have my word, brother, if that's what you want. That's it. All done. No more drugs.* You released him then. He got to his feet and stared at you in shock, and I wondered if he would accept your promise. Finally he nodded and said: *Then it's done.* He called off the others and they limped away into the dark.'

'They just left?'

Laurie gave us a weak grin. 'The action lasted less than thirty minutes before they took themselves off to lick their wounded pride. You lot, however, spent the next few hours still howling and punching at thin air. One time you even linked arms and got me down to join you and we tottered around in a line like we were dancing some kind of ceilidh. Finn kept shouting *shields* and telling us to hold on tight.'

I shook my head slowly. 'What a bloody stupid situation.'

'Aye,' murmured Laurie. 'But this time no one got killed, thank God. No one got their head pulped.'

We lapsed into heavy silence and it was several minutes before I peered around the summit and something turned in my stomach. 'Where's Hope?'

Magnus frowned, but had no response. He cast his gaze across the hill and panic welled in me. I forced myself to my feet and Laurie clambered upright too.

'Hope?' he called.

'Hope,' growled Magnus.

'I don't remember seeing her,' I garbled. 'Only at the end. She said something about Jamie and she was over there...'

I turned towards the eastern cliffs and even as I did, Madri let out a little cry and I saw her lurch backwards with a hand flying to her mouth.

My world slowed. Magnus shouted in alarm. Madri turned and pointed behind her towards the edge of the cliffs, her face contorted in shock.

I remembered now. *What are you doing?* I had demanded. *Going to Jamie*, Hope had replied. *Going to Jamie.*

I stumbled towards Madri. She was gesticulating, and tears broke from her eyelids. I could feel Magnus and Laurie hurrying behind me. I made it to the rocky section, then caught my foot and fell. Gasping in pain, I hauled myself upright. As I did, I glanced to my left and saw another figure emerging through the rain. I whipped my eyes back to the cliff edge and took a few more staggering steps to close the distance to Madri.

And then my brain kicked in, and I stopped and looked back.

What was happening? What games were being played? The figure was *Hope*.

She began to move towards me, alarmed at the sound of our panic. Madri was still shouting and gesticulating, and I tried to gather my wits.

'I don't understand. Who's down there?'

I could see the grief in Madri's eyes. It was grief for me.

'I'm not sure,' she garbled. 'The light's too poor. But I think… I think it's your friend.'

Stunned, my legs took me across the last few metres while my brain tried to sift through the confusion. The land opened up dizzyingly, and I had to drop to my knees and crawl the last inches. Rocks below. Rocks everywhere. Vast blocks of granite, thrusting out of the ground, broken over millennia.

And there in the heart of them, curled motionless below me, I could just see the outline of someone I thought I knew. Blue jeans. A lemon jumper and cream coat.

And hair so red.

Given up to the winds.

Dear God. Anna.

LXVI

They could not remove me from the edge.

They tried reasoning, they tried shouting, they even attempted physical force, grabbing me by the shoulders and hauling me backwards. But always I fought them off and crawled back to the edge.

I wept and called her name over and over again. My tears fell into the vortex along with all the raindrops, and maybe some found their way to her. I considered climbing down. In moments of clarity between the emotions, I peered along the cliffs and tried to calculate routes off the hill. But the light was still dim and the rocks slick with rain, and I knew I could not trust myself to make it to the bottom safely.

Perhaps that was the point. Maybe I was *supposed* to fall too and join her amongst the debris. Just like I had been *supposed* to fall with my family right off the edge of that bastard Great Slab in Langdale. They'd left me behind all those years ago and I'd been forced to stare down at their broken bodies from the heights above, as I stared now at Anna's.

There was almost certainly an easier route by descending the main slope to the barns and then traversing along the foot of the cliffs. But the comedown from the henbane still weighed on me like an anchor. Though I might cry and weep and struggle, my bones barely had the energy to rise, let alone plot a course to her.

Why did you come back? At one point I shouted that question down to her. *Why?* I had watched her little Fiat depart and wind away along the lane to the Haddington junction. How far had she got? When did she reconsider? Had she returned to the car park and waited for me as the night descended and the rain came in?

Morning coalesced and now I could see her more clearly. Her white plimsolls, which were such poor footwear on upland ground. The shapeless jeans she wore incessantly. And that lemon jumper, which only Anna could like. I wished I could reach down and ease a curl of red hair away from her face, but I feared what I might find beneath.

It was Hope who first stated that we must leave, and I hated her for it.

The men had ceased attempting to get me away from the edge and were packing up and checking the summit for untoward objects dropped during the night. Madri remained sitting beside me. She knew I wouldn't do anything stupid now, but she still wanted to keep a check on me.

Just once she asked, 'Was she special to you?' and I gave no answer to such a stupid question.

When they had performed their tasks, they assembled around me and the clamour grew for me to forsake my vigil.

'We have to go, Finn. It's getting light.'

'If anyone sees us up here now, we're buggered.'

'There's nothing we can do, Finn. She's dead.'

She *looked* dead, but I couldn't bring myself to accept it.

Somehow – through tenderness and sympathy and hostile warnings – they hustled me back from the edge and got their arms around me.

'That's right, Finn. You know it makes sense.'

'It's for the best.'

Real fury erupted when we got to the car park, and it was not directed at me. The whole Clan was splintering. Magnus hurled accusations at Hope for bringing henbane onto the hill, and she snarled back that we were only in this situation because of his obsession with the berserker madness. I said nothing. I was too crushed by the sight of Anna's Fiat Uno parked in one corner, waiting for her return. They put me in the back seat of the Volvo and left me there while they continued to strut and point and shout at each other, until another vehicle passed along the lane and they realised that it was madness to be drawing such attention to themselves.

Magnus and Laurie came either side of me on the back seat and hemmed me in. Perhaps they did it on purpose to ensure I had no second thoughts. As Hope took us back along the road and we passed an isolated house with its lights on, I had an unstoppable urge to leap out and bang on its door and tell the occupants that someone lay beneath the cliffs of Traprain.

'She doesn't deserve to be abandoned there,' I protested as I struggled with them. 'Someone needs to know before it's too late.'

'It's already too late,' Hope said heatedly from the front.

'Damn fool,' Magnus cursed, grabbing my wrists. 'Don't you get it? You turn up there spouting about a body and – hey presto – the police will have a photofit in no time. Then what will you say when they interview you and show you a picture of your own face? Because they will interview you, Finn. You're her tutorial partner. They'll want to speak to you.'

I hadn't thought about that and the new information subdued me. We dropped Magnus where his van was parked further around the hill, then Hope took us on the turnings back to Edinburgh's ring road and across the Forth to Fife.

With hindsight, perhaps I should have fought harder. Perhaps on the summit I should have kicked and cursed and found a path down the slick rocks to Anna. Because I was soon to read in the *Edinburgh Evening News* that life had lingered in her.

Life… lingered in her.

I had allowed them to cajole me from that hill while her life – perhaps – still flickered.

They dropped me outside Sallies.

'Don't say *anything*,' one of them had implored me. Then Hope pulled away and the Volvo headed up North Street and turned left just before the cathedral.

That was the last I ever saw of the Clan.

LXVII

The police did interview me.

I was told to meet two of them in a small office next to the bursar's, and they went through a series of questions. But their lines of enquiry seemed cursory and, even though they scribbled whatever I said into notebooks, their expressions betrayed their disinterest. A foolish student had fallen off a cliff. It was hardly a case that would sky-rocket their careers.

I sat in that room and told them endless lies. All except one central truth, which I will never forgive myself for voicing. I said that Anna had purchased her car because she wanted to follow in the footsteps of early Christian saints and Traprain Law – I believed – was closely linked to the life of St Mungo. The two officers made assiduous notes, but it was obvious that they had no idea what I was talking about. Later I found out that Charles had corroborated this information in his own interview. Yes, he said, Anna had gone looking for saints, and it was all such a terrible tragedy.

A week dissolved. I was given leave of absence from lectures, and I wilted in my room. I wandered the pavements and paths of St Andrews and ate mechanically in Hall. Other students looked at me and whispered their condolences and that only made everything worse.

Then the *Edinburgh Evening News* printed its piece and some would-be good Samaritan took great relish in drawing my attention to it. It broke me.

I sought out Father Haughton in his office and told him I was leaving. He said he understood my emotions, but wanted me to know I was a good student and a theologian of promise. He urged me to consider taking the rest of Candlemas away from the university and returning in September to begin my first year again. I thanked him and wished him well, although I knew I would never be back.

I found Charles in his room on the second floor and told him he would make a worthy minister for many.

'Always keep her in your prayers,' I whispered.

'Of course I will,' he replied. 'Every day.'

He extended his hand, but I took him in an awkward hug and wished him success with the rest of his studies.

I did not call on the Clan. They had gone to ground, and I had nothing to say to them.

I walked along North Street to the bus stop, carrying my kitbag. It was the same bus to Leuchars railway station that I had taken those few weeks ago when Hope caught up with me just in time and hugged me in the gangway to the accompaniment of wolf whistles. But she was not in my thoughts now.

My mind was filled with Anna's joyful face as she talked about the meanings of the gospels. I thought about her family in Tennessee and her church and the bright future that should have been hers. I heard again the tenderness in her voice as she found me books in the libraries and brought me food when I could not leave my room. It was this inherent care that had killed her. And that knowledge, in turn, killed me.

As the bus rumbled past the Student Association and the School of Medicine and the rolling greens of the Royal and Ancient Golf Club, I sat on the back seat and I did not look back.

And I wept for my friend.

LXVIII

For thirty years, I have been haunted by two awful enigmas.

Did I kill Anna? On that night of violence, deep in henbane visions, was it the real Anna who came to me and held me close and attempted to herd me away? I shoved her when I saw Hope. That moment will live with me forever. I had waged bloody warfare on waves of imaginary warriors across that summit, but perhaps that one shove caught a *real* Anna off balance and sent her tumbling over the precipice.

And the other mystery: how long did she linger? Could I have saved her if only I had possessed the courage? In the weeks afterwards, I tried to discover evidence of the definitive time of death, but no autopsy reports were made public, and only two other local papers covered the story. They led with news that a student had fallen on Traprain Law, then spent most of the articles reminding readers of the Viking hoard of hack silver that had been discovered on the very same hill.

*

During these last three decades, I have existed. That's pretty much the only way I can describe it.

I've worked hard enough and kept a job down, one that sends me on journeys around Scotland. I've got to know the country more, perhaps even to understand it.

I married. Then realised what a huge mistake it was and petitioned for divorce after fifteen months.

Seventeen years ago, they discovered Blaine deep in the sludge of Finlaggan loch. He was roped and weighed down by rusted chainmail, and the front of his skull had been smashed. There was a media frenzy for a while, but no one came forward to denounce us. No 46er, no Justus. The circumstances around Blaine's murder were as imponderable as the lives of the Norse lords who had long ago governed the kingdom of Dál Riata from those lochside ruins.

For many years I forced myself to forget about the Clan. I boxed them up and stacked them away in a part of my brain that I didn't want to visit. But the rise of the internet proved too much of a temptation.

I found Magnus Engstrom easily. He was some kind of insurance broker in Birmingham. I remembered how much he had loved the romance of Scotland, and I thought his job sounded as far from that as it was possible to get.

Although I looked, I never found a single reference to a breakthrough in the search for the berserker drug of the Vikings. I guess his dream of academic success and adulation perished with so much else that night on Traprain Law.

I came across a picture of him on his Facebook feed and it floored me. He appeared happy enough, brandishing a champagne glass at some social shindig, but gone were the curls, gone was the light in his eyes. Gone was his magnificence.

On and off, I dipped into his social media and snooped on him for the best part of a decade. Then, about four years ago, his feed was closed down. I searched more widely and came across an announcement that Magnus, beloved son of Mairi Engstrom, former Home Secretary, had died of pancreatic cancer aged forty-seven.

There was no reference to his brother in the brief obituary. In fact, I had to search hard for him and eventually discovered his name in the lower echelons of non-executive directors of the Engstrom paper business, based back in Uppsala, Sweden. So he never took his cherished path into Parliament. Something stopped his smooth progress. Maybe it was his mother. Perhaps he had a change of heart. But I wonder if that beating he took on Traprain knocked the confidence out of him, brought him down to the world of the rest of us mere mortals.

Madri was simple to find. She owned her own apothecary and alternative medicine business, and on her website she used her full name of Madrigal. I remembered her cursing her parents for giving her such a pretentious moniker, but it suited her. It always had.

Even at fifty, she was beautiful in the profile picture on her site. Her silver strands had colonised her entire scalp and they flowed down over her shoulders, accessorised by giant silver earrings and blood-red lipstick. There were videos of her giving online lessons about pagan medicine, ancient cuisine and seasonal cooking. I played them often just to hear her voice again.

There were other photos showing off her photogenic family. A handsome barrister husband and three children who were already taller than her. One, I read, had just started at St Andrews, and I think I was pleased for her.

I never found Laurie. No matter how hard I trawled the web, he never came back in the search results. Perhaps it is for the best. He always was a mystery. A connoisseur, a storyteller – a killer. I will simply remember him as the man who brought the faeries to us and danced with wild abandon around our fires.

And what of Hope? I left her until the last to seek. I spent years avoiding her, even after I had begun to spy on the others. When I finally found the determination to seek her, she escaped me. Whatever I tried, I could not locate her. Thousands of Hopes pinged back in my Google and Facebook searches, but none looked like the woman in the scarf with the midnight hair and the eyes of such grave magnificence. Perhaps America is just too big a place to find one individual.

This failure bludgeoned me for a while, but I came to accept it and perhaps even to be grateful that she was gone. Too many emotions lay along that path. Too much hurt.

Probably I would have creaked into retirement and then into my autumn years and that would have been the end of it. But then, four months ago, something quite unexpected occurred, and it threw me completely.

Hope found *me*.

One day, I logged into my professional social media

account, the one that listed my job title and work credentials, and there was a message from someone called Hope Fallon, Professor of Medieval European Studies in the School of Humanities and Sciences, Stanford University. I knew instantly that it was her.

Dear Finn,

How can thirty-one years have gone in the blink of an eye? I've spent a very long time summoning up the courage to write to you.

Now I've started, I really don't know what to say. Should I ask how the last three decades have been for you? Should I reel off a list of life events that have happened to me?

I have a daughter. Marissa. Seventeen now and as beautiful as that sunrise over Iona. Her father walked out on us three years ago, and it's been a bumpy journey.

My work takes me all over Europe, but never to places as beguiling as those we shared. Sometimes – apart from Marissa – I think I left the best of me back there round those fires.

Should I say I'm sorry? I am. Heartbreakingly so, but I know that words like that are so insubstantial.

I am coming to St Andrews next year. A personal trip, nothing to do with my studies. It's been a huge decision.

I've avoided the place consummately, and that's not easy when academic symposiums and conferences pop up there all the time.

I want to ask if you would like to meet? I know that's an incredibly presumptive thing to suggest, but there it is – I've said it now. Perhaps a coffee or a walk, or whatever else you might suggest.

I will understand if I don't hear from you. I have spent half a lifetime trying to understand and to accept the paths we trod when we were young.

Take care of yourself, Finn. You are in my thoughts.

Hope

For over a fortnight I sent her no response and then I finally managed to cobble together a holding message, saying it was nice to hear from her, but I would like to take some time to consider her suggestion.

She stirred up so many emotions again. Recollections that had lain buried for too long, burst once more into my conscience and I fretted and paced and turned to my whisky.

Finally, late one Friday night almost thirteen weeks ago, a voice came to me. I think it was Anna's.

'*Write it down,*' she whispered. '*Write it all down. Use the words, use the memories, to find yourself again. Then decide if you want to see her.*'

And so I did.

I began that very night with that first line: *Life lingered in her*. And I think Anna was happy that I started it all with her.

Each night, when the day job is done, I've sat at my desk and pored over my memories. Once more, I've joined the Clan. I've laughed around their fires and listened to their myths. I've told their story.

And I've lived with Anna too. I've conjured her in my mind. I've reflected on her movements, her smiles, her chatter and her beautiful soul. Perhaps, I hope, I have brought her to life again.

I am sure she has been with me on this journey and, as the pages have unfurled, she has told me things.

She wants me to live. Maybe she even wants me to forgive myself. She is up there in heaven right now and only dear, cherished Anna would still keep wishing God's love on me.

Faith, hope and love abide; but the greatest of these is love. 1 Corinthians 13:13

Perhaps I will return to St Andrews.

Perhaps I will walk with Hope.

Perhaps.

Acknowledgements

Writing novels – probably for most authors and certainly for me – is a solitary experience. I tend to work in large blocks of time each day, concentrated into a few months of focus. I disappear into my stories and only come out to eat and sleep and maintain the everyday administration of life. Sometimes I even think I live more closely with my characters during these periods than with the real people around me.

That said, I could not have written *When We Were Killers* without the advice, expertise and kindness of a select group of individuals:

Thank you first to J.P. Orsi, a graduate of St Andrews, who readily furnished me with all the background stories of life at the university. Some of the key scenes – especially the foam party and the drinking game on the stairs of Sallies – were created directly from his recollections, and I hope I've portrayed these annual customs with appropriate accuracy.

Thank you too to Mike Dougan. A great friend of many

years, who offered advice and enthusiasm during the critical early stages of story creation.

Then there's Dave Follett, a lifelong friend and the first reader for all my novels. He's reviewed first drafts of The Pantheon series and *When We Were Killers* and always helped me shape them better before submitting to my publishers.

Thank you, as always, to Laura MacDougall, my agent, and to Peyton Stableford, my brilliant editor at Aries and Head of Zeus. When I submitted a bulging 130k-word draft of *When We Were Killers* to Peyton, she used her skills and tenacity to show me how much better it could be with a wordcount closer to 95k. The resulting story – I hope you'll agree – is tight, fast and compulsive.

Then there are my family members who have given me the space and understanding to allow me to disappear into my fictional world. A huge thank you to my parents, who turned their spare room into a temporary writing space whenever I visited and left me undisturbed. And my gratitude – as ever – to Jackie (and Albert) for their support and patience, and for reminding me that my real world is fundamentally better than my fictional ones.

If you'd like to connect, I'd love to hear from you. Please message me on: cfbarrington.author@gmail.com
You can also find me at:

www.cfbarrington.com
Facebook – @BarringtonCFAuthor
X – @barrington_cf
Instagram – @cfbarrington_notwriting

Thank you for your company.
C.F. Barrington

About the Author

C.F. BARRINGTON was raised in Hertfordshire and now divides his time between Fife and the Lake District.

Want to read more from C.F. Barrington?
Discover the Pantheon series.

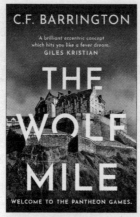
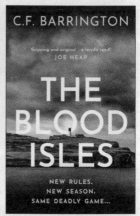

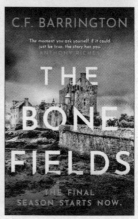

Squid Game meets *The Hunger Games* in this epic thriller series where modern-day recruits compete with ancient weapons in a deadly game across the streets of Edinburgh.

Available in eBook, Paperback and Audio.